THE ART OF
BREAKING
GLASS

THE ART OF BREAKING GLASS

MATTHEW
HALL

ORION

The right of Matthew Hall to be identified as the author
of this work has been asserted by him in accordance with
the Copyright, Designs and Patents Act 1988.

First published in Great Britain in 1997 by
Orion
An imprint of Orion Books Ltd
Orion House, 5 Upper St Martin's Lane, London WC2H 9EA

A CIP catalogue record for this book is available
from the British Library

Printed in Great Britain by
Clays Ltd, St Ives plc

For Matt Gaynes;

for my father, Sam;

and for Cecilia

I'd like to thank all the people who have helped me, at one time or another, with this novel; however, to be properly inclusive, such a list would be longer than the novel itself. A partial accounting would have to include Carl Brandt, for untold services rendered; law enforcement veteran Marc Ruskin for always being at the other end of the phone; his colleague Jim Fitzgerald of the FBI for his many kindnesses; Laurie Liss, for her magic; and Fredrica Friedman, my editor, who made it a much better book than it was when she first saw it. I feel privileged and grateful to have worked with you all.

Special thanks must go to these readers who, over time, offered help and suggestions: Cecilia Petit, Mickey Hawley, Tracy Davis, Jessica Bagg, and Lydia Redmond. I'd also like to thank WFMU, 91.1 FM in the New York/New Jersey area for teaching me everything a freeform radio station can be, and Moira, Perry and Rae, and Agatha and Ozzy for keeping me sane during the long winters.

All men should have a drop of treason

in their veins, if the nations are not to go soft

like so many sleepy pears.

— *Rebecca West*

All politics is local.

— *Thomas P. "Tip" O'Neill*

PART

ONE

I

The trick was not to think.

Bill Kaiser stood on the roof of the Marque, a fifty-story apartment tower a few blocks north of the UN. Aesthetically, it was an unfortunate piece of modern architecture, of use to Bill solely because it was adjacent to the Montclaire, home of Senator Arvin Redwell.

The night was sharp with a static clarity. There was ice in the air, a strong steady wind from Canada. Above him, the stars were clear.

The trick, he knew, was to empty one's mind completely.

Bill was a tall man, thin, with a wiry chest and long, well-muscled legs. His hair, naturally a light brown, was dark now, and cropped short, in a manner almost too severe to be conventionally fashionable.

In his mind, he heard music — Nietzsche Prosthesis, three chords, over and over, louder than God. It was what the twentieth century had in place of Wagner. It was like hearing electricity breathe.

A garage driveway ran between the two buildings. At its narrowest, it was just over ten feet wide. Bill stepped to the edge, peering down into the chasm between himself and the senator's roof.

Fifty stories, straight down, if he missed. But he wouldn't.

Bill was hungry. There was a sandwich in his black daypack, egg salad with bacon and mayo and pickles, just like his mother had made in their apartment on Forty-seventh Street. They would bring them to the old Central Park Zoo, sit and watch the seals, his mom in her inappropriate loud dresses. He'd been carrying it all day, but he hadn't had a bite, not yet. He needed to be light.

He knew he could jump it. Piece of cake. But if he missed, he died.

Ten feet. It was not that much. He walked again to the far end of the roof, readjusted his backpack, stretched and restretched his limbs just as if this were a track meet, back when he'd cared about such competitions. But the old exercises helped; as he worked each muscle group, he could feel the current within. He pictured himself making it, landing and skidding along the dark roof. And then he felt the bottom fall out of his stomach, the wild plummet, bricks scraping him as he tried to grab a window, the concrete rushing toward him, his knee, his chin, and then his brains everywhere, extinguished, a one-way ticket into the realm of pure electricity.

One or the other. Right now.

Bill sucked in air, backed to the far edge of the roof, and began to run. For one moment he felt like an animal, free and mythic in the moonlight. And then the edge of the building, the half-foot wall at his shin. He kicked off, launched himself into the night.

For a long moment he was disconnected from any solid matter, running silently through space, cold air bucking his face. He looked down the chasm, the sheer brick walls and white concrete below him, felt gravity's pull. He kicked, until he could actually feel his body rise, readjust upward, sheerly by dint of muscle work alone. In that instant he knew flight was possible. It was just a matter of balance. And then he landed on his feet on the Montclaire, walked the kinks out, looked up at the stars smiling down. Everything was in tune.

He tried the roof entrance. Locked. He pulled his long black flashlight from his pack, unscrewed the head, uncovered the electric raking tool and tension lever, made quiet work of the roof access door, and entered the building.

He knew he was taking a risk: there was a brand-new closed-circuit camera in an all-weather pod facing the door. Bill had seen it with his binoculars from the roof of the Marque back before sunset, but in his experience something as innocuous as a single door opening on one of several video screens at two in the morning would pass unnoticed.

Bill worked his way down six flights of stairs, entered the hallway, stepped quietly to apartment D.

A week earlier there'd been a security man at a little table, checking invitations for the senator's wife's Metropolitan Opera benefit. Alma Redwell was a soprano; Bill had never heard her, though he actually liked opera. A hundred and fifty guests, including a handful of senators and bank presidents, the mayor, and Edward Mackinnon, the real estate magnate. All the usual war criminals.

Bill had worked his way into the relatively unsecured computers at the senator's PR firm to get himself onto the guest list. Then he'd merely arrived at the door wearing a decent suit and a press pass. His name had been on the list; the security man had wished him a pleasant time. He had slipped through the crowd of money-eyed men and glamorous women, and all he could see was a prison, or rather, a chain of prisons, beholden to no one, stretching from coast to coast. Both the mayor and Senator Redwell had run their most recent campaigns on the issue of law and order, together calling for more prisons, more cops, more guns, more "safety." The fact that crime was actually down in the city had not deterred them, primarily because Edward Mackinnon was a major contributor to both their campaigns. The Mackinnon Group had apartment and office buildings all over the city; Edward's most recent acquisition was Straythmore Security, Inc., a very hot, very aggressive private prison–building company hatched out of a think tank in Utah. After the election, it had been a surprise to no one when the Mackinnon Group announced it was their intention to purchase a building from the city and build New York's first private, for-profit prison.

Part of the problem was the current city administration, endlessly willing to sell New York's treasures to the lowest bidder. Of course, Edward Mackinnon, the man who had managed, against spirited neighborhood opposition, to tear down the Phipps mansion, the Hammerstein Theater, and the Museum of American Immigration, all to put up his god-awful apartment and office towers, would find a scheme to take them up on the bargain. Bill found the entire proposal merely sad, the usual level of corruption at play, until he began to investigate Straythmore.

What he discovered scared him deeply.

Simply put, Edward Mackinnon's new company did not want merely to build prisons. They saw privatization as the future of all American law enforcement. The police, the station house, the judges and the courtrooms and the prisons and the guards — all would be property of, or employees of, Straythmore Security. They would be paid by government contract. Straythmore — or its competitors, if such there were — would run the law enforcement business, from top to bottom.

It's not that Bill was such a fan of the United States government — far from it. But at least in theory, they were accountable — that was the point. Bill had never voted for Straythmore Security, and he had no intention of letting them — in effect — run his country, much less his city.

The plan was to build five "satellite corrections modules" in New York, one in each borough. The older neighborhoods contained abandoned factory and school buildings: large sites the city was willing to sell cheaply. Of course, the whole prison project was right now in its very early stages; a letter of agreement had been drawn up between Mackinnon and the city, stating Straythmore's intent to acquire their first choice for the Manhattan site.

The Carnegie-Hayden Library-Lyceum.

The Lower East Side's most majestic antique building. The flower of the last century's noblest thinkers, the expression of a hundred years of utopian idealism. They were going to tear down a glorious symbol of hope and faith in humankind, rip out what had been, and still could be, the spiritual center of a neighborhood, to put up a prison.

Bill was not about to let it happen. Everything about it was wrong, and Bill was just the man to make it right.

The main lock was a six-pin Hampshire. He opened the second lock with the electric pick, then unrolled his sixteen homemade Hampshire picks, worked through them, threading each in as carefully as a tap needle through a spinal column.

Finally he pushed the last pin up, the cylinder turned, and the moment the door left the jam the Armall keypad inside began to beep out the seconds. Bill slapped on the light. Arvin Redwell's apartment looked huge and cold and forbidding. On the alarm panel, a red light blinked angrily as it beeped.

An Armall 2060 multiplex radio link, series J, which meant a six-digit code. Bill considered the liquid crystal readout.

SYSTEM ARMED, it blinked, and then next to that, ENTER CODE and digits representing seconds counted down — 27 26 25 . . .

Bill had suffered through several books both by and about Senator Redwell, preparing for this moment. Long an advocate of privatization of government responsibilities, Arvin had endured a tiresome childhood under a brutal, disapproving father. Throughout his educational years, he'd been a mediocrity. As he'd matured, he'd begun to find strength in a nasty form of cunning. It was obvious in the way he'd claimed Alma, his second wife. He'd first seen her in concert the day he'd been appointed chairman of the oversight committee and assumed real power for the first time. Sitting in the audience, his first wife beside him, he'd been consumed by desire for her.

Mister Family Values.

After the curtain calls, he'd gone backstage, met Alma, and carefully set up an assignation with her, while his wife chatted happily with Alma's husband, not six feet away. If the scene had been in a movie, Arvin Redwell would have thundered against the immorality of it from the Senate floor.

Bill punched in the date of Redwell's ascension and first sight of his future wife: 03-24-89.

The machine didn't stop beeping. The angry red light kept flashing. SYSTEM ARMED ENTER CODE 21 20 19

Damn. The numbers were right: at the party, he'd noticed that the zero, two, three, four, eight, and nine keys were smudged ever so slightly with gray. The other keys were bone white, never touched at all. And Bill knew he'd punched them in right — that wasn't the problem. Backwards, he decided.

89-24-03

The beeping went on, implacable: SYSTEM ARMED EN-TER CODE 15 14 13

Bill thought of the opera house, Arvin and Alma meeting back-stage, both married to other people —

09 08 07

European, Bill thought. Fuck. He'd heard Alma at the party: that rich Italian accent. He punched in 24-03-89.

The beeping stopped. The red light turned green. On the liquid crystal display it now read SYSTEM READY.

The alarm defeated, Bill walked to the window, looked at the street. No traffic this late. He relaxed, the old emotions came back, and he savored the beauty of it, the sheer thrilling gall of being alone in someone else's apartment, of invading a world.

The paintings, what there were, were all hunting pictures redolent of English gentility. Nothing worth all that alarm protection. And on every shelf and table, little ceramic figurines of shepherds and lambs and ducks, and somewhere, he was sure, sad-eyed children and drunks in battered top hats.

He took off his leather gloves, put on surgical rubber gloves, slid open the medicine chest.

Arvin Redwell, Bill learned, owed his stellar good humor to antidepressants. The most recent prescription was less than two months old. In the kitchen, Bill found an impressive array of wine-glasses, bottles of wine, and books about wine. He stepped into the study, admired the view, turned on the man's computer, and was confronted by a screen request for a password.

He tried a couple of obvious ones and was denied access. He dug into his black backpack and took out a rubber-banded fistful of diagnostic disks. He tried the first, quickly saw it wouldn't work. Same for the second. The third one got him in, thereby embedding a program that created access into the hard disk itself. He read through a few memoranda. They weren't terribly interesting; he did it because he could. Then he became aware of an additional level of cipher security in the computer, probably for sensitive documents, but that didn't matter. He already knew everything about Arvin Redwell he wanted to know.

He turned off the computer, opened his black backpack, and took out his tools. He used his ratcheting screwdriver on the desktop's metal cover, slid it off, exposing the hard drive and ribbon wires and the various cards. These were green silicon panels filled with computer chips that added features to Redwell's machine.

There were two spaces open in the card bus of the computer. That made everything infinitely easier.

Bill took the bomb from his backpack, cut through the tape, carefully opened the bubble wrap. Inside was a paperback-sized silicon panel, layered on each side with a molded sheet of C-4. Everything looked to have traveled well. The explosive-encased computer card clicked firmly into Redwell's machine as if it were finally home.

Bill screwed it in place, connected the ribbon wire that would allow it to communicate with the hard drive. There were two wires he left jutting into air. He pulled a tiny red light out of his backpack, threaded the wires into either side of the socket. Then he turned the computer back on.

Nothing blew up.

Bill used his diagnostic disks to add a new chain of commands to the password file. Then he rebooted, retyped the sequence of commands he'd created, and pressed enter.

The red light lit. That was all he needed; he turned off the computer, unclipped the light, and wired on a blasting cap; he plunged this directly into the C-4, slid the steel computer box shut, worked the screws tight with the ratcheting screwdriver. Then he repacked his backpack, making sure the room was clean of his presence.

He placed the chair behind the desk the way he'd found it, re-traced his steps through the musty apartment, reset the alarm and relocked the apartment door with his picks, his fingers sweaty in the gloves. He kept the stairwell door from slamming behind, went up one flight of stairs, set one foot on the next, and then, somewhere above him, he heard voices, an echoing murmur.

He froze. Footsteps coming down, two people. And then, from below, unmistakably, the sound of crisp static on a police radio.

His mouth suddenly contained no saliva. He continued up, attempting total silence. He made it one flight, slipped out onto the next hallway. The sign said 46.

No cops. Good.

Sometimes, these things happened. One always had to have contingencies. He walked down the carpeted hallway, past silent apartment doors. He could go through one, wait, and then work the fire escape. But that might involve hostages: bad idea.

All right, then, another default. Bill always tried to have another default. He considered the elevator. Apartment building shafts were notoriously difficult. Punching the button would be the ideal way to signal his precise location. Next to the elevator was a small utility room containing the incinerator chute. Bill looked inside, thanked his stars.

Across from the incinerator chute was a small air duct. The chute was worthless to him — sending anything down it was a stupid trap. But the air duct was perfect — just four Phillips-head screws between him and safety. Bill took out the ratcheting screwdriver, pounded out the four screws. He removed the grill, zipped everything that even smelled like a burglary tool into the main cavern of the daypack. The computer disks he broke in half and ripped into pieces. He unzipped a side pocket, took out a thick sheaf of paper pamphlets. They were rather the worse for wear — they'd been in his backpack for months — but they existed, and that was all that mattered.

There was a straight-edge razor in the pocket as well. He slipped that into his shirt pocket.

He pulled off the Phillips screw head, jammed the ratcheting screwdriver into the daypack and stuffed that into the air duct. He screwed the air-duct panel back with the inch-long screw head.

He was ready.

He peered out the door. Nobody to be seen.

Clutching his pamphlets, he walked boldly out of the incinerator room. The hallway was silent.

He crept to the stairwell door, opened it, and listened.

Nothing. For a long moment. He went in, climbed a flight of stairs, and then out of nowhere a voice three, maybe four flights above him said, "Hold it, I hear something."

It was like lightning through his heart, but Bill was prepared. He walked out onto the forty-seventh floor hallway. Empty, thank God. He walked straight to the incinerator room, opened the door, put the pamphlets in his mouth, and began to strip off his shoes. He jammed them down the incinerator chute — now, he didn't care. He threw the jacket down next, and then ripped off his shirt and pulled down his pants.

He heard the stairwell door slam open, knew there was at least one person on the forty-seventh floor with him.

Perfect. He stripped off his underwear and socks, dropped them down the chute. The pamphlets were still between his teeth.

He had saved the razor blade for last. He held it in his right hand, set it a quarter of an inch away from the blue vein in his left wrist. He thought of prison, thought of Arvin Redwell and the others, and he pressed down into his skin, sliced down, a quarter of an inch, a half an inch, three quarters of an inch, and then the blade slipped.

He was bleeding. The blood was definitely beginning to ooze.

Bill wanted to laugh. There was something hysterically funny about this. And then a voice said, "We know you're in there, we're going to give you to three to drop your weapons and come out."

He took a pamphlet — he was amazed how hard he'd been biting them — and wrapped it around the razor.

"One."

The cut on his left wrist was shallow, but it was bleeding. The nice thing was, even as he did it, it all seemed so logical.

"Two."

He was beginning to bleed everywhere. He took the razor in his right hand, bowed his legs, pulled up his penis and testicles. He put the blade of the razor to the bottom of his scrotal sack.

"Three." He started to cut. And then everything happened at once: the door slammed open and two New York City cops screamed "DROP IT" and pushed guns into Bill's face. They were confronted by a wild-eyed naked man covered with blood, a thick stack of pamphlets between his teeth, clutching his genitals in one bloody hand, shouting, "I'll cut 'em off— I'll cut 'em off— I'll cut 'em off—"

The first cop lowered his gun. "Oh, Jesus, get the AIDS gloves — let's take this guy to Bellevue."

II

Charley was babbling again, there in the back of the car. Outside, thin snow covered the ground, and the sky was a sharp morning blue, and Charley was watching it all, putting the sounds and the pictures together in his head. Rick was droning on and on about selling some big house; Sharon tuned him out, checked her son in the rearview mirror for a moment, watched his lips move. Caaws, he was saying. Caaws and Hawsees. And then the scene shifted, she was on the Psych ER and there was a girl on the ward covered in scabs, jutting off like scales all over her. Then it was time to leave the ward, and Sharon walked out through the metal detectors into her childhood house in Oneonta, the swing set cold and barren outside, and there was a door in front of her, wooden, and she approached it, all she did was get closer, and then she woke up.

The room was black, and for a sharp moment she didn't know where she was — her mother's apartment in Oneonta, or her old place upstate, or anywhere else in the world. Outside her window the dark form of the Empire State Building seemed to coalesce and make itself prominent, black against the blueing night sky. She was in her apartment, she was in her own bed, and then she thought of Charley.

Twelve seconds, she figured. Twelve seconds between actually stopping sleep and first thinking of Charley.

Better. Better than yesterday, she remembered. Better than usual.

She lay back in the bed and allowed herself, now that her mind had opened the subject, to remember her son: his fine blond hair, his mispronunciations, his smell. He really did have Rick's eyes.

Or would have. She looked across the dark room at the lump on the chair that was her purse, thought of Charley's little Mickey Mouse zipper pouch nestled at the bottom. She couldn't explain it, but there was a weird kind of safety in having it there. She turned on her side, rubbed the long scar under her chin, looked at the red digital clock — five forty-eight; once again, better than average. She could almost say she'd gotten enough sleep.

She'd come not to trust sleep since the car accident. In the last year and a half, she'd routinely awakened several times a night, Rick and Charley, living or dead, around the bend of every turn of thought.

When she moved to New York, she'd thought the city's constant motion and sound would further damage her ravaged sense of sleep, but oddly enough she'd adapted fairly rapidly to the continual low-level welter of traffic. Her apartment was on a sidestreet in the East Twenties, a room and a half on the seventh floor, looking north, and even the ambulances yelping around Bellevue three blocks away didn't really faze her the way she'd worried they might when she signed the lease.

She lay back on her pillow and switched on the clock radio.

Classical music. It made for smooth awakenings, she found, but after a while it made her sad, and she flipped around, found one of the college stations that had salsa. Rick's tastes had been locked in what radio programmers called classic rock. After living upstate most of her life, Sharon found the multiplicity of radio stations in the city an odd bonus she hadn't been expecting. It was impossible to be sad with salsa playing; Sharon listened to the heartbeat dance rhythms without understanding a single word.

Finally she planted her feet on the cold wooden floor and hoisted herself up. She was wearing a shapeless flannel nightshirt that was still, pretty much, white. She took up the ancient plaid robe that had once been her father's, shouldered into it in such a way as to have her arms come out the sleeves and not the holes, and padded into the bathroom.

She looked in the mirror, decided there was no way, this morning, she could convince herself she was anything remotely near beautiful. She had shoulder-length dark brown hair with a tendency to curl slightly, a long straight nose, and strong cheekbones she'd inherited from her father. Her body was long and thin. She cranked the shower's hot water all the way, with just a scrinch of cold.

An hour later, she was ready to leave the house. She finished her tea, splashed water in the cup, rubbed it with an unsoaped sponge and set it on the rack to dry. She pulled the sheet and blanket up the bed until they lapped unevenly at the bottom edge of the pillow, declared the bed made. She opened the refrigerator, looked inside — an unopened quart of water, a couple of yogurt containers, a lump of tinfoil that probably contained chicken. She let the door slap shut, Charley's drawing flapping gently in the slight breeze. The paper was beginning, very subtly, to discolor.

She closed her drawstring bag, hoisted the strap over her shoulder, aware once again of Charley's little zipper pouch nesting hidden inside. Today, she promised herself. Today she would talk about it. She locked the door, took the elevator down, and walked out on the street.

The light was beautiful this morning — calm and shining and quiet, the sky still young and light blue. She looked at the river, spent the moment she spent every morning avoiding even glancing at the half-built Mackinnon Group skyscraper going up on the next block.

Uncle Ed.

When she'd been apartment hunting, Sharon could have called him — she probably could have had her pick of his rentals, and she was sure he would have cut her a break financially. But she chose not to.

She'd found her wonderful little apartment in the *New York Times*. It was precisely the neighborhood she'd wanted; the building was funky and old and didn't have a doorman, but it was hers.

She turned north, up First Avenue. The slant of clear sunlight and the cool snap of breeze against her face made her remember mornings like this in Tivoli. The village hadn't even had a stop-

light; Rick thought that renting a post office box made his business mail seem somehow more official, so every day Sharon and
Charley would walk together to check the box, Charley breathing
on his yellow duck mittens, watching his breath come out in fog.
They would pass the firehouse, dogs on porches following their
progress. Sharon and Charley had both loved those mornings —
the two of them together in a world of quiet, Sharon keeping her
strides slow because of Charley's short legs. Now, Sharon saw
that if she and Charley had lived in the city, they'd never have had
that time together — not four blocks of quiet, not every morning. Some days Rick would announce he was stopping for the
mail on the way to work, and Sharon and Charley would give each
other a glance of palpable disappointment. Rick never caught it;
it sailed right past him, intangible, like astrology or ultraviolet
light. Sharon privately thought Rick had missed a lot of things,
always living in the here and now. The world, she'd thought, was
full of mysteries, and Rick had shown curiosity about only a small
handful of them.

Now, a year and a half later, Rick and Charley in the ground upstate, Sharon didn't feel that the world had mysteries. Mysteries
implied something hidden behind something solid. Now, Sharon
felt that the entire world was made of sand, that it could disinte-
grate at any moment, for any reason.

She beat a blinking red light across a street, looked through the
window of the magazine shop at the clock on the back wall —
eight-ten; she was fine — and then took in the newspaper headlines. She saw the Kurdish refugee who ran the newsstand watching her, and she smiled — one thing they always had lots of at
Bellevue was newspapers — went in, and purchased a pack of
Necco wafers.

She continued north on First, noticing the way the damaged
people began to accumulate as she got closer to Bellevue. She
slipped under the Greco-Roman arch they'd put up to make the
entrance distinct from the rest of the gate, joined a small herd of
humanity, nurses and doctors and a few ragtag patients, walking
down the concrete path and in through the double doors. This put
them in the old edifice; a few of the herd peeled off to offices here,

but the bulk tromped right through, down a long corridor lined with photos and artwork, into the new building.

This could have been an airport — waiting areas and counters and tall glass windows that overlooked a parking lot. Sharon walked past the medical emergency room, took a left at the elevators, opened a thick steel door to a blank, bare hallway. The sheetrock was badly scuffed, with fist-sized holes punched through. Halfway down was another door; Sharon knocked, and one of the police officers saw her through the small glass window and let her in.

"Morning, Sharon." The cop toasted her with his blue paper coffee cup.

"Morning, Hector," she said with a smile. She stepped through the metal detector, a plastic frame. A beep sounded, and the light went from green to red because of her belt and the keys in her purse. She kept walking, took a left into the room toward the nurse's station. There was a man on a gurney and a woman cuffed into a wheelchair on one side — new arrivals. Along the opposite wall were plastic seats; a few patients sat in these, conversing or scratching or muttering to themselves. As she walked by, a few voices went up — Miss! Nurse! Excuse me! "Give me a minute, guys," she said to everyone, looking specifically at two of her patients from yesterday: an energetic black man whose face lit up in a smile when he saw her, and a white girl with bad skin who looked at her with dull, dead eyes.

Sharon had actually grown to like the sour smell of the psychiatric emergency room. It was permanent, a constant state, as if once a month someone lovingly spackled the walls with a careful mixture of urine and vomit. At the very first it had revolted her, but there was no other smell quite like it and she had come to miss it when she moonlighted on other wards.

Of all the places Sharon had ever worked in her life, this was undoubtedly her favorite. Medical emergencies came to the ER down the hall; psychiatric emergencies came here. The ward was shaped like a long flat C, the patients inhabiting a lengthy hallway surrounding the nurse's station and quiet room. Sharon had been warned from the start that the bottom end of the C was not visible from any other point in the ward; she was always careful coming around that corner, because nobody could ever predict what was happening over there. All day, every day, Hector and Michael were in attendance at the entrance, with their badges and guns and bulletproof vests on at all times. They put new patients through the metal detector, checked their possessions, kept responsibility over those patients brought in after having broken one law or another. Sharon liked them; mostly they drank coffee and complained.

The patients were a different matter; Sharon liked them as well, but for different reasons. Whatever was going on in their lives that had brought them here had just happened; they were still raw from it. They came in screaming and went out quiet. It wasn't nursing so much as intervention. Sharon always felt that reality was a lot more tightly compacted in the Psych ER than in the wards upstairs, and she appreciated it for that.

There was a seventy-two-hour limit on the patient's stay in emergency; during that time he or she was seen, usually once a day but sometimes more, by an attending psychiatrist and a social worker. Except for Garber, who ran the place, the shrinks were all rotating residents. They were here to get life experience, rather than share the benefits of their own.

That was one of the reasons Sharon felt comfortable on the Psych ER. She knew things the doctors didn't necessarily know. Originally she'd wanted to be a doctor; her mother had convinced her to go to nursing school to keep her in Oneonta, a fact she'd come, over time, to resent. She'd gravitated naturally to psych nursing. Before she'd met Rick, she'd been working toward a Ph.D. in clinical psychology with the eventual goal of doing one-on-one therapy with patients. He'd not been in favor; she'd pressed on for a while, but motherhood had finally proved too much of a full-time job. After Charley died, she had not been motivated to go near those books and papers. Here, on the Psych ER, she wasn't interested in any theoretical analysis of her patients; the populations changed too rapidly for any of that. Mostly she liked to listen to the patients explain themselves, if they were coherent enough to talk. As a rule they told great stories.

Sharon slowed in front of the quiet room, peered through the small glass window at a young man five-point tied to a wheelchair, howling to himself. The noise was barely audible outside the door. She walked on, through the next door into the nurse's station.

Inside, two women looked up. Patients were forbidden here, but everyone knew the only thing stopping them was a sign on the wall.

"Morning, guys," said Sharon, taking off her coat and hanging it and her bag on the wall.

"Yo," said Crystal.

"Good morning, Miss Blautner." Hermione was a crisp, starched older woman who always wore nurse's whites, though on this ward one didn't have to. She had been there longer than anyone, and regarded the place as, functionally speaking, her own. Sharon didn't really believe Hermione liked her, though Crystal insisted the woman had said good things about Sharon when she wasn't around.

"How was the night?"

"Lost four, picked up twelve." Crystal handed Sharon the intake log, on a clipboard.

"Ugh," said Sharon.

"We are," Hermione said primly, "over capacity."

Crystal pulled the clipboard back from Sharon. "We're losin' five more. Freedman, Taggart, and Chusid are goin' up to the schiz ward. Grein is being released on her own, pending she stays on her meds. Garber decided Tuttle is not a dual diagnosis —"

"What?"

"— gets out soon as his paperwork gets done." Crystal set down the clipboard, cracked her gum loudly.

"The guy is totally delusional." Sharon slumped into a chair. "He thinks machines are following him around, reading his mind."

"Garber says he's just a junkie hiding from people he screwed over."

"Total paranoid delusional system —"

"He saw some movie on the tube last week. Says that's where the guy picked it up."

Sharon opened her mouth, shut it, and swallowed. "I've been talking to Tuttle for two days. I think he's totally authentic."

"May I remind you that you are not yet a doctor," Hermione said, not unkindly.

"Right, right, right," Sharon said.

"Dual diagnosis is tricky," Hermione said sweetly. "If a drug addict wants to quit, the city has methadone clinics waiting." She checked her watch. "Excuse me, ladies." She stepped out.

Sharon looked at Crystal. "It's about numbers," she said, dismally.

"Course it's about numbers, girl. City says Bellevue can't touch normal junkies — depressed junkies, suicidal junkies, schizophreniform junkies, they go up to dual diagnosis, they get a bed, meds, anything they need. Your normal junkie, he's got to go out, find himself a program, and wait on line. That's the mandate."

"Tuttle's a schiz!"

"Girl, obviously somebody's keeping some list somewhere, we been sending too many of them up there. Garber's got to turn away a few, look like he's being a good little gatekeeper —"

"Junkies don't come here!" Sharon exploded. "Junkies don't come to the Psych ER at Bellevue just to run away from the problems of their lives —"

"Don't get pissed at *me*." The two women looked at each other, and then simultaneously burst into laughter. "Get a grip," Crystal said, as the laughter died.

"Sorry," Sharon said. "Garber's a dick. We got anybody cool today?"

"I ain't been out hardly at all yet."

"Well —" Sharon pushed away from the desk. "Let's do it." She went to her coat, dug around in the pocket, found and opened the Necco wafers. "Want one?"

"You know I hate them things."

"Later," Sharon said, and walked out onto the ward.

At first, Milt Slavitch was just another of the sick and bloody and mutilated people stacked on gurneys in the emergency room hallway. Sometimes while he waited he said "please" over and over again, until it built into a sharp staccato prayer; the rest of the time he just stared at the overhead lights and spoke so deep in his throat no one understood him. Four stitches on his left wrist, three on his right, and three crossing the perineum up behind his testicles. When, finally, his bandages were in place, the doctor waved him away in dismissal and went on to the next case, a gunshot wound. The two cops pushed his gurney through the maze, took a right and then a left down the hall into the Psych ER.

Immediately the metal detector began yelping. "He's clean," one of the cops said, "or was." Hector turned off the overhead, scanned him with the handheld, waved him in. Hermione walked over, set the gurney against one wall. "We have clothes for him?"

"Came in without," said the cop with the clipboard.

"Nothing to check at all?"

"Just his leaflets," said the tall cop.

"And his stitches," said the other cop, and there was muffled mordant laughter between the two men. Hermione did not smile. The patient's lips were moving. Hermione bent slightly to hear.

"Please don't put in any more chips . . . please . . . no more . . ."

"No one's going to do anything bad to you," Hermione said, turning and looking out over the ward. Brian the fat intern hadn't gotten in, yet — he was younger than most, and tended to arrive late and flustered. The social worker was already in her first meeting of the day and booked for the next two hours, and Crystal was doing meds. Sharon had spent the last fifteen minutes explaining methadone maintenance to Tuttle. "Nurse Blautner?"

Sharon excused herself and came over, glanced at the well-built man on the gurney, his bandaged wrists. "New guest to the party?"

"In a word." Hermione didn't smile. "A prelim mental status, please? He's been here before, we're still awaiting his charts."

"Why doesn't that surprise me?"

"I'll get them to you as soon as they come in."

"My pleasure," Sharon said, and turned to the patient. "Would you rather be in a chair? That would be more human, right?"

Bill looked at her through wide-alert eyes. "No chips," he said. "Please, no chips."

"I didn't say chips, I said chair."

"I don't think he's going to be doing much sitting," the cop said, and handed her the clipboard. She read the crabbily written first sheet, glanced at one of the paper leaflets, got the gist.

"Sitting's not contraindicated. Would you gentlemen care to help me?"

Sharon leaned over the patient. He was a handsome man, dark and wiry, with deep, intelligent eyes. "We're going to untie you from this, and put you in this —" She touched a long wooden wheelchair reminiscent of a thirties tubercular sanatorium. "Okay?"

"What'd you do with FDR? Shoot him and dump him off the boat?"

"We're not terrorists," Sharon said, "and they're not that old, though they look it." She smiled. Damnit, Bill thought. This one's bright. "Officer, could we lose the cuffs?"

The cop stepped up, fumbled with his keys. "Shiva, lord of the dance," Bill said, low in his throat. He was still staring into her eyes.

"I'm sorry?" She hadn't made sense of what she'd heard.

"All those weather assholes on television, they're all false prophets. They think it's a science. They don't fucking know."

"Absolutely," Sharon said, "often they don't. Sit up?"

"Read the leaflet. Shiva taps the symbols on his fingers — tap —" He tapped his thumb and middle finger together. "And the world begins, and he starts to dance to the music he's making." Bill sat upright, turned his upper torso gently, bandaged wrists in the air like a Greek dancer. "Before he made the first sound, there was a whole other universe, right? And it ended. Right?"

"Right," Sharon said, because actually that kind of made sense, at least to her.

He looked at her. "Creator, destroyer. He gives, he takes away." Tap. "In the beginning was a word, a sound, a vibration. Light — particle or wave? Pinball — threat or fucking menace? Same shit. In Genesis, light is a sound."

"Right, that's Genesis's answer to the problem," Sharon said, and then was sharply aware of Hermione watching her. Something unspoken passed between them that Sharon only partially understood. "Why don't you get in the wheelchair," Sharon said to the patient, "we'll take you to the bathroom, let you do whatever you need, and then we'll talk."

"Read the leaflet. When you pray you look up. Christians think it's the closest thing to God, Rah Rah Rah the old blue and white, but that's not it at all. Every time you look up, you see Shiva's dance, beaming back down at you. Everything else is electricity, always trying to make the connection, always trying to make everything complete."

She smiled. "So who are you in all this?"

He smiled back. "I'm the stick that stirs the drink." And with that, he pushed himself up off the gurney, hobbled to the chair, and sat down. "Electricity's constantly seeking to make the connections, clouds dance to Krishna's cymbals, and the fucking weather assholes just don't fucking get it." There was a moment of uncomfortable silence between the cops and the nurses. "Well?" Bill said, expectantly.

"To the bathroom," Sharon said.

"To the bathroom!" Bill said, with a flourish.

"To the bathroom," one of the cops said, and Sharon pushed the patient along at the head of the little parade.

Bill nodded at the dance pop coming from the radio, walked to the can, and sat, muttering darkly about chips. Sharon, keeping an eye on him discreetly from just outside the half-open door, took a moment to look quickly over the leaflet. Hermione approached.

"I'm not sure you're aware," she said softly, "that Dr. Garber published a paper two years ago on markers for genital self-mutilation in schizophrenics."

"I had no idea."

"He tends to take an interest in these." She nodded toward the bathroom, in which Bill was humming.

Sharon faced Hermione. "Thank you," she said.

"Just so you know." Hermione did not smile, turned, and readied a pillow on the wheelchair.

Sharon resumed her delicate surveillance as the patient wrung out a washcloth, cleaned himself, cleaned the uncleanable steel plate in place as a mirror, washed his hands again and then came out and sat back in the chair.

"Do the stitches in your groin hurt?" she asked.

"I don't feel the chips when they're off." He became quiet.

Sharon and Hermione exchanged a slight nod. Sharon bent down to the patient's eye level. "If you don't mind, it's policy at this point to tie you in. You can wheel around, talk to people or whatever, but we don't want your stitches ripping —"

"You don't have to. I mean, really, you don't," Bill said, but Hermione was already at work. Sharon joined her — wrists and ankles, all with one long white cloth belt.

"This would seem to be all about punishment," said Bill.

Sharon smiled. "Yes, I'm sure it feels it. You'll get out of it, as soon as we trust each other. Let's lose all these authority figures, and just have a little talk, okay?"

"Can't fool me," said Bill. "You're an authority figure, too."

"Not much of one," she promised, then got behind the chair and pushed it up past the door and down the hallway to the offices. Room A was in use; she backed him into B so he could face her, then slipped around, shut the door — "privacy," she said — and took her seat behind the desk. Sharon started the way she always started:

"I just want to talk with you about what happened that got you in here, and how to get you happy and healthy and back out into more normal surroundings."

"Anything you want to know about me, read the leaflet."

"I did." Sort of; it was a complicated collage of typing, writing, and badly reproduced photographs of clouds over New York. "I'm more interested in you." She watched his eyes. He was smart, she saw that. Twisted. "So," she said, "who are you?"

"My name is Milt Slavitch. Which you already know."

"Not how it's pronounced, no, I didn't." She looked at the form. "And you live at 438 West Tenth Street."

"Uh-huh." It was an empty lot, and had been for some time.

"No phone?"

"I used to have one. They disconnected me."

"Any animals?"

Bill smiled pleasantly. "Just a pair of ragged claws —"

"Scuttling across the floors of silent seas. You and J. Alfred.

What I mean is, do we have to worry about feeding a dog or a cat or a lizard during your time here?"

"Nope. Just me alone."

"What sort of work have you done?"

"Well, I'm an engineer," he said.

"Electrical?" No answer. "Architectural?" He just stared. "Genetic?"

Close. "I wear a little cap and make the train go."

"Ha ha ha," said Sharon without any laughter in her voice, and then there they were, grinning at each other across the desk. "I mean what do you do for money?"

"I repair things. You know, appliances, electrical systems. Stuff that's gone wrong."

"Repairman." Sharon made a note on the small pad on her lap, put a star in the margin to return to it later, and then thought, well, let's do it. "All right — pardon my being direct, but what was going on in your life that made you decide to cut yourself?"

He said nothing. Sharon sat back and waited, hands in her lap, watch faced up so she could include it in her view. A minute passed, and most of another. At two minutes she would have said something, but he spoke before she needed to.

"There's an office building," he said. "On Park. North of Grand Central. With an extremely elaborate garden in the lobby."

"Uh-huh," Sharon said, because he had provided space for her to do so.

"There's a flower they have there, it's from Brazil. Twice a year it heats up to a hundred and thirty-seven degrees Fahrenheit. Two nights, coldest part of winter, it changes its metabolism from plant to animal, generates and burns amino acids, and — flame on."

"Wow," said Sharon. "Why?"

"Cold night, right? Got these one kind of bugs, down there. Flies. They're drawn to the warmth. They go in, get pollen on their wings. Next night. Cold again, flowers heat up. Flies go in, brush the pollen onto the stamen of a different plant."

"Ah," Sharon said, was aware of the risk even as she went on. "So this is a story basically about sex."

"A hundred and thirty-seven degrees Fahrenheit, two nights a year." He said it angrily. "All that effort trying to make the circuit complete, and it's in a fucking office building on fucking Park Avenue. The nearest symbiotic flies are forty-two hundred miles away."

"It must be sad to be that lonely," Sharon said. When she'd first started this, before she married Rick, she'd been afraid to let the patient in on her interpretation of the give-and-take between them. Over the years she had gotten more casual, and her assessments were better for it. "Is that," she said not at all gently, "why you cut yourself?"

He clammed up. Well, they had to talk about it; anything else was shooting the shit. But then, under his dark growl of a stare, a flash of doubt shivered through her: she seemed to be assuming he was yet another borderline case, cutting himself for the dual purposes of masochism and manipulation, telling her anything he might think she wanted to hear. But he was talking about himself in tangential metaphors; borderlines tended to be too self-obsessed to bother with that.

Well, then, clear it up. "Did you want to die?"

Bill tightened his lips, considering. "Don't we all, on some level?" he said finally. Sharon didn't answer. Her throat felt dry. He was watching her eyes. "I mean," he went on, "that's the big kabloona, the only question worth answering, yes?"

"There are other questions," she said, not necessarily caring to elaborate on what they might be. "You live alone?"

"Yes, I do."

"Do you enjoy it?"

"We're all alone. Human condition. It's natural."

"Would you say you've ever been in love?"

Of all the questions she could have asked, that one he had not been expecting. Kat. Ekaterina von Arlesburg. "There've been people. There was someone. It never worked out terribly well."

"Oh? Why not?" She kept herself poker-faced.

He let out a long sigh, staring at her. "Well, reciprocation's sometimes a problem."

"On their part? Or —"

"Let's not talk about that, okay? This is all ancient history, school-day afternoons and shit —" He and Ekaterina, wandering through the Guggenheim, talking about Cubism: all of life exploding in slow motion, just as it always had, captured on a flat surface for the first time. She'd always understood him, back at school, and then later.

Sharon watched him carefully, trying to read him, giving him the silence to explain himself.

"There was someone who reached out for me, okay?" he said finally. "Many years ago, I was in one of my subterranean periods, and she sort of dug down and found me —"

"Is she in your life now?"

There was a pause, which told her all she needed to know. And then he said: "She couldn't go where I went."

"Oh? Where was that?"

He grinned. "I wanted to keep power out of the bedroom and in the civic arena, where it belonged."

Sharon heard the resolution in his tone. Whoever she had been, he hadn't tried to cut off his testicles because of her. "Tell me about your family."

Bill smiled. "Old New York radicals for generations — we shot presidents, we were philanthropists, bootlegged whiskey —"

Uh-huh. "Parents alive? Mother? Father?"

"Depends which father you mean — the one who smashed things, or the asshole —"

"You mean, the one who smashed things wasn't an asshole?"

"The real one," Bill said. "From Harvard to Thorazine. Actually they were both assholes. Neither one of them lasted very long."

"So you were raised by your mother . . ."

"She died last year." It was funny saying that. He thought of her vomiting on the street from the chemo. Rainy fall day.

"When?" Sharon asked. "Around now? Or —"

Bill was silent. Yes, Sharon thought, around now. She sighed. "Milt, I sort of need to know how she died." If she'd committed suicide with a razor, his risk level was immediately going to elevate way high.

"She came to this fucking building and she fucking died, the way poor people always do."

"No no no, I mean what manner, what cause —"

Bill looked at her oddly. "Cancer," he said at length. "Ovarian cancer."

Sharon searched his face for emotion. "What did she do?"

"She was an actress-singer-dancer." Something inside told him not to say all this, and at the same time he remembered her voice in his head, saying it just that way. "Mostly, she danced."

"Ballet? Or —"

"Broadway."

"Really?" Sharon was always intrigued when people had connections to that world. "What was she in?"

Bill looked at her. "You know. Musicals. Chorus stuff. Do we have to talk about this?" He seemed profoundly uncomfortable.

"Well I'd like to — I mean, obviously she was important to you —" Bill said nothing. "It's something to be proud of — your heritage, and all." She thought of her father, thought of the Mackinnon Group logo, pushed all that away. "When you were a kid, did you do things with your mother?"

"She used to take me to art museums," Bill said, and then mumbled something, more to himself than to her.

"What?" she asked.

"I said there go the fucking chips again."

"Tell me about the chips."

"You already fucking know about the chips." Now, out of nowhere, he was furious.

Hoo, boy: affect was labile as hell. Sharon was glad he was tied up. She held his eyes with her own. "If I already knew, I wouldn't ask. Do you think somebody did something to you?"

"They put in fucking chips, okay?" He was violently angry. "First time I was ever fucking here, they put in chips so they'd always know where I was."

"Chips," Sharon said, beginning to get the idea.

"There's a fucking satellite way above the world, and when they want to track someone, they put a chip inside, it runs off the body's own internal electricity, they press a button, the chip completes a circuit, and the satellite tells them where you are every minute. Read the pamphlet — it's all in there."

What a rough way to live your life, Sharon thought. "You believe you have electricity inside you?"

"Of course I do. We all fucking do —"

"In any specific place?"

He looked at her as if she were profoundly stupid. "It's everywhere! It's in me, it's in you, it's in every piece of matter in the universe — it's the great unifier. It keeps tables from dissolving into piles of molecules, and molecules from dissolving into piles of atoms, and atoms from dissolving into quarks and neutrinos, and you know what they are? Pure fucking electricity. The mind and breath of God."

Sharon couldn't have agreed with him more. "So where'd they put the chip?" Bill was silent, mouth locked with tension. "Were you trying to release it when you cut yourself?"

Again, nothing from the tortured man across the desk.

"Is it in your bloodstream? Or —"

Nothing from the man.

"Or the other place you cut."

"You already fucking know." He hissed it out.

"Tell me."

He whispered to get the words out: "It's in the center of my testicle." He blushed violently crimson. "Sometimes I feel it in one, sometimes I feel it in the other. It holographs itself back and forth." He looked Sharon in the eye. "They've got it all set up so there's no way to figure out which."

"And the only way to get rid of the thing —"

"Is to cut my fucking balls off. That's it, that's the choice they've given me. If I want freedom, I have to castrate myself."

Sharon let that sink in, thought of Freud, all his later work about what we keep repressed in order to build civilization. This guy had simplified it down to its most basic form.

"Does it cause you pain?"

"When they want it to." She had to strain to hear him.

"Is it hurting right now?"

He nodded yes, his lips white. Sharon watched him, felt the kick of empathy she often felt when confronted by someone in pain.

Schiz or schizoaffective, she was thinking, fairly high-functioning, but with a big-time delusional system.

"Does it speak to you? Do you hear it say anything?"

Bill shook his head no. "It causes me to act. It's not like an instruction, or anything."

"It doesn't command anything?" He shook his head no. "Ever hear voices? Or see things that normally aren't there?"

Bill considered. "No, not at all."

"And the electricity — do you ever feel physical pain that you associate with it? Does it" — she debated words — "concentrate in any part of your body, hurt you in any way?"

"That's not the way it works at all. I'm talking about something totally different —"

And at that moment there was a knock on the door, and Dr. Garber opened it before Sharon could ask who it was.

"Nurse Blautner, excuse me," he said to her chest. "I thought you might appreciate my expertise in these cases."

"Well, we were in the middle of our conversation, here —"

"Fine," Garber said, shutting the door and perching himself on the edge of the desk. "You know," he said to Bill, "I've written papers on cases like yours."

"Dr. Garber is head of the psychiatric emergency room, here." She tried to sound thrilled, ended up sounding goofy.

"How do you know what my case is?"

"Ah, well, just from the police record and the medical report. You know, it's interesting, but all the people I've ever encountered who cut their genitals with a sharp instrument or scissors" — Sharon cringed; everything about this was wrong — "well, they all had similar traits in their background."

"Perhaps," Sharon risked, "we can discuss all this after the assessment —"

Dr. Garber turned and gave her a look of complete bafflement. "But I'm here now," he said.

"So you are," said Bill, affably, from his position tied to the wheelchair.

"Well, I just wanted to ask you —" He shifted his glasses.

"Sometimes we find a pattern of vandalism, a malicious attitude towards valuable property —"

"Hmmm," said Bill.

"Coupled with a divided or disorganized home, and no same-sex parent or role model."

"Sounds like me all over," Bill said helpfully.

"May I ask you a personal question?"

"Of course."

"Do you have any memories of being abused as a child?"

"No," said Bill. "None. May I ask you something, doctor?"

"Certainly."

"Do you have any children?"

"Actually, no," Garber said. "Not yet."

"I can't tell you how glad I am to hear that," Bill said, the pleasant smile still on his face.

Something in Garber's eyes froze. "Well," he said, and got up off the edge of the desk. "We'll talk again, on the ward, I'm sure. I trust I've been helpful, Nurse Blautner —"

"Terribly," Sharon said.

"Doc?" Garber turned. Bill's smile was dazzling. "When I was standing there with that razor, ready to lop off my balls, you know what I was really thinking?"

"What?"

"I was thinking there are too many assholes in the world already."

Sharon bit her lip. Garber flashed teeth, shut the door behind him. The air was oppressively thick for a long moment, and then Bill said, "What nuthouse did he escape from?" and they both — Sharon couldn't help it — burst into long, loud laughter.

III

Three hours later, Sharon was in the nurse's station reading through Milt Slavitch's newly arrived charts. He had first come to the hospital five years before, and again two years later. The situations were all similar — he was caught someplace he shouldn't have been, leaving his leaflets. When cornered, he cut himself.

There was no way to tell from his charts if he'd ever been taken anywhere besides Bellevue.

In both of his previous visits, his listed profession had been re-pairman. The first time he'd said he was unemployed; the second time, he'd been fired from a job the week previously. Addresses were different with each visit. He didn't seem to be able to carry on a working relationship with the phone company.

Sharon attempted to decipher one of the leaflets. Both sides of the photocopied page were crammed with typing, writing, diagrams of satellites and their orbits, and black-and-white photographs of clouds. The gist seemed to be that certain cloud formations occurred when certain satellites were overhead, and that those combinations of heavenly events in turn caused or stopped (it seemed to shift from example to example) various polit-ical changes, both in New York and in the world. Most of the pho-tos had dates; the most recent was two months old, a cloud vaguely in the shape of a cross that purportedly appeared in the sky the day of the pope's recent arrival at Kennedy. Several of the cloud pho-tographs had a view of the Empire State Building in the distance. Undoubtedly they'd been taken downtown, south of her place, be-cause the view from her apartment window was not dissimilar.

Deluded, yes, but there didn't seem to be a great deal of anger in the thing. It wasn't a warning of some dire prophecy. If any-thing, it seemed gentle, pointing out correlations between things that, in truth, had no connection whatsoever.

Mr. Slavitch's previous diagnosis had remained consistent, with variations, in every visit: schizophrenia, paranoid type, stable, sub-chronic with acute exacerbation; 295.30 on the DSM-IV classifica-tion. Sharon got back to her own assessment: speech was rapid, she wrote, and jumped from topic to topic. Affect was labile, without euphoria. Except for chronic delusional system, subject seemed fully oriented, alert, and without memory impairment.

Sharon stopped, looked back through the charts. All three times he'd cut himself when confronted by the police. Sharon leaned back in her squeaky chair, considered the question of a factitious diagnosis. But a few things militated against his doing it all on pur-pose: on one wrist, at least, he'd cut himself quite seriously; his delusions were remarkably similar in each of his hospital visits, and his cluster of symptoms all fell within the range of legitimate schizophrenia. Fakers tended to say yes to everything, to go for big, juicy symptoms they thought were uncheckable — aural and visual hallucinations, visitations from God. As with any lie, their stories would change over time. Low-key or high-key, real schizophrenics tended to be more consistent.

But she kept staring at those confrontations with the police, and she continued to wonder: he was obviously deeply intelligent — he could well know how to slip past the checks in place that usually caught the factitionals.

And then the more she thought about it, the more certain she was that he was crazy, all right. She'd read tons of the literature, and she'd been around enough cases — real, and a handful of factitious — over the years. After a while, you got to be able to hear it in their voices and see it in their eyes.

She looked at the patient disposition papers in the old charts. The first time he'd come he spent three days on the Psych ER, and then three days in the ward upstairs before being released. The second time, he'd spent three days on the Psych ER. Garber must have been happy to have another little statistic that said average stays were decreasing.

Sharon finished the assessment section of the form, unlocked the cabinet, and took out a drug slip. She filled in everything so all Garber would have to do was sign, clipped it with her assessment, walked onto the ward.

.The patient's chair was set against the wall. "Sharon," he said, "are you my Charon, guiding me through this Stygian darkness?"

She checked that her clipboard faced down so he couldn't see her paperwork, squatted by him. "That's my job. How you doing?"

"I finally figured out what this place feels like."

"Oh?"

"Evil summer camp," said Bill. "Some kind of summer camp where all the arts and crafts are lung tar painted on canvas, and in shop you carve ashtrays out of human sinuses."

"Ugh, that's awful," Sharon put her hand to her stomach.

"It even smells like summer camp," he went on happily. "Vomitous pork chops and limp string beans and pond scum. You know? And all the counselors are trying to hide that they smoke, and are all drinking and screwing each other all summer."

"Were you a kid, or a counselor?"

"I only went once, we were rich for, like, half an hour. Lutece after the wedding — fucking pig thought he could fucking buy us. Didn't fucking know who he was dealing with. Did not have clue fucking one."

There it was again: the tower going up on First popped into Sharon's mind — Mackinnon Group. "There are times when we think that the world is made of sand," she said. "And there are times when we know it's not." Okay, simplistic, but he seemed to be listening. She stood, rattled her papers. "Let me go do this. Anybody you want to meet, talk to them. Or I'll introduce you."

"Thanks," he said. She walked the length of the ER, knocked on Garber's office door. "Who is it?"

"Nurse Blautner."

"Enter." Sharon pushed the door open. Garber was standing, considering the frame of one of his diplomas.

"I have a drug order for Milt Slavitch — I was thinking neuroleptics, preferably Haldol." Nurses and social workers could examine the patients, assess their conditions, and do group and single therapy with them, but they couldn't prescribe medications. That was up to doctors. Sharon had no problem with that — they were the ones who got sued when things went wrong. "After your consult, I mentioned suicide contracts to him — I think he's a good candidate." She clicked a pen, held it and the slip out to Garber.

Garber turned his head without moving the rest of his body and looked down at Sharon. "Far be it for me to distrust your assessment," he said slowly, "but as you are no doubt aware, I have a great deal more experience than you in these matters. Just eyeballing him, I think Milt Slavitch may not be sick at all."

"Well, I considered a factitious diagnosis —" She kept her smile in place. "As far as I can see, he may think he's pulling something over on us, but he's also obviously ill —"

"I think he delights in fucking with authority."

"A man who believes the government has planted a computer

chip in his testicle might well think authority is fucking with him."

"Perhaps, Nurse Blautner, it should." He took the clipboard out of her hands, flipped through the pages. "Three times he's been confronted by police, three times he's cut himself. Maybe if we just let the cops take him to Rikers, it'll reality-check him. Be like shock treatment, aversion therapy. Confront him with his worst fears, let it run its course."

You punishing little bastard, Sharon thought. What, you heard us laugh and got pissed off? "Police have declined to prosecute."

"That could change with one phone call."

Sharon opened her mouth, shut it again. Nothing she could say seemed large enough. Bellevue had accepted this patient; it was her job to be the patient's advocate, to shepherd him through the system. And then she saw the hole in his logic. "Either he's sick or he's not. Sign the order, I'll hold it pending a test consult." She saw his skepticism, went on: "Based on his previous actions, we have every reason to believe he'll attempt suicide at Rikers. God knows it happens. And how would that look in the papers? 'Wrist-Slitter Rejected as Fraud by Bellevue Kills Himself in Prison'?"

That did it. Garber blinked twice and swallowed. "Well, we could at least run another course of electroshock."

"That we could," Sharon said. "If the neuroleptics don't work." Electroshock could be quite helpful with severely depressed patients. Milt had had it his first visit; for that, they'd have to find him a bed on the wards. She held out the pen and drug slip.

He took them, signed off on the clipboard, and handed it back. "It's always good to work with someone," he said then, "who retains the strength of their convictions."

Sharon smiled grimly, and he waved her away. She slipped out the door, stalked back across the ward. Milt was where she'd left him. "We're going to get a psychologist in," she said, "give you some question-and-answer tests — real basic stuff, just a conversation, not a medical procedure at all." Bill watched her carefully. "Those'll probably give us the go-ahead to prescribe medication — neuroleptics. There are side effects. You know about them? —"

"Extrapyramidal? Tardive dyskinesia? Constant uncontrollable swinging motions for the rest of my life?"

"Fifteen percent chance, if we have to do long-term."

"Did the dingbat think I needed them?"

That meant Garber. "Look," Sharon shifted in close, "we had a laugh during the assessment, and that's fine. But one of my tasks is to socialize you to this little universe — bizarre as it might be." She had his attention. "Dr. Garber can make life difficult for anyone he doesn't like. I think he's threatened by intelligent people — anyway, I had to go to bat to keep him from mucking around in your case. That's part of my role, here."

"But I've aroused his curiosity."

Sharon nodded. "Because of the whole police thing — you know, how you came in." Get off that. "So I think it's important you practice a bit of impulse control when you're around him. You can ventilate with me, that's fine. I'm on your side, here. But him —"

"Last time, he had a beard, didn't he? What, three years ago —"

"I wasn't here."

"A beard and a penchant for electroshock. Where were you?"

Pause. "Upstate," she said. Her smile felt brittle and false. Bill said nothing, just looked into her eyes. Finally she broke away. "So you don't have any problem with the idea of medication."

"I detest it. What if your life always boiled down to 'Take this shit or we'll shock you'? But I'll be a good little soldier."

"Glad to hear it." She started to rise.

"Sharon?" She stopped. "I'm sorry you have such a jerk boss."

Sharon suppressed a smile. "What can you do?" she said with a slight shrug of her shoulders, and started to go.

"And you know what?" She stopped, waited. "To be absolutely truthful, I actually rather enjoyed summer camp."

She smiled. "I didn't," she said, and then she was gone.

Bill watched the air where she'd been, the closed door of the nurse's station. Even with the tests coming up, somewhere inside, for no reason, he felt innocent and pure and strong.

* * *

"So," Sharon was saying, "I actually had another dream of Charley, last night."

Across the desk, Dr. Julia Phillips said nothing.

"He was alive, he was fine — it was in the car before the accident. And then in the dream suddenly I was here, and there were all these people that needed tending in the ER."

"And how did that make you feel?"

Sharon thought about it. "Like I had work to do," she said. In her mind, she flashed on Charley, his little white coffin, the funeral upstate four months after his father's. He'd survived the crash and two operations, died on the table during the third. She shoved the image aside. "Meanwhile, work has been so hectic —"

"You mean on the ER."

"Crystal's a delight," she went on. "Nothing fazes that woman. She knows Garber's an asshole, and she just lets him ride."

Dr. Phillips froze slightly. Garber was technically superior to both of them at Bellevue. It had taken a while for Sharon to get comfortable talking about him to Dr. Phillips, even though the psychiatrist was on the ethics committee, in-hospital. "And you can't do that," Julia said.

"Umm, no."

"Why do you think he irritates you so?"

"Well, he treats me like an idiot, and I'm halfway through my Ph.D." She heard herself sounding defensive as she said it.

"Have you had any thoughts about picking up where you left off with that?"

Sharon debated various responses, finally shook her head. "The whole point was to be a shrink, see patients. But I don't want that much responsibility over anyone, right now. I mean, I just don't think I'm that great at handling it."

"Which leaves you working under Garber."

"Right. That's what I've chosen. Right." Sharon thought of Charley's little Mickey Mouse zipper pouch, lying at the bottom of her bag on the floor next to her chair. She had promised herself as she came up in the elevator that today she was going to bring that up, but if Dr. Julia Phillips wanted to hear dirt about her Bellevue colleague Garber, so be it.

"But the thing is — the man's just one long unfulfilled promise."

"Does that remind you of other men you've known?"

"Not really," Sharon said. "I mean, kind of. Rick made good on his promises. As a rule."

"He promised to be with you forever."

"That's not his fault. I was driving."

There it was again. For a long moment neither said anything. "Anyone else?"

Sharon knew whom she meant. Funny, she had absolutely no desire to talk about it. "Well —" Her voice came out an octave too low. She cleared her throat. "Well, my father," she said, as if it were perfectly obvious.

Dr. Phillips said nothing.

"Dying as he did," she said. The next logical thing to say was about the Charley bag, but the moment had passed, or at least she allowed herself to feel it had. "I mean, my being so young, and all. Mom used to lie and say it was an accident, but when I was sixteen I got really fed up and made her stop."

"You were still angry at him."

Sharon considered that. "I don't think I am, anymore. Well, on some level, maybe. Probably. It goes back and forth." This all seemed an intellectual exercise. "I mean —" She searched for words. "My dad got screwed. He got screwed out of what was rightfully his. Mom says he was prone to depression—he'd always had periods where he would shut himself in his study and not communicate." Sharon looked at the floor, looked about three feet above Dr. Phillips's right ear, and then at her eyes. "He spent years of his life working with his partner Eddie on this computer program, invested all this time and money, the partner screwed him out of the rights to the thing, he got majorly depressed and shot himself." Sharon thought of her father in his T-shirt out in the sunshine, building the swing set in their backyard. She wondered if the memory was of a real moment, or if she'd conjured it up in a dream. "I blamed myself — I mean, that's obligatory. When you're nine years old, you don't know about money, business partners suing each other, any of that shit. You don't understand." And then she said nothing for a long time and stared dully at the surface of the desk.

"But now you blame the partner —"

"Well, Eddie went on to become Edward Mackinnon and make millions of dollars in New York real estate. He's a salesman. He was always a salesman. Dad was the computer genius. Edward Mackinnon made a mint off my dad's program — if he'd known squat about computer programs, he'd have stayed in the computer field. He wouldn't have had to diversify into luxury buildings in New York. And now, I read that his next big project's supposed to be a prison —" She shook her head.

"You don't blame your father in all this?" she asked gently.

"Well, of course — he pulled the trigger, no one else."

Dr. Julia Phillips glanced at the clock behind Sharon, made a show of discreetly checking her watch. "So —" she said. "It was an unfulfilled promise . . ."

"Well, yes —" Sharon didn't like the juxtaposition. Not at all. "But to put my father and that asshole Garber in the same sentence —"

"Sometimes we're not angry at the people in front of us. Sometimes we're angry at people in our heads."

Of course Sharon knew that was true. But later, taking the elevator back down from the sixteenth floor, she couldn't shake the elemental truth: if Garber was the beneficiary of any residual anger she might feel over the death of her father, then he should consider himself one lucky bastard to be in such august company.

Sharon had eighteen minutes left of her lunch hour; she headed into the cafeteria and took up a tray. Maybe today there would be some wonderful surprise.

There wasn't. Meat loaf, fish filets, stuffed shells in red sauce, squalid fried chicken under orange heat lamps. Sharon spent a long, blank moment watching the washed-out ears of corn float serenely in their dingy water. Then she got angry at herself: this was silly. All morning, she'd been thinking fondly of a chef's salad in a paper bowl with Russian dressing. The counterman was waiting. "Chef's salad, please," she said.

The counterman pointed dismissively toward the wrapped paper bowls. He tapped his spatula against the metal steam table. "Hot food," he said to the next woman on line. Sharon took up her bowl of salad, scooped a plastic tub of Russian dressing from the cooler, spigoted herself some iced tea from the machine, paid, and found a seat at a table. She opened her book, a flashy new hardcover collection of Jung's thoughts on healing, recently sent to her by Rick's mom. She was in the act of pouring pink dressing on her salad when her light was blocked.

There was a man in front of her. He had dark hair and a mustache and a white jacket. She'd seen him in this room before, and had thought absolutely nothing of it.

"Hi. Excuse me, can I ask you something?"

Sharon froze in mid-motion. "I guess so," she said, not at all sure of herself.

"I see you in here all the time —"

He was holding a copy of the *New England Journal of Medicine*. He was waiting for an acknowledgment. Sharon had none to give.

"I've noticed that book you're reading at the bedsides of a couple of my nicest, most intelligent terminal cancer patients —"

Sharon leaned back. He had a high forehead and a strong chin.

"I always wondered what a normal person would say about it."

He wasn't unattractive. He looked young, unruffled, as if life hadn't beat him up yet. She scraped out the rest of her dressing onto her salad with a white plastic knife and set the container down. "It's good," she said. "Sort of a pep talk for the spiritually traumatized." She didn't like the way that sounded.

He grinned and shook his head, his thick eyebrows knotting. "And you are reading it because — ?"

"One of my patients recommended it to me."

"Where do you work?"

"The Psych ER" she said and felt like she'd been caught in a lie. Psych ER patients tended not to do a lot of reading.

If he saw the discrepancy, he didn't show it. "You like it there?"

"I have my fun," said Sharon. He was waiting for her now to reciprocate, to ask him where he worked, and even as she recognized the fact, she noted his finger holding his place in his *New England Journal* and made a conscious choice not to. Just because he asked did not mean she had to ask back. She looked at her salad, trying to figure out how to get back to it.

"I'm Frank," the man said rather hurriedly, as if afraid the conversation was going to die.

"Sharon," Sharon said, because it was kind of difficult not to. At least he hadn't offered his hand.

"You know the other question I had about you?"

"I can't imagine."

"I've seen you here — mostly afternoons, I guess —"

"Go ahead," she said.

"Well, I can't help but notice that you always seem to be eating exactly the same thing — chef's salad, Russian dressing, iced tea." He got it out. Sharon could see that it actually had taken effort. Now he paused, as if expecting to be congratulated on his powers of observation. Sharon waited.

"I was kind of wondering why."

Sharon smiled to herself — it was a big, fat, lazy softball, and she swatted it out of the park. "Because," she said, "I like it." She took up her fork. "And now, I'd like to get to it. So —"

"Right," he said, and smiled. He had a nice smile, Sharon noticed — wide and straight and clean. "Well, see you 'round," he said, managing to completely ignore his defeat. He touched the table with two fingers, a gesture that made something in Sharon's stomach crawl. Then he walked casually away and out the door.

Sharon took a bite of her chef's salad. It was exactly the way it always was — crunchy and mushy and sweet and salty all at once. Baby food for adults. She took another bite, found herself feeling slightly guilty for trashing poor Frank.

And then she had the idea: what if, wherever he was now, he was somehow aware of the moment of guilt she was experiencing on his behalf? What would he have thought?

Then, without warning, came the corollary: what if that had, in fact, been his intent?

No, it couldn't be. Even an avid reader of the *New England Journal of Medicine* could not be that clever.

And besides, he had way too nice a smile.

IV

Senator Arvin Redwell sat between the mayor and Edward Mackinnon in the City Hall conference room, privately amazed that he needed to be here at all. His assistant Lamar had been nattering on ineffectually for fifteen minutes, Edward obviously bored and the mayor in his usual amiable fog, and the senator had finally had enough.

He held up his hand; Lamar stopped mid-word, reminding Arvin all over again why he liked the boy. "Look," Arvin told the assembled community board members and redevelopment activists, "it's not that we're trying to ram this thing down the throat of this neighborhood, or that neighborhood. It's that we feel this spot on the Lower East Side of Manhattan is ideal —"

This was met by a loud chorus of boos. Finally an older Irish lawyer in a rumpled suit with a certain dignity stood up and waved the crowd down. "Arvin, you and I go way back, so let's cut the baloney. You take a neighborhood that's totally shot to hell, like the truly awful sections of the South Bronx, it makes a lot of sense to put in a prison. It gives jobs, it's an anchor for other businesses, fine. Even though, right now, polls say a majority of people don't feel another prison is the answer, if you were to tell me you were opening this thing in the South Bronx, I'd say go for it. Go be a pioneer, save the world, start something new up there. But you want to do it somewhere safe, somewhere established. So for that you're going to rip out blocks of affordable lower-middle-class housing, displace thousands of people, and build this thing that looks like Dachau — I don't see it helping the neighborhood. And I'll tell you what — the only reason you want to do it on the Lower East Side is because you couldn't get away with it any other place. Well, I'm going to fight you." The crowd burst into applause around him. "And Edward —" He pointed at Edward Mackinnon, who straightened his back behind the table. "This goes against everything you've ever said about the importance of maintaining the continuity of neighborhoods. This is taking a neighborhood that has been evolving organically for years and just putting a lid on it. Edward, you wouldn't want your kid growing up next to a prison. Have you really so given up hope on the low-rent areas of this city that this is the only way you can devise to make money off them? This thing you want to build will cast a shadow on everyone who lives in that area — don't you see that? Or was all your other rhetoric simply lies?"

Another sustained moment of applause.

"But Edward —" he went on. "More importantly — do you know who you're in bed with, here? These people want to privatize everything — the judicial system, the cops — everything. Is that really your philosophy?"

Edward sat up, pulled the microphone closer. "I'll be the first to concede Straythmore's long-term goals might now appear out of the mainstream — but who knows? When Ford built the first car, I'm sure the vision of a nation of interstate highways was a foreign concept to a lot of people —"

"But private police forces? Corporately subcontracted judicial systems? Is that a vision you support — I mean, it must be, you bought a huge stake in the company —"

Edward shook his head. "I bought into the best privatized prison building company in the world today. They're aggressive, they have short-term goals, and, yes, a long-term vision, I'll grant you that. But in the short term, they didn't have the wherewithal to really expand into the urban markets. That's why we're a great combination."

"But what about checks and balances? Don't you see their long-term vision runs counter to the spirit of the Constitution and Bill of Rights of this country? There can be no authority higher than the independent judiciary — except Straythmore Security? I don't see that written anywhere in the law books, Edward."

"I'm not a constitutional scholar — but I don't think we should stop a company just because ten, twenty, thirty years down the line they might seek new forms of business. Listen, I have to be accountable to my shareholders. Whatever Straythmore's long-term goals are, I have to worry about the Mackinnon Group making a profit this quarter, and the next, and the next. That's where my responsibility lies, ultimately. And this will help do that."

The rumpled man just shook his head. "So now you've got a letter of intent to buy the Carnegie-Hayden building, a crumbling old pile the city's been trying to get rid of for years, the perfect place to begin your new little empire. Well, I can see the fix is in. We let this building go, we won't be able to hold on to any of the others. But if I had the money, I'd offer the moon for it just to stop you."

Edward looked at Arvin with a discreet half-smile. For all his eloquence, the rumpled man had just destroyed his own argument. Because nobody was ever going to do anything with the Carnegie-Hayden building. In terms of everything Edward Mackinnon knew about marketing, it was the perfect site — convenient to the Tombs, the city prison downtown, yet not so close as to create any public perception of trying to set up as a direct competitor. And it was situated in a neighborhood well past its prime; they'd be able to buy whatever land they might require when the need to expand arose. But — even better — symbolically, the Carnegie-Hayden represented a kind of corporate philanthropical vision from the past; the fact that the building was a crumbling ruin in need of tearing down showed precisely the limitations of the old ways of doing things. Maybe it had once been beautiful, but now it was just a rattrap, and when they moved the wrecking crews in, nobody — Edward was sure of this — would finally care.

Manhattan had to be first, to establish that Straythmore was the acknowledged leader in the field, but the city had made it clear that, in its current budget crisis, it was quite willing to sell off a great many things it regarded, fairly or unfairly, as white elephants. Edward already had his eye on a shortlist of choice city-owned properties in Brooklyn and Queens — the old Knickerbocker Terminal, the vast Prometheus Textile factory space — beautiful old buildings whose time had come and gone, and yet there they were, still standing. All perfect for Straythmore's "satellite corrections modules" and the gradually expanding role in neighborhood law enforcement that might well inevitably follow.

If, down the line, he could find sites as ideal as the Carnegie-Hayden in the other boroughs, the other cities, the other markets he intended to hit, he'd rip out them all.

The attractive Korean woman started with the Bender Gestalt Test, motor and visual skills, not Bill's favorite, but one that he rather appreciated. Organic neurological symptoms were not to be desired; he copied the little squares and squiggles fairly carefully, though he had fun crowding everything into one corner of the paper. As the square was thought to represent the male, and the circle the female, he made sure to keep his squares consistently small and open-ended. His House-Tree-Person drawings were an embellished combination of several from textbooks back in his basement. And then they moved on to the Rorschach, a subtle, complicated, fluid test Bill loved more than any other.

There were no right answers. That was the beauty of it, really. Millions of people had given their replies to the ten inkblots Hermann Rorschach published in 1921, a year before his untimely death. A huge baseline had been established, coupled with a voluminous literature describing how differing symptoms displayed themselves in people's responses to the inkblots. Bill had studied it extensively.

It always surprised him how lacy and beautiful the actual images were, especially the colorful ones — there the gossamer reds and golds and greens shimmered like angels' dresses.

Card I was perhaps the scariest, the most like a Halloween mask. Bill knew that perception of forms was the standard for reality testing; schizophrenics tended to make forms from unusual sections of detail. "I see an arm, kind of gnarled, there —" He gestured. "It's rotting. It's rotted off. And that's the hand — closed." Ego boundary disturbances. He pointed an inch away. "But it has a hole in it, there's muscle missing — that's the white." Bill debated various barrier-versus-penetration responses, suddenly found himself thinking: not too much, don't want Sharon to think I'm a complete fuck-up. Depression, he remembered, and plunged into the black areas, the way they looked like animals frozen in time. He'd get to inanimate, animal, and human movement later. They went over his responses for a while, and then with the next card he latched on to the slightly lighter shades of black, and began to introduce the idea of color shading as form, one of Exner and Wylie's eleven signs of suicidal ideation.

After this, the Thematic Apperception Test, which involved making up stories to go with ambivalent drawings, and then he'd be done. The only test he'd never been able to get a handle on from the literature was the MMPI, 550 questions that nailed things down scarily well, but it was expensive, it took a week to be scored by some company out in Jersey, and it wasn't usually given without a guarantee that eventually, down the road, somebody somewhere would get paid.

"To tell you the truth," Dr. Amy Soong told Sharon over the phone an hour later, "treatment potential is pretty good. He's not faking — his shit runs deep. Lots of body image distortion, a fair amount of maternal and death imagery. He gave seven of the eleven Exner-Wylie suicide determinants — they call for eight, but close enough. But he's smart as hell, vast supply of knowledge, he cares about virtually every field of human endeavor. A bit socially isolated, but not a lot of sexual immaturity. Is he dangerous to himself and others? Yeah, I'd have to say. But he's creative — I'll give him that. And actually, rather sweet. You'll get my report by five."

Sharon thanked her and hung up the phone. It was so odd — if she'd finished her Ph.D. in Clinical, she'd get to do testing like Amy. But Amy dealt with symptoms on paper in an office upstairs, while Sharon dealt with people. She finished measuring cc's of antipsychotics into little cups, then edged her tray of liquid meds through the door of the nurse's station. She felt like some kind of neuroleptic barmaid, carrying eleven plastic-lidded Dixie cups filled with various combinations of medications and cranberry-raspberry juice. She walked past Andrew Sentoro, in exactly the same position she'd left him in before — hunched over, one hand on his crotch, the other up toward the ceiling as if he were orating Shakespeare or catching a fly ball. She'd tend to him later — there were pliable catatonics who pretty much went where you led them, and there were resistant ones. Those took extreme patience: they fought you every step of the way. Andrew was resistant as hell.

Sharon started at the front. Carmen was thirty-nine, a grandmother, and heard voices that talked about her everywhere she went. She'd been brought in by her husband with bruises all over her arms and shoulders.

Sharon sat next to her. "I brought your medication first," she said, "so you could see nobody'd done anything to it."

"You can't trust nobody around here." Carmen drank her cup down. "They're all dogs. Steal your meat right off your plate." She made a motion to spit, but her mouth was too dry from the meds.

Sharon stood. "We'll talk later," she said, and saw Malcolm approaching, all pumped up.

"That thing with my tongue, it's happenin', it's happenin'." He was terrified.

"Look — you're not on medication that does that."

"I feel it, I feel it, my tongue's curlin' up like a roll a toilet paper."

"Lithium doesn't cause that. You're on lithium. There's nothing in you that would do any of that stuff." Malcolm was manic depressive, and a rapid cycler — this was his fifth manic phase this year, and his third hospitalization. Now twenty-eight, he'd been treated with antipsychotics as a teenager in Venezuela and had begun to have the first signs of extrapyramidal side effects — uncontrollable movements of the tongue and lips. Garber had been ready to put him on more of the same — antipsychotics were helpful in high manic phase — but Crystal had made the point that this was a textbook case where you didn't have to take the risk. The last thing they wanted was the poor guy to get the full-blown symptomatology and spend the rest of his life uncontrollably swinging his arms.

Malcolm paced back and forth, scratching under his drawstring pants, his hospital shirt flapping open around him like a sail. "I don't need this shit," he sputtered. "I got four hundred thousand dollars coming to me from a bank on Thirty-third Street." He stamped away, furious.

Sharon walked to the card table. Walter was deep into the gin game with Fletcher, Shabazz, and Rodriguez. He was one of the Psych ER regulars, a homeless man who came in every few months when the paranoia got too much. Sharon interrupted the game to give him his juice, which he drank down greedily.

Sharon looked over the table. "You gentlemen've been playing for a while —" Fletcher banged his cast to scratch his leg; he'd broken it in a suicide jump. "You should let somebody else in."

Shabazz had the weight-room build of an ex-con. "We're just playing, ma'am," he said. Rodriguez muttered something in Spanish that Sharon didn't get, and they all laughed.

"Half an hour, gentlemen," Sharon said, checking the clock. "Whoever's behind then has to give up their seat. Got it?"

None of them said a word. Sharon went on down the hall.

The drugs had varying degrees of effectiveness: as a rule, they ameliorated the psychotic symptoms, which allowed patients at least to understand and participate in whatever decisions were made on their behalf. For relatively low doses, liquids were easier than pills — they couldn't be cheeked and then spat out later. Sharon also had to watch for anyone who went to the bathroom immediately afterward. Often they would try to make themselves vomit.

Crystal bustled onto the ward with pills for the megadosers and immediately was caught again by red-haired Malcolm. "I need a smoke," he said. "They're sending a chopper to get my money."

"You'll get your meds as soon as we finish the blood work."

"UNESCO wants my blood, you know that? United Nations. I'm gonna speak there when I get my money."

From across the room, Sharon and Crystal traded a glance — sometimes bipolars in manic phase were charming, if loud. Sometimes they were just a pain in the ass. Finally she got to Bill, sitting in his chair at the back.

"Last one," she said, showing him the tray.

"Rotten egg," Bill said. "You're like a stewardess — the way you walk with that tray. All these people's minds pitching and rolling around you, it's great how you keep balance."

"I take that as a compliment," Sharon said. "This is for you."

"Impressive, you can keep your calm, not get cynical."

"I'm pretty cynical," she said, trying to defuse whatever construct he was building.

He looked around. "Then why do you work here?"

Good point. Sharon searched for a reply, found one. "I'm so cynical I think this is normal."

"That's not cynicism, that's penance." Sharon considered it intellectually, and then the logic caught up with her — Charley, of course, Jesus — and the emotion came and she took it like a body blow, tried not to show it in her face as the liquid fear formed out of nothing and exploded in her heart. How had he known that? Was her wound that obvious? He was watching her eyes.

Bill saw their thoughts jump parallel as dolphins for a moment. Exhilarating. "Yeah," he said, because it was the next thing to say, "we all create our own prisons."

There was a chair next to him, so she sat. Halfway through the action she tried to make it look casual, but it didn't work. "What's yours?" she said, still holding the little plastic cup with the red juice in it.

"New York, every inch of it. I've got a basement where I keep my brain. Superman's fortress of solitude. This place is where you get to be Supergirl."

Sharon shook her head. "Naah, Supergirl didn't work out for me. Now I'm just Lois Lane." She held up the cup. "Ready?"

"I take this stuff, will you untie me from this chair?"

"Sign a suicide contract, agree not to screw around with your bandages in any way —"

"All right all right all right," said Bill. "I'll do it."

"Deal," she said, opening a straw, poking it in the cup, and holding it for him to sip.

"This isn't Thorazine," Bill said, after the first swallow.

"Nope. Haldol."

"Thorazine tastes like shit," Bill said and took another pull on the straw.

When he finished, Sharon pushed his wheelchair away from the wall and undid the long cloth bands around his chest, wrists, and feet.

Bill stood and spent a long elaborate moment stretching his bandaged wrists up to the ceiling.

"You stretch like a dancer would," Sharon said. He was strong, well muscled and lithe at the same time.

He dropped his arms. "I didn't get it from my mother, if that's what you're asking."

It had been in her mind. "Well, you know, the milieu —"

Bill shook his head dismissively. "Mom didn't dance much after that last show at the Hammerstein before it went down. It's not as if we stretched every morning, okay? It's not like we did little exercises together."

"Well, what did you do?"

That stopped him. He thought about it. "Before she married the asshole? Or after?"

"Before," Sharon guessed.

His first impulse was to keep the answer vague, to delve equally into truth and nontruth, but then he remembered the apartment in the West Forties, the smell of the mornings there, and it was all around him, those days. "Woke up," he said. "Got myself some cereal, cranked up the Mr. Coffee so it would be there for her and whoever she was with, which was usually someone. If she was alone and she needed to get up, I'd bring her a mug of coffee with a jolt of vodka in it. Her eye-opener."

"How old were you?"

Bill shrugged. "Twelve, thirteen, fourteen? Mom didn't like sleeping alone. Sometimes when she was drunk enough, she'd come into bed with me, just to have a body there."

Asshole Garber sometimes called them right. Sharon kept her face absolutely free of expression. "Must have been confusing," she said.

"Naah, it was just mom."

There was a lull then, a pregnant pause, and Sharon thought to herself, all right, why the hell not? "Yeah," she said then. "I had the whole single-parent thing too." Of course, in my case, we didn't sleep together . . . but she didn't say it. "It's weird, when you become a parent to your parent."

"Mom or dad?"

"Mom. Dad died when I was a kid." His brains all over the back wall.

"Your mom ever remarry?"

"Nope," Sharon said. "Nope, nope, nope. You have a stepfather, though —"

"Had. They were only married like three years. He's had two wives since."

"It's funny, your mom sounds like a case, but you speak about her with real fondness."

"Hmm," Bill said. "Well, she gave me things."

"Like what?"

Something in him was guarded. She could see it in his eyes. "Like art," he said. "And politics. Her morals were impeccable." And then something in his eyes changed, became kinder. "Like for instance, did you ever consider the relationship between the viewer and the painting in a museum?"

"Well," Sharon took a stab. "You look at it, you learn what it's trying to say —"

"No no no. Everyone who looks at a painting changes it fundamentally in some tiny subatomic electrical way." Sharon looked skeptical. "Seriously — the painting changes you, and at the same time you change it. You leave imprints on each other."

"I don't think that's really the case," Sharon said gently.

"It's nothing you see." Bill sounded entirely reasonable, as if this had been in *Scientific American* last week. "Different combinations make different things happen — I mean, consider some horrid securities criminal who buys a three-hundred-year-old Rembrandt oil, and he gets it home and hangs it on the wall, and as he looks at it, just by interacting with his particular gaze, it curdles into a blood red sheet?"

Magical thinking, Sharon thought. "You have quite an imagination," she said, and at that moment Malcolm, little red-headed Malcolm, stumped up to the card table, put his hands under it, shouted, "Fuckin' niggers take my fuckin' MONEY!" and up-ended everything, sending cards and newspapers flying.

The uproar was instantaneous. People who seconds before had been lost in worlds of their own came back to earth with a snap and began to scream. Fletcher was howling with pain under the edge of the wooden table, the weight twisting his leg in his cast. The three other card players were up and shouting at Malcolm, backing him to a wall. "Shit," Sharon said, and then: "SECURITY!" She ran to Fletcher, got him out from under the table, helped him belly his way through the knot of people. She looked up just in time to see Rodriguez slam Malcolm's chest with one punch, and then another. Crystal appeared out of nowhere, followed closely by Brian, the rotating psychiatric intern, his stomach chugging as he ran. Malcolm came back up holding a chair, began to swing it in front of him so no one could get near. "I want my MONEY!" he shouted. "I want my fuckin' MONEY, you scumbags!" And he smashed the chair into Walter, who went down bloody and stuttering in pain.

Sharon kicked through the door into the nurse's station, took a vial of clear liquid from a locked cabinet. She popped the top off a syringe, filled and capped it, and went back out onto the ward.

Hector had carved Rodriguez away from the pack with his nightstick, was now walking him backwards and shouting at them all to sit down. That left Malcolm holding his chair up against Shabazz, in fighting stance, hands open in front of his face, looking for a way in to grab the chair and take the man apart.

"Me and you, asshole," he kept saying. "Just me and you."

Brian the intern was pale. No help there, Sharon thought, not for the first time. She walked up to Shabazz with the needle in the air, like a gun. "Get away from him," she said.

"Gonna pound the mufuck."

"You touch him, we'll bang you for assault. You'll go one-way to the prison ward."

"You listen to her, honey," Crystal said from the other side.

For a long moment Shabazz did nothing, Malcolm red-faced in front of him, visibly shaking with rage. And then his hands lashed out, took hold of the chair, yanked it out of Malcolm's hands, and hurled it high against the wall. It tumbled down onto the upended wooden table, came to rest on the floor. Shabazz stormed away, past Malcolm to the front of the ward.

Sharon watched him go, found she could breathe again. "I have to give you this, Malcolm," she said then, and at that moment, something clicked in Andrew Sentoro's head, a complex combination of memory, chemicals, and inappropriately triggered animal instinct, and little Andrew, trapped and mute and frozen in one position for two days, went from a state of catatonic stupor to one of catatonic excitement in less time than it takes to unlock a door.

The noise he made when he picked up the table and swung it over his head was a total unleashing of repressed rage. He smashed it once against the chickenwire-glass window of the nurse's station, then hauled it back and smashed it again and again until the wire dented and the glass snapped and splintered, the panes cracking loudly into blades.

Sharon heard the sound and winced her eyes shut against it and was instantly surrounded by the memory of broken glass everywhere around her — every particle of air had contained a shard as the car whipped across two lanes into the moving semi. She was sinking, something in her was sinking deep and hard. And suddenly there was no blood in her stomach and in her head, she was dizzy, and she couldn't trust her legs to keep her up.

Bill followed every step, watching from the side. Her face turned death-mask white, she thrust out an arm for balance, and the syringe flew from her hand and skittered across the linoleum, and he went for her just as she fell. He caught her, and for a long weird moment he struggled with her thin limp body, as in a pietà, trying desperately not to lose her and have her head smack against the floor. He was aware of the noise of Andrew slamming the table into the window; three feet away, Malcolm was flat against the wall, giggling. Sharon seemed to be unable to draw a full breath and her eyes were half open; he could see her fighting. He lowered her gently to the floor, and looked around for the syringe.

It was in the far corner. He ran over, scooped it up, and then the table hit the wall and fell to the ground behind him, and Bill spun around in time to see Andrew Sentoro wrestling his pants down to his thighs. He fell on Sharon and pinned her head with his hands and clamped his lips over hers, his naked groin grinding against her.

Sharon's eyes opened, and she looked over at Bill, and all he could see was her terror. He set the capped syringe down by her head, put one arm up against Andrew's windpipe, grabbed one of Andrew's hands away from her neck and pressed the balled fist high up against the man's spine and pried him off her. The man's large white penis bobbed under the fluorescent lights. By that time, Hector and Crystal had each grabbed a leg, while Bill struggled against the man's teeth and elbows, and Sharon wriggled out from under him and found the syringe. She popped the cap off, checked for damage. "Hold him," she said, jammed the needle deep into the muscle of his naked thigh, and pressed the blue plunger.

Ten seconds passed. Twenty seconds. Strings of obscenities poured from Andrew's mouth. After forty-five seconds he seemed to relax. Then the fog rolled in over his eyes, and they knew it was safe to let him go.

"Thank you," said Sharon, leaning up against a wall, still catching her breath.

Bill shrugged. "Anytime, Sharon," he said. "Anytime."

V

"Garber's always doing this," Sharon was saying. "He creates situations, and then leaves them for other people to deal with. I hate men who do that." Out of nowhere she remembered the wood grain on the swing set at their first house; she sipped her margarita.

They were at Puerto Vallarta, a noisy Bellevue watering hole. Sharon and Crystal only came here when they were in bad moods: the chips were greasy, but the margaritas were undeniably great, and it was midway between Sharon's apartment and Crystal's subway.

"Guy had maids," Crystal said. "Betcha he had maids. Black

ladies older 'n his mother picking up his shit where he dropped it. Got used to thinking someone'd always be there to catch his dirty underwear before it touched the ground."

"Hey, I didn't come to Bellevue so I could be on his little 'team' and take hits whenever he screws up." Sharon sipped her drink. "I could have stayed upstate at Dutchess Community — nice quiet suburban population, run a couple of rehab groups, do some teen counseling —"

"Drive past that graveyard every time you need something from the supermarket —"

Sharon grimaced. "Not quite that bad, but right, that part sucked. I mean, Rick's family were really good, *are* really good —"

"But you need them like they need salmonella."

Sharon smiled. "More or less. Though I stay in touch." She thought of Charley's plastic Mickey Mouse zipper case, nestled quietly between her feet at the bottom of her bag. Once again, she initiated the laborious effort to push all that out of her head. God, the exertion always felt the same way. And then she noticed some-one crossing the restaurant toward them, curly hair and a strong chin, and Sharon suddenly felt trapped in her chair.

He caught her eyes, smiled, continued to come over as if she'd invited him. "I'm glad to see," he said when he got to their table, "that you do indeed have other things besides chef's salad."

Crystal looked from Sharon up to the guy, and then back, a half-smile playing on her face. She hid it by sipping her drink.

Sharon felt called upon to say something. "Hi," she said.

"Hi," he said. "I'm Frank." He said it to Crystal.

"I'm Crystal," Crystal said. "She's Sharon." This was accompa-nied by an unsubtle point of her thumb.

"That, I know." He turned to Sharon. "How you been?"

"Surviving quite adequately, thank you." She tried to keep it arch, complete, someone who didn't need anything or anybody.

"Doesn't sound much fun."

"It ain't," said Crystal, looking directly at Sharon, who made a face back at her, all gritted teeth and flashing eyes.

"You both work in the Psych ER?"

"Uh-huh," said Crystal.

"Surgery gets really predictable — they come in sick, you take stuff out, they either die or they stumble on — but Jesus, in Psych, you guys must have stories —"

He trailed off, and there was a brief, expectant pause where everyone looked at her. Sharon considered Crystal, laughing behind her eyes, and thought: all right, might as well be adult about this.

"Yes," she said, "you can ask anybody what the voices in their heads are saying now, and by and large, they'll tell you."

"What do they usually say?"

Sharon considered it. "Your basic constant uncontrollable stream of babble, either for or against themselves."

"Or 'FUCK YOU FUCK YOU FUCK YOU' — we get that a lot," said Crystal helpfully.

"Command hallucinations —"

"You mean, like, 'Kill the President —'?" Frank imitated a crazy person, badly.

"Cops love those guys — they send them straight up to the forensic ward on eighteen, keep 'em behind bars," Crystal said. "Do not pass go, do not collect two hundred dollars."

"We had a pyro, she had voices telling her to set fires," Sharon recalled. "She was very sweet, once her meds kicked in."

"Had she wet her bed?" Frank asked. "Been cruel to animals?"

"Big three," Crystal said.

"Actually, yes." Sharon said. "Three classic markers for a serial murderer, she had them all. But she hadn't done anything that we knew about, so basically she just got better and left."

"And right now, she's somewhere out there —"

"Not taking her meds and hearing voices," Sharon said, and they all laughed.

"Surgery, stuff like that never happens. May I stand you ladies a round?" He gestured at their almost empty glasses.

"Sure," said Crystal. "No," said Sharon. Again both Frank and Crystal looked at her and waited expectantly.

"Well, why not," she said, finally, to Crystal. "I hardly ever party anymore, right?"

*　　　*　　　*

Sharon was under the curly-haired man, spread wide, her ankles over his shoulders, and he had his eyes closed, and he was pounding deep inside of her, slamming her with his thighs again and again. His arms were pressed tight at her temples, his palms holding her wrists down so the only choice she was able to make was whether to keep her eyes open or shut. She shut them, and even as she hated herself for hating herself so deeply, the pleasure inside her mounted, the sensations grew more and more beyond her control.

She opened her legs wider, gave up trying to control anything, gave in to him. She wanted to lose herself; that's all she asked. Take this mortal body of hers and use it and rip it and leave it in a pile on the floor. She didn't want an identity; she wanted an orgasm, and this man, pinning her down, forcing himself faster and faster into her, this man was shredding everything she knew and cared about herself, leaving her with only one out.

What was his name?

Phil. That was not it. It was a valiant stab, but it was not it. She searched her mind, hated herself for this sudden, stupid Freudian mental block.

She opened her eyes, looked up at his face. It was a violent shade of red; his eyes shut, his expression at once mindless and determined. There seemed no room anywhere in it for pleasure.

Frank.

Yes, of course. Frank DeLeo, M.D. All those margaritas at Vallarta's, and then Crystal had left, and then the taxi ride to — where? The Nightmare Lounge. One of those clubs. Then more beer and tequila, listening to him talk loudly about how he and his ex-wife should've never ended up in court, she hadn't given him a chance. He was attractive, and not without charm, but he was younger than she, in a loud foolish way that wasn't really all that amusing.

She'd gotten drunk. And in one of the dark little rooms of the club, when he'd started to kiss her, she'd kissed back. And now here they were, back at her place at two in the morning, with him trying to gain his identity, and her trying to lose hers.

Damnit, one bad evening, and all her self-destructive impulses came crashing out. She hadn't had sex in, what, ten months? Almost eleven. And that had been exactly the same — a horrible, drunken one-night stand she'd used to punish herself for even contemplating the idea of being with someone new.

She closed her eyes again and instantly her mind conjured up the blue-flowered wallpaper that had been above their bed in the house upstate. She winced to get it out of her head, struggled daintily with her wrists, hoping he'd clamp down, and when he did, she found herself thankful — at least he knew to do that — and the knife-edge of pleasure began to grow again, deep inside. She reached for it as if it were a sacrament, wanting to be consumed by it, wanting nothing more than to feel that power surround and engulf her, wanting nothing more than to explode.

Then he began to make noises, guttural, gnashing throat sounds, and then he changed registers and there was a keening, childish kind of wailing, high pitched and inarticulate, and he slammed her and slammed her and slammed her with his orgasm. He quickly pulled his cock out, holding onto his condom, rolled off her, and stared at the ceiling, breathing hard.

Sharon looked at him and thought to herself: damn. Whoopee for him, and here I am, again. She wondered if he had enough chivalry to attempt cunnilingus, or if she was just supposed to be satisfied by his amazing masculine prowess as it had already presented itself. He had not, in the hours they'd been together, proved the most perceptive or sensitive of men. In her mind she pictured Rick, and then Charley, and abruptly she wanted him gone.

That would be the best thing.

She thought about the bathroom; she thought about privacy, of shutting a door and being alone. Unfortunately, she was lying next to the wall. She sat up, looked at him spent by her side. "Ummm," she said, "I'll be right back, I just want to . . ." She pointed toward the bathroom, grimacing inwardly to herself about being so prim and decorous after what had just transpired between them. The bed bounced as she got out.

He seemed to have no reaction at all, besides lying there like a large beached fish.

She grabbed her very old, very unsexy ripped plaid robe off a chair, wrapped it around her naked body, and skittered into the bathroom. She shut the door and leaned against it and closed her eyes and felt for a long moment that she was going to vomit. She held her stomach and gritted her teeth, and the eruption in her belly subsided, and she stood and looked in the mirror.

She was shocked by what she saw. She looked like some ancient madwoman at Bellevue. Her hair was a rat's nest of tangled knots and curls. Black mascara ringed her eyes like she'd been crying. Her eyes were red and blotchy and they hurt.

She turned on the shower, hot all the way and a touch of cold. She stuck one leg in — it was fine — then stood under the rushing water and closed her eyes and felt it cascade down her body.

When she came out, ten minutes later, she was secretly hoping to find he'd left, but he hadn't. He was standing in his jeans. "Hate to run, but I should really probably sleep at home, tonight."

"I have no problem with that." And she didn't.

"Thanks." He scratched his chest. "Use your bathroom?"

"Go right ahead." She went to the window and sipped her water and dried her hair with the towel and watched moonlit clouds rushing above the Empire State Building. She wished she were one of them, scudding along the surface of the world, evanescent enough to pass around solid things without getting caught.

Charley'd never seen the Empire State. Not even once.

There was a racket of flushing, and Frank came out of the bathroom, ostentatiously zipping his pants. He opened the refrigerator, looked inside, shut it again. The drawing on the door rattled in the breeze.

"This your son's?"

"Mm-hmmm." Sharon toweled her hair.

"Must be incredible to go through that whole experience —"

"You survive."

"I don't know." He shook his head. "It would sort of make me want to latch on to anything that came my way."

Sharon stopped what she was doing, slowly lowered the towel.

"I mean, you're doing really well with it — I can see that." He wasn't looking at her. He was looking at Charley's drawing, and just by his viewing it, Sharon began to feel it being defiled.

"I just know," he continued, "I'd be looking for answers in everyone I met —"

"Don't worry, Frank." She finished with the towel, draped it over the chair. "I'm not."

He looked at her wide-eyed, stepped forward. "I'm sorry, I —"

"Look." Sharon took up her brush. "I said before — I'm not looking for a relationship. And I'm not going to get all weird on you because a year and a half ago I lost my husband and my son."

Frank said nothing, standing open-mouthed at the refrigerator.

"You have a really busy job," she continued. "So do I. Maybe we'll see each other around Bellevue, that's fine —"

He took her in his arms, held her stiffly, kissed her cheek.

"I think you're a really remarkable lady."

He's saying this because I'm letting him off easy, she knew.

"The sex between us was amazing." He looked into her eyes. "I've never had anybody respond to me the way you did."

Sharon considered that, debated whether or not it was a compliment. She hadn't been responding to him; he'd just been someone off whom she could bounce her self-hate. But she did not say it. And then he touched her face, ran his finger along her scar, down the side of her cheek by her ear, followed the line under her chin. It was a forced intimacy, an act Sharon hadn't known anyone would ever do, and she was repulsed, but at the same time something was alert inside her, something deep.

She shuddered, hoped he hadn't seen it, stepped back. There was a look in his eyes she couldn't read: it reminded her of hawks.

"Well." He took a step back. "I should get going." Awkward silence as he dressed. "I'll call you in a couple of days."

"Right," Sharon grinned, a quick, worthless flash.

He came close, kissed her slowly. She found herself not wanting to give in to him, but she did.

He took up his coat, held it with two fingers over his shoulder like Frank Sinatra. She walked him to the door. "Bye," he said, with the grace to be awkward.

"Bye," she said and shut the door behind him. She stopped in front of the refrigerator, spent a long, numb moment looking at Charley's rough little picture, her finger idly rubbing the scar that ran down under her chin. Then she turned away, not feeling much of anything, and sat on her uncomfortable wicker chair and looked out the window at the Empire State Building and the sloped roof of the Citicorp Center and the sleeping city in between.

Maybe this was all she deserved, these bruisers who pounded her and took their pleasure and left. She'd had a good man, and a child, and she'd lost them. It wasn't that she wished she'd died in the accident, though the idea sometimes snaked around her for days on end. It was as if the fact she was still walking the earth were somehow a mistake, some kind of cosmic clerical error.

She thought of her father, his big hands pushing her in the swing set he'd built. It had taken him weeks, what with all his other work. And she and her mother had left it sitting in the yard for the next family, when it came time to leave.

That bastard Edward Mackinnon was still walking around out there, in New York. No clerical error for him. Sharon thought of Charley's Mickey Mouse pouch sitting like a stone at the bottom of her bag. It was reassuring to have it there. It gave her control.

The apartment felt cold and empty and dank, like she'd broken something she'd spent months building. Frank DeLeo, M.D., she knew, was the answer to nothing. The problem wasn't his; it was hers. Sometimes she wanted to feel something, needed to feel something, and she tried. And afterward, all she wanted was her little life back, eating the same things and keeping to the same streets and going through the same routines day in and day out. It was survival, pure and simple — no emotion, because emotion, she knew, could hurt. Sometimes she enjoyed it, sometimes she endured it, and sometimes she just wanted to let it go, to lie down and not wake up and see how that changed everything.

That's what her father had done, pushed beyond his own personal edge, and sometimes the pull of that ran deep.

VI

When Sharon entered the nursing station at nine the next morning, Crystal gave her one look and shook her head. "Up to me, I'd tell ya go home, get twelve hours of sleep —"

"I'm okay," Sharon said, stifling a yawn.

"Was it worth it? I sure hope it was worth it."

Sharon poured coffee for herself, blew on it. The steam puffed away and disappeared and then continued just as it had before. "I don't know," she said then. "He's easy to say yes to."

"So?"

"So I'm not sure it's a great idea to keep saying yes to him."

Crystal thought about that. "See, you know me, I figure you've been saying no so much, you could use the practice."

Sharon juggled that in her head. "Maybe," she said and sipped coffee. "Borrow your paper?"

"My bag." Crystal gestured with her elbow. Sharon took it and her coffee, kneed the door open. She was immediately approached by a tattooed older man with sleep-crumpled steel gray hair. "Miss, ya got a cigarette? Please, I'm begging ya."

"No smoking on the ward." She fumbled in her pocket. "You want a candy?"

"No cigarettes at all?" He already had his hand out.

"Sorry." She peeled off three Necco wafers, deposited them in his hand. "Drink a lot of water, it helps."

He shambled off to take the Necco wafers as if they were pills. Sharon walked the ward to see who was where.

The room was quiet, even somnolent. Everyone was either asleep or groggy, on their meds. No one seemed to be demanding her attention, but they would, they would. She took a chair in the corner so she could see as much of the room as possible, made herself comfortable, drank her coffee, and opened the paper.

"Bomb Scare Clears Nun Rape Court" was one headline. God, that poor nun. "Gay Basher Found Bashed": "Convicted gay basher Anthony Jankovich, thirty-two, was found beaten to death seven blocks from his home in Kew Gardens, Queens. He was released from prison Thursday after serving four months for a gay-bashing incident in Tompkins Square Park last year." Some kind of justice, Sharon thought, and turned the page. And then someone sat down next to her and said, "Do I dare disturb the universe?" and even before he spoke she knew it was Milt.

Sharon smiled. "Depends on what you want in life."

"What I really want? A strawberry malted with extra malt."

"And what are your associations with that?" Always a reasonable question.

"Totally obvious. When I was sick as a kid, Mom used to promise me a malted when I got better."

"That way you had something to look forward to besides going back to school," Sharon said with a smile.

"Spoken like a true mother," Bill said, and watched as the smile froze on her face. Then she looked away and it disappeared.

"So." She busied herself refolding the paper and set it just so on her lap. "Other than wanting a malted, how are you feeling?"

Bill considered the question. "Really?" he asked.

"Unexpurgated truth."

He bit his lip. "I've been thinking —" he started, and then closed his eyes and lapsed into silence.

She waited.

"It's weird, getting older," he said, and he shook his head. "You ever feel you've lived beyond your time? Like you knew everything about a world, everything there was to know, but it's changing beyond your grasp, and you can't catch up, you're not meant to catch up —"

Sharon had several responses to that, but the one she allowed was: "What world?"

"New York, this city."

"Nobody could know it all."

"Not all — but all the rules, all the players. And if you don't know them, you know how to get to them, how to wire the connections." He looked at her. "You haven't been in New York very long, have you?"

"About a year. Is that why you cut yourself?"

"I used to be able to direct things. I used to be able to — fix events, things would happen a certain way —" His hands made looping gestures in the air. "No surprises. I *knew*." And then he bashed his palms together, again and again. "It's so hard for me to express. It's like — there's my brain, all my normal stuff, and over top of everything is this dead layer of cold, numb shit."

"Those are the meds. Your body's still trying to figure out what to do with them. We won't know what's going on for a day or two more." The standard line. "Nobody can control everything — that's not the way life works, that's not in the job description. But you're obviously a very capable man. Like yesterday, I really appreciate the way you helped me out. You were great."

"Well, you seemed so weird when that guy smashed the glass."

"I didn't know that stuff could break." Sharon heard the defensiveness in her voice.

"The way you froze — like you were trapped, or something. Like in a nightmare."

"Or in a building," Sharon risked. "With pamphlets."

He mulled on that, not looking at her. "I hate it when there's no way out," he finally said. "I hate it. Those scars are from glass, aren't they?"

Sharon touched the scar where it ran under her chin, realized she was blushing.

Damn.

"Yes," she said. "Car crash a couple years back." Keep it light.

Bill said nothing for a moment, watching her intently. "And then you came to New York."

"More or less." Purposefully oblique. Not that it seemed to be doing any good. "When I was a kid upstate I always wanted to live here." Why did that feel like she was saying too much?

The words lay heavy as stones between them for a long cool moment, and then Bill said, "You lost something, someone, some kind of universe. You lost it, it's gone, and now you're here."

And Sharon couldn't help it; she nodded. She shouldn't have, but she had no choice. He'd caught her; they both knew it. And in acknowledging it, she felt something opened up between them, and she wanted him.

She looked away, but she didn't get up, didn't walk across the room, which she then realized was her second mistake, which only reaffirmed that nodding had been her first. Damn, suddenly she had slipped behind, was desperately trying to play catch-up.

"What were you feeling when you cut yourself?" Back on track.

Bill considered the question seriously. "There's a kind of panic that builds up, like all of your parts are spinning away from each other, faster and faster, mutating their way into separate destinies — you cut, and it's the only thing that holds you together. Suddenly there's a center, there's gravity, one thing follows another." Sharon thought of the Mickey Mouse bag at the bottom of her purse, a dense little center of gravity she carried everywhere she went. "Family?" he asked.

"What?"

"In the car."

She debated what to say, realized her pause gave the answer.

He was watching her. "Husband?"

She closed her eyes, was damned if she was going to cry.

"Sharon — not a kid —"

Abruptly, she stood. "I'll talk to you later."

"Sharon —"

But she was already walking away. He stood, ran after her. "Sharon, I'm sorry —"

She turned, tried to smile. "It's okay — really." She wiped her nose.

"If there's anything I can do —"

"You're a gentleman," she said, and now her smile was real. She pointed at the nurse's station. "I've got a million things —"

"We'll talk," he said, and she nodded, went through the door. He stood, feeling foolish, knowing he'd said the wrong thing, thinking of a million things he should have said instead.

VII

"That wasn't so painful, now, was it?" Arvin was on his cordless, pacing back and forth across his living room. He reached out to wipe dust off one of the Hummel figurines. "I told you, a little bit of humiliation, and now we know every decent argument that can be hurled against us. And I think this ad answers most of them." He walked back to his desk, looked again at the proof sheet.

Edward, at his townhouse on the other end of the phone, was less convinced. "These Straythmore Security guys, they're so used to building prisons out in the sticks — they've got to watch the zeal thing in this market. I mean, maybe all that think-tank stuff will come true—in which case, we'll own the business — but in New York or Chicago or Los Angeles that can't be the point of the exercise."

"Right — well, that's why they needed you, Eddie. You know how to crack a city open and put up a building."

"Yeah, but this ad —" Edward returned to the subject at hand. "First of all, they're wrong to put in a picture. Should be just headline and text. Second of all, I want a quote from you."

Arvin stared out the picture windows at the bridges over the East River, lit up against the night. "All right, I'm game. Write something up, I'll approve it."

"Thank you, Arvin, that'll help."

"My pleasure. Listen, you get your invitation to the Goncharov debut at the Met? It's a benefit —"

"We'll be there."

"Good man." Arvin hung up the phone, wandered into the kitchen, topped off his glass of wine. Alma had rehearsals; he was sure his staff in Washington had e-mailed reports for him to read. He stepped into the office, dropped into the chair, and considered the view from the window.

The computer didn't entice him at all.

Finally he picked up a copy of the *Washington Post* and began to read an article on the new labor department statistics.

People were scared of New York. That was Arvin's gut feeling. Foreign investment in New York had been flat for the past two years, and Arvin was sure the people that mattered were scared to invest. It was important to send a message to the rest of the world that New York was not some haven of depravity, that the powers that be were tough on crime.

That way foreigners would come and spend money to live in

Edward's buildings, and his campaigns would never be wanting for contributions, and all would be right with the world.

It was all about perception, he knew, but perception was all.

The moon was high over the Empire State Building when Frank got off the bed, opened and shut the fridge, and started hunting through the dark kitchen drawers.

Sharon sat up, adjusted the sheet to make the bed slightly less of a mess, caught her reflection in the dark window, and spent a moment trying to adjust her hair. "What are you doing?" she finally asked, at the noises he was making in the kitchen.

"Opening another bottle of wine."

"Don't do that. We'll both be a wreck tomorrow."

"You wanted more." Well, yes, actually, she had. And, kind of, she did. "And besides," he said, "I have a present for you."

"Wow, really?" she said, and instantly hated how much she sounded like a child.

"Uh-huh." He came to her with the full bottle tipped up like a penis. She held her glass and he filled it. "Two, actually."

"You waited all this time?"

"I wanted you to appreciate them." He offered the two wrapped packages with a flourish.

She held them on her lap, savored their weight, picked up the smaller package. "No —" he stopped her. "Bigger one first."

She pulled off the shiny red and green wrapping paper and marveled at the bamboo picture frame. "It's wonderful!" She set it on the bedside table, wiped a smudge off the glass. "It fits right there perfectly — Frank, thank you."

Frank smiled indulgently. He'd bought it because he'd thought it would fit her kid's drawing, get it off the damn fridge, but he didn't want to bring that up now. "Open the other," he said.

Sharon flopped the package back and forth, raised a quizzical eyebrow, and tore into it. She pulled out a long, thin scarf.

"It's beautiful." It was. Soft silk shot through with textured spiderwebs, black against black, and endless — it just kept coming out of the wrapper, draping over her thighs.

He raised his glass. "You like it?"

"How could I not?"

He gestured; she clinked her full glass with his, and they both drank. "I saw it in a store window —" the same thrift shop where he'd found the frame, but no need to tell her that — "and I thought it might have several — uses."

"Uses?"

"Let me show you." He kissed her lips. Then he set his wine-glass on the floor, took hers from her hand and set it on the night table, and smiled at a golden square of refracted light prismed through the wine onto the glass of the empty frame. He gathered the silk scarf, touched it to her nipples, one and then the other, until each stood erect, the areolas wrinkling in anticipation. He took a mouthful of wine, took each nipple between his lips, let her feel the cold liquid, let a little dribble out his mouth, down her chest. He swallowed and licked up the tears of wine with a broad, flat tongue.

He pulled back and grinned and looked into her eyes and they were connected; he could see that.

He lowered the black scarf over her eyes. Her tongue licked her lips nervously as he wrapped it three times around her head. Her forehead was covered, and her eyes; a half inch of fabric hung in the air below her nose.

She couldn't see; he knew it. He had worked the wrap out perfectly in his office, with the door locked, that afternoon. He tied the scarf middling tight in back. She still had not said anything, which he considered remarkable. Good girl.

For her part, Sharon had at first been intrigued by her reactions to all this. Fear had been a part of it, but fear like what one felt on a roller coaster, fear based on a rush of adrenaline, not dread. She'd found an odd sense of power in letting him do these things to her. When he'd covered her eyes, the smell from the scarf had been strangely familiar, and then surprisingly so: it was an old-lady smell, the merest trace of a long-dead perfume. It so intrigued her she'd spent the last few minutes thinking about that, not him — a condition that had suddenly felt absurd when she'd realized he was going to bind her hands.

He took one wrist, kissed her palm, and tied it to the wooden frame with the scarf. He made the knot tight, did the same with the other. He sat back and watched her rib cage move, her breasts rising and falling. She was testing the limits of the wrist ties, finding them immobile.

He sipped from the wineglass, held it up to her lips, let her sip as well. Then, very tenderly, he kissed her.

"Do you trust me?" he asked.

There was a long pause while Sharon considered the question. "I trust you not to hurt me," she said finally.

"— and if I wanted to hurt you?"

Something about the way he said it made her nerves jump, and her heart was beating. In this anxious space, some part of her wanted him to devour her completely. "I would trust," she said, "that you would respect my limits." It was hard getting those words out; it opened a vast complex of emotions. She felt singularly alone; she wanted to spit in his face, cut free and run, but she couldn't, and that made it interesting.

In one gesture he pulled the sheet away and exposed her, utterly naked. "Open your legs," he said, and took another sip of wine. "Knees bent. Right." She complied perfectly. Long thin legs, a lovely ass and flawless round breasts that fit her torso beautifully — she really had a great body, he thought, and drained the wine. He set the empty glass on the bedside table, took up her full one from the floor, drank off the top half inch.

Then he held the glass between her thighs, careful not to touch her, and tilted it until a stream of cool white wine poured down onto her vulva.

She'd had no idea what would come next, but the shock of the cold was so surprising to her that she yelled "No!," cocked back her legs and lashed out, smashing her right foot full into his shoulder. The impact made him spin, the wine from his wineglass sprayed the headboard, landing with a wet slap against her cheeks and chin. He grabbed an ankle; she kicked again, hit his right hand across the bedside table, the wineglass fragmenting into shards, the picture frame tumbling, a cascade of shattered glass.

Sharon, blind, felt herself sinking inside: she was going to vomit, but she couldn't vomit, not tied like this — Goddamn it. She thought about breathing, getting oxygen in and out and in, and then she started to shake and twist her head to get the blindfold off, but it wouldn't come.

It took Frank a moment to realize that the glass had broken in his hand, and as he pulled one piece out of his palm, the blood welled up in a clean line behind it, and it wouldn't stop coming. He sat heavily on the bed, looked at his palm, and said, "Fuck."

"Frank, get me out of this right now."

He wasn't listening. "Fuck," he said, and now he was angry.

"Frank — Now, damnit, untie me!"

He was a fucking surgeon, and if there was anything the fuck wrong with the tendons in his hands —

"Frank — I'm not kidding —"

Fucking bitch didn't have to fucking kick like that. His hand hardened into a fist, blood welling up between his fingers, and he raised it high and brought it down, hard, against her jaw.

When Sharon walked in, what she mostly felt was guilty for how late she was. She passed Crystal, who grimaced at her, and then the grimace turned to open-mouthed wonder as she caught sight of the bruise climbing up above the floral silk scarf around Sharon's neck. Sharon nodded — she hadn't meant to, but she did — and scooted on toward the nurse's station. Before she got there, she saw Milt coming toward her, concern all over his face.

"Sharon —" He searched her with his eyes. "What can I do?"

The statement surprised her. "I doubt anything —"

"I hope the other guy looks worse."

"You know what?" Sharon said. "I hope so too." And then Crystal bustled up, touched Sharon's arm, and held the door of the nurse's station open for her, and she went inside.

Hermione was in Crystal's chair, surrounded by charts, when Sharon came in, making a show of taking off her coat and acting like everything was normal. "Sorry I'm late, guys," she said. "I had what it's safe to say was a rough night."

Hermione was up at once. "Are you all right?"

Sharon considered the question. "Well, I feel stupid."

"It was Frank, right?" Sharon nodded. Crystal was furious.

"Should we think in terms of rape?" Hermione's voice sounded comforting, but her backbone was pure steel.

Sharon shook her head no. "We had already made love. The fight happened after."

"He did not press his advantage?" Hermione was insistent.

She remembered him naked, breathing hard, his fists. She hadn't seen his eyes. "I've got some bruises, but that's all."

"Asshole," Crystal said, and slumped into the ratty yellow chair. "God, I feel like such a shit."

"Why?" Sharon and Hermione said it at the same time.

"I told you to see him — I pushed you every step of the way —"

"Who knew?" Sharon said, feeling inside that she'd known all along. "Guy drank too much wine and got out of control." She stood, poured coffee. "Though I'll tell you, now that eight-month first marriage makes a lot more sense."

"You could press charges, you know."

Sharon had thought of that. But the idea of standing up in court and having to explain — God, no. And he hadn't raped her.

"No, let's just trash him through the grapevine," Sharon said, and they all laughed.

After he'd stormed out the door, it had taken Sharon half an hour to wriggle out of the ties, crying the whole time, terrified. Once she'd worked one hand free, abruptly she found herself laughing hysterically. She'd forced herself to clean up, then she'd taken a shower and a sleeping pill. When she woke up the next morning, the idea of seeing movies or wandering through museums alone had been infinitely depressing to her, so she'd come into work. "If I get tired later," she asked, "would you all mind if I took off early?"

"Go to it!" said Crystal.

"Fine, fine," said Hermione.

"Thanks, guys. Now, what is to be done?"

VIII

Mrs. Jeremiah Tolchin, Veronica to her friends, was the first to admit she was a stickler for routine. At her age, surprises were rarely positive things. Her husband's death five years before had been a rude surprise — she had been older than he — and during their fifty-eight years of marriage they had shared a running joke about all the putative champagne and dancing girls he would get to after her demise. She found widowhood to be essentially what she'd always secretly feared it would be — one long, bleak footnote to their life together, a period to be endured. There were joys in her world now, but they were small ones, ones that were hers and hers alone, that never made her want to run and share them with Jerry.

She was wearing tan slacks and an old blouse from Chanel that she'd had for years. She finished buttoning a not utterly obnoxious sweater her daughter-in-law had bought her two Chanukahs ago and began feeling through the dark closet with the tips of her fingers for her tweed coat. She found her failing vision perhaps the most irritating thing about being eighty-two; she liked to tell her friends that when Jerry died, he'd taken her eyesight with him. She felt the coat, pulled it unceremoniously out, and draped it over her shoulders. Diego, downstairs, was always very handy, holding her coat for her so she could put it on properly before she ventured outside. She felt through her purse, making sure her keys, wallet, and pills were all together. Then she took up Jerry's old cane — her hip had been hurting her again this morning — and stepped out her door to the fourteenth-floor foyer.

She worked her way down the hall to the elevator, pressed the button, and started to put on her kid gloves when she noticed the smell. Her eyes may have been going, but her nose was still sharp as ever; even so, at first she could not for the life of her identify what that smell might be. Subtle but pervading, it was putrid and slightly sweet, and a memory came to her of the war, all those bodies, and how hungry she had been. She pushed it all aside — it did no good to remember — and concentrated on the smell.

Of course it was coming from that horrid incinerator room;

someone had left their newspapers all willy-nilly in there, and the door couldn't shut. Veronica had lived there long enough to know that once a smell got hold in that room, it was difficult to get it out — it just spread and spread like an infection in an open sore.

Why they had to have incinerators in apartment buildings she never knew. It just bothered her — always had. Jerry would have said it was because of her time in the camps — well, what of it? She could no more control that than she could control her dreams.

The elevator came, and she took it down to the lobby, and there was Diego in his too-tight jacket, and as he saw her he rushed up to help, dear man.

"Let me get that for you, Miz Tolchin —" He took up her coat.

"There's the most vile odor coming from that little room next to the elevator on my floor —"

"Odor."

"If you could send one of the boys up, I'd be grateful."

"I'll tell Manny right away."

"Thank you, dear." Manny, she found, tended to be a slothful fellow, but she held her tongue. Firmly in her coat, she made her way past the security desk to the front door. Diego opened it, and a cold wind blew in and made her think of Chanukah. And then she realized the holidays were coming, and she smiled.

The staff of the Montclaire were always blissfully efficient in the month before the holidays.

"What it looks like," Bill was saying, "is one of those marks violists get? Brown patch under the jaw where they put their instrument?"

"Really? They get a mark?" Sharon adjusted her scarf.

"Next time you're around Lincoln Center, keep a watch and you'll see it." They were sitting in the blue chairs, their backs to the Psych ER wall.

"So if I just carry a viola case for a week or two, I'm set —"

They both smiled. "There's your answer," said Bill, and he turned the page of the newspaper. Something caught his attention, and then he said: "I'm getting out of here today, right?"

"It's not up to me," she said carefully, as she always did when patients asked. "I mean, your seventy-two hours are almost up, but there are various treatment options. We're doing a release assessment" — she checked her watch — "pretty soon." That was actually one of the reasons Sharon had dragged herself in, today — Garber had had a hate-on for Milt from the start, and Sharon felt she should be there in case he needed an advocate.

"Because tonight Laila Goncharov is singing *Götterdämmerung* at the Met —"

"You're an opera buff?" Sharon was surprised.

"Well, I've been working my way through Wagner —" he said, slightly defensively. "You know WHBN? 98.6?"

"I don't think so."

"Best radio station on the planet. No commercials, totally listener supported, totally freeform — they'll go from Coltrane to Nietzsche Prosthesis to the love duet in *Götterdämmerung* in the time it takes for a normal radio station to cue up Led Zeppelin."

"Are they the one that plays salsa early in the morning?"

"Café Con Leche. Spanish show. But there's a guy Wednesdays until noon, he plays rock, jazz, and always a little opera —" But he could see she'd stopped listening. "What?" he asked. She was staring down at a picture in the *New York Times*.

The headline said "Van Gogh, Kandinsky Fetch Highs in Fall Auction." Below that, Sharon had immediately recognized the stern jaw and patrician cheekbones of one of several well-dressed people in a crowd shot. "Oh God," she said, "Edward Mackinnon."

"Where?" Sharon gestured. "The builder?" Bill asked.

"Mm-hmm," Sharon said, noncommittally, but she pulled the paper closer, off his lap, and looked hard. There was a young, attractive woman behind him, holding a little boy's hand. And then Mackinnon: gray at the temples, dignified, his face still thin. "Those types always age well, don't they?"

"You know him?" Bill asked.

Sharon paused. "He and my father were business associates when I was a kid." She said the words delicately.

A grin played around the edges of Bill's face, never reaching fruition. "And yet, you work," he said.

"It couldn't have ended worse, shall we say." Suddenly she was furious. "I mean, I hate the bastard, okay? He screwed my dad into the ground."

He was watching her carefully. "Figuratively, or — ?"

She looked at the picture for another moment, and then gave it back. "It's ancient history, Milt. Don't even worry about it."

Bill sat back. "Sometimes it's better to talk about these feelings of anger. Hold it in, you end up in places like this."

Another moment where they looked at each other — and when the laughter came, it was pure and clean and honest between them. "I'm the nurse, you're the patient, that's the deal. Got it?"

"Yes, ma'am." Then Bill saw her face change, and followed her gaze. Hector was making his way through the ER, locked on Sharon. "This just came for you." He held out an envelope.

Sharon knew immediately who it was from, but even so she was shocked to see his name and the hospital address embossed in the corner, and suddenly her heart was pounding, and she wanted to be a million miles away. And then she just held the sealed envelope, and another emotion took over — the gall. The sheer fucking gall.

Bill watched all this. When she looked back up at Hector, she was shaking with rage. "Who brought this?"

"You know, that doctor. Curly-haired guy."

"Shit!" Sharon walked quickly to the other end of the ward.

Bill watched her disappear, turned back to the paper, looked for a long time at Edward Mackinnon's smiling face, his wife, his little son hiding behind his leg. Then he read the article.

He was pleased and gratified to learn that Edward Mackinnon had purchased the van Gogh.

Fifty-three point nine mil.

Serious money. The kind of money you could do something with.

It made him think.

Sharon opened the door into the staff bathroom. No one there; good. She seated herself in the farthest of the three cubicles and opened the letter.

Sharon —

I hate myself for what happened last night. I feel utterly crushed, humiliated, mortified at what transpired between us —

Between us? Sharon found herself getting angry all over again. Like I'm complicit in your bullshit. She forced down the dangerous black thought that somehow she had been, and kept reading.

— and I feel I owe it to you to make amends.

A gaseous bubble erupted up her throat, she tasted saliva tinged with bile, and she swallowed it down. She didn't want to be here. She didn't want to be reading this. She scanned down the letter. His handwriting was like a child's. It was someone she didn't know at all.

We can start with a phone call, or a letter back, or coffee, or a drink — but I want to see you again. And I hope that, somewhere inside, you want to see me.

She sat there for a long moment, sparks and little one-celled creatures swimming before her eyes, and then folded the paper once, made a crisp edge with her fingernail, folded it again, edged it and folded it, and began meticulously to rip it into little strips of confetti. She dropped the handful of paper flakes between her thighs into the toilet, and only then realized she had to pee. She did so, stood, and flushed and watched the confetti swirl around in the yellow water until it all disappeared.

Then she adjusted her scarf in the blurry steel plate above the sink and opened the door to get on with the business of the day.

Manny hated this shit. Fucking old ladies and their fucking noses made him go clean out nonexistent smells, cater to their every fucking whim. Pile of shit, this whole fucking place.

He opened the incinerator chute, tried to see down with a flashlight. That didn't work. He took up his broom, stuck it down the chute, then passed it up. All clear, either way.

He sat on the newspapers and sniffed. Okay, yeah, there was

something, but it was pretty fucking minor, by him. He shined his light into the air grate, saw something blocking it, inside.

Shit. Rich kids in this building, fucking up everything. He pulled out a screwdriver, got the grate off and reached in.

Black backpack with a sandwich in it, yeah, kinda nasty. Some kind of tunafish, some shit like that. And then the rest — real nice long metal flashlight, some other stuff. He was at the point of thinking he might keep them for himself when he remembered: sicko prowler, few days back. "Burglary tools," he said to himself and wondered if there was any way he could maybe just keep the flashlight.

Sharon and Hermione were in Garber's office, trying to argue the man into getting Andrew Sentoro a bed upstairs, when the intercom buzzed. Garber picked it up, grunted, and eyed Sharon.

"It seems the police are here to arrest your Mr. Slavitch."

Sharon was up and out the door. Whenever the police came in to pick someone up, they came in packs, and there was a phalanx of blue surrounded by the crowd at the far end of the room. All of that, Sharon thought, to pick up one lonely schizophrenic. A gaggle of cops were bantering with Hector by the metal detector, hands on their gun belts, as if insanity were an infectious disease they might catch if they went in any deeper.

"Hector, who's in charge, there?" she asked.

"Lieutenant, robbery division," said one of the cops, pointing. Dark-haired guy, good cheekbones, talking to Crystal. She pulled up the scarf at her neck. Two cops were jerking the buckles tight on Milt's straight jacket; he looked up at the ceiling like a man in prayer. "Lieutenant," Sharon asked, "what's up?"

The cop looked at her warily. "This is Nurse Blautner," Crystal said, because of Sharon's own plainclothes.

"Dennis Kincaide." He offered a hand, and Sharon shook it. Thick black eyebrows and a mustache. "Perp was brought here three days ago?" he said. "Building guy found burglary tools he stashed before the cops got to him."

Goddamnit; her heart dropped into her stomach. She tried to formulate a sentence about how maybe they weren't his, but even as she had the thought, she knew they were. Somehow it only supported how competent Milt had always seemed.

But to what end? "Listen," she tried again. "However he got in, the man's a paranoid, his purpose for being there wasn't theft. He's got these end-of-the-world-type pamphlets he makes up."

"Well, but, you find that pattern of equipment at a scene, that's attempted robbery, that's a prison term right there."

Shit. "He's already cut himself when confronted by police," she said. "He'll try suicide again, I promise you."

"Alls he has to do is rip his stitches out, he's a goner," Crystal added.

"Well, we're keeping him in the building — what floor's the prison ward, fifteen?"

"Nineteen," Crystal corrected.

"Courtroom up there's not in session till Monday," Sharon said.

"Right, right, nineteen." He made a mental note. "Book him, then straight into the prison ward, keep him on watch." He looked around. "Anybody here talk to him a lot? Get to know him?"

"I did," Sharon said.

"If I could —" He led her away from the group for privacy. "What's your take?"

"He's smart, he's decent, and he's very nuts."

"Talk about politics much?" Sharon was mute. "The government?"

Sharon lowered her voice. "It's part of his delusional system. He thinks he's being tracked by satellites." For some reason that sounded bad. "We got a lot of that," she added. "His case has more to do with castration anxiety than anything."

"He ever mention any senators, any judges?"

"Nope, not at all."

"'Cause that building he was in is just chock-full of important people." One of the cops walked up to the lieutenant, radio in hand. "Lieutenant, Brannock wants a word with you."

The man took the radio and said "Kincaide here," and Sharon

turned away and cut through the crowd. "Excuse me —" she said. "I'm a nurse —" She slipped between two officers and sat next to Milt. "Well, big guy, I'm sorry it's come to this."

She'd intended to sound light, but it came out strangely bitter. He sat looking up at the ceiling, seemingly oblivious, withdrawn deep into himself. And then she saw his lips move, and he mumbled something, but she couldn't hear it.

"You want to try that again?"

He licked his lips, wet them, his eyes still on the dirty gray acoustic ceiling tiles, on the cross of metal directly above his forehead. "That's not why I was there," he said, very distinctly, and then: "They're not touching me," and she didn't know whether he meant they hadn't gotten to him, or if he was promising some awful retaliation if they did.

The funny thing was, she believed him. "They're going to take you upstairs," she said, suddenly sounding stupidly chatty, as if this were all the most normal thing in the world. "They've got a whole booking area right here in the building, so it's not like you have to go downtown to the Tombs or anything like that. And then the ward on nineteen" — she'd shied away from calling it a prison ward, though that's what it was — "I mean, there's security in the front." Cops, guns, bars. "But once you get past that, it's just like the rest of the wards upstairs. It's better than this place — you'll have a bed and everything."

"You've never been there," he said to the ceiling.

"Bullshit," she said. "I've moonlighted shifts there, I've run meetings there, done therapy—"

He lowered his chin, looked her directly in the eyes. "I've got too much to do to go there."

"Look, it's not going to be the rest of your life, it's a temporary thing —"

"You don't know." He said it quietly, almost under his breath, and the force of it chilled her into silence.

"No. You're right," she said finally, "I don't." She uncrossed her legs and shifted to stand, and then their eyes met and there was something pleading in his, something powerfully intelligent and in need of help, and angry as she was at him, she held herself in check.

"It's more complex than I think it is, isn't it?"

His nod came from someplace deep, and took a long convoluted moment to reach the surface; when it arrived it was so slight as to be imperceptible, but she saw it.

"What were you doing there?" She said it quietly, so that no one around them could hear.

He said nothing, emotions rippling like flags behind his eyes.

"You're scamming me, right? You've been scamming me from the start."

"No." Bill said it quietly, dead earnest.

"Well then, what were you doing in that building?" No answer. "Come on, goddamnit, tell me." Her voice was low, just above a whisper, her fury as solid as iron.

"I was there to fix something." She searched his face. "If they take me," he said evenly, "I'll have no choice but to kill myself."

"Don't give me threats —"

"It's a fact." And now he turned his gaze upon her, and she could see he meant it.

"Just tell me why."

"We are in a war," he said finally, and he smiled gently, as if somewhere inside some hard and cold thing suddenly found itself oxidizing. "And I have to do my work."

"And what is that?"

He straightened his back. "I repair things, keep them even," he said. "I connect the circuits that otherwise don't get connected. I keep the balance. That's my work."

Sharon's mind was clicking along at a furious rate. "In the universe? In the world? Or —"

"Manhattan Island." And he smiled, he suddenly seemed light enough almost to laugh. "That's the battleground. That's where I live. And that" — he leaned in close to her ear — "is where you live, now, too."

Sharon sat looking straight ahead, her heart pounding a notch harder than it should have been. "Enjoy the city, Sharon," Bill said, and then Lieutenant Kincaide cut through the crowd.

"He's been Mirandized?"

"When they put him in the jacket, Lieutenant."

Bill looked from the cops and the lieutenant to Sharon. "Sometimes I wonder," he said, "if patriarchy isn't a cult."

Sharon cleared her throat. "Sometimes I do too, Milt."

Their eyes met. Bill opened his mouth to say something more; no words came. The lieutenant looked from Sharon to Bill and back.

"All right," he said, "let's take him upstairs." Two cops wearing rubber gloves hoisted Bill up roughly by the brown leather straps across his back. He stood, a more handsome, more dignified man than the people around him, and turned toward Sharon.

"I'll see you." He almost whispered it, and then he kept his eyes on her, head turning, until the cordon of blue officers tightened around him and she couldn't see him anymore and they marched him down the hall toward the exit.

IX

At first, various officers had jutted their faces into Bill's and asked him questions, some nicely, some snidely. He ignored them all. Finally the lieutenant with the mustache sat down, opened a bag of long pretzels. "Want one?" he asked. "Sorry about the jacket — you can take it with your mouth."

Bill stared at him, no flicker of anything on his face.

"Ah well." Kincaide shrugged, took a bite. "Why that building, Milt? Who were you trying to get?"

Bill said nothing.

"Pamphlets were kinda rudimentary — if you don't mind me saying. But the tools — that flashlight! Beautiful piece of work, electric lockpick and all. You make that yourself, or what?"

Bill said nothing.

"And you even slit yourself — that took guts. Shows you're committed. All those nice little shrinks and nurses are one thing, but you and I — we're both pros, Milt."

Bill just stared at him.

"Who do you work with? That entry technique, you're not some kid out joyriding. You know your stuff. C'mon, Milt, you give me some names, your life gets easier. Who else is in your crew?"

Bill didn't say a word.

"Who fences your shit? Just tell me, man. You got to get rid of it somehow."

Bill didn't answer.

Lieutenant Kincaide shook his head in disgust. "You think the Tombs is rough, upstairs is all the dregs too diseased for that place. Nastier than shit. But you don't have to go — you give me names, you get a private room, twenty-four-hour guard, no bars on the windows, adjustable bed, your own TV. Just give me a name."

Bill didn't even move.

"Give me something — anything, just a crumb, so I can tell my boss I got you talking — you'll never see the prison ward."

Bill stared at the spot right between his two thick dark eyebrows and didn't say a word.

"That's it." The lieutenant stood, walked past Bill, and opened the door. "Jennings, take this sumbitch upstairs and throw him to the fucking wolves."

The single entrance and exit to the prison ward involved two sets of sliding prison-bar doors monitored at all times by police in a steel and glass booth. Bill was taken past the first set of bars; they slammed behind him, and he waited as the officers unloaded their guns barrel-down over the metal boxes of sand. A bank deposit drawer extended out from the booth; the cops placed their guns and ammo in it, along with their paperwork. The receipt for the prisoner was handed back through the drawer, and then the second barred door opened and Bill found himself, for the second time in his life, behind bars.

They were approached by a huge, fat, dumb-looking skinhead in hospital whites. "Milt Slavitch," one of the cops said and handed a piece of paper to the orderly.

"They give you his charts from downstairs?"

"Naah, nothing like that."

"Figures. Any outbursts?"

"Nope." The other cop shook his head. "Okay," the fat man

went on. "You guys can go. You" — he checked the paper in his fat white hand. "Come with me — 6A."

Bill followed him down a hallway of white-painted cement block, past the glassed-in nurse's station. Next to it was a locked door, from behind which Bill could hear muffled but undeniable screaming. "Quiet room one." The fat man cocked a finger at the door, and then: "Quiet room two." He pointed out another one. People filled the passageway, large men and scrawny men, some diseased, some tied into wheelchairs, some standing and staring in a neuroleptic daze. They passed room after room, each with four beds. The windows were caged — black sheet metal with small squares cut out — but even through that Bill could see that the views of the city were glorious.

"Your bed, guy." Bill followed the fat man into one of the rooms. In back, near the window, was an empty bed, not a hospital bed but more what one would find in a military barracks. A black man was lounging on the far bed, reading a horror book. Bill sat down and the bed creaked under his weight. "Better than the floor in the psychiatric emergency room," he said with a smile.

"Yeah, most people come from there get happy when they see a real bed." The man turned his back to the window so there was nobody behind him. "You missed lunch. Dinner's at six-thirty. Activity room's down the hall, any attempt at disruptive behavior means quiet room. Any attempt at sexual activity with any of the other prisoners means quiet room. As you know, you are under arrest; fact that you're in a hospital is a privilege that can be rescinded at any time. You unnerstand everything I just told you?"

"I get the gist."

The fat man cracked his gum loudly, started to walk out. "Guy?" Bill said.

He stopped without turning.

"You wanna get me out of this jacket?"

The man reading the horror book shot out one loud snort of laughter. The fat man turned, looked at Bill through pudgy eyes.

"I got to use the can, man."

Pudgy sighed. "You attempt to self-mutilate, you learn what it's like to eat, sleep, and shit in restraints, all right, buddy?"

"Gotcha."

"Stand up, face the wall, don't move till I tell ya." Bill did. The man came up behind, undid the buckles, stepped back three feet. "Now take the jacket off slowly, hand it to me." Bill did so, and then flexed his arms out on either side, stretching his muscles. "Arms down." Bill dropped them. The man rolled the jacket into a tight log. "All right, face me." Bill did. "Show me your palms." Bill did. "Open your fingers." Bill did. "Turn 'em around." Bill did. "Clasp hands behind your neck." Bill did. The man stepped closer. "Head back." Bill did. "Open mouth." Bill did. The man looked inside. "Lift your tongue." Bill did. "Stay," the man said, took a look at the floor around Bill's feet. "Take one step to your left." Bill did. "Other foot." Bill did. The fat man cracked his gum again. "All right, you're free to do what you need to do." Then he turned and walked out.

The black man took a plastic jug of water from under his bed, swigged some down. "Come the revolution," he said, "I'm gonna feed that shithead to my pit bull."

Bill stretched his body to the skies and went out the door.

As in the Psych ER, the patient population was not expected to have change for a pay phone; an outgoing-line-only phone hung on the wall in the main corridor. The people waiting were largely polite, save for one impatient, smelly man who was talking incessantly about what he was going to do when he got his hands on that bitch Connie. Eventually the man in front, a black muscle builder with a neck like an oak tree, said, "Excuse me" into the phone, covered the mouthpiece, turned to the nervous talker, and said, "WILL YOU SHUT UP?" at the top of his lungs. He got back on the phone, said, "Like I was saying," and continued to plan his defense.

The nervous talker turned, muttering more loudly now, and limped away, which made the line shorter.

The phone was situated uncomfortably high, with no chair anywhere near it. A large sign above announced the rules: local calls only; ten-minute limit per person.

Bill dialed; after four rings, the answering machine picked up. Silence, and a beep — if anything it sounded broken. Bill spoke quickly.

"Ten large for a favor. I'm at Bellevue, I need you to bring some stuff ASAP. Anything from Chapter Seventeen of the red book ought to do it. Whichever's the easiest — don't make it fancy, just quick and dirty, and no metal. Make it like a present for me, you know, wrapping and all, recruit a kid to bring it to Sharon Blautner, she's a nurse at the Emergency Room, first floor. Sharon Blautner. Today, okay? Not tonight, not tomorrow. Timeliness is what the ten big ones are for. See you soon." He debated saying more, reluctantly pressed down the switch hook.

Then he dialed another number, the beeper he'd given Lobo years ago. When it answered, he pressed 666.

That was that. That was his fallback. It would either work, or it wouldn't, and he'd have to think about suicide in earnest.

X

Lobo was on his hands and knees on the plush pink carpet. Raoul and Theresa had spent the last fifteen minutes climbing all over him, between his huge arms and through his legs, all around the living room. Raoul would pull Lobo's nose, and Lobo would puff his cheeks out, and Theresa would gather up all her thirteen-year-old dignity, poke his cheeks with her fingers, and Lobo would exhale like a horse, and the children would squeal with laughter, and then it would all start over again. Periodically Celeste would yell from the other room for them to quiet down, she couldn't hear her soaps. This always occasioned great seriousness of purpose, and Lobo and the kids would all put fingers to their lips and glare at each other darkly, and then the laughing would start again. Thus when Celeste again called for Lobo, at first he ignored her and burrowed his face into Raoul's fat little tummy.

"Lobo," she said from the doorway. "One of your beepers just started." He shook off the kids, stood, and followed her down the hallway. "I think," she said, "it's the one you got from Bill."

*   *   *

"What can I say?" Sharon said, and touched her chin. "Bruises, I'm a basket case." She shook her head. "Everything sucks."

Dr. Julia Phillips, across the desk from her, said nothing.

"I mean, I just let my self-hate — take over," Sharon said. "I mean, I've always had those fantasies — you know, sexually —" Sharon found herself looking at the floor; she really didn't want to say anything more about that. "And then there's this really intelligent patient on the ER — I don't know. Something about the guy just makes you want to help him — I don't feel that a lot from this population. It's not like dealing with children — you know that." The woman was like stone. "They're not cute."

"And this one is?"

"Well, in a different way —" She leaned back in the chair. "Yes, I'd say he was cute. Bright."

"Is this the one you mentioned in our last session?"

"Did I? Yes, Milt, right." Sharon looked out the window at the sea of buildings of Manhattan. All those possibilities. "Anyway, they took him away this afternoon. I mean, they arrested him." She lapsed into silence.

"What'd he done?"

Sharon laughed, kind of embarrassed. "It turns out he really is a pro. I mean, he's sick, I can see that. The building where he cut himself? They found burglary tools." Some part of her shrugged at the last two words, as if putting them mentally in quotes. And then she looked at Julia. "The funny thing is, of course he would know what he was doing. I mean, on some level, he's presenting at one thing, but he's actually totally another. But the real thing he is, is so far removed from conventional — I mean, he's nuts. He's nuts. He may not be nuts the way he said he was, but he's nuts." She leaned back. "Brilliant, but nuts."

Julia said nothing.

"You know, I remember my dad being so patient." Sharon shook her head. "When he was trying to take you through something. A problem, like math homework, or his work. He was always teaching by example." Sharon lapsed into silence, remembering her father, his hands. "Mom never got that from him," she went on. "She just saw it as an inability to communicate. But the horrible thing is, when one parent dies, the other parent's view of the relationship becomes the predominant truth — you know that. But Mom wasn't as bright as Dad. I mean, beautiful back then, right, but she didn't really understand him. To this day, she talks about how difficult it was to really know what my father was talking about. But I always knew. He was way out there, he was a computer genius, he was a mathematician, but he had this great ability to live what he was thinking. He would never explain, he would just sort of — do."

Julia Phillips said nothing.

"Even his suicide. He didn't talk about it. He didn't call Edward Mackinnon and tell him what he was going to do, or why, or any of that. He took the shotgun and just — did it."

Julia Phillips said nothing.

"Which is why I know this guy Milt is really as dangerous as he presents. I mean, he's sure as shit capable of anything — suicide, you name it. Because he's got that. He's not just being. He's doing. And whatever it is he is in fact doing — it's out there. I know." Sharon leaned forward in her chair. "I know because I've seen it before."

Walking out of Julia's office, Sharon was seized with the sudden fear that she was going to run into Frank. In the elevator, she fully expected it to open on eight, Frank's floor, and then was deeply thankful when it didn't. Finally she reached the lobby and scuttled through the maze of hallways back to the Psych ER.

Safe. Crystal and Hector were dealing with a starved-looking longhaired man with a broken nose and bruises all over his face. "Can't cross the blue line," Crystal was saying. "That's the rules, okay?" And then she saw Sharon. "Yo. Someone came for you."

Sharon looked at Crystal. "It's not —"

"Not Frank. Some kid. I put her in B." She pointed.

"Okay." Sharon walked over, knocked, and stuck her head in. There was a dark-haired girl, thirteen or so, with an odd dignity, in a perfect blue Sunday dress embroidered with little flowers.

"Hi, I'm Sharon. You're looking for me?"

The girl licked her mouth, started to speak, and nothing came out. Sharon shut the door, and sat down to be at eye level with the child.

"I have this to give to Bill Kai— Milt Slavitch." She blushed, pushed a shopping bag a little toward Sharon.

Suddenly, Sharon saw, she was scared.

"Bill Kai?" she asked.

The girl blanched slightly. "Milt Slavitch. He's my cousin. Bill Kai is this guy at school I know."

Interesting. Sharon eyed the bag. "And who are you?"

"I'm Laurie Leskovich. Milt's my mother's sister's son. Every once in a while, he gets weird, and he ends up in the hospital — my aunt says good riddance to bad rubbish, but I can't say that — Milt's always been real nice to me. So that's why —" She gestured at the bag.

"What is it?"

"It's kinda like —" She licked her lips, and then she was emboldened. "It's kinda like when you're in camp? And your folks send you a care package?"

"How nice!" Sharon didn't touch the bag, finally decided that perhaps there was some kind of family resemblance.

"Is he going to be in trouble?"

"Yes, he might be," she said. "But Milt's a pretty strong guy. He'll be fine." What an odd thing to say, she thought. But true. "What do we have here?" She pulled the bag over.

"Oh, like food he likes —"

A fat clear baggie wrapped tight, containing Fig Newtons and M&Ms and cashews. Sharon looked it over, didn't see anything amiss. A lot of dark jawbreakers, individually wrapped in plastic, a pair of heavy socks, and three plastic liters of soda.

"Just food?"

"Well, and socks," the girl said, and stood. "So, unh, could you take all this stuff to — to wherever he is? For me?"

"Not so fast. First, let me get your name and address — just in case there's a problem."

"Sure," the girl said, and sat back down. "Laurie Leskovich" — she spelled it — "148 West 207th, New York, New York 10034."

Did it sound rote? Sharon couldn't tell. "Bronx?"

"Inwood." She stood.

"Where do you go to school?"

"JHS 52, 650 Academy Street." Sharon believed her, but wrote it down anyway. "I have to go," she said.

Sharon stood, lifted the bag. It was light. "I'll see what I can do." She opened the door; the girl spent a moment adjusting her winter coat.

"Thank you very much," she said and offered her hand. Sharon shook it. Then she walked back through the metal detector, which did not go off, and was gone.

Sharon stood for a moment, holding the bag. She stepped over to the metal detector and waved the bag back and forth in the doorway. The green light didn't change. Sharon sat down, went through the bag, considered each item. She unrolled the socks, checked to see if anything was hidden. They were a newish pair of long white athletic tube socks, slightly damp to the touch, as if they'd been pulled out of the drier too early. She smelled them; they smelled like socks. She looked again at the candies, checked the soda bottles. The plastic caps were factory sealed.

She passed it through the metal detector again. The light stayed green.

She thought of running it by the lieutenant, but she'd bent the policy before, they all had. People often left books, letters, even foods in the Psych ER when they were taken up to the wards; if the nurses liked them, very often the books and things would find their way upstairs. Sharon had even seen Hermione do it once or twice. This case, while a bit different, felt much the same. She walked back to the nurse's station, the bag dangling from her hand.

Had she looked more closely at the plastic liter bottles, she might have seen that the bottom shells had been reglued with epoxy. But she might not have — at their apartment on Seventh Street, Lobo had been as careful as he could be, given the time in which he had to work.

*   *   *

Crystal was wiping her glasses. "So ain't you tired yet?"

"I'm leaving, I'm leaving. I had therapy, and I've just got a couple errands to run —"

"You don't want to go back to your place, you can stay with me, you don't mind the kids and the mess," Crystal said.

"I can't hide from my own apartment — that's silly."

"Good girl. Call me, you change your mind," Crystal said.

Sharon waited forever at the ground floor elevator bank, trying hard to stand proud in case Frank was anywhere in the vicinity. On the way up, she vaguely wondered what to do about dinner. The cafeteria, she saw, was out.

The door opened onto the prison ward's corridor. Directly across was a large sign: NO FOOD FLOWERS OR GIFTS BEYOND THIS POINT. That, she knew, was for the masses.

The only cops visible were the two in the glass booth behind the bars. One of them — the cute one — she'd seen before, the times she'd worked up here. The other was new. Sharon walked through the metal detector, which stayed green. When she got to the gate, she waved her Bellevue ID. The cop nodded, smiled at her, and the first gate crashed open with a loud screech.

Sharon stepped in, and the gate shut behind her. "Always a pleasure," the cop said, his lips forming the words and his voice coming from a tinny speaker above her head. The bank drawer rolled open. "ID, please."

Sharon dropped it in, leaned back against the buckets of sand. The cop she didn't know was writing her information into the log. "What brings you here today?" the metallic voice continued.

"Oh, some stuff for the nurse's station." A lie, but a serviceable one. The bank drawer slid back out. Sharon clipped her ID back on her sweater, readjusted the scarf around her neck.

"Take care," the cop said, the inner door slammed open, and she stepped onto the ward. Instantly a gaunt white man, all elbows and Adam's apple and scrawny naked chest, was flapping at her side.

"They took away my guns, and all my dogs —"

"I'm not a doctor."

"No no, but, they came to my house —" Lots of people in the

hallway, no sign of Milt. "— took away my dogs, I mean, those dogs, but they were like pistons, you know, I mean, fuckin *there* —" Sharon hustled along, but he loped along right next to her. "They felt nice, you know, the whole water thing and the shower —"

Sharon finally wheeled, turned on this guy full force. "I'm not your doctor, now GO, or I give you quiet room."

"I can't jerk off here," he said. "California, we used to make the movies —" He had this look on his face she could hit.

She didn't have to. "This man bothering you, ma'am?" The scrawny man looked up, and Sharon realized she had not known Milt Slavitch was quite so tall.

"Well, actually —" she started, because some answer was needed. Bill reached out, grabbed the scrawny man's throat, pushed him against the wall, and looked in his eyes.

"Don't . . . Fuck . . . With . . . Her." He said it with a forceful deliberation that sent something cold deep into Sharon. There was a fury in his voice she had seen before; in this universe it made sense. Bill threw the man into the hallway and he scuttled off. He would not, Sharon knew, bother them again.

"I brought you this," she said, and handed him the shopping bag. "It's not from me —" she added quickly. "It's from this little girl named Laurie —" She was watching for an emotional reaction to the name, but he was too busy with his face in the bag, he was doing something with the socks, ripping them apart and tying them into knots, and then suddenly he ripped the baggie open, and there were M&Ms and cashews and Fig Newtons spilling all over the floor, and he came up with something in his teeth, a white nozzle thing, and then — *crack* — one of the soda liters opened, and he jammed it in his underarm and then cracked another open, and he held the two liter bottles in his hands, and he was pouring them both on the floor, and the smell hit, pure chemical like a refinery or an oil leak, and where the two liquids met, there was a wrenching, hissing noise, and then suddenly there was fire all around them, Bill next to her with this white bit of plastic in his teeth. Sharon just stood there in shock, because, fuck, she'd been duped.

Bill held the bottles together, splashed them back and forth until they were surrounded by a ring of flame — it was smoky and hot and she found herself yelling at all the pajama-clad people to keep back — the flames were up to their waists, and she was so glad she didn't wear stockings to work; stockings were plastic and when they melted in a fire it was a disaster, sepsis became inevitable. You died of the sepsis, you didn't die of the burn. Bill threw the two bottles far down the hall toward the exit, and they landed, liquid glugging out, and everywhere it splashed was flame a second later. Bill hurled all the little hard candies and the rest of the contents of the shopping bag down the hall towards the guard post and the gates. When the black candies hit the fire, thick black smoke billowed out of them, all out of proportion to their tiny size. Bill opened the last soda liter, saw the look on her face, stopped, and plucked the plastic nozzle out of his mouth and said, "Stay with me," and she just opened her mouth in frustration, there was nothing else she could possibly do. A fire bell was ringing somewhere behind her, and then another. "Sprinkler system," she thought, and looked up. He screwed the nozzle on the Pepsi bottle, hoisted the bottle upside down, squeezed off three streams of liquid that, when they hit the fire, turned into a cloud of flame. He covered his right hand with one sock, dabbed the other into the flaming liquid, and pulled it onto his left. The flame sputtered mildly five inches from his fingers. "Sorry about this," he said and spun Sharon around and grabbed her across the throat with his right arm, the upended bottle in his right hand by her ear, his left hand outstretched, holding the burning sock. When he squeezed the spray trigger, the liquid hit the burning sock and blew into a line of flame ten feet across the hallway to the white concrete block wall, and then stuck, licking deep into the pits and crevasses. "We're walking," he yelled and pushed her forward, and when he stepped, she stepped, and then finally the sprinkler system dribbled out a little, and then a little more, and then turned on full force above them.

Sharon was shocked. The water didn't seem to put out the fire — it almost seemed to make it combust more, spread it around, burning slicks of chemical fire flowing in rivulets. All her childhood in upstate New York she had heard about Lake Erie catching fire — she'd never been able to picture it, but now she could. The water shushed valiantly into the smoke, but it just kept rising, pushed by new smoke from below. Milt was forcing her toward the exit, and for a moment she could see the blue uniform of one of the cops up ahead in the hallway, but then Milt pushed her directly into the smoke, and she couldn't see anything, and she prayed they wouldn't shoot.

They were at the barred gate now, billows of smoke issuing out into the elevator foyer, and Sharon could see maintenance workers and cops. "OPEN THE DAMN DOOR!" Bill roared, and Sharon saw through the bars cops with guns out, looking straight at her. "OPEN THE DOOR OR I BURN HER!" Bill pulled the trigger on the spray bottle, and a dragon's breath of flame shot through both sets of barred doors, and the people outside stood back. There was a commotion in the ward; in Sharon's peripheral vision, somebody came charging up, and Bill saw it too and turned and there was a huge white man with a shaved head and a fire extinguisher and Bill blasted the fire extinguisher. Flame enveloped it; the man dropped it, backed away from the flames. "Get away!" Bill yelled, and the man ran. Bill turned back, Sharon still trapped in his arms, and yelled "OPEN THE FUCKING DOOR BEFORE WE ALL BURN!" and now the smoke was too thick, but Sharon got glimpses of her friend back in the booth, hands on the controls, and Bill pulled his arm back just before the jail cell door rammed open.

Bill pushed Sharon through, and the wiry dog man tried to claw his way out with them. Bill kicked the man's naked chest, pushed him back in the ward, yelled "SHUT IT!," and the gate rammed home. He grabbed Sharon back — she had just stood there, frozen, little rivulets of liquid fire flowing around their feet — pointed at the outside gate, and yelled "OPEN IT!" Nothing happened for a long moment, so Bill sprayed a line of fire across the glass, and then turned the nozzle on Sharon — she closed her eyes and winced in his arms — and the gate crashed open. Bill sprayed a slash of fire at the ground in the elevator foyer, and Sharon could see people run back around the corner to get away, and there were cops with guns out, drawing a bead. They stepped out together, Sharon in the headlock, and at that moment the elevator arrived, and Bill yelled "GET OUT GET OUT GET OUT!," and more cops emerged with guns drawn, and Bill held Sharon tighter, sprayed the floor with fire to keep them back, and then dragged Sharon backwards into the empty elevator, and sprayed out the door until it finally shut.

He looked at her, and said almost defensively, "I tried not to burn anybody —"

"You ASSHOLE!" She hit him in the shoulder, stomped in a circle, and then faced him again. "What does THAT have to do with ANYTHING?" she said, and the elevator began to move, going down. Bill pressed the emergency override, then pressed stop. The elevator shuddered to a halt.

"I had to get out." He said it almost plaintively.

"Why? WHY?" No response. "WHY ARE YOU DOING ALL THIS?"

"I'm trying to" — he gulped in air — "take care of the city — like an angel hovering over everything, every little piece —"

"You lying PRICK!" she said and hit him in the shoulder again.

"Look, I don't have time for this." He turned back to the control panel. "Bellevue has twenty-four floors, right?" The counter ended at twenty-four. "No more floors above that, right? And no thirteen."

"I'm not telling you a thing," she said, and then: "Bill."

That stopped him, but only a moment. "Milt," he said back.

"Not according to the delivery girl. Who was she, your kid?"

"I don't have a kid. I tutor kids. Those are the only kids I know." Bill turned the elevator back on, pressed eleven. "The great thing is, I'm in a hospital," he said, half under his breath.

Sharon hadn't understood him, and didn't care. "You know, there are going to be cops absolutely everywhere," she said.

"Probably, yeah."

"I mean, you're never going to get out." She took a step forward. "I think you should surrender to me."

He looked at her. "You do, huh?"

"Absolutely. Give me that blowtorch thing, and we'll get off at eleven and march out —"

"I'm sorry, Sharon, I don't think that's feasible right now."

Sharon faced him. "You're going to end up dead, okay? I mean, within the hour. Bam, today, last day of your life." She took a step closer. "But if you give up, it's like a whole other chance, a whole other life —"

"I'll make my own chances, thanks." They had just passed twelve. Bill hit the stop switch, and the elevator shuddered to a halt in its shaft. "Help me."

"No."

"Then I'll do it without you." The handrail around the wall of the elevator was narrow. Bill set the spray bottle under his arm, clambered up with one foot on one side, another along the back, and hunched his neck up against the ceiling. He pushed, a panel lifted, and thick crumbling dust fell from the square hole. He put the bottle up first, struggled through until he was on top of the elevator car.

He looked around. The light from the skylights above was miasmic, but there was just enough to see what he needed to see.

Hospital elevator banks, Bill knew, were designed differently from practically all others. In apartments and office buildings, it didn't matter how much space stood between two separate elevator shafts — in fact, they designed them as tight as possible. In hospitals, they couldn't. On every floor, allowances were always made so that in an emergency a patient on a stretcher could be moved out of a stuck elevator, shifted across a thick balcony into a working car.

All the elevators were in use; huge lumbering machines ferrying people down from the fire. Bill looked up to see that his elevator's counterweight was about eight feet above him.

Damn. The counterweight rode a track like a guillotine blade up and down the back wall of the shaft; when the elevator was at the top, the weight was at the bottom and vice versa. Stopping at eleven, Bill had met it in the middle. Not, however, close enough.

"Bill?"

It was Sharon. Bill said nothing, watching the elevator in the next shaft descend below him.

"Don't jump, okay, Bill?"

In the next shaft, the elevator was on its way back up from the bottom, and there was no way it wasn't going to stop at eleven. He grinned at Sharon. She really was lovely down there, standing in the middle of that box all alone.

"It is Bill, isn't it?" He put a finger to his lips.

He'd been right; the elevator next to his was two floors down and slowing. He heard a man's voice inside say "Lock and load," and the wicked steel sound of rounds being chambered, and he knew they were riot cops coming for him.

There was a look of pleading in Sharon's eyes. He held the roof edge with his burned left hand, extended his right into the elevator, and took her fingers in his. Then he shifted, brought his face down as far as he could, and kissed her knuckles. And then he drew himself up and was gone.

The elevator rose to meet the eleventh-floor door and stopped, four feet below his own.

As the door opened, Bill dropped gently down onto the new arrivals' roof as the cops inside all thundered out, their noise masking his own. He unscrewed the nozzle, set the open bottle on the elevator's roof door so it would overturn if anyone opened it. He held on to the elevator's central cable — actually two cables, less than an inch apart — and stepped gingerly to the far edge, overlooking the third elevator shaftway.

No sound came from behind him. It amazed him that Sharon hadn't said a word.

He looked up and saw the third elevator descending above him. He looked down, noted the counterweight against the shaft wall rising in its track. Above him, the bottom of the elevator was coming down fast, closer and closer. He considered the sheer futility of what he was attempting, remembered General McClellan, demoted by Lincoln for doing nothing. The elevator passed his head, passed his chest, passed his knees; that was when he forced himself to jump at the back wall of the once again empty shaft.

It was the same type of double cable, and it was moving, greased and slippery and dirty, and when he grabbed it, he dropped, skinning the backs of his hands against the wall. He must have slid down about ten feet; when the counterweight slammed into him it rattled back and forth in its track but kept rising. Dust and grease covered the steel slab. Bill held on and rose, floor by floor, as the elevator sank farther and farther beneath him.

There was nothing below him now but air.

Bill got one foot on the rising counterweight, and then the other, and now he was standing. Across the shaft, the closed doors of floor after floor passed in a stately fashion; water dribbled down from nineteen — the sprinkler system, he guessed. Above him, smoke-diffused light from the skylight illuminated a metal catwalk; above that, he could see the top end of the elevator works, huge wheels that ran the double cable, powered by the motors and drums far below. At the center of the catwalk a small and exact square hole was cut for the main elevator cable to pass up and down. And then the counterweight slowed, and stopped, and Bill gritted his teeth: the elevator had opened on the first floor.

Three subbasements. Damnit. The elevator was at the lobby level, there were three subbasements below it, and there were three floors above Bill to the top of the shaft.

He set his feet up against the wall, held on to the double cable and pushed himself up, grabbed tight, and walked with the balls of his feet step by step up the cinderblock wall. Above him was the grid, the steel catwalk. Three more body lengths, the top of the shaft closer and closer, five feet from his grasp —

The cables shuddered, and then, far below, the elevator door shut and the cable in his hands started to descend, slowly, and then faster, and his feet slid and it ripped his hands and there was no place to go, nothing to do but leap.

The catwalk was a metal grill like a subway grating, and his fingers went through and he immediately made fists and held, but his hands were bleeding and greasy, and the grip was impossible, he could feel himself slipping.

And then, hanging there, he realized he was trapped. He could hear the central elevator cable hum, two taut steel ropes moving at bone-shredding speed four inches behind his right shoulder. His fingers were sweaty and bloody and hurting and useless. He was going to hang like this for — who knew how many seconds, and quarter inch by quarter inch he was going to slip, until he fell and died, and that would be that.

The grid was interrupted by a heavy metal panel. This, he knew, was a trapdoor to facilitate repairs — all elevator shafts had them. Unless the workers here were incredibly sloppy, it was undoubtedly bolted shut.

He bent his neck back and pulled himself up and tried to press the steel panel open with his forehead, grunting with the effort, and it didn't budge, and his fingers were sweaty and slippery, and he would have given anything for a place to stand — the thought was so overpowering it made him dizzy. Then the central cable slowed to a stop, and he looked at the hole it traveled through. He'd have to use it. He didn't have a choice.

Come on, God. Pure electricity. And he found himself making promises: Get me through this, connect the circle, and I'll stop. I'll finish and I'll stop and I'll leave.

He looked down to see where the elevator was. That, he realized, was a mistake. He tightened his left fist, let go with his right, and grabbed the central cable.

The two strands were well oiled, but they were also filthy, gritty and slimy at once. He grabbed the edge of the cut square of catwalk — the edges were sharp; they bit into his flesh — and then forced his right hand up through the hole, next to the cable, realized he didn't have enough room, shifted his arm into the corner of the little square. This allowed him to get his elbow through, and he clamped his fingers into the top side of the grate. Now he was hanging from above, and he let his left hand go, shook it out, dangling in space, and then somebody downstairs pressed a button, the wheels above him came alive, and the elevator cable started to move.

He grabbed the grid with his left hand, pulled like hell to position himself away from the thing as it gathered speed down. It was running the skin off his elbow and the back of his arm. He held on tight and prayed that it would stop, prayed with all his might, but it didn't. Then finally it shuddered to a halt, and he didn't care anymore. He forced the rest of his arm up the hole; it was slick with blood, which actually made it easier. He scrabbled his fingers along the top side of the panel, reaching desperately to find the latch before the elevator started to move again. The cables would slice his torso open in this position. And then he felt it, and he wanted to cry.

A bolt. Thank God, a bolt.

He shot it forward, hurled his leg up and kicked the panel with his foot.

It raised and then fell shut with a clang, and Bill suddenly found himself overemotional, sobbing with happiness. Then he heard the fits and starts, and the elevator wheels began to turn. The downward momentum forced his arm out, ripped his skin on the sharp edges.

He grabbed the grid, pulled himself away from the moving cable, and then bashed the steel panel with his forehead, and it went up, thank God it went up, and he clambered up and pushed himself through and lay on his back.

He wanted to laugh and he wanted to sleep and he lay there looking up at the sunlight coming through the bird-shitted panes of glass. His arm was bleeding, it was a mess, but it didn't matter because it felt so good to breathe.

He gulped in air, sat up, and looked around. The works of the three shafts were housed under one long angled shedlike roof, broken up by skylights. He climbed a ladder to an access walkway above the shafts. At either end was a door out onto the roof.

Cautiously he pulled himself up and looked out the skylight window. It was late afternoon outside, dusk under an iron gray sheet of cloud. The roof was at eye level, black tar paper, with various skylights and vents and a huge air-conditioning unit and a sloping stairwell entranceway door about thirty feet away. And then, as he watched, the stairwell door slammed open and two cops in full riot squad gear, with helmets, danced out, guns drawn, one covering the other. They ran for the air-conditioning unit, the largest structure on the roof, and disappeared behind it.

The wind slapped the door open, thirty feet away. Bill stared at the doorway and waited for a hand to come out and close the damn thing. When none did, he gritted his teeth and kept low and turned the knob and pushed his door open with his shoulder. The minute the wind hit him, he ran.

It was a cold afternoon, calm under the thick gray clouds, the air cool and alive around him. He was halfway there when he heard the word "Freeze!" and he kept running, and a shotgun exploded somewhere behind him and he threw himself into the doorway, slammed his shoulder into the cinderblock, reached back out and pulled the door shut behind him. He jammed the bolts home and ran down the stairs.

He bypassed the first door he came to, ran down a flight and debated the next door, but something in him didn't like it and he flew by that one and went down another flight. He opened that door, crossed a linoleum hallway and entered another door. This room smelled horrible. He was surrounded by sacks of garbage piled up shoulder-high in plastic hauling carts.

Most of the bags were black. Some were red.

Bill ripped open a black one, found it full of computer paper and lunch residue and coffee cups. He tried another, and found plants and flowers and dirt.

And then he turned his attention to the red bag waste. The first one he ripped spewed syringes and bloody clothing and something that looked like a chunk of liver. He tried another, and was rewarded by a set of green operating scrubs, stiff with dried blood.

Dried was okay; he didn't mind dried. He pulled the pants on, dug deeper into the bag, and pulled out a green shirt. This was still moist in places, but he put it on anyway. Then he dug out a mask and one plastic bootie. It took him a long time to find another plastic bootie, and when he did, it didn't match — it was probably sized for a woman. He stretched it on, then stood at the door listening for sounds of any kind, didn't hear any, and stepped out the other entrance.

Across from him was an ice machine and Styrofoam chests. He was almost past it when the idea hit, and it made him grin. He took a chest, filled it with ice, and slapped on a lid.

He went back into the room with the garbage bags, found what he was looking for, and stepped out into the main elevator foyer. When the elevator came, it was empty. At nineteen, the door opened and Bill could see that the emergency was over. Cops and firemen were standing in groups, chatting. An orderly pushed a man handcuffed to a gurney onto the elevator, and Bill recognized the huge black man who had been on the telephone earlier. Bill turned away, but the man was staring at him, and when the elevator opened at eight, Bill followed the nurses out. He left them quickly and walked down a hall of patients' rooms. He turned a corner and liked the sign on the door before him: DOCTOR's LOUNGE.

Inside one man sat reading the *Times* with his legs up on the table. He looked at Bill, nodded, and went back to his reading. There was a coffee machine — Bill set down the ice chest, helped himself to a cup, put in sugar and milk, and sipped it. At the back were lockers and two showers.

Bill found a towel, and went into the shower room. In the wastebasket by the sink was a disposable razor. Bill fished it out, stripped down and turned on the shower and gingerly tried to clean up his scraped and battered body.

A few minutes later, a man entered the stall next to his and turned on the water. Bill shaved himself as well as he could without a mirror, turned off the water, and toweled himself gently around his wounds. Then he put on the same green operating pajamas, stiff with dried blood, and went back into the lounge.

Bill took up his ice chest and noticed that the showering man had left his ID and a pair of tortoiseshell glasses sitting on the table. Bill palmed them and left. He put on the glasses — they made everything curve and elongate in a headache-inducing way — clipped the ID to his pocket, held the ice chest in front to cover it, and walked purposefully back down the hall.

There was a small crowd waiting for the elevator; the five-o'clock exodus. When the door opened, Bill saw patrolmen and a couple of riot squad cops at the back, but the rest were all hospital personnel. He smiled, shouldered into a niche between two nurses.

The lobby was jammed with angry people, all talking at once.

"What's the story?" Bill asked no one in particular, his heart pounding in his chest.

"Cops're looking for somebody," one big-haired woman said

and cracked her gum. "Got checkpoints at the exits slowing things up."

A well-dressed man emerged out of the mob, looked at his watch. "Excuse me — I've got to get out of here — I'm a doctor —"

"We're all doctors, guy —" a voice growled from further up in the mob, and around them people laughed.

It took five minutes for Bill's little pocket of humanity to move up to the doors, where two cops were checking IDs and ushering people through. Bill chose the younger one.

"Is this going to take long?" he asked, when it was his turn.

"Name?" The cop eyed his bloody shirt.

"Ed Kuransky," Bill said, for that was the name on the ID clipped to his shirt. He wiggled the card, then held up the ice chest in front of it, opened the lid, and stuck it under the cop's nose. "I gotta get this liver to St. Luke's in twelve minutes."

"Go, go," the cop said, and waved him off. Bill walked through the doors and cut between ambulances onto the sidewalk and marched with the crowd up toward First Avenue, trumpets and violins and choruses all coming together so loud in his head he was actually surprised the people around him couldn't hear it.

It was almost dusk when Arvin Redwell awoke from his nap, and for a full four seconds he thought he was in Washington, at his house in Georgetown, until he heard Alma humming scales from the other room. New York. He debated going back to sleep, but the thought of the report he had to read forced him off the bed and into the bathroom. And there, urinating, he caught sight of his wife in her slip, shaking her fingernails in the air.

"How much time do we have?"

She frowned. "Two hours — a little less."

"I should really do a little work," he said. She said nothing. "If I had this whole evening . . ."

"Come to the Met, make yourself seen, stay as long as you like, and then go. I'll say something came up."

Another compromise, but fine. He zipped up, flushed, and touched her arm. "Thanks."

"Don't even think about it." She went on into the bedroom.

Arvin Redwell walked up the hall into his office, sat, and turned on his computer. His window commanded a stellar north view of the East River. The afternoon was fading, the windows of Manhattan lighting up, people in their kitchens with their hopes. He had always liked that view. The time and date appeared on the computer screen. Arvin Redwell typed his way into the e-mail program, perused the unsecured postings that had been sent while he was away. Nothing that wouldn't wait.

Then he asked for the secured e-mail. The machine asked for his access code, as it always did. He typed it, hit enter.

A complicated series of electronic transfers took place inside the machine; an instruction in the form of an electric pulse was sent to the capacitor, which amplified the charge, and sent it on to the blasting cap. This fired, igniting the thick wad of plastic explosive, which then blew up and outward with tremendous force.

To Arvin Redwell it seemed that in a split second the computer had become an inferno on his table before him, and then he was part of that inferno, that incredible heat, and the table was gone, and he was no more.

PART

TWO

XI

"So. Let's go back to the beginning." Kincaide sat back in the little room, stroked his mustache. "Girl you've never seen before comes into the ER, hands you a bag of what look like food items, asks you to take it to Milt, or Bill, on the prison ward."

Sharon was rubbing her temples, her eyes closed. More than anything she wanted just to lie down.

"Yes," she said, feeling the depths of her hopelessness.

"And you know it's against the rules to bring anything to a prisoner on that ward, but you do it anyway."

"I told you I scanned it. It looked like food."

The other man in the room spoke up: "And you'd known Milt Slavitch — or Bill Kai — how long?"

"Three days."

"You're sure of that." That was Brannock, the lanky older man in a dark suit to her right, just beyond her peripheral vision.

"I would be happy to take a lie detector test," Sharon said.

"There's no reason to be hostile," the man said evenly, and Sharon hated him for it. "Is there a reason we should think you're not telling the truth?"

"I never saw him before." Sharon heard a tremor in her voice. She thought of getting her compact, pulling herself together, but all that was in her bag, hanging with her coat in the waiting room.

"And what were your feelings for him once you met him?"

"Professional," said Sharon, her head up.

"Obviously they were more than that. Or you wouldn't have acted so unprofessionally, broken so many rules for the man."

Sharon felt herself beginning to slip: the catch in the throat, the welling of tears behind her eyes. It wasn't Milt, or Bill, whatever his name was; it was these assholes, the way they piled insinuation on insinuation until they'd trapped her in a prison of words. She felt just as jerked around as she had in that elevator. And then the anger came back, and it was good to feel something besides small and wrong and hopeless.

"Look. It's my job to develop a rapport —"

"I think you developed a lot more than that," the lanky man said, and Sharon wanted to turn and hit him, but she didn't. She scratched the scar under her chin, and then there was a knock at the door, and a cop stuck his head in. "Brannock, it's your wife."

"Right there." As he left, Sharon looked for a wedding ring, and didn't see one. Kincaide brought out a bag of long pretzels.

"You must be hungry, Sharon — please." He gestured. "Take one. You've been here forever."

Sharon pressed her hand to her stomach, shook her head no.

"So you hang with Milt, Bill, for three days. And at one point he saves you from" — he checked the papers on his desk — "that guy Andrew who jumps you. Wouldn't it be natural to talk about getting together outside, about maybe having a drink or coffee or something just to, you know, thank him?"

"It didn't happen," Sharon said, definitively.

"Not even a glimmer? You talk together, you laugh — Crystal told us that. People saw you interacting —"

There was a perfunctory knock, and a cop stuck his head in. "Lieutenant?"

"'Scuse me." He walked out, and left Sharon alone in the scuffed white room, and all at once she felt like she would never have the energy to lift herself out of this uncomfortable plastic chair.

She was numb to everything, right now: emotions seemed a

privilege she could not afford. She felt a million miles away from herself.

Kincaide came back into the room, sat, and said nothing, staring right at her, and Sharon smiled at the thought that this felt like a therapy session, with neither of them talking.

"What's the smile?" he asked. She shook her head. It wasn't worth explaining.

"Sharon, can I ask you a favor? You were carrying that bag" — he gestured vaguely at the other room — "when you went into the prison ward. I wonder if you'd let me take a look through it."

At first it seemed a mild request, and then Sharon remembered Charley's Mickey Mouse bag. She swallowed, and there was something nasty at the back of her throat. She wasn't sure what to say.

"I'm sorry — no."

"See, I think you're innocent — duped into this, as you say — but Brannock's kind of a tough old mule. I think it would ease his mind a lot if I could say you'd cooperated with me."

How many pills were in it? Eighty? A hundred? "I can't."

"If you've got nothing to hide, Sharon —"

"If I had anything incriminating, I would have given it to Bill when he got out of the elevator. That's the only way I could have made my story stick, right?"

Kincaide was silent.

"Right?" Sharon repeated, suddenly angry.

"Well, yeah —"

"Well, then, check the shafts. Find Bill, ask him."

"I'd rather ask you."

"Okay — no, you can't."

A simmering pause between them. "May I ask why?"

Sharon looked at the black linoleum between her feet for a long moment. Then she looked him in the eye. "Did you ever lose a son, Lieutenant Kincaide?" He said nothing. "Did you ever have your family die around you?" Obviously not. "Well," she said finally, "call me when you have."

*   *   *

When he got to the Lower East Side, Bill walked south, ideas buzzing around his head like electrons around a proton. He entered a building a block and a half from his own, trotted down the stairs. There were four entrances to his place; this was the northernmost. He crossed the basement, went through a heavy steel door, bolted it from inside. This left him in total darkness: he extended his knuckles, touched the old bricks on either side, ambled quickly forward, counting his paces. At two seventy-five he slowed; he knew in the complete darkness there was a metal fire door to his right, with no external bolts or locks and no knob. He knelt, felt for the metal plate of an electrical outlet, flicked the panel up. Inside, a blue Christmas-tree bulb cast a weak hidden light, revealing a scavenged, broken-looking computer numeric keypad. Bill pressed a six-digit code, heard four bolts ram open.

Bill's basement had once been a speakeasy. Speakeasies had been a hobby of his when he was sixteen — researching them, sitting in the big room of the New York Public Library, working his way through the twenties in the *New York Times* on microfilm, then tracking them down and hiding things in the abandoned and forgotten ones.

His basement was a mess. The main room was cavernous, with filing cabinets against one wall and a wooden workbench the length of the opposite side. In the center was his desk, completely covered with clipped bits of newspaper and magazines and soldering guns and multimeters and about four computers' worth of bits and pieces, hard drives and monitors and circuit cards, all surrounding his main computer, which was, as always, on. There were phones in various stages of disarray, and beepers and manuals and alarm system components and coffee cups and locks and keys and tools.

Bill walked by the desk to a stereo on the top of the filing cabinet, hit the radio switch on. WHBN was playing some kind of discordant alterna-jazz, squawking rude sax squeals and clamorous guitar. He turned up the volume until the noise filled the windowless brick room. Then he dumped his coat and newspapers onto a chair. It was warm in the basement; as he took off his shirt, he found himself captivated once again by the luminous beauty of the

Jackson Pollock drip painting on the far wall. He took a step closer, and another, until the strands of color began to reach out and caress and entangle him, and he was safe within their grasp.

The city eternal.

Ekaterina was responsible for his having it; somewhere in that painting was her gaze. Sometimes he wasn't sure if he'd kept it for its inherent beauty or for the lingering resonance of her.

Beyond was the kitchen, with a long restaurant stove that had been left for scrap when Bill found the place. It had taken him almost two weeks to get the grime off. Next to that was a small room, probably once an office. Bill's bed was in there, an unmade mattress and box spring on the floor. Through another door was a large, cavernous space that had been the main room of the speakeasy. Anyone else would have made it their own; Bill blamed rats for his rejection of it, but the fact was he simply felt more comfortable living in a messy warren of cramped spaces. There were rattraps in the corners of the large room; once every couple of weeks he'd fill the sink with water, dump the cage in, and drown the beasts. He kept a steel locker and a refrigerator in there for storage of his more volatile drugs, chemicals, and compounds.

Bill considered the question of Sharon. Totally different from Ekaterina, vastly more honest, a different kind of intelligence altogether. And strong: if she wasn't strong, she wouldn't survive. That made the circle complete; he tore himself away from the lowering fog of the Pollock, put on a pair of black leather fingerless gloves — after years of training himself, he always felt safer when he was wearing something on his hands, even when fingerprints didn't matter — and turned his attention to his computer. He had built and rebuilt it himself, most recently wiring in a cellular interface along with the conventional modem. He took the cover off his keyboard, typed his password — had he typed anything else, the hard drive would have automatically begun reformatting itself, erasing everything — modemed to the *New York Times* on-line database, set up some search parameters, keyworded "Mackinnon, Edward," and went to take a shower.

Forty-five minutes later, Bill sat on the edge of the tub in his basement, blow-drying his newly blond eyebrows and hair. He checked himself in the mirror, set the dryer aside, opened a jar of vitamin E capsules, bit the tip off one, and squeezed the thick yellow oil onto his frayed and scabby arm. Then he took up the gauze bandage, slathered the inside with aloe vera, pressed it over his wound. He stood, checked the bandage in the mirror.

He was stalling. He didn't like it, but there it was. He put on the black tie, checked himself in the mirror. He knew what he wanted to do, what the next logical step had to be, and he knew precisely how foolhardy it was.

At the computer he downloaded the list into a file. Then he threw on his long black coat and left the basement, heading uptown.

Stick around, Sharon thought as she walked out of Bellevue. Don't leave town. We want to have you available to us so we can drive you mad at our whim, asking the same questions over and over.

Of course Sharon had agreed, because, she thought exhaustedly, she always agreed. Could you not leave town? Could you wear this blindfold? Could you let me use you as a human shield?

She walked up the Bellevue walkway, onto First, and then came to a dead stop. She had no idea where to go. Home was unappealing: the thought of sitting in that apartment gave no warmth to her soul. And then she knew what she wanted to do, and she walked resolutely forward, up toward Second Avenue.

She thought of Bill, she thought of that kid who'd brought her the bag, she thought of those cops, and the truth was inexorable: Goddamn, she'd been a fool, hadn't she?

She caught sight of the Mackinnon Group skyscraper going up down the street, and as she crossed the avenue to evade it, its very existence drove her to wonder if perhaps foolishness was an inherited trait. Sharon had always thought that the lesson of her father's death was not to fuck up the way he had, but perhaps that was unavoidable; maybe it was a matter of twisted family destiny.

The thing was, she thought, she had spent her life trying to make everything right. That had been her childhood — attempting to create a universe for her mother in which there would be some kind of solace, some kind of justice. Night after night, Sharon would listen to her mom in the other rooms of the house, knocking into doorframes and talking back to the television set as she got drunker, and Sharon would lie in bed and build elaborate fantasies in which Edward Mackinnon would finally be forced to pay for his crimes against their family. She wanted to be the hero; she wanted to heal her mother's pain. When she was ten and eleven and twelve years old, she'd wanted that more than anything in the world.

One day when she was fourteen, she came to her mother with a plan. She'd read in the paper that Edward Mackinnon had taken his company public — that anyone could now buy stock in it. All they had to do was buy some, and they'd have access to the records in the company's files. They'd be able to figure out what part of the profits came from her father's computer program and sue the company. And Sharon's mother had said, No, dear. Edward Mackinnon was just being a businessman. It was your father who was weak.

On Second Avenue, Sharon shouldered open the door to the Starr Bar.

She had been in once before, when she'd first moved into the neighborhood. She sat at the end of the bar, asked the young Irishman for a Booker's, three ice cubes, water back. The bourbon was sweet, and then it was harsh, and country-and-western music began to emanate from the jukebox in the corner.

It hadn't been that she'd wanted to wreak revenge on Edward Mackinnon — destroy him the way he'd destroyed her father — though at times her anger had led her fantasies into that area. After a while it had become an unfulfilled wish for a conversation between her and her old uncle Ed — she'd wanted to show him how his actions had consequences even he could not understand. It was a matter of enlightenment, of wishing she could unload everything in her brain into his, so that he'd be able to comprehend what she knew as everyday truth. And it all boiled down to one phrase: You Just Don't Treat People In That Manner.

And now she wanted to say it to Bill Slavitch, or whatever his name was. She felt used, and abused, and somewhere out there she had the feeling he was laughing, and she didn't like it at all.

Standing in the shadows of the tree-lined street, Bill checked east and west with his binoculars. No one was walking toward him within half a block; if he was going to do it, now was the time.

He slipped between parked cars, trotted up the two steps to Sharon's front door. The exterior door only required a quick working with a piece of metal Venetian blind; the interior door had a more complicated buzzer and plate, but he had no need to go that far, this time. He stepped inside, stood in the battered tile atrium, looked over the mailboxes. These were the old-fashioned kind, with a small viewing window stamped out above the keyhole. With gloved fingers he took up the envelope in his coat pocket, ripped it open. Inside was a note rubber-banded tightly around a swizzle stick; he slid it through the little window. It dropped into the box.

He was out on the street a second later, walking west.

The evening was mild as Bill Kaiser trotted up the steps to Lincoln Center and joined the throng. He passed by the fountain, noted the differences in the audiences peeling off into one or another of the theaters — the lithe gay men and long-muscled young women with their hair pulled back gliding into the New York City Ballet; the married couples and older singles attending the Philharmonic at Avery Fisher Hall, and then, at the back, the ones exuding wealth from their tanned faces, jewelry clattering on bony white arms and long, well-bred necks: the operagoers converging for this evening's performance at the Met. Bill headed into that crowd, his black coat flapping around him, his tux a perfect fit. He stood on line behind a couple trying to remember where they'd first met Letitia — Rome? Santa Barbara? Tivoli? Bill looked at the well-dressed couples, and for once didn't feel subversive, being here; merely lonely.

This was to have been his reward, and he tried to reinvigorate it with the meaning it had held when he'd been hanging from one

arm in that elevator shaft. The love duet at the end of the prologue — that's why he'd survived, that had been his strength. And
then the couple ahead finished and Bill stepped up to the ticket
window.

"You're holding tickets for Redwell."

The man behind the glass said, "Credit card order?"

"No, comps," Bill guessed.

The man found the envelope and fanned two tickets out and
said, "Curtain goes up in two minutes; enjoy the opera."

Sharon worked the key in her building's front door, finally got it
open — a little tricky, nothing too hard — shut it behind her, and
smiled at the tiny atrium. "Oh, you again," she said, which was a
joke — the building saying it to her, but also her saying it to the
building. Then she spent a moment fiddling with her mailbox key
until finally the funky old thing creaked opened, and she took her
mail and unlocked the atrium door. Waiting for the elevator, she
flipped through junk mail with sad-eyed dogs from the humane society, a notice of a lecture series on new AIDS treatment techniques, a schedule for Film Forum. And then, not in an envelope,
she found a weird twig of paper wrapped around a swizzle stick.

Plastic swizzle stick, with a vaguely sinister red cat's head at the
top. She unrolled the note. The handwriting was crabby, odd, almost illegible:

> *Sharon —*
>   *Karma: what you give out, you get back sevenfold.*
>   *See you 'round.*
>   *— Bill*

The elevator door dinged and opened and waited, and Sharon
stood frozen under the fluorescent hallway lamp, unable to
breathe.

He'd come here. He'd put this here. He knew where she lived.

Just the thought of it made her want to run out into the night.
She looked back at the doorway, suddenly afraid he was watching.
She could sleep on Crystal's couch, or maybe get a hotel room.

Then the elevator door started to close, and she stuck her foot in, got on, and pressed her floor, debating even as she did if she should get off at seven and walk up a flight, as if somehow he could be monitoring her every action.

Going up, she looked at the evil little plastic cat's head and felt as if the floor were going to open on a hinge beneath her, send her plummeting.

She read the note again, her hands shaking in the thin light. And then the elevator door opened, and she realized she should have gotten off at another floor, because now she was trapped.

She stuck her head out, looked both ways.

The hallway was empty. She walked quickly to her door, checked the knob, checked all around.

Nothing.

She let herself in, flicked on all the lights at once, opened the closet and kicked through all her clothes, and checked behind the shower curtain.

No Bill. Just her apartment, exactly as she'd left it.

One message blinking on the machine. She didn't want to play it, but finally she willed herself to press the button.

Garber: "If you could be in my office ten-thirty tomorrow morning, there are several aspects of your behavior this afternoon that need to be discussed."

Sharon closed her eyes and sank to the bed and concentrated on breathing. "Fuck," she said out loud, "they're going to fire me."

Just putting it into words made the muscles in her shoulders go rigid, and her fingernails dig into her palms. She thought she would explode, blow apart at the seams, and that would be that. And then her breathing returned, the pitching and rolling in her stomach subsided, and that was the awful thing: that she was still here, that everything was just so fucking normal.

Alone in the world. That was how she always ended up.

She walked into the kitchen: Charley's drawing flapped in the breeze: a house, messy trees, big yellow sun. She opened the top cabinet above. The Booker's was behind the Windex. She got a glass, poured in two fingers, corked the bottle. Then she pulled her bag over, opened the drawstring mouth as wide as it would go, and upended it on the white blanket. The long bag vomited forth everything inside.

Losing the job. It was too nasty even to think.

At the bottom was Charley's Mickey Mouse bag. She took a long mouthful of bourbon, swallowed it, felt the fumes rise in her head. Then she unzipped the bag.

Most of the pills had been crushed to a coarse off-white powder by the constant shifting of stuff in her drawstring sack.

The funny thing was it only captured her imagination when she wasn't looking at it. The physical reality of those pills and chunks of pills and crushed gelatin capsules and indeterminate powder never made her want to get a glass of water, pour it all in, mix it up, and glug it down. But on the bus, in the bathroom at work, on the elevator going up to see her shrink — suddenly the whole idea would overtake her, and she wouldn't be able to shake it for great lengths of time.

She wondered if her father had ever regarded his shotgun that way, and she realized — of course he had. He must have looked at it every time he walked into his office, there above the mantelpiece.

She had heard the noise from upstairs — hugely loud, two explosions on top of each other. So surprising against the calm of the night that her math pencil had actually leapt out of her hand. She'd run downstairs, turned the corner, approached the door —

And that's all she remembered. She didn't know a thing about what happened next, which scared her. She had images in her head, but she honestly didn't know what was real and what was received.

Both barrels. Had she really heard two blasts? Or was that just her filling in the story, extrapolating? The top of his head had been torn off, blood and brains and bone and hair all over the wall behind him. She had an image of what that must have looked like — but whether it was memory or fiction, she had no idea.

There were things she knew she'd invented — a bone white skull bowl rocking back and forth on the floor. She didn't know when she added that touch, but years later she realized it couldn't have been like that. And she'd always had a picture of blood coming up from the cavity of his brain in a steady stream, like water rising from a fountain. The first time she'd ever worked in a medical emergency room, she'd realized people just didn't bleed that way.

Back when life had been normal, Charley had fixated on the Mickey Mouse bag; for months he'd carried it from room to room for some private reason of his own. Rick began to refer to it as Charley's purse, which had made Sharon angry — the boy would grow up however he grew up; nobody could do anything about that. After the accident, Sharon used it to keep all his pain and antiseizure pill bottles in one place. In the twilight four months of Charley's life, as the doctors despaired of ever repairing the damage, the list of pills in that bag just kept growing. After Charley died, Sharon had gone back to her mother's in Oneonta and taken hours at the closest emergency room just to have something to do. There'd been plenty of pills of all kinds around; that was when she began to build the suicide pack in earnest.

She'd looked for chemical antagonists, things that couldn't be taken together. By the time she moved to New York, the toxicity in that bag could have killed a fair-sized roomful of people.

And all she'd ever done with it was carry it around and remember it at odd moments and be reassured that it was there. She'd even contemplated the taste, which would be wicked, sharp and chemical — vile. There'd been a period, right after she'd lost Charley, where she couldn't pour out a glass of water without seeing herself mix in the pills. But she'd never actually done it; she'd never gotten any of it to the vicinity of her lips.

Sharon took another sip of bourbon and stared into the bag. And then she rose, walked to the sink, calmly opened the cabinet, took down a glass, and filled it with water.

Man, she'd loved that job. That was the shame of it — she'd finally found a job in a place worth fighting for. And, once again, she'd been too much of a fuckup to keep it.

Charley was gone, Rick was gone. New York, the job, it was like she just couldn't hold on to anything.

She set the glass on the bedside table, held the bag of crushed pills over the glass, and slowly tipped her hand.

When the white-yellow dust hit the surface of the water, it

spread out immediately, suspended at the top, and the larger chunks began to sink, and then more and more.

It was fascinating to see the way the different pills acted, the fragments cartwheeling down. She took another sip of bourbon, just watching. And then she took up the glass of cloudy water, raised it to her mouth, touched the cold glass to her lower lip.

A tiny taste of something bitter and astringent met her tongue.

Out the window, the Empire State Building blasted its lights into the night. She was aware of her heart beating, of her pulse rocking through her arms. And then something inside backed up and exploded: this was insane, this was bullshit, this was precisely the sort of behavior she'd been trained to deduce and intervene.

She stood, holding the glass, walked carefully into the bathroom, terrified to spill a drop, to lose control. She emptied the glass into the toilet, her teeth clamped hard on her lip.

Damnit, killing herself would prove to the world that she really was a victim, that she was the victim Garber and Frank and Mister-Karma-Bill thought she was. But they were wrong. She wasn't that person. She knew that.

She stepped out into the kitchen, washed the glass in the sink with too much soap, set it on the rack to dry. She knocked back the end of her bourbon, washed that glass as well.

The Charley bag was still on the night table, half filled with poison. She shook the contents into the toilet, flushed and flushed and rinsed the bag out and jammed it deep into the laundry hamper. Then she came back out, fished the television remote from where it had fallen behind her bedside table, and pointed it and clicked on the TV.

Nazis marching, earnest American soldiers stepping carefully through ruined French towns. She pressed the channel up, and there was the news, firetrucks, a zoom up to a smoldering gaping hole in an apartment building. Cut to some stock footage, Arvin Redwell shaking hands, photo ops, pacing back and forth behind the podium during his last filibuster, what a despicable man. And then Sharon realized: no, wait, it seems he's dead.

Live again, the camera panned back down to a black woman

standing in front of a canopy, the canopy said "36." That rang a bell, and even as she turned up the volume, a clammy chill injected itself into Sharon's chest, lingered in her stomach: 36 what?

She waited. A bombing. A senator dead, in his East Side apartment building. At last, the woman said it: 36 Sutton Place.

The Montclaire.

Sharon's heart was hammering as she scrabbled through her wallet, took out the card. Detective Michael Kincaide, with his numbers. She thought of calling Bellevue to double-check, but she knew she was right. She'd been poring over that file for three days. She dialed the first number on the card, realized the second was a beeper, almost hung up to try it, but then someone picked up.

"Kincaide."

"Lieutenant, it's Sharon Blautner —"

"Sharon — you see the news?"

"The dead senator — that's the building Bill was in."

"Anything you want to tell us about that?"

"He did it," she said. "He did it, and he knew the bomb was going to go off today, and that's why he had to escape."

"Uh-hunh." Distinctly cold. Sharon wanted to tell him to go fuck himself. Instead she said: "He left me a note. In my building."

"He was there?" Urgency in his voice. "Read me the note." She did. "It came wrapped around this nasty little swizzle stick," she said, "like pushing me through fire was some kind of party."

"Sharon, you tell me — you think it sounds like a threat?"

She debated. "It's more like an iron law he's laying down. My problem is that after today I have no idea which side of it I'm on."

"We got one bomb where this guy's been already, tonight. You don't mind, I'd like to treat this as a bomb scare."

"My God, Lieutenant —"

"Got a Baggie? Put everything he sent in it, touch it as little as possible. Bring it. Get your stuff, pull the fire alarm, and get out."

"Lieutenant, you're scaring me —"

"I'll leave my cellular open, you see anything, you call me. I'll be right there, okay?" He got off the phone. Sharon pulled out an unused Ziploc, dropped the note in, and sealed it up. Then she spent a long moment standing in the middle of her apartment, thinking, If I was going to save one thing from this place, what would it be?

Charley, she thought, and started to collect every photo and drawing from the walls.

XII

"Been a while," Bill said.

"Certainly has, my man, certainly has." The dealer was a blondish man, wiry, about Bill's height. "What ya need? Got that smack, got that crack —"

"Heroin," Bill said. "I'll take a couple nickels."

"Nightzone, cleanest smack around. You need works?"

"Naah." Bill got out his wallet, gave the man a ten-spot, received two glassine envelopes in return.

"You want downers? I know you like them reds —"

"No, I'm all right on that stuff, for now."

"Anything you need, you know where I am, Third and Avenue B."

Bill looked him up and down again. "Thanks, Paulie, I'll find you." He left the man, turned the corner, headed east. A block later he found a sewer grating, dropped the glassine envelopes down it, and turned south under the night sky, toward the Carnegie-Hayden.

It was hard to believe that this desiccated husk of a building had ever represented anyone's utopian dream, but at points throughout the last hundred years, that was precisely the hold the Carnegie-Hayden had in people's imaginations. Bill stood across Avenue C and looked up at the six-story edifice. Well-scrubbed, it would have seemed palatial: now, graffiti covered the broad entrance steps and climbed halfway up the arched windows. Only one small annex was still in use; otherwise, the huge original building was empty, locked and fenced; homeless men slept in cardboard boxes at the top of the steps.

It always amazed Bill: human beings forced to sleep in the cold outside a vast uninhabited building. He shook his head in wonder.

Originally founded by Andrew Carnegie six years after he built his famous concert hall, the initial idea had been simply to put up a library under Carnegie's usual method: he built and equipped the building; local authorities provided and maintained the site. In this case the local authorities, aided by a group of successful New York businessmen, got together to expand the initial concept to include a gymnasium and a special library and lyceum devoted to the textile and garment-manufacture sciences. This, in turn, brought in a private contribution from Charles Hayden, he who later funded the famous planetarium uptown at the American Museum of Natural History, to include works on applied and theoretical sciences.

The Carnegie-Hayden Center, as it was named, was a place of citywide self-improvement for generations of students, workers, and businesspeople, both male and female. It also was a part of its time and place: in the days when anarchists and socialists and millennial utopianists harangued the masses from the Lower East Side's halls and streetcorners, it became a debating society for the new world aborning. Margaret Sanger gave speeches there, as did Emma Goldman and Eugene V. Debs.

In the forties, a flood caused portions of the library holdings to be removed because of water damage; eventually all the books were consolidated into the New York Public Library system. The last book was moved out in '52, and theatre troupes joined a Catholic medical clinic already using the space. By the sixties the skylit top floor had been colonized by artists, a day-care center inhabited the annex at the building's west end, and the larger of the two auditoriums became the near-legendary Pink Panther discotheque. Warhol's crowd created a scene there that lasted for years.

It had been part of his mother's litany of stories from back before they'd left the Lower East Side and moved to midtown. Bill had heard it so often that he actually felt he could remember the drizzle on his skin the day his father left for the last time, could recall the day his mom first took him inside the Carnegie-Hayden.

He couldn't, of course. He'd been an infant, not even a toddler. But he could picture it — Helen, his mother, lying on the bed, trying to keep Bill from crying as his father methodically smashed every breakable object in the apartment. All her records, every dish, even the demitasse cups: that's the way she'd always told it.

Then the man had packed a suitcase and walked out. When the police came, an hour later, she told them he had gone back up to his country-club friends at Harvard, and then she'd held her son close, surrounded by broken glass and china, and the two of them had watched the sun rise. When she saw the old Ukrainian lady across the street unlock her security grill and open her shop, she realized a new day had begun, and she knew precisely what she had to do. She dressed, and then dressed Bill, put him in his pram, and walked through drizzling rain to the Carnegie-Hayden.

She'd struggled the baby carriage up those steps, feeling she was doing it precisely the way her grandmother must have done it with her father. Nobody helped her as she maneuvered her way through the double doors. Nobody thought to question a woman pushing a baby carriage up the marble stairs at eight in the morning. Nobody did a thing as she stood in front of the long chiseled lists of local contributors, lifted her baby out of the carriage, took off his right mitten — he was right-handed, she'd tested it time and time again — and touched his tiny fingers to the deep crevasses of one of the names cut in the marble. This is yours, she whispered. This is your great grandfather. He helped create all this. These are your people; this is who you are.

There'd been a plan to save it, a brilliant proposal by a Jesuit named Fenton Digby that would have restored the Carnegie-Hayden's role as a physical and mental health center for all of lower Manhattan. The plan had worked its way through the bureaucracy, even receiving informal approval from the city council, before ending up in the back of some file cabinet in City Hall.

The Panther closed in '74; for the next few years the ballroom became a gay Latino juicebar. As a kid, Bill had come to any number of parties there, with his mom. After the police raided the club, the building was chained shut; one night in high school Bill snuck past the boarded-up door and gave himself a tour. By the time he found the swimming pool, half full of trash, he had come to decide that Digby was right: this building, alone, could save the Lower East Side.

It could be a clinic and a school — all at once. The nightclub could pay for the hospital beds. It could make enough profit to feed itself, cover its own losses. The idea expanded and expanded in his mind, leaving him breathless as he walked from one garbage-strewn marble hallway to another.

All that was needed was money.

And now, the powers that be wanted to rip it down and put up a prison in its place. Bill shuddered at the insanity of it: the reason it existed at all was to keep people out of prison. That, from the start, had been the whole point.

The problem was, the concept of the nation-state was in disarray. Nations had allegiances; their governments were supposed to be accountable to the people and thus represent some kind of fundamental national character. But nation-states were backwards and old-fashioned; corporations had become the new nation-states. And corporations were completely unaccountable and had no allegiances to anyone or anything, except their profits.

It was awful, the cynicism, the lack of faith in people, the pure and absolute corrosion of hope.

In every neighborhood where Straythmore wanted to put a prison, there was a building like the Carnegie-Hayden, built on the hopes of an earlier generation. One building at a time, they could be Digbyized, turned into a growing network, that would do more for each neighborhood than any prison possibly could.

Digby had never intended his plan to stop at just one building.

How much would it cost to implement something like the Father Digby plan? How much would it cost to stop them on their first beachhead, save one building, make it prosper, make it the pulsing heart of a thriving community? How much to create a template that could be repeated as needed all over this broad and majestic country?

Well, Edward Mackinnon had purchased a van Gogh for fifty-three million. Bill looked at the massive handcarved building and thought to himself what fifty-three mil could have done.

One van Gogh.

The more Bill thought about it, the more it seemed like an even trade.

*   *   *

When the clock radio went off, Sharon incorporated the salsa into her dream; then it became too insistent, and she woke up. Her heart was pounding and her mouth was dry and then the world rushed in and something in her chest began to writhe with anxiety.

They hadn't found a bomb, but the damage was done. Now everyone in the building was scared to live near her, and she couldn't completely trust her own home.

Damnit. She took a long shower and emerged feeling closer to normal. Then the phone started in.

Kincaide. "Just wanted to let you know I passed your name on to Martin Karndle, the FBI agent assigned to the case. I'm sure he'll want to interview you — you'll be getting a call."

Crystal. "You seen the *Post*? There's a quote from Garber, blames you by name for helping Bill escape."

Oh, God. "Why does he want me in, this morning? Why doesn't he just fire me on the phone?"

"Who knows what they're thinking, they're so scared."

That brought the anxiety back. She was dressed and almost out the door when the phone rang again, and this time she figured it had to be her mother; everyone who could possibly call had already called. She picked up the receiver.

A man's voice. "Sharon Blautner?"

"Who is this?" It sounded like Bill.

"Ah, this is Ben Q. McAnn of the *New York Times*. I'd like to ask you some questions about the escape yesterday —"

"Listen, I can't talk to you now, I have to get to —" She stopped herself before the word "work"; she suddenly had a picture of photographers with those big 1940s-style flashbulb cameras hovering around the Psych ER hallway. "I've got to go."

She hung up, sat on the bed, her drawstring bag in her hands, her heart beating hard. Then she marshaled her thoughts, stood, and put on her coat.

Outside it was a cold fall morning, the clouds gray and low with threatened snow. Sharon observed two guys sitting in a car across from her building, thought perhaps they were reporters. They seemed to take no notice as she walked by.

She turned the corner onto First, checked the clock on the back wall of the newsstand, saw she was on time, and then looked down at the headlines of the papers and immediately felt like she was naked on the street in a dream. "REDWELL DEAD IN BOMBING," said the *News*, with the subhead: "Suspect Flees Bellevue." The *Times* had a banner headline: "SENATOR REDWELL IS KILLED BY BOMB AT HOME; SUSPECT SOUGHT." The *Post*, which had always supported the man's policies and campaigns, had a picture of him ringed in black, under which were the words, "HE GAVE HIS LIFE."

Sharon bought all three, was reminded of the Necco wafers by the Kurdish man. She shook her head, and continued on her way.

There it was: on page two, the *Post* quoted Dr. Harold Garber as saying that Sharon Blautner, a nurse who had only been at Bellevue a short time, had "aided in the escape."

The dread in her stomach seized her so suddenly she didn't even remember to avoid looking at the Edward Mackinnon skyscraper up the street.

Edward Mackinnon was not in the mood for aesthetics, but aesthetics had already interrupted his concentration twice thus far, and they weren't even out of the morning, yet. On his desk, the *New York Times* was open to Straythmore's full-page ad, complete with the quote from Arvin. "No, no, no," he was explaining into the phone, "the tone of the next ad has to be — it's terrible, it's a tragedy, the man was a friend, Straythmore Security can help stop this. Because the truth is, your company has been offered a stage to make its point —" There was a knock at the door, and his wife Melissa led Theodore reluctantly into the room. Mackinnon said, "Hold on," clamped his hand over the phone receiver, and barked, "What?"

Theodore hid behind Melissa's thigh, chewed on a finger. "Ted wants to see the van Gogh again," she explained.

Edward Mackinnon said, "Stuart, let me put you on hold," punched another button on the phone, and buzzed the outer office. "Van Gogh's at the gallery, right? Is it uncrated?"

"No," said a British voice over the line. "They're hanging it this afternoon."

"Thanks, Jenny." He looked at his child. "Ted, it's gonna be in an exhibition with a lot of the other pictures we have. We're doing that so that everybody can see it. And it takes time to set up a show like this. But the minute it's up, you and Mommy and I will go down and see it before anybody else gets a chance to."

Theodore came out a little bit from behind his mother's thigh. "When will that be?" he asked.

"End of the week," Edward said, and thought to himself, If I'm not in Atlanta, or — oh Jesus — Washington, now. Where were they going to do Arvin's funeral? "Ted — Daddy's got to work. Mommy'll take you to school."

"Lucretzia's doing it. He's got practice for the school pageant later."

"Right, right. Have a good day at school, okay?"

"Okay," the boy said, and he and his mother turned and walked out the door. Melissa shut it as she left.

Mackinnon jabbed the blinking button. "Ah, just saying good-bye to the little monster. Anyway, I'm sorry about Arvin, he and I had a wonderful relationship, but I can't believe we paid all that money into that political action committee of his, got him on-line with this new prison project — and he gets blown up in his own house —" Edward sighed. "Life," he said, "just ain't fair."

Dr. Harold Garber lived in one of those ugly, white-brick, thin-walled apartment buildings that had sprung up all over the Upper East Side during the sixties — middle-class housing at its most for-mulaic, Bill had always thought, down to the useless little terraces facing the street. Bill was lying on the roof of one, looking through binoculars across Lexington Avenue at another, watching Garber and his unattractive wife bustling about in their apartment, getting ready for their workday. It was obvious they were married: Bill could see it in their unspoken morning choreography, the way he shaved with an electric razor in the living room while his wife disappeared into the bathroom, the way he talked at her as she sorted papers into her briefcase, the way he waited at the door as his wife washed the coffee cups in the sink. Then she turned out lights and they left the apartment.

Bill watched the building entrance; a minute later, the couple stepped out from the lobby onto the street. Bill tracked them as they walked to the bus stop. The crosstown was there; she ran and caught it. He stood as the bus rumbled off and then strolled past the subway entrance and hailed a taxi downtown, to Bellevue.

Bill spent a moment contemplating Garber's building, watching the doorman pace back and forth in the morning chill. He double-checked his equipment, made sure he had the IDs he'd need to get in. He put the binoculars away, brushed the pebbles off his uniform, walked calmly back down the stairs to the street.

Getting into Garber's apartment would be a piece of cake. What he'd do when he got there, he wasn't sure yet, but he had a few lovely little ideas.

Garber's nasty little dig at Sharon in the *Post* had been, finally, just too much.

XIII

The New York agents all had mugs, and the Washington agents had cardboard cups in little plastic holders, and all the coffee had long since turned cold while they debated the Bureau's psychological profile, waiting for Martin Karndle. Finally he walked in the door, waving his own well-thumbed copy.

"Sorry I'm late folks, but the director's been getting calls from all the senators and congressmen who ever talked to him at a dinner party, they're all shitting bricks that they're next. I am meant to convey to you that everyone above us in this organization's great chain of being is extremely desirous of an arrest, preferably in the next five minutes." He sipped his coffee, made a face. "Alton, what do the fireboys say?"

An elegant black man in his early forties plucked a notebook off the table. "First off, the technologies behind the escape fire and the explosion were two entirely different beasts — only thing they've got in common is that they were both sophisticated pieces of work. Bomb in the computer was actually software driven, so far as they can tell. Not motion sensitive or a timed device. The chemicals in the escape were inert apart and extremely volatile combined. This is not run-of-the-mill stuff — whoever made them up, we're talking some high-level chemistry work — they had to have had a fair amount of experience."

"Ed, what have you got on the good nurse Blautner?"

A beefy blond younger agent pulled a page from his file. "Well, surprising thing is, she's rich. She's got just under half a mil in a CD in a bank in Oneonta, upstate."

Whistles and sighs around the room. Karndle cut through: "Gentlemen, she's a widow; the accident seems to have been legitimate; her husband and son were undoubtedly insured. No recent hefty deposits? Or withdrawals?"

"Eight hundred and fifty bucks to Crystal Santiago, five weeks ago. A check for the equivalent amount entered Blautner's New York account on Monday last week."

"Fine," Karndle said. "Alphie — phones?"

A short agent with wiry hair and glasses sat up in his chair. "She's called her mother in Oneonta twice, with no answer. She's had incoming from various people — a lot of reporters. She's in the book. Thus far, no sign of any connection to Bill."

Karndle tapped a pen against the papers before him. "John — Herbie — get your gear. The rest of you, anybody who has not read even the boring, stuffy footnotes at the tippy end of this here psychological profile is holding the rest of us back, and there ain't no room for that on this bus. In fact" — Karndle picked up the profile, waved it at them — "if this thing has anything on the ball at all, I think Nurse Blautner may be key."

At nine-fifty, Sharon wanted more than anything for the meeting with Garber to be over. At ten-twenty, she was ready to kick in his door and have it out, but she forced herself to wait. At ten-twenty-seven, Sharon knocked and was buzzed in. She was not surprised to find a meeting already in progress.

Hermione was there, and Dr. Julia Phillips — her presence was a shock — and Garber and an older, well-tailored man Sharon had never seen before. Garber cleared his throat, gestured. "Dr. Eakens, Nurse Blautner." Sharon shook a strong white hand, murmured hello. It felt like a wake. Garber looked at his desk and said, "Sit down, Nurse Blautner." She took the logical chair, across from Julia.

Julia was cool, very cool.

"There will, of course, be an investigation by the police of yesterday's incident," Garber began. "At this time they have yet to file any charges" — he looked at Sharon — "though I think it's safe to say that could change at any moment —"

"Well, actually, no, probably not —" Sharon interjected, but Garber rolled right on.

"But even if they don't" — he looked at the gray-haired man — "we have Bellevue to think about. The fact of the matter is, Nurse Blautner ignored a hospital regulation, and by doing so endangered the lives of patients, staff, police officers —"

"And myself," Sharon added. "That counts for something."

"We must protect Bellevue, Nurse Blautner. It is the job of the police to worry about facts. We must worry about appearances. From this moment, your employment at this hospital is terminated."

She'd had no reason to expect otherwise, but even so, a sickly, crawling feeling started in her stomach, and suddenly she was dizzy. She took a breath. "Julia?"

"I'm here as a representative of the ethics committee."

"Not as my therapist."

Julia's facade didn't crack. "No, unfortunately not."

Sharon's eyes widened. "How very ethical," she said at last.

"There's no reason to be vituperative —" Garber began, but Sharon looked at Hermione.

"I've done good work —?"

"Very good work."

She turned to the older gentleman, who had not yet said anything. "Doctor, whoever you are, were my files satisfactory?"

The man crossed his legs. "Given the relatively brief time of your employ, I'd say yes, they were."

"It'd be nice if I could get a letter from somebody in this room attesting to that fact."

No one said anything. Sharon waited, but nobody said a word. "It'd be nice —" she started again.

The man cleared his throat, interrupting her. "I'm afraid," he said, "in the current situation, Bellevue is not in a position to write such a letter."

Sharon was very aware of her breathing. "So basically you're not going to do even the tiniest thing to support me, you've already trashed me in the papers, and I'm never going to find a job as a nurse in this town again."

Nobody said anything.

"Right?"

Nobody said anything.

"Right?" she demanded.

Hermione's mouth opened and shut. Sharon stared at her in wonder — she'd always had a backbone of iron; now she just appeared to be an old lady. "It will be difficult," Hermione said, almost whispered, and then, "I'm sorry." Sharon shut her eyes and she was plummeting down someplace empty and hollow, deep inside.

When she blinked open, they were all still there, watching her as if she had just been found to have some fascinating new disease, as if she might suddenly break out in plague boils or reptile skin.

"Look," Sharon said, "I made a mistake. I thought I was doing something completely harmless, and it turned out I was wrong. I made a mistake, now I've got to fix it." She stood up. "Is there anything else you have to say to me?"

Garber cleared his throat. "I'm afraid I have to ask for your Bellevue ID."

God, how petty. Sharon's eyes bored right into his, but in the end, she unclipped the laminated card from her pocket and set it down on his table. She'd always hated that photograph of herself; now it stared at her accusingly.

"And any keys you may have."

Sharon spent a long moment with her key chain, disengaging the keys to the nurse's station and the drug closet. She set them next to the card. "Okay?" she asked. "Are we quite done?"

Guilty looks back and forth among everyone, and then Julia faced Sharon. "The question has been raised precisely how to handle this incident with the press."

Garber sat up. "I have already taken steps to let the media know it wasn't Bellevue procedures that were at fault —"

"Just me." Sharon felt the air around her shaking with tension under the fluorescent light.

She looked up to find Julia watching her like a hawk. "Dr. Garber," Julia said, "I think that's so wrong. It's obvious Nurse Blautner had no intention of doing this on purpose —"

"I've taken books up there," Hermione said. "Everybody's done something like this once or twice."

Garber didn't like this at all. "Someone's got to take the heat for this thing —"

Hermione shushed him with a gesture. "What if it turns out Bill had nothing to do with the senator's death? You'll have made a huge deal over an escape — an elopement. A spectacular, dangerous elopement, I'll give him that — but that's all it was."

Julia chimed in: "Fire Sharon — but for God's sakes stop hamstringing yourself in public with this."

There was silence. Garber sat in his chair, slump shouldered behind his downturned mouth. "All right, okay, fine," he said finally. "But mark my words — it'll cause us more problems later."

Sharon closed her eyes and breathed a sigh of relief and felt suddenly woozy, but it didn't matter. It was over; it would pass.

They were talking about something else now, names she didn't know, but Sharon had lost the context. She struggled after it for a brief moment, and then she realized it didn't matter. She didn't need to know who they were talking about. She stood, and her head was dizzy and she felt unsteady on wobbly legs. She opened her mouth to say, "Can I go now?" but what came out was something else: "Can I say something?"

They stopped talking and they all looked at her with varying degrees of irritation. "I liked this job." She licked her lips. "I really did. I —" There were tears somewhere behind her eyes, but she was damned if she was going to let them out. "I was happy here. Happier than I'd been in a long time."

"You should've thought of that before you took those explosives upstairs," said Garber.

"Shut up, Harold," Hermione angrily waved him down.

"It's a good place," Sharon said, and swallowed. "Too bad." She slipped through the door and closed it gently behind.

She walked sedately across the Psych ER. Patients all around clamored for her attention, women tied to wheelchairs and men mumbling to themselves and a black kid screaming his lungs out, and all Sharon wanted was to get back in business, find out what their stories were, but she couldn't. It was absurd, it made her want to laugh, but she was too sad and angry.

Sharon walked by them all and stepped into the nurse's station. Crystal looked up from her paperwork. "'Bout what you thought, huh?" she said, looking into her face.

"Been fun, Crys." The black woman hugged her, rocking her gently. Sharon snuffled and pushed Crystal away, got a tissue, and blew her nose. "This sucks," she said and rubbed her eyes. "I think," she said, "I'd like to get out of here now."

"I think that's probably a good idea."

"Anything lying around that's mine —"

"I'll throw in a box. That way I know I'll see you again."

Sharon slipped into her coat, shouldered her bag. "'Bye, Crystal." She kissed her cheek. "I'll call you."

"You better." Sharon stepped out and walked past Garber. There were more cops than usual clustered around the metal detector by the exit, and some suits. Bringing someone in, obviously; well, that wasn't her problem anymore.

"I'm sorry —" Hector said as she walked by him.

"I am too —" She looked into his eyes. Hector had always been a gentleman, but she didn't want to chat. "Excuse me —" She pushed her way through the crowd, to the hall outside. Immediately two large men in suits turned in, and blocked her progress.

"Are you Sharon Blautner?"

Sharon looked up at them. Tall, well muscled, good haircuts. "Depends — who are you?"

"FBI." They both flashed badges. "We'd like to have a conversation with you."

"Can it wait a little?" The men continued to look earnest. "Because right this minute I'm not in the absolute best of moods."

There was a slight pause. The two maintained eye contact with her. "Are you saying you don't want to talk with us?"

Hmm, Sharon thought, bad idea. She sucked in air. "No, no," she said equably. "Let's do it."

"Please follow us." They got on either side of her, took a left out of the ER, which was strange, and then another left.

"The exit's that way," Sharon pointed right.

"Reporters out there, Ms. Blautner. We'd like to spare you."

"Right. Well, uh, thanks. Lead on."

They led her out on a loading dock, helped her down steps to a waiting black Plymouth. Sharon had never had anyone put her in a car before, but these guys were pros. They pushed her down, gently folded her in, and one guy used his hand like a skullcap to keep her head from getting bumped. Sharon found herself next to another man, about her age, wolfen, with a lean and angular face. He looked like a particularly avaricious car salesman, or possibly a bond trader. "Sharon Blautner." He extended a hand, and Sharon shook it. "I'm Special Agent Martin Karndle, FBI. I'm here to coordinate the investigation into Mr. Slavitch's role in the assassination of Senator Redwell —"

"I spent a lot of time with Lieutenant Kincaide yesterday."

"We know that. But I'm now the main official here."

"Head honcho."

"Right. And I'd like you to forget you ever told the story to anyone else, and tell it to me for the first time."

HBN was playing a string quartet as Bill sat at his worktable, comparing the schematic against his own wiring in the open razor. He resoldered one connection, checked his work on the multimeter.

Good. He spent a long moment trying to close the black plastic shell, rearranged some of the newly added components to fit. When he tried it again, the razor locked shut with a satisfying click. He opened it back up, glued the edges, clicked them into place, wiped the sides, and left it to dry.

If he'd had time he would have stopped for lunch, but he didn't. He promised himself something quick from a salad bar when he got back outside. He turned his attention to the next task on his list, picked up the thin sheet of metal, debated again how to make the letters, finally decided to do it the hard way. It took half an hour to sketch what he wanted. Then he fired up the oxyacetylene torch and began to cut the shapes to fit.

The FBI's offices were in a steel and glass tower just north of City Hall. In the first room they took her, Sharon told her story to Martin Karndle and three other men. In the second, she went through it again, to two men who had flown up from the Behavioral Science lab at Quantico, Virginia. They were surprised at the depth and detail of her observations until she explained she was halfway through her Ph.D. One of the agents had suggested she finish it, and she'd smiled. Like any self-respecting psychoanalytic institute licensing board would ever approve a shrink who'd been implicated in the death of a senator. That made her want to go home and curl up and die.

Now she was in a cramped windowless office with a desk, two chairs, a computer, and another of the agents, who was typing up notes. He had tried to make small talk, but after five hours she had no conversation left.

She'd just finished the *News*'s comics when Martin shooed the agent out, shut the door, sat at the edge of the desk, and looked down at Sharon, and the whole gesture reeked of casual authority, like a guidance counselor befriending a troubled teen.

"Sharon, we've been debating how to proceed here, and we think you may be able to help us. This guy Bill — highly intelligent, highly motivated. Obviously very sophisticated, in his choice of tools. According to the Behavioral Science boys, he's not doing it because Satan tells him to, and he's not doing it to make himself famous. Some people vote; he bombs."

"All I know is that he's not done with me," Sharon said to the man's left suspender.

Martin Karndle grinned. "You did him a favor. You made it possible for him to get out. We think he thinks he owes you." He shifted and looked her in the eyes. "We'd like to cover you — phones, in case he calls, agents as necessary — discreetly. Most of the time, you won't even know they're there, but you'll be the safest person in New York."

"It'd be hard to say no to that. When the note came, I freaked."

"Good. Well, then —"

"But if he sees that I'm constantly being escorted —"

"We're expecting him to be watching."

"Right now he likes me — he wants me to like him. But if he ever feels betrayed I promise you, I will feel the full force of his anger." They were both silent. "What if I said no?"

He shrugged. "We'd do it anyway."

"Well then, formally, I'd like to say no. Because if he even catches a whiff of it, you'll have made my situation a lot more dangerous than it is now." She shook her head. "So if you're going to do it, it'd better be so well done I don't even know you're there."

Bill lay on the scratchy black roof of the Durkheim-Nimitz Foundation Building, his back to the darkening gray afternoon sky. Five stories below him, periodic taxis slicked their way east. He'd been there almost an hour, lying in his black coveralls, looking with binoculars through spaces in a foot-high windbreak of cement blocks he'd set up before lunch.

That afternoon the building directly across the tree-lined street had been a hive of activity. A crew of good-looking young men and women were busily at work on the first and second floors, opening crates and centering pictures and adjusting lights. Every so often one or two of them would come outside, sit on the marble steps, and smoke or swig down a bottle of water.

On the third floor, Bill could see the office, a book-lined area with neat desks and cordless phones and bulky desktop computers. Above that was Gregor Fontin's apartment, a duplex. French Empire furniture spackled with ormolu, Rich Lady OP77 Yellow on the walls, tables with flowered fabric skirts. Bill wondered, not for the first time, why people bothered to have decorators, when they always made everything look the same. Above that, on the top floor, was a bedroom, in the same florid and overwrought decor.

Shame the man lived here, Bill thought. That made it tricky.

No wooden water tank on the top of the building, of course — five-story buildings usually got their water pumped up from the mains under the street.

That made things more difficult still.

There was movement in the office, and then Gregor Fontin marched into view, a cordless phone to his ear, and began to pace back and forth. He was a tall, balding man with a gray beard and fine clothes. Bill watched as he was handed a small painting by a younger man in ornate suspenders. Fontin set the painting on the desk, adjusted a light, and the two men stared intently. Through the binocs, Bill saw it was a Picasso, probably early. The two men conversed, fingers gesturing. Then Fontin set it aside, disappeared for a moment, and when he came back he was shrugging into his coat.

Bill checked his watch. Four-twenty-eight.

After two minutes, the front door opened and the two men exited and walked together up toward Madison. At the corner, Fontin hailed a cab. They got in and drove off, and Bill was ready.

He zipped the binocs into one of the coverall's pockets and then stood up and walked casually east, stepped over the short wall to the next brownstone roof, and went in the stairwell door. He was in a dark little space at the top of a townhouse converted into apartments. His suit was precisely where he'd left it, hanging from a light fixture in a garment bag. He stripped out of the coveralls, slipped into the suit, put on his plain-lens glasses, and trotted down the stairs of the brownstone. Behind one door, he heard a child crying as a television blared loudly in Spanish. Given the neighborhood, Bill suspected a housekeeper having a bad day with a white employer's kids.

Bill stepped out of the building, dumped the garment bag in the recycling bin, and walked up the block toward the gallery. He tried the door; it was locked. A sticker announced "Armed Response Security by AADCO." He pressed the buzzer.

A voice crackled through the box. "Who is it?"

"Fire inspector," Bill said, and waited.

He was buzzed in and met at the door by a thin young man with a ponytail. Bill handed him his ID, which the man pored over. "What can I do for you?" The man looked him up and down.

"Just a quick inspection of the fire safety systems; citywide update; you should have received a letter about three weeks ago —?"

"Doesn't ring a bell."

Bill opened his briefcase, flipped through a great pile of official-looking forms, and pulled out a business letter. At the top was the letterhead of the New York City Bureau of Fire Prevention. The thin man skimmed the letter and handed it back.

"Follow me," the man said, and led him past a desk into the gallery. Bill took from his briefcase a different form and a clipboard, stood for a busy moment filling in half the page, then turned it over, slipped it in the clip, and took out a flashlight.

There were ladders up in the main room of the gallery, and large modern paintings, some mounted, others leaning against the walls waiting to be hung. They were all by what had been the hot artists of the eighties. The room was dominated by a huge blue Schnabel bristling with broken plates; next to that, one of David Salle's ironically pornographic works, juxtaposing women and clowns. Across stood one of Eric Fischl's less interesting blurry memories of a white, middle-class baby-boomer boyhood, and on the back wall, a Jeff Koons portrait of himself in bed with Cicciolina.

Nothing that wouldn't be missed, Bill could see. He aimed his flashlight at the halon nozzles set into the ceiling, counted them, made a note on his blank page. "Halon system," he said and took out a tape measure. "Mind if I pull over a ladder? Some early models get condensation from the gas, it hardens, clogs 'em right up."

The man helped Bill move the ladder. Bill climbed up and investigated the nozzle. Perfect. "Nah." He smiled down. "You got the good kind; you're fine. Gallery goes up to the second floor?"

Upstairs were crates in the center of the room, and the white walls still smelled faintly of paint. Bill dutifully shined his flashlights at the nozzles in the ceiling, scribbled notes, and then inquired about whether or not he could see the tanks.

"Right this way," the thin man said, and led him down a flight of stairs into the basement. Against one wall were six torpedo-shaped compressed gas tanks. Each stood chest high; each was labeled: "Basement," "1st floor," "2nd floor," "Office," "Apt. 1," "Apt. 2." Bill measured the diameter of the coupling where the tank joined the pipe, made a note, and looked around the room.

Sculptures had been stored down here, as well as boxes of old exhibition posters and catalogs. Off to one side was a carpenter's bench with well-organized tools.

Fine, fine indeed.

Bill scribbled some notes on his form. "We ran a total test of the system about a year ago —"

"Kind of square footage you got here, you should do it every six months," said Bill, and then clicked his pen closed and locked the clipboard into his briefcase. The thin man used this as a cue to ask, "Is there anything else we can help you with?"

"No," Bill said, with a final glance around the room. "No. I've seen everything I need."

XIV

It was dark by the time Sharon left the FBI's offices and caught a taxi uptown. She sat for a time, looking out at the cold, brightly lit windows of Chinatown. Then she asked the driver to put on the overhead light and took out the long yellow envelope of documents they'd given her. She found the first draft of the Behavioral Science lab's profile of Bill and began to read:

Subject has a deep and abiding disrespect for authority; though careful to present whatever front is required, he regards all authority as an enemy. Politically, he might brand himself an anarchist. He regards himself as a friend to the small, and a scourge to the large. Subject is bright, and highly motivated. He is a long-term planner, with great patience, obviously highly resourceful.

Subject may be responsible for a great many open cases in the New York area. Look for bombings connected to progressive and radical political issues such as AIDS and other health-related funding, housing and other community-oriented issues.

Sharon turned the page. They went on for a bit about Bill's probable family background, postulated a complicated relationship with a narcissistic mother. All this was familiar to Sharon; she'd told them the basic facts of it over turkey sandwiches five hours before. Then they went in for more guesswork:

Subject is highly educated, with emphasis in explosive and flammable chemistry and computer software programming and technology. Education could not have been completely self-administered. Education level: Chemistry seems at or beyond college level, while the computer knowledge would suggest a postgraduate or corporate education.

Alternately, though witnesses gave no evidence of this, his knowledge suggests a military background. His antithetical attitude towards authority may have derived from a stint in the military — look for maladjusted computer technicians who got into trouble with military justice.

She tried to picture Bill in military clothing, parading on some concrete field down south, and for some reason the idea made her laugh out loud.

As she turned the corner onto her block, she saw an Eyewitness News van parked in front of her building, with reporters lingering outside her front door. The taxi slowed; she didn't say a word, trying to figure out what to do, how to play this, whether to avoid it completely.

He stopped behind the double-parked Skycam van. "Three twenty-seven's right there," he said and ran his finger along the buttons at the bottom of the meter to turn it off and print the receipt.

She wanted to go home, to be in her apartment. She was entitled to do that. And she would, reporters or no.

What had Karndle said? "Use the media to send the message you want to send."

How about the message of someone being harassed by the media?

She paid the taxi, tipped him, got her keys ready, got out and took a deep breath, and walked up the sidewalk, avoiding the eyes of the men with video cameras and headphones. And then:

"That's her."

"Nurse Blautner —"

She heard her name, and the adrenaline surged inside, fear pounded in her chest, *he's going to see me*, and she had to force herself to keep walking toward the door. There was a camera to her right, dogging her. She didn't run; she kept even steps, as if she didn't understand what language they were using.

"How did it feel to be held hostage?"

The old, dented doorknob.

"Did he hurt you?"

She worked the key, pushed it open, tried to shut the door behind her, but the man with the camera was there, filming the back of her head. "Did you know he was dangerous?" the man asked, as Sharon unlocked the second door.

"Did he talk about Senator Redwell?"

She got it open and slipped through. She jammed the door shut behind her, heard the lock click, and knew she was safe.

She took the steps because she didn't want to stand there waiting for the elevator, finally got to her apartment. Out the window, the Empire State Building beamed at the sky.

God, what was becoming of her? The phone machine blinked angrily from the bedside. Fourteen messages — she had to count it twice to be sure. She had no desire to play them, to call anyone, to do anything but sit.

After a while the radiator heat and the noisy New York silence began to feel oppressive; she put on the radio, and the little apartment was instantly filled with the booming voice of the classical station's newsman: "Police and FBI agents continued to sift through the wreckage of Redwell's apartment, looking for further clues —" She slapped the tuning knob, sent the needle careening down the dial, stations bubbling through her speakers as they passed, and then she remembered: WHBN, 98.6.

She found it. There was a woman talking in a low, confident, smoky voice: "— Nietzsche Prosthesis," she was saying, "off of *Rage and Tarmac*, which I still think is their best album, that was 'Ask the Animals,' and as I'm sure you all know, the Nietzsches have just announced tour dates. They're going to be in New York in six weeks, and believe it or not we've got tickets to see them, and — let's see, something really hard — what's a good question —"

Sharon looked out at the rooftops of Manhattan, and thought, somewhere out there, Bill is probably listening to this.

"— Okay, totally unconnected to Nietzsche Prosthesis, here it is: which is usually longer, the femur or the tibia?"

Well, shit, I know that, Sharon thought.

"That's the question. I'm not asking about the bass player's previous bands, I'm not asking about who played what on which song. The number here is 789-8854 —"

Sharon went to the phone and dialed it.

"Here's Ironclad Alibi, from *Songs of Distress*." Churning guitars started, with a fiddle over top. On the phone, the station was ringing. Sharon spent a moment trying to hold the phone to her ear and reach across the room to turn down the radio, but the cord was too short, and then the station answered: "WHBN," said the girl with the smoky voice.

It took Sharon aback. "You're the disc jockey."

"Yeah, we're one of those dinky noncommercial all-volunteer outfits. You calling for the tickets?"

"Well, the femur is always longer, except in deformations —"

"You got 'em; hold the line." Sharon was put on hold, the same music coming from the radio and the telephone, and then the music got softer for a moment, and over the air the smoky-voiced girl said, "No more calls, please; we have a winner" and clicked off to let the music play. It got louder again, and then the disk jockey returned to the phone. "So I need your info," she said to Sharon.

Sharon gave it to her. "I've never won anything from a radio station before," she said, when they were done.

"Cool," said the disk jockey. "They're a great band."

"Listen — you have somebody on in the mornings?"

"Salsa in drivetime, and then different people every day."

"Okay — Wednesday? There's a guy around noon —"

"That'd be Erik Moore; he's the station manager."

"Do you think I can talk to him?"

"Yeah, he's still here, I think. 789-6511."

"Can you transfer me or something?"

"Our phone system is unbelievably primitive."

"Okay, thanks."

"Enjoy the show."

"Thanks." The disk jockey hung up. Sharon started to dial, hung up, and turned the radio down to a low murmur in the background. Then she dialed the number again. It rang and rang, and a man answered. "WHBN."

"I'm looking for Erik?"

"Hold on." He put her on hold, and she listened to the radio over the phone. Then, a male voice: "Hello?"

Sharon suddenly realized she had no idea quite what to say. "Hi, my name's Sharon Blautner?" she tried. That didn't bring any response, and she pressed on. "I have this complex problem, maybe you can help — your station is listener supported?"

"Yes, ma'am."

"That means people give you money, right? Send you checks, right?" She was aware she sounded incredibly stupid, but that didn't seem, right now, to matter. "How does that work?"

"Do you ever listen to us?"

"I have — Café Con Leche, the salsa show in the mornings."

The man sighed on the other end of the phone. "Well," he started, "we don't accept corporate or government sponsorship. We don't run any ads. We have a marathon once a year, annoy all our listeners and make them cough up to keep us running. We've been here since 'sixty-four."

"Okay, this is going to sound weird, but — is there any way to trace a listener?"

A long pause on the phone. "You mean — through the radio?"

"No, no, no — I mean, somebody who's contributed — you know, a supporter — or someone who won tickets —"

Another long pause. "Truthfully, I don't see a reason in the world why we would —"

"No, no. Look. Do you have a news department?"

"Nope." He was becoming curt.

"Well, you know the senator who was blown up?"

"Not personally."

"No, but — this is going to sound crazy, but I'm connected to the case. I spent the day being interviewed by the FBI —"

Silence, and then: "This is getting a little weird for me —"

"No, really, this is all true. I'm the nurse that got fired — I accidentally made it possible for the guy to escape —"

The man said nothing for a moment. Sharon heard a noisy rustling of paper. "Go on," he said.

"The guy — Bill or Milt Slavitch — he's a listener of yours."

"Of the station?"

"No, of yours — Wednesday noon."

"That is me," he said. The noise got louder.

"What are you doing?" she finally asked.

"I'm looking through newspapers. I'm trying to find a question to ask you to see if you're legitimate —"

"My name's Sharon Blautner. I'm a registered nurse, New York State license number 668592. Four days ago, this man Bill was brought to the Psych ER at Bellevue, I did a psych assessment, spent three days talking with the guy, he mentions you play opera, they find burglary tools, take him to the prison ward, this little girl comes in with a shopping bag, it looks innocuous, I take it up, I break a rule, I give it to him, suddenly there's fire all around, he takes me hostage, nearly gets me killed, escapes, and now I'm out of a job!"

It was the first time she'd said it all in one sentence, and no matter how tired she'd been when she got home this evening, now she was absolutely furious.

"Okay," said Erik Moore. "So what do you want me to do?"

"I'm responsible for him getting out — I've got a personal quest to find the guy."

"Because he killed the senator?"

"Well, first off, because he lost me my job. But yeah — you can't just go killing people you disagree with politically, right?"

"If they're pricks like Redwell, it's a fine idea by me —"

Sharon debated that. "Look, I think Senator Arvin Redwell was an ethically compromised scumbag who consistently sought out the lowest common denominator — but I'm a nurse. You don't let the scumbags die just because they're scumbags." That was true. That much she knew. "So, he's a listener — don't you have a program guide you send to people's homes? Or a contest thing — I just won two tickets to some band I never heard of —"

"You won the Nietzsche Prosthesis tickets? Good for you."

"What are they?"

"Alternative culture heroes of the minute — actually, they're not bad. We've had people calling all day for those tickets."

"Maybe he won tickets once, and you sent him tickets to his home — that would mean you had his address —"

"Not how we do it. We leave them at the club under your name."

"Basically I'd like to pick your brain, have a conversation — if he's a contributor, maybe you have some kind of record —?"

"Listen, I was about to head home, and I have a bunch of work to do there tonight — why don't you come into the station tomorrow, and we can talk — sometime in the afternoon?"

"That'd be great."

Pause on the line, and then: "You're not going to drag the FBI in here, are you?"

"Not if I can help it."

"Because our disk jockeys would heartily resent it —"

"Erik, I promise you — I know just how they feel."

The woman had been very gracious over the phone when Bill had called. Yes, they were one of the few clubs of their ilk that stayed open late. Usually an appointment was necessary, but no, tonight he was in luck. When could he get there?

Bill walked into the hotel, kept his cashmere scarf up around his chin as if still cold from outside. The lobby was as striking as he remembered it, with fresh cut flowers and tapestries and marble. A beautiful, well-dressed family spoke French around him as he waited for the elevator; it came, and the youngest daughter eyed him sweetly as they got on. He got off on three, walked down a hall and through a frosted glass door.

The woman who greeted him wore a little black dress and had an accent Bill couldn't trace. She led him into a private room and told him to disrobe. He perused a list of musical selections; heavy on classical lite. He debated Ellington and Monk; Ellington was calmer. They put it on for him, he lay down, arranged the towel over his groin and put the protectors over his eyes.

The problem with tanning, Bill found every time he did it, was that it was just so fucking boring. He lay on his back under the lights and stared at the darkness under his eyelids and wondered how anybody who didn't have to do this to change his appearance ever put up with the colossal waste of time.

Finally, at the halfway point, he turned over, removed the eye protectors, and began flipping through that day's *New York Times*, thoughtfully provided by the salon. On the back of the last page he came to Mackinnon's ad.

Full page, black text on a white background: THE MAN WHO BROUGHT YOU THE SAFEST BUILDINGS IN NEW YORK NOW INTENDS TO MAKE NEW YORK SAFER FOR US ALL.

And then, much small-print drivel about the prison.

Somebody, Bill decided, should publicly point out the inaccuracies of this thing.

It required an answer. And, Bill thought, he was just the person to do the job.

Erik had packed his bag for the gym that morning, intending to go after his day at the radio station, but slicing east through the dark cold of Houston Street he walked right by it. He was not in the mood.

He had a stack of new alternative CDs to preview for the station, but the idea of working his way through them this evening was completely uninteresting. It had been the finest part of his job throughout the six years he'd been station manager, but lately the new bands he'd been hearing all seemed the same — a slightly younger crowd mapping out the same 'new' territory, starting out on the tiny independent labels that this year's crop of major label bands had left last year, on their own climb up the ladder.

But that wasn't what was bothering him, and he knew it. He turned down the sidestreet, decided against a stop into the bodega for groceries, unlocked the door to his apartment building, and sprinted up the stairs to the third floor. The elevator was so slow, and had been broken so often, he had fallen out of the habit of using it. He thought of Janine, wondered if she'd be around tonight for dinner, felt a glimmer of hope that she wouldn't, and immediately squelched the notion as unfair.

Their door was a gray steel monolith with two locks. He spent a long moment noisily unlocking it, and Artemis ran up purring and rubbed his ankles. He hung his coat, leaned to pet the cat, noted the lights on in the living room. That didn't mean anything; he and Janine were both sloppy about things like that. He walked into the small kitchen, Artemis clipping along right with him at every step. He opened the refrigerator, and then noticed the cat dish.

"You poor cat, you have no water!" The cat danced in tight figure eights at his feet. Eric washed out the cat dish, filled it with cool tapwater, took an ice cube from the freezer and dropped it in;

it cracked and tinkled. Artemis batted the ice cube with her paw, and then hunkered down and drank voraciously. Eric topped off her food, petted her bony black back, and unzipped his bag to take out the CDs. And then Janine walked in from the bedroom. Suddenly she was in the room with him, and it gave him a start.

"I didn't think you were here!" he said.

"I'm not," she said. "I mean I'm leaving in a minute." She was fiddling with an earring; she offered her cheek to be kissed, and he kissed it. She smelled of all her usual smells — perfume, and cinnamon gum, and menthol cigarettes in her hair from her coworkers. They both pretended he didn't know she occasionally smoked. She spent a moment in front of the mirror in the hall, trying to get her earring to dangle just right.

She was tall, with a helmet of carrot-red hair cut into bangs and shaved very close at the back of her neck. Her makeup was, as usual, dramatic. She wore a green and black turtleneck, a black skirt, and green and black striped stockings.

It was not what she'd put on that morning. "You look great," he said.

"Thanks," she said absently, and began minute adjustments of her hair in the mirror. And then, almost as an afterthought: "I'm meeting Gillian at Maladroit."

"God, remember that place?" Eric thought of the dark red room, the small tables, a candle on each one. "We haven't been there in months."

"Well, she needed cheering up," she said, defensively.

"Oh? What's going on?" He tried to be casual.

She turned away from the mirror, and faced him for the first time. "We got the first batch of samples in from Hong Kong, and half the dye lots were wrong."

Maladroit? Because of the fucking dye lots? And then what, dancing at the Rainbow Room? But he didn't say any of those things. Instead he said, "You didn't feed Artemis when you came in."

"Oh, right, shit —" She turned toward the kitchen.

"I did it." And they exchanged a look, but he turned away and picked up a fist of CDs. "I have to get through these tonight."

"Make a pile of the good ones for me —"

"Of course." She came over, and he held her, and once again something inside him melted slightly, a tiny dizziness he still felt when she touched him. He kissed her lips lightly, careful not to screw up her makeup. Then he let her go. "Come back soon."

"I won't be too late." Emphasis on the too. Her coat was a long gray cashmere capelike thing that wrapped elegantly around her; one small but pleasant aspect of her work in the fashion industry was that her clothing was routinely wonderful. "'Bye," she said, and left, and he locked the door behind her. He listened as the sound of her heels clattering on the stairs faded below him, and then felt utterly alone, and unsure what to do next.

He punched the CD player on, and flipped through trying to figure out where to start. He knew himself — usually, no matter how down he was, one good song, one keeper, and he'd be bouncing around his living room and all would be right with the world.

And then he caught sight of the file cabinet by his desk in the corner, and something in him froze, and he remembered being on the phone, flipping through newspaper. He exhaled a long sigh and thought: might as well look at the damn things. Maybe I'm wrong.

He put the CDs down on the dinner table, and opened the bottommost of the file cabinet's four drawers. There were folders — old tax returns, by year; a bunch of clipping files of different stories he'd followed in the newspapers; a file of typed-up raps for his radio show. And then he found it: a green folder that said "SS." He pulled it out, sat down, and opened the folder.

Twenty-six plain white envelopes, the address laser-printed, each one sent to him at the station.

Sooner or later, he'd known this would happen. Sooner or later, someone would ask the right questions, and he would have to come up with some kind of answer.

He picked up an envelope at random, opened it, pulled out the newspaper clipping, unwrapped it from the swizzle stick, and began, once again, to read.

*   *   *

The first thing Bill did when he entered the dark apartment was take the knives off the kitchen wall magnet and put them at the bottom of the laundry hamper. He lowered the blinds, then looked in drawers and closets for any other weapons. He didn't find any, but he did uncover a cache of brutal pornography that confirmed everything Bill already knew about Dr. Frank DeLeo.

Then he opened the circuit box, flicked all the switches off. The refrigerator shivered to a halt. He unscrewed the overhead bulb so that it no longer connected to the circuit, left it hanging. He did the same to several other light fixtures, stepped back out, relocked the door, and went downstairs. He trotted across the dark street, sat on a stoop, and waited.

A couple of men went in who might have been Frank; Bill allowed them time to get upstairs, and then tried Frank's number from his cellular phone. No answer. Finally a curly-headed man in a leather jacket came hustling down the street, entered the building, disappeared into the elevator.

Bill gave him time, and then tried the number. The second he heard the line open, he hung up and shouldered his bag of tricks. It took him seconds to get into the building; he debated the stairs, decided the cameraless elevator was safer. On the sixth floor he got his tools ready, and knocked on the door.

"Who is it?" The voice was male.

"Electrician," Bill said, hands on the instruments in his coat pockets. The locks clicked and snapped; the man opened the door with a candle in his hand. "Dr. Frank DeLeo?" Bill asked.

"Yeah?" Bill raised his right hand, blasted Frank full in the face with the Mace. The man covered his eyes, instantly sobbing, and Bill pushed him in and kicked the door shut. He took the ether-covered towel from his pocket, smothered it over Frank's mouth. The doctor was struggling mightily, bullish shrieks coming from his throat; he was strong, trying to bite through the towel. Bill wrestled him to the floor, held him down, was debating whether to go for the syringes when he felt the man give slightly, relax, and slump. Bill whipped out rope, wound the wrists together, tied them above his head to the bed's elaborate brass footboard. He pushed the ether towel deep into

Frank's mouth, tied the man's feet with another length of rope, anchored them to the radiator at the other end of the room.

The man on the cold wooden floor was battling to stay conscious, shaking his head under the towel. Bill opened his bag to set up his syringes and the rest. When he turned back, the towel had slipped, and Frank was looking right at him.

"Please — don't kill me —" His speech was thick, like he'd bitten his tongue.

Bill, solemn, shook his head. "Not what I'm here for."

"You're the guy that escaped —" He spat the word out.

Bill said nothing, stepped over him, and knelt at the foot of the bed. Veins had distended in Frank's wrist, under the rope. Bill slid the needle in as deftly as he could, pushed the plunger.

"What's in that —? What are you —"

"Sodium Pentothal. And don't worry, asswipe — it's sterile."

"What do you want me for? You want Sharon —"

"I'm here because of what you did." Frank was fading. Bill replaced the towel over the man's face, popped the cap on the syringe filled with Seconal, stuck it in Frank's thigh muscle, and emptied it. Then he hit the circuit breaker back on, fixed the lights, found an oven mitt and a cookie sheet.

The man, Bill was glad to see, was solidly asleep.

Bill took the propane torch from his bag, fired it up, and adjusted the flame until it was a clear blue knife jutting into the air. He knelt, ripped Frank's Brooks Brothers shirt open. The man's chest was muscular, and slightly hairy — altogether attractive, Bill was sure. He thought of this man on Sharon, pummeling her, and stuffed the ether-soaked towel deeper. Then he took up his pliers, held the first of his three metal constructions to the propane until the sheet metal edge of the 1½-inch-long first letter glowed red, and brought it down firmly onto the skin above the sternum, just below the man's collar bone.

The hot metal hissed when it touched the skin, and Frank writhed slightly, and moaned from deep in his throat, and the smell of burned flesh and hair eddied gently up into Bill's nostrils.

He lifted the letter. The skin beneath it had turned an angry burned purple red and begun to welt. There, identifiable forever, was the letter "I."

The first word was done. He had two more to go, and then, after tonight, no woman who slept with Dr. Frank would ever be able to say she hadn't been warned.

"Mom —"

"Sharon. Hold on." Sharon waited, looked out at the lights of New York, and felt the tension tighten in her neck as her mother banged around the apartment in Oneonta. A cupboard closed, and then suddenly she was back, the repeated scratch of a lighter and then the flare of a cigarette in Sharon's ear. "I think Puffy's sick," Sharon's mother said. "She threw up before. But they didn't teach you about animals, right?"

"She get into the garbage cans again?"

"They keep things clean here, not like in New York. How are you making out?"

Damn, she didn't know. Sharon forced the words: "Seen the news?"

"Up the street at Ted's, but he always has the sound off."

"Mom, I lost my job."

There was a long pause. "I made fifty-two sandwiches today —"

"Mom," she said, "I lost my job."

"I heard you the first time." There was anger in her voice.

"You didn't respond —"

"What do you want me to say? You fucked up another thing?"

"I can't talk to you when you've been drinking."

"Sharon, I put in a full day of work at Ted's —"

"Did you ever go back to that therapist I arranged —?"

"You're just like your father, you know? Always thinking the answer can come from some expert outside —"

"Well, it sounds like you could use a meeting —"

"Don't give me that bumper-sticker bullshit, Sharon. I'm not the one who just got fired."

Sharon said nothing, thought of her mother's daily life: the bar, the sandwiches, the constant glass of vodka. It would never end because no other employer would let her drink all day. It was a Teflon-coated existence, completely impervious to attack. And at that moment, Sharon thought of pouring herself a bourbon, and never being attacked again.

"Aww, honey, I'm sorry." At first Sharon thought her mother was talking to the dog, and then realized with a start that she was saying it to her. "Why are we fighting? Listen, come back, you can sleep on the couch, get another job at Fox Memorial Hospital —"

"No, Mom," Sharon said decisively. "No. I've got too much to do here."

Breaking in was simple. Though Bill no longer had a right to be on the eighth floor of the warehouse, he had once co-owned the burglar alarm business it contained; that was the company with which he, Lobo, and Ekaterina had founded Linnet Communications, and it was the first chunk they'd sold off, once they began to specialize in the interoffice computer and communications business. Now it belonged to Belkstrong, an alarm-installation chain.

They hadn't bothered to relocate to another building, which was good, because Bill still had core keys for all the common doors.

Right before he and his partners sold it, Bill installed the fanciest, most complex alarm system then available over the entire Linnet warehouse floor. Basically it was the same system the FBI used: next to each door was an electronic display keypad that, at the touch of a button, randomly jumbled the numbers on the keys. This prevented anyone from figuring out the code simply by watching: every time the keypad was used, the location of each number was different.

Bill was grateful, once he got to the door, to see that they had not bothered to change the hardware of the system. That was lovely, because Bill had left himself a trapdoor; if it was still in operation, he would not have a problem. He pressed the electronic keypad on, waited as the computer assigned numbers to the individual keys, and then tapped in a thirty-eight-digit number, completely from memory.

The computer recognized the code he'd embedded, and the door buzzed. He turned the knob and stepped into the office.

It was not as he remembered it: when they'd had Linnet, they'd tended to keep things as bare-bones as possible. Now, the office section of the warehouse had been painted, and Museum of Modern Art prints blared colorfully on several walls.

It was odd being back. For a moment he remembered the feel the place had had, the work they did, the fights. Lobo had always been straight, but Ekaterina had been so adept at keeping her various lives separate; even in high school, no matter how much attention she gave you, there was always another agenda somewhere in the back of her mind, another angle being covered. Finally, he had found it no way to live one's life. He shook off the memories, stepped into the warehouse proper. He'd expected things to be organized differently, and they were, but not by much.

He found a rolling canvas cart, tugged it to a high stack of shelves that contained various sizes of alarm sirens. The largest ones were larger than any in his experience; he'd need several, to do it right.

Piece by piece, he began filling the cart with the equipment he wanted.

XV

WQXR was playing classical music on the radio, and morning light flooded the East Side apartment. Lois was in the living room, trying to finish the employee pension proposal she'd been too tired to read the night before, and Garber was wandering in and out in his underwear with his coffee cup, buzzing around her like a fly.

"I just don't see why," he said, finally.

Lois looked up from her reading. "I told you. You know my parents. It was a way of allowing myself some privacy."

"We've known each other two years, been married one, and only now you tell me of this account —?"

She set her papers down. "It didn't matter." She looked out the window at the white brick building across the street. "I've had it since I was sixteen — we went through all this last night."

"And how much is it, precisely?"

"I'm not sure — about two thousand, a little more —"

"See? You're not telling the exact amount. It's still a secret you're keeping from me."

"I lost the bankbook, all right?" Suddenly she was angry. "You're acting just like my father."

"Well, I think you should close it out, put that money in the joint account —"

"We'll see," she said, and got back to her reading.

Right. We'll see. Those were always her last words, the ones beyond which no argument could go. He stood for a moment, coffee cup in hand, watched her underline something and turn a page.

Jesus God, she pissed him off. Garber drained his coffee, shoved the dirty mug in the sink, and stomped into the bathroom. He brushed his teeth, trying to think of just the right line, and then just the right way to phrase it. He rinsed.

"I don't see why you have to have your own account, along with the joint account," Garber said, out the bathroom door. And then the zinger: "I just don't want to replicate your parents' bad marriage." Garber turned on the electric razor, effectively drowning out her response. The buzz was slightly different, but he didn't really think of that when he touched the shaving head to his right cheekbone, and took the full force of fifty thousand volts, straight to his brain.

If the Sheffield Arms Hotel had ever been glamorous, that time was long gone, and now the ornate hulk at 148th Street was a single-room occupancy place no more or less squalid than anything else in the neighborhood. On the ground and second floor was La Lengua Larga, a Chino-Latino rice and beans joint where Lobo took lunch practically every day.

There were two ways of getting into the second floor dining room: one was up the stairs from the restaurant's lower room, which had a lunch counter and a few tables. The other was through the door in the back, which led onto the second floor of the hotel. Lobo was built like a linebacker; when he flexed his arms, his muscles rolled like bowling balls under his sleeves. He walked upstairs, set his tray at the first booth, and then pushed open the door into the bathroom.

Empty. He went in the stall, pulled up the heavy lid of the toilet tank. On the underside, a bandage of masking tape spiderwebbed out, appearing to hold it together. Lobo pulled the tape away, and an envelope came off with it. He set the lid back on the tank, sat on the can, and opened the envelope.

Eight five-hundred-dollar bills and — he counted them — sixty hundred-dollar bills, none of them new, many wrinkled. He took off his money belt, spent several minutes loading the bills into it. Then he flushed, straightened his clothing in the mirror, walked out, and sat down at his lunch. He was delicately cutting plantains into his black beans and rice when Bill stepped through the connecting door from the hotel and sat quickly across from him.

"You." Lobo looked at him, pushed his food away.

Bill pulled the scarf down from over his mouth. "Great to see you too, old buddy."

"The whole point was not to see *you*. You're in all the papers, I don't want anything to do with you." Lobo fixed him with a look of disgust.

"Still riding on the money from Linnet?"

"We're comfortable."

"Kids okay? Celeste?"

"Everybody's fine. Look —"

"So what you're saying is you've known me since second grade, five years ago we sold legit burglar alarm and office communication businesses that I brought you into, you walked away with over half a mil plus perks, I never ask a thing from you without paying my way, and now you won't even have a conversation with me?"

Lobo squinted, steel-eyed. "What do you want, Bill?"

Bill took four napkins from the dispenser, began playing with them. "You still tight with your man Enrique? He still have that compressed gas business?"

"So far as I know."

"Think he'd do me a favor?"

"I think he'd do me a favor. You he wouldn't touch."

"Well, how low am I on your shit list?"

Lobo said nothing for a moment, and then said, "What you need?"

"Dummy tank and a blank tank of nitrous oxide."

Lobo whistled. "What, you got a high school student, you're trying to get her clothes off?"

"Very funny, big guy."

"What size?"

Bill held his hand shoulder-high off the floor. "Today."

"Yeah, okay, okay, I can do this. That it?"

"Should be." Bill had crumpled up the napkins; he threw them at the ashtray. He missed. "You ever speak to Ekaterina?"

"Twice a year, Christmas cards."

Bill debated that, let it go. "Well, that's all I wanted. Listen, I really appreciate everything you do for me."

"I'm a family man, Bill. I mean, I know we came up together — you sneaking me into that private high school of yours to teach me the rock-climbing wall — but now you're too much for me."

Bill nodded, sad truth at the back of his throat. "Later." He stood, rearranged his cap and his scarf. He started to go.

"Yo." Lobo's voice stopped him. Their eyes connected. "Watch your ass," the big man said, and Bill smiled and walked out the back door.

Lobo ate a little of the meal; after a while he palmed Bill's crumpled napkin and went back to the bathroom. Wadded inside were four more hundred-dollar bills.

Sharon felt like she was on a mission as she marched up the steps past the lions into the grand limestone New York Public Library, and then felt pretty foolish when she trotted back down them ten minutes later, ignored the taxis, and walked through the cold to Times Square to catch the subway uptown. Theater memorabilia was stored at the Library of the Performing Arts, at Lincoln Center. She left the subway, walked past the Metropolitan Opera, around the reflecting pool and its oversized Henry Moore, to the library.

Inside was a clean white space with a calm, busy hum. She kept her voice low when she spoke with the goateed young man behind the counter: "I'm trying to find a playbill for the last show at a particular theater — the Hammerstein."

"You know the name of the show?"

"'*Sergeant Was a Lady.*'" They both turned to look at the speaker, a grizzled older man with thick glasses and an improbable hairpiece.

"What?" Sharon asked.

"Musical. Flopperoo." He made a swirling-drain gesture with one hand. "They closed that show to tear it down." The young man with the goatee sailed off into the stacks.

"Did you see it?" said Sharon, wide-eyed.

"'Course I did. I saw everything. Still do."

"You remember it?"

He shrugged. "Romance, World War One, doughboys. It was a dog. If I remembered all the dogs I ever saw —"

"Did it have an actress — a name like Kai?"

"That'd be Kaiser. Singer/dancer. Helen Kaiser. She was getting a little broad in the beam by then." The goateed man returned with a faded program. "That's it," the man said.

On the cover was a cursive logo, with a drawing of two men and a woman in World War One costume coming out of the "y" in "Lady." Sharon flipped through, careful of the brittle pages. The ads were old, the cars and fashions out of date.

"You're not thinking of reviving it, are you? 'Cause I got people you could talk to —"

"No, no, no. But thanks." She read the credits page — Helen Kaiser was alphabetical, below the title — and then found her biographical sketch: her character had been Genevieve. This was followed by a short list of Broadway credits, a handful of off-Broadway, some television, and a confession that she was the voice behind the Cook's coffee jingle. And then the last line: "But the role Ms. Kaiser most relishes is that of mother to her absolutely wonderful six-year-old son, Billy."

Sharon's face flushed, and suddenly her heart was in her mouth. God, there it was. "Can I Xerox this?"

"Machine's over there," said the goatee. "You might also try *Theater World* for that year —"

But Sharon wasn't listening. She walked over in a daze, put in a quarter, and made a copy and then just sat at a long wooden table and read through the bio over and over until she got to the point where she could begin to think again.

Damnit. Damnit damnit damnit, he had actually been telling the truth.

Theater World had supplied a photograph from the play, a picture of a woman in profile that could have been Bill's mother, and could have been anybody's mother. Sharon had then looked at pictures of Helen Kaiser in earlier roles, and the more she saw the more marked the resemblance between mother and son became. She had idly wondered if there was somewhere she might find old phone books, and had been directed back to the main branch of the New York Public Library, on Forty-second Street.

She got off the bus at Times Square, rewalked the two long blocks to the library. The microfilm division was in the grand room on the third floor; they had phone books going back to 1874. Sharon picked out a carrel, got a microfilm spool for the year of *Sergeant Was a Lady*, and zipped through, looking for Helen Kaiser.

Half a column of Kaisers. No Helen, no Bill.

She scrolled through the year before. No Helen, no Bill.

She tried the year before that. No Helen, no Bill or H or B or anything.

She went up ahead, to the year after *Sergeant*. Nothing.

She gave back her spools of microfilm, put on her coat, walked out of the building.

The air was cold, and the sky looked pregnant with snow, and if Sharon had thought about it, she'd have realized she was hungry, but she didn't.

Kaiser must have been a stage name.

She walked south down Fifth, looking at the way the sidewalk sparkled in front of her, ignoring the fashions in the department store windows. If you're in show business in New York, she reasoned, and you've had any success in that world, it's probably the chic thing not to be listed.

Bill's mother, narcissistic piece of work that she must have been, would have opted for the chic thing. And then she stopped in her tracks and looked up at the Empire State Building, and a grin spread across her face, and she said, out loud, "Yes!" and looked around for a pay phone.

There was one across the street. She ran against a yellow light, beat it, fished out a quarter, and called the Psych ER.

"Crystal, it's me."

"Man, you got this place in a uproar, FBI's interviewed us —"

"Tell me about it. Listen —"

"You listen. Garber's in the hospital, real weird thing. He got himself electrocuted."

For a moment Sharon didn't understand, and then she did, and froze. "Like, a shock?" she asked, tremulously.

"Some kinda device, like it was done on purpose. They took him to Mount Sinai, he got some stitches, they were worried he'd cracked his skull, but he's fine. Some question about his memory, but you know the deal with electroshock, they get it back."

A taste of his own medicine. Sharon shut her eyes against the cold, and then the fear was in her heart: they'd also talked about Frank. But Bill had never seen Frank. And — she was sure of it — she had never even mentioned his name. "You there?" Crystal asked.

"Yeah, I'm here. Listen, I have a favor, I need you to pull some records for me, about a year ago we had an oncology patient named Helen Kaiser, she died at Bellevue —"

"Bill's mom?"

"You got it."

"I'll take a look in microfilm — but ain't that the kind of thing the FBI'll be doing?"

"I don't trust them. I don't trust anybody, right now," Sharon said. "I have to take care of this myself."

*   *   *

On the way to the Museum of Natural History to place his little device, Bill debated the next step, then checked his watch. He would have loved to wander the museum, see the dioramas he'd been so fascinated by as a child. But the shame of it was, today he simply didn't have the time.

Somewhere around noon, the drugs began to wear off, and Frank groggily woke up, driven out of sleep by the persistent pain all over his chest. At first he didn't understand that he was tied, and then he did, sharply, and the memories and edges of memories of the night before flooded his mind, and instantly he was terrified.

He shook the towel off his face, and looked around to figure out how to get his hands free. His chest itched, and it hurt — that was a mystery — and he wanted to scratch it.

He tried to untwist his wrists, pull them through the rope, but every time he moved, it tightened. He was furious and scared — what kind of asshole would leave him tied up like this? — until finally he was able to unscrew one of the brass crossbars in the footboard, and free one hand. He got the other loose, sat up to untie his ankles, and only then did he realize that his chest was some kind of burned, bloody mess. He stood, shaking blood into his feet, and hobbled quickly to the bathroom mirror.

There, backwards in the mirror, branded in dark red scar tissue, were well-formed, readable letters making three clear words, stacked in a pyramid from collarbone to sternum:

I
HIT
WOMEN

He went back into the living room, sat in a chair, waited for the nausea to subside. He picked up the phone, put it down, stood, and paced. Then he picked up the phone again, started to make a call, and then hung up, furious. He went back, looked at himself in the mirror, the letters staring back at him, backward.

My chest, he thought. My beautiful chest. And only then did he begin to cry.

XVI

There were album covers all over the walls of the studio, and a velvet painting of Elvis, and a pair of football shoulder pads hanging from a ceiling fixture, and a Balinese demon mask high in the corner. Fast percussive jazz played from speakers hanging in every room. Sharon walked on, past boomerang fifties furniture and a much-put-upon couch and several electric guitars and amps in various states of disembowelment and, behind glass, a small radio studio, turntables and soundboards and a microphone all surrounding a young woman, headphones on, busily flipping through albums on her lap.

Sharon debated tapping the glass when a tall man came in from around the corner. "Sharon Blautner? I'm Erik Moore."

She shook his hand. He was lanky and blond and intense looking, with very hip tortoiseshell glasses perched delicately on his nose. "Come into my office. I'll show you what I figured out about your problem."

Erik's office was a mess — piles of compact discs and tapes and stacks of paperwork and posters all over the walls for weirdly named bands on tiny independent record labels. "Here," Erik pointed out a computer half buried in CDs. "Every year, two weeks in March, we have the marathon. If Bill Slavitch has —"

"It's Kaiser, I just found that out," Sharon interrupted.

"Whatever name he contributed under, we'll have his info on these —" He held up a handful of 3¼-inch disks, popped the first into the computer, and called the address list onscreen.

He word-searched "Kaiser" and came up with a woman, Jennifer, who lived on East Ninety-eighth. According to the computer, she had pledged thirty dollars, paid it, and had been sent an HBN T-shirt, bumper sticker, refrigerator magnet, and program guide. "I know her," Erik said. "She comes to our benefits. Your guy's white, right?"

Sharon nodded.

"This woman's from Tanzania — I doubt they're connected."

The previous year yielded nothing. Nor the year before, nor the year before that.

"As a rule, only ten percent of the listening audience ever actually gives money," Erik said, as another search came up blank.

"Damn," said Sharon. "I was really hoping —"

The chair squeaked under Erik as he leaned back. "Well, there is one more thing — I guess I'm a bit hesitant to bring this up —"

"It can't be more embarrassing than my barging in and wasting your time —"

"No, no, that's fine — I assure you." Abruptly, he stood and began to pace. "This radio station serves as sort of an intersection for a lot of different subcultures — artists and musicians, of course, but more than that — politicos from all over the city, AIDS activists, squatters rights activists —" He was shaping something invisible in the air with his hands. "People on the fringes, people on the edges. That's our audience. And some of them are way out there" — he gestured, a whirlwind hand around his brain — "crazies. And marathon is not the only time we hear from them." He crossed the room to a steel closet, reached in back, and took out a brown cardboard file.

He sat back down, and set the accordion file folder on the desk. It stood by itself. "These are our nuts. We've got a couple of people who think that everything we say that comes out their radio is directed personally at them. We have people who think we can help them in their battles against the evil fascist landlord banker police state, and then get angry when we can't. We've got a few people who become a bit too enraptured with various of our female deejays. And then —" He took up a manila envelope, shook his head slowly. "Man, part of me does not want to do this."

"Please," Sharon said, quietly, "whatever you've got —"

Erik Moore leaned back in the chair. "For several years now, somebody," he said, "has been sending me swizzle sticks."

*　　*　　*

There were two separate recipes Bill was cooking at once; one was easy, and one was not. He loved life when it got like this: he, alone in the kitchen, making things to explode.

Not really bombs, neither of them. One would be quiet, and one would be liquid, and both had to be manufactured from scratch.

Logistically, what he was contemplating was a nightmare. But he didn't want to involve anybody else.

Not yet. People always tried to talk him out of the really big ideas, he'd found. Like Linnet: Ekaterina had been very comfortable working with her contacts to fence the antiques and paintings he and Lobo stole. When Bill suggested a legitimate business, they'd both scoffed. After he'd gotten it up and running, only then had they seen how ideal a profit-making machine it could be.

With this project, he'd need help down the line, that was obvious, but he couldn't think about that. All he could do was set it up and hope that when it started to run, people might be drawn to its motion.

"I started hearing stories about five years ago." Erik sipped his tea. "Certain community organizations were getting anonymous contributions — significant money, a grand, two grand — never less than five hundred. Envelope always contained cash wrapped in a news clipping, and always — always — a swizzle stick."

"Swizzle stick," Sharon said, and tried to keep still, though her heart was beginning to pound. "With a plastic cat's head —"

"From the Pink Panther — famous old disco from the sixties. Pretty cool because that place hasn't existed in years and years."

"He sent me one — I mean, he put one in my mailbox —"

"See, I did a few radio bits about the 'anonymous angel' who was keeping these various community, day-care, and homeless-support groups alive. He must have heard it, because he started to send them to me — usually wrapped in a newspaper article about one of these groups, some cause they were fighting for. Then marathon came, that year, and money arrived with a swizzle stick — like, a grand. Ever since then, he always gives like that, every marathon —"

"So," Sharon said, "this guy is your biggest contributor —"

"No, he's not — we get people who do more. You'd be surprised. Anyway, I began to see a pattern with the swizzle sticks he was mailing me — they obviously related to some specific triumph or tragedy of citywide neighborhood politics — I mean, when the prenatal clinic was refunded after that fierce battle with the HHC — that merited a swizzle stick. Eventually it was forced to close — damn shame, but that's another story. When the Landmark Squat won their court case, I got another swizzle stick. Until that one, I thought it was celebratory — I thought someone was sort of saying "Cheers!" through the mail. But then I was talking to Hamilton at Landmark Squat, and it turns out they could not have won their court case without the anonymous money that turned up in an envelope with a swizzle stick. And then there was an article in the *Post* about a tutoring program in East Harlem that had survived on anonymous grants, and they mentioned swizzle sticks right there in the article. That's when I realized that whoever this was wasn't just reacting to events — he was shaping them." He took a sip of his tea. "And then — well, this gets complex." He got up and began to pace. "Used to be this vicious drug dealer Karma Delgado on Second and C — you live around here?"

"I'm pretty close, Twenty-fifth Street."

Erik smiled. "In the minds of most Lower East Siders, nothing exists above Fourteenth Street. Anyway, he and his dog both disappeared — I got one swizzle stick on that, wrapped in a blurb from the *East Village Shadow* mentioning his disappearance, and then another when they found him dead."

"God!"

Erik nodded.

"And he was murdered?"

"Cops said it was a massive overdose, but there were bruises on the body, like somebody had knocked him out. He was an asshole, and he was disposed of."

"But that doesn't mean —"

"Once, it doesn't. But this's been going on for years."

"Other murders?"

"Well — consider the history of the Carnegie-Hayden. Huge old

pile off Avenue C — in a just world, you could really create something great there for the whole city to use — that was the original
intent. But as it is, it's kind of a magnet for urban utopianist activist
types. Every time the building's changed hands, the minute the
new owner announces plans to tear the thing down, I just wait for
the swizzle stick. And it comes — and the guy dies. Harry Ashlam,
heart attack, Derrick Gianelli, car accident — I got swizzle sticks
on both those guys. You know where the Pink Panther was, don't
you? Where all these swizzle sticks came from?"

"I'm afraid not —"

"The Carnegie-Hayden. It was this famous sixties hangout in
the grand auditorium of the Carnegie-Hayden."

In her mind, Sharon felt the blocks begin to tumble together.
"And he's responsible for all those real estate guys and drug dealers
getting murdered —?"

"Well, we can't exactly say we know that — I mean, it's not like
they were stabbed with swizzle sticks —"

"I mean, but if it's Bill —"

"Whoever he is," Erik said, "I've always admired him."

Sharon said nothing, let that swirl around in her mind.

"I mean, if he's the man who got rid of Karma and that asshole
dog of his — that alone, the city should give him a medal. And the
other stuff — the tutoring project, donations to build that safe
house for battered women, helping to pay for after-five day care
when the city cut funding —" Erik was shaking his head. "He's
made this city a better place to live."

"You want to protect him."

"Assuming he's done all this. He's hard-core, but he's on the
right side." He was watching Sharon. "And you're going to go to
the FBI, tell them all this, and eventually they'll nail the bastard,
his life will be over, and then all the vulnerable programs he's
helped all over the city will get pummeled." He shook his head. "I
guess it's progress."

Sharon licked her lips. "Look, I don't care about his transcen-
dent political vision — he's hurt people, and it's not good enough
that some of them were schmucks. I'm not a schmuck, and he hurt
me." She stared into his eyes. "He's sick, Erik, and the probability

is he's going to eventually decompensate, if he's not doing it right now, and then he'll be perfectly capable of blowing up this radio station if you play the wrong song." She sighed. "I know what you mean," she went on. "I find a lot of things about him admirable. But we've got to bring him in, Erik — and you know stuff about him nobody else knows."

Martin's office was airless and tight; sitting, Sharon felt tiny. "Have the Behavioral Science guys finished their report?"

"You never really finish one of them — you keep plugging in new information." Martin spent a moment reading through papers, put them down. "Got anything new for us?"

"Bill's last name is Kaiser — I found his mother." Sharon explained about finding the play, gave him a photocopy of the bio.

"Sharon Blautner, girl detective. Very good. Very, very good." He leaned back in his chair and smiled at her. "Anything else? Any other stops during your day?"

Erik had asked for twenty-four hours; Sharon had agreed. She shook her head no. "What's the deal with Garber? Crystal told me he's in Mount Sinai —"

"Yeah. Listen, you know a Frank DeLeo? Dr. Frank DeLeo?"

Oh, shit. "Uh, yeah —"

"When was the last time you saw him?"

"Three nights ago. I told you this. We — had a fight."

"And he hit you."

"Yes."

"And Bill Kaiser knew he hit you?"

Oh, God. "What did he do?"

"He knew he hit you?"

"I came in with bruises."

"And you told him it was Frank DeLeo?"

"I never said who it was."

"You're sure of that?"

"Absolutely. It would have been completely unprofessional."

Martin Karndle sucked air through his teeth. "Do the words 'I HIT WOMEN' make any sense to you?"

Sharon just sat, frozen into place.

"Last night Frank DeLeo was tied up and branded by Bill Kaiser. Those words, like a sign on his chest."

Sharon didn't breathe, emotions rushing inside. "Branded?"

Martin Karndle handed her a Polaroid photograph. Yes, Frank's chest. He'd been ever so proud of it.

Not anymore. Fear rose in her stomach. The letter, her reading it there with Bill sitting next to her. Frank's stationery. "Actually, he might have figured it out," she said, and explained.

"It turns out Dr. DeLeo actually does have a history of battering women. He told us it was why his marriage broke up — his wife took him to court."

Sharon nodded. "That fits," she said. "What's he going to do?"

"Plastic surgery. It won't be perfect; he'll always have a reminder."

How odd, Sharon thought, but she didn't say it. "And what about Dr. Garber? Something put him in the hospital —"

"Fifty thousand volts, right in the head. Another Bill Kaiser special — he stole the guy's electric razor, took it apart, and put in the guts of a stun gun."

"Ugh." Sharon shook her head.

"So basically, he's maimed two people, both of whom hurt you."

"I'm sorry for them both — I didn't want those things to happen."

He just stared at her.

"I didn't ask for this, Martin."

"Not even a little bit?"

Sharon sat silent.

"I mean, to law enforcement, it sure looks like you're calling the shots here —"

"I didn't tell him, 'Go escape from the prison ward, go electrocute Garber, go brand Frank.' You know that, Martin."

"Well then, why's he doing it?"

She debated all the reasons, closed her eyes. "Because he loves me," she said finally, because it was ultimately the truth.

"And do you love him back?"

Sharon shook her head. "Of course not. He scares the shit out of me." She looked at him. "How can you love somebody when you have no idea what they'll do next?"

And even as she said it, she thought of the gentle, plodding predictable life she'd had upstate with Rick, and how it had always vaguely surprised her that he wasn't more like her father.

XVII

Five eleven Barrow Street was a glum forty-story postwar office building at the back end of the financial district. Bill entered the lobby at precisely five o'clock and worked his way through the noisy babble of homebound office workers like a salmon heading upstream. He was wearing a gray jumpsuit and kneepads and sunglasses and a bicycle helmet, and a long black canvas bag that went across his back on a strap. He was almost at the far elevator bank when a fat man in a blue blazer hustled up, dinged his shoulder with a fat finger. "Messengers sign in at the desk," he said, and turned, expecting Bill to follow.

Bill made his way to the security desk, signed something illegible with his left hand, and caught an upbound elevator. At thirty-four, he waited outside the locked men's room until an executive ambled out, caught the door just before it closed.

He locked himself in a stall, took off the pads, unzipped his gray coverall, revealing a bright blue Con Ed jumpsuit. He stuffed the coverall and bike helmet into the bag, fished out a blue plastic Con Ed recording computer, zipped, and walked out. He knocked on the clear glass door of AADCO Security, was buzzed in, and marched to the desk. The secretary motioned him to wait, pushed buttons and spoke into the headpiece.

"AADCO — Hold please. AADCO — He just left for the day. . . . Thank you. AADCO — Hey, Bob, she's still here, I'll connect you." She pressed the buttons, and turned her attention to Bill. "Yes?"

"Con Ed —" Bill had his ID out in the same hand as the computerized meter reader. "We're having a reciprocal surge-and-drain meter problem —" He pulled out a flashlight, flicked it on at the ceiling. "We've got it tracked down to your wires."

"You know where to go?"

"Yes, ma'am." The phone was ringing again.

"Okay, go on," she said, punching another button. "AADCO —"

Bill walked into the office.

It took a few minutes to scout the office's full dimensions. Sales desks in the front, a corridor of offices, storerooms loaded with boxes and brochures. And then, in the back area, the computer room, a glass booth containing five mini-mainframes. Outside was a semicircular bank of computer terminals and telephones; in front of that was one man opening the lid on a cup of coffee. Bill walked purposefully into the computer room, turned on the flashlight, and spent a moment considering the computers they were running. As he walked out the man with the coffee was standing. "Hello? Can I help you?"

Bill fingered the ID on his shirt. "There's a power reciprocation problem in the building. The meters downstairs are out of phase, I'm just trying to thumbnail assess your usage, see if your lines were affected —" He held up the hand unit. "You'll be getting a letter if we find any discrepancy."

"Uhh, well —"

Bill was already walking away. "Usually it means a credit," he said, waved, and was off.

He smiled as he passed an attractive power-suited woman, entered a copy room, and spent a long moment following the electrical lines along the walls with his flashlight and entering data onto his handheld device. There was a door at the back, and Bill opened it: a shallow closet loaded with pens, Post-it pads, business forms of various sizes. No help there. He strode back out, rapped loudly on the next door down the hallway, and listened carefully. When no one answered, he opened the door and looked in.

An empty conference room. At the far end was another door. He stepped in, walked past the oblong table and empty chairs, and tried this second door: a walk-in closet, four feet deep, the three walls lined with deep shelves holding computer paper, stationery, old computer terminals. He turned on the overhead light, knelt, considered the bottom shelf. Perfect.

He shut the door behind, spent a few moments unburdening the space below the bottom shelf of its contents, wedged himself in near the wall, and finagled the boxes back into place, covering himself. Before he fixed the last one, he took out the book he was reading, Pliny the Elder's *Natural History*, opened it to his bent page. Then he pulled the last box in against his head and shifted around so he was on his side. It was airless, but he didn't mind that. He adjusted the flashlight, found his place, and began to read.

God, what had she been thinking?

Outside the window of the cab, New York was speeding by, the driver had reggae on, and Sharon looked at the streets full of people rushing out of office buildings into the cold and felt they were on another planet, that she was a million miles from them, racing through the darkness on some uncharted asteroid all her own.

He'd electroshocked Garber; he'd branded Frank. Edward Mackinnon was next; that was as inevitable as rain. And Erik's view of Bill had stayed with her: why, when Ed had only brought misery to her family, should she lift one finger to help him?

The cab sped up, changed lanes, and slipped in and out of the other cabs surging north like sharks. Suddenly the homebound businesspeople on the street seemed malevolent, and Sharon had contempt for them all. And then the night felt curiously familiar, decisions made, questions answered and put to bed. Upon this rock I will build my — well, not church. Fortress. All those people, each in his or her own individual fortress, buttressed by options chosen and accepted and forgotten, nothing new to learn. The same New York night as any other.

And she was just like them, except that once upon a time in her life, she'd had Charley. She weighed the gravity of that, aware of the empty space on the seat next to her in the cab, this messy blond boy, not perfect, but a pretty damn good version of the human condition to have been blessed to know.

To have been blessed to allow life.

They were stopped by a red light, and Sharon thought of the dingy white walls of the Psych ER, Bill's eyes dancing after her, Ed Mackinnon and his family staring up from the newspaper, the beautiful young wife and the little boy in the blazer —

Fuck it, she couldn't do this.

He was going to do something to Mackinnon, for her, and she could not let him.

There was a clock in a deli. Two minutes to six. The light turned green, and the driver roared across the intersection. Sharon saw a street pay phone up ahead. "I'm sorry, but stop the car," she said.

He turned down the reggae. "What you say?"

"Just stop anywhere up ahead —"

"You say Twenty-fifth Street —"

"I'll get out here." He yanked the car over to the next corner, the telephone far behind them. She paid the man, and checked the seat before she shut the door. There was a phone catty-corner across the street. She ran between cars, got to the phone, and dialed 411.

"Edward Mackinnon," she said. "Office and home, everything you've got. East Sixties off Lex." She'd walked by that building several times when she first came to New York. The operator gave three numbers; she dialed the first, got a receptionist, and was told he was not in. She hung up, dialed the second.

"Mackinnon Group." The secretary had a British accent.

"Hi. This is Sharon Blautner, I'm the daughter of Allen Blautner. Please — it is urgent that I speak to Edward Mackinnon."

"Excuse me, could you say that again?" Sharon did, more slowly. "And what is this in reference to?"

"I'm an old family friend," Sharon said.

"Hold one moment." The woman clicked off. Sharon leaned against the sticker-covered metal wind protector and waited.

There was a shoe store to her right. Sharon looked at the window display. Then she realized that the two fashionably black-clad young women working in the shop were in the midst of a heated argument. She watched as their fingers shook, hands waved, and mouths jabbered silently behind the glass.

The phone clicked back. "Mr. Mackinnon is in a meeting. If you care to leave a message, he'll get it at the first available —"

"I'm at a payphone, and this is an urgent family matter."

There was a pause. "You want me to tell him that."

"Blautner. The name is Blautner. Sharon Blautner."

"Hold." She clicked off again.

On the other side of the glass, the older woman made sharp, cutting gestures as she spoke. The other had picked up a stack of shoe boxes and was standing, red in the face, boxes up to her chin. And then two young women, office workers, bright from the cold air, pushed open the door and entered the shop.

Sharon watched the two shop women freeze. The older woman got busy behind the counter. The younger looked for a place to set her boxes, decided against the table, decided against the chair, finally set them back on the floor, dusted her hands on her black pants, and pasted a big smile on her face for the customers.

There was a click, and then, on the phone, Edward Mackinnon's throaty growl: "Sharon Blautner, I haven't heard from you in years!" That voice — oh, Jesus. Her unc Eddie — damn, the same. Suddenly she felt tiny again, next to this big man. "How's your mother getting on?"

Sharon felt things swirling inside of her. How was her mother? "Fine," she lied, and found the lie bitter in her mouth. Why was she doing this?

"Saw your photo in the papers this morning — sorry you've had some bad luck." Paternalistic bastard. This was not a good idea.

"I have to talk to you because the man who escaped — Bill Kaiser —" This was hard. "I think he may try to threaten you."

"Actually, the FBI's already called — it seems he took notice of my picture in the paper while under medical treatment —"

"Right — right," Sharon said, slightly deflated.

"Believe it or not, we've grown accustomed to these sorts of security problems — had quite a few, over the years. One gets used to a certain level of — active paranoia, I think we'd say. I wouldn't worry too much about it. Now I'd love to talk to you, I'd love to see you again. You must be — what, thirty, by now?"

"Thirty-two," Sharon said.

"Thirty-two, my goodness. Well, come by the office, we'll have coffee together — next week?"

"I'd prefer it sooner," Sharon said, wondering why she'd prefer it at all.

"Tonight's impossible, we've got an enormous fund-raiser I wish I didn't have to go to," Edward Mackinnon said. "Tomorrow — let's see, can we crack open the schedule —" He put his hand over the phone, and Sharon heard muffled conversation with someone in the room, and then he came back. "How's seven-thirty?"

"In the evening?"

"In the morning."

"Is there any other time?"

"Really — no, not tomorrow."

I'm trying to save your life, and you make me get up at six in the morning. "All right," she said.

"It'll be great to see you again," Edward Mackinnon said.

"Right," said Sharon. "Tomorrow." She got off the phone, wondered, 'Why am I doing this?,' and then looked around, realized she was in a neighborhood she'd never seen before, and wondered where, in the city, she was.

Eight-thirty on a crisp fall Friday evening in Manhattan. The city was full of pleasures: boom boxes playing salsa in the bodegas; grand cru wines being uncorked in glamorous restaurants. This was the moment people worked for all week long. The theaters were filled with light and sound; taxis streamed downtown carrying harried two-career couples on their way to parties; singles who had pined all week, hoping for a phone call, now put on fashionable black clothing and made their way to bars and clubs.

Under the huge blue whale at the Museum of Natural History, the big band was playing quiet dinner music while the guests dined on poached salmon and tarragon chicken at five hundred dollars a head, all to raise money for the museum's twenty-first-century fund. Edward Mackinnon was sitting between Melissa and Letitia Whitney-Vanderbilt, now eighty-seven, with her much younger male escort. Across sat the mayor and his wife, and Les and Shel Gargiulio, longtime supporters who owned a chain of liquor stores throughout the city. Edward had focused most of his attention on the devilishly charming Letitia; the Gargiulios, as always, he left to the mayor.

Letitia was telling a particularly amusing story about a luncheon she'd attended with Winston Churchill when the sirens abruptly began. They sounded like a prison break in an old movie — the rising and falling wail, ear-splittingly loud. The orchestra tried vigilantly to play through it, but the noise level increased and increased. Gradually, table after table fell silent; Letitia adjusted her hearing aid, and then became confused. "Is there a fire?" she asked Edward.

"I've never heard a fire alarm like that," Edward said, and then the words started.

"EDWARD MACKINNON FINALLY FIGURED OUT HOW TO MAKE MONEY HOUSING THE POOR — BUILD PRISONS! ARE YOU GOING TO LET NEW YORK CITY BE CARVED INTO SEPARATE PRISON BUILDINGS FOR THE RICH AND POOR? ARE YOU GOING TO LET NEIGHBORHOODS BE CONDEMNED AND DESTROYED SO THAT EDWARD MACKINNON'S CUSTOMERS CAN HAVE A PURELY PSYCHOLOGICAL FEELING OF SAFETY? ARE YOU GOING TO LET THE CONSTITUTION AND BILL OF RIGHTS OF THESE UNITED STATES BE FLUNG DOWN AND DANCED UPON FOR PROFIT? FIGHT BACK!" And then the prison break sirens began again, screechingly loud.

Melissa and the mayor were staring at Edward — indeed the whole room was. Abruptly he stood, red-faced with anger. Melissa stood too, uncertain of what he would do next.

The sound was coming from a tall, velvet-covered box in the corner behind the bandstand, almost invisible in the dark room. Edward stepped to it, stuck his face directly into the offending noise, and knocked the box to the floor with one powerful swipe of his arm.

*   *   *

Erik had spent the evening trying to work on a series of rants for his radio show, but the image of Sharon at the station kept interrupting his thoughts. He often found himself surrounded by people who considered every little problem in their lives a crisis; it was refreshing to meet a woman in the midst of an honest-to-God crisis who seemed capable of treating it merely as a problem to be solved. These thoughts scattered when Erik heard the key in the door; he noted the time — eleven-forty — finished the sentence on the computer, saved everything, and got out of the program. Janine entered and shed her wrap. "Hey," she yelled, and he called back, "Hey." She disappeared into the kitchen, and he heard the refrigerator door open, the squeak and pop of the cork being pulled from the bottle. "Wine?" she called.

"No thanks," he said. He had enjoyed the straight edge he'd kept all evening; no reason to dilute it with fog now.

"Place is clean." She came into the living room with her wineglass, looked at him for the first time. "You cleaned up."

"The urge came over me," he said.

She looked at his eyes, set her glass down and sat next to him. "What's up?"

"How was your evening?"

She was trying to read him, he could see. She knew he was keeping something from her. He waited to see which way she'd go.

"Busy," she said, and sat back. "Charlayne's an idiot." She sipped her wine. "She was the one who totally screwed up the fabric orders. She was blaming it on Hong Kong, but I found the paperwork." Lipstick on her glass. She'd obviously just reapplied it.

For him? Or as a result of someone else? Or was he paranoid?

She caught him staring. "You were writing when I came in."

"Just a rant for the show."

"Want to read it to me?"

That stopped him. Something warm opened in him, and it felt like old times, but all the same he had the inescapable feeling of being patronized.

"It's not really coherent, yet —"

"I used to love it when you'd read to me —"

He remembered. He playing Daddy to her little girl. And then when she wanted to rebel against Daddy, he got that side of it, too.

She started massaging his neck. "You are so tense. I was giving Gillian a shoulder massage in the office today and I thought she was tense, but you're like steel cable."

She created little dysfunctional families she could be the hero of everywhere she went, and she didn't even see it.

Her fingers jabbed at his shoulders. "Listen, I have to go to Hong Kong with Gillian next week for factory visits —"

"You never go to those things —" And then, "Gillian?"

"J.C. put us together —"

"Bullshit." That's why she was being nice. He stood, crossed his arms. "It's going to happen again, and we both know it."

"No, really."

"Janine — don't lie."

"We talked about it, Gillian and I. Real busy trip, everyone exhausted every night — I don't think you have to worry."

Erik looked at the ceiling. " 'Don't think' — that has a nice firm feel to it."

A devilish look crossed Janine's face. "Just because she's never been interested in you —"

Erik shook his head. "Don't even start that shit."

"I know you. I know what you want."

"No." He just looked at her. "You think you do." He got his coat. "Go. It's fine. Do whatever you need to do. I'm going up the street for a beer."

"I'm not gonna follow you, Erik."

He turned, walking backward. "I don't want you to."

"You always say I don't talk about things. I bring this up and you leave —"

"This wasn't talking about things, this was presenting a fait accompli."

"Erik —"

"Really. You've been clear from the start, you're being honest with me, I always said, just don't lie —"

"I may be asleep when you come back —"

"If you're not, we'll talk," he said, just to get out.

" 'Bye," she said, a little timid wave, very waiflike, very little girl.

He went out the door and down the steps, and a phrase formed in his head that had never quite put itself together before: too old to be a little girl, and too immature ever to be a woman.

Bill had fallen asleep with his watch in his underarm so that when the soft vibrating of the alarm began, it tickled him awake. One A.M.: the sirens had done their work by now. He regretted not being there — it would've been fun. He spent a long uncomfortable moment slowly pushing away the protective boxes that hid him, and wormed his way free. He had left the light on in his stuffy little closet, and it was still on. Nobody had been in.

He unzipped his blue Con Ed suit and had a flash of himself as a child, his mother stripping his snowsuit off his legs. The coverall underneath was light, black, tight-fitting. He stuffed the blue uniform into his black canvas bag, took out a standard issue Israeli-made CNB gas-mask, fixed the snout of the mask over his face and pulled the straps tight over his head. Then, crouching low, he pushed the door open.

The conference room was dark. He'd been hoping to hear a radio going, something to give him a bit of sound cover, but no such luck. He walked across to the next door, took the flare gun from the bag, checked the load, and stuck it into a zipper pocket on his right side. Then he unwrapped the first cardboard paper-towel tube. It was heavy; dangling from the mass inside was a section of dowel on a string.

Bill opened the door. The hallway was half lit; an office on off-time. Sounds of sporadic computer typing came from his right.

Bill felt his heart hammer, a steady iron drill. Something acrid in his nose, a slight eddy of burning plastic. He grasped the first cardboard tube in his gloved right hand, took the dowel in his left, pulled the two apart. There was a slight frazzle of something in the tube, a slender spume of gray smoke. He took two steps into the room, hurled the cardboard tube at the man sitting typing at the computer. It went end over end, fifteen feet, clomped him on the side of the head, and dropped under the desk. "Hey!" the man said, startled, his hand to his head. The man stood up, picked up the tube — and immediately dropped it and covered his face in his palms. "My eyes! My eyes!" he screamed, and curled fetal on the floor. An older man ran into the room, took one look at the situation, and ran at Bill, and then the gas hit him and his legs turned to rubber and he fell on his side on the floor. He started to heave, and brown-gray vomit burst from his lips.

Bill put the other CS gas grenade away. Fifty-thousand cubic feet of invisible gas in a nine-hundred-square-foot area seemed like enough.

The man who'd taken the full hit of gas had vomit down his shirt; the older man was trying to stand, hands still at his face. He started to run jaggedly down the hall. Bill tackled him, pulled him jerking and howling into the conference room. He pressed the flare gun into the man's temple, told him to shut up, and the man did. Bill took out strips of cloth, gagged him, and tied his wrists and ankles. Then he went out, dragged the heaving man into the room, tied him to his coworker.

Bill walked swiftly into the glass computer booth. He took from his bag a hammer and chisel, knelt, positioned the chisel at the hard drive, and smashed the hammer down. Then he jerked the chisel back and forth, effectively pithing the first computer.

Primitive, he knew. He could have done it from the keyboard, but that would have told them more about himself than he wanted them to know.

He chiseled into the hard drives of the next four, leaving gaping holes and twisted metal and plastic where the computers' main memories had been. Then he stuffed a small bag of his homemade explosive mixture into every computer, lit the fuses one by one with a lighter, and walked out of the room.

When the explosions started, the rapidity sounded like gunfire. The mixture in the bags did not trigger the smoke alarm, which was as he'd planned it. He retrieved his cardboard canister, then got the hell out of there, barreled out past the elevators and slammed into the stairwell — no reentry on this floor — and began climbing the stairs up, two at a time.

Eight flights later he stood on the roof, breathing. The wind was freezing and blustery; puddles of rainwater had frozen into slick runways of ice. He stepped to the west side of the building, the lights of bridges visible in the distance. He'd estimated the drop to the warehouse next door as five stories; piece of cake. He wrapped the rope around his waist, belayed off a vent pipe, lowered himself slowly backwards, off the edge.

Bill drove slowly up the street, looking for any sign of stakeout, satisfied himself there was none. He parked twenty feet from the gallery. It was one-fifty in the morning, cold and windy. He took the stepladder and the first tank to the door, considered the locked metal box that surrounded the alarm bell. Picking the lock would have released a refrigerator-type plunger switch, setting off 120 decibels. The box had vents in the front and sides; Bill climbed the ladder, carefully snaked two flexible rubber hoses through the metal slots. He covered the rest of the vents with masking tape, connected the hoses to the tank of aerosol insulation, hit it on. It took about fifteen seconds to fill the bell casing with quick-drying plastic foam insulation. He took the ladder and other equipment back to the stretch, pulled out the hand truck with the big tanks strapped on, pushed them up to the door, took out his picks, and got to work.

The first lock was a piece of cake; the second was a brand-new Fordham; after a nerve-wracking fifty seconds, he was in.

Something inside the gallery was beeping; the bell outside clicked feebly, frozen. Bill wheeled the hand truck with the tanks into the main room of the gallery, ignored the Schnabel and the Fischl, and then was stopped by the van Gogh.

Even now, when he didn't have time for it, it was an astounding painting: a brutal face, eyes filled with sad and tender intelligence; gnarled, overworked hands.

He tore himself away, took the back stairs down, two at a time. The alarm system was next to the halon fire extinguisher tanks in the basement. Red lights were blinking furiously on the front of the alarm control box. He pulled out a crowbar, wrenched and popped the box's lid, found the lever and shut the thing off.

It stopped beeping, but a small green light on the inside panel told him it was still on.

Behind the panel, he knew, a computerized autodialer was frantically trying to dial the headquarters of AADCO securities to alert them of his presence in the gallery. But he also knew it would never reach them — the computers it was trying to contact were not going to answer.

He bumped the hand truck down the stairs into the basement. Against the wall were the five tanks he'd already seen. Over each was a handwritten label. He found the one that said "1st floor."

It took him twenty-eight seconds to uncouple the large tank of halon gas from the receiving pipe. The tank was heavy; he lowered it gently to the floor. He wheeled up the tanks he'd brought, wrestled his large tank off the hand truck, shoved it in under the first-floor label. The connector screwed easily onto the top; he rigged up the smaller piggybacking propellant tank, turned it on.

Then he banged the empty hand truck upstairs, turned his attention back to van Gogh's portrait.

Close up, he could see how quickly the artist had painted it. He'd concentrated on the face; there were bare bits of canvas visible at the sides and top, where details were less important. It was shocking how much it showed the other paintings to be the slaves to commerce they were. Edward Mackinnon didn't deserve to own it, and it did not deserve to die.

He pulled it away from the wall, and a flood of marbles crashed noisily to the floor; an old gallery trick to unnerve people who toyed with art. Bill had no intention of toying with it — he intended to steal it. The hanging wire, he saw, was screwed onto the wall; he cut it with wireclippers, caught the picture in his abdomen when it fell. He covered it with a tarp, set it on the hand truck, and bungee-corded it in.

He wheeled the truck past the Schnabel and the Fischl and the faux sexuality of the immense photograph of Cicciolina, thought of condemned prisoners watching the best of their ilk go free. At the door, he took the flare gun from his zippered pocket, pointed it at the ceiling of the gallery room, and pulled the trigger.

The canister shot up, slammed against the ceiling, ricocheted to the floor. Then the material inside ignited, exploded into red sparks completely illuminating the room, and the canister began to shoot around the floor like a pinball, billowing black smoke.

The fire protection system went into gear, and Bill watched for three seconds as the reddish corrosive acid shot out of the ceiling fixture, coated everything on every wall around it. Bill backed away, afraid of the caustic chemical spray hitting him, but at the same time transfixed as he watched the Schnabel turn from blue to bloody rust. He reloaded the flare gun, backed out the door with the painting, sprinted up the street, opened the van, and shoved the hand truck in. He drove out of there as sedately as he could, his heart pounding in his chest, Wagnerian trumpets blasting in his head. Behind him, under the tarp on the floor of the stretch, the sea captain stared sadly up at the new world rising.

XVIII

When the salsa went on, Sharon opened her eyes and then closed them again, still tired. She'd been up until three, rolling and turning in bed, Edward Mackinnon at the beginning and end of every thought. Six-fifteen in the morning; three hours of sleep. Not enough. She debated calling Edward Mackinnon and canceling this stupid appointment she'd made.

She forced herself out of bed, padded stiffly into the bathroom. She looked like a bloated ghost in the mirror. She just wanted to close her eyes.

Hadn't the phone call been enough? She'd warned him. Did she have to suffer through the masochism of chitchat over coffee with the man who had betrayed her father? She'd call and reschedule, and go back to sleep. God knows she needed sleep; that was more important than staring at the black hole in her life that was Edward Mackinnon.

And what would she do after? What could she do? She pictured herself walking alone all over Manhattan in her gray coat, wind blowing under the gray sky. Too much wine with lunch, dead asleep by three, awake and hung over by nightfall.

Or maybe not. Maybe a movie. A double feature.

Hiding.

How useless. She didn't want to go, she'd spent half the night torn about going. Enough was enough. It's not like I can make a difference, now, she thought. I did my bit, he knows the deal, it's in the FBI's hands, to hell with it. And then the phone rang, and it so startled her she banged her thigh on the edge of the sink.

She ran hobbling to it, picked it up. "Hello?"

A woman's voice, warm and British: "Sharon Blautner, please."

"This is she."

"This is Jenny calling for Edward Mackinnon, there's been a bit of an emergency, and he's asked me to call and cancel your appointment this morning —"

"Is he all right?"

"He's fine —"

"His family?"

Hesitation, and then: "There was a break-in at a gallery, several of Mr. Mackinnon's paintings were vandalized —"

Paintings. Bill, the newspaper, the Psych ER. Oh, God, no. "Mr. Mackinnon just bought that van Gogh —"

"I don't have any information on that." Her tone turned icy.

Sharon held the phone and considered, the tension knotting into a ball in her stomach. "Tell Mr. Mackinnon," she said finally, "that I'll be right there."

The man found the ramp with ease, but the door was more difficult; it took him a moment to negotiate his dog through, and then he was inside. He followed the voices, the dog leading him around the corner and into the main room of the precinct.

He had been here before: a tumble of talk and activity. He got to the counter, cleared his throat, and said, "Excuse me."

"Over here." The voice was young, and white. The man put one hand against the counter, walked three steps in the direction of the voice. "How can I help you?" the white voice said.

"I sell pencils on the street —" The man waited for a reply; none came. He unzipped his coat, unzipped the coat underneath, took an envelope from the side pocket. "Guy came up, gave me this, told me to bring it here." He lay it on the counter.

The white cop took it up. A plain white business envelope, sealed, no writing anywhere on it. "Said to give it to, what, Kinnade? Kindade? Some name like that."

"Kincaide?" The man nodded. The cop wrote "Lt. Kincaide" on the front, tossed it aside. "I'll see he gets it," he said.

"You do that." The old man turned, walked a couple of steps, and then turned back. "Young man?" He fished around in his pocket, came up with a ten-dollar bill. "Young man, this a twenty?"

The cop looked. "No sir, that's a ten."

"A what? A ten?" He made a fist. "Damn. Guy said he was giving me a twenty — you believe that?" He stuffed the bill back in his pocket. "People ask you shit, you just can't trust 'em. In-credible." He zipped up his coats. "Damn. C'mon, boy." He gave his dog a tug, and the animal was up at once to lead him.

He made it out the door and down the ramp, not smiling in case there were any other cops watching. Only halfway down the block did his features melt a little, warmed by the nine other ten-dollar bills pressed tight between his sock and his ankle.

Sharon rang the doorbell of the beaux arts double townhouse and waited, looking up and down the block. Trees and bay windows and an older, dignified woman in a maid's uniform walking two lily-white bichon frises, ribbons in their hair, one pink, one blue. One of the dogs ventured off the curb, squatted between a Range Rover and a black Mercedes. Sharon watched the woman wait, patience etched in deep lines on her face, and then remove a plastic bag from her purse, bend down, and pick up the dog's turds. She knotted the bag and hid it in her newspaper.

Something about the woman's calm managed not to make this ignoble. Sharon thought about jobs, thought about nursing, and then the buzzer buzzed. A man's voice — not Edward — said, "Who is it?"

"Sharon Blautner," Sharon said to the metal grill at the side of the door. The door opened and Sharon found herself confronted by a cop in blue, a large man in a suit, and Martin Karndle.

"Martin — hello. Is — Mr. Mackinnon —"

"Sharon, there was no need to take a taxi. We could've made a completely secure transfer. If you'd just coordinate with us —"

"Sorry," she said, and obviously the subject was closed.

They walked through another heavy locked door, into a pale yellow drawing room, with delicate antique furniture and an over-stuffed flower-print couch and a huge exuberant painting on the wall: red, white, and blue, French flags. It took Sharon a moment to remember the name: Fernand Léger. Sharon saw, through an arch, the dining room, a table for twelve. They marched her past it, up the stairs.

Edward Mackinnon was waiting at the top, and when he recognized Sharon she watched his face light up with what appeared to be honest pleasure. "Sharon Blautner —" he said, and the voice was the same, it really was him. And then Sharon found herself in a bear hug with Edward Mackinnon. "It has been donkey's years —"

Sharon felt herself blush, which made her blush more. "Good to see you," she said, and the weird thing was, it was actually true. He was wider than she'd remembered, bulkier, and his hair was white, and his skin looked rubbed raw, a slightly sunburned look.

Edward Mackinnon. God.

And then stomping down the stairs from the third floor came a blond little boy. He stopped when he saw people below him, and Sharon waited for him to be intimidated by all these strangers in his hallway. Instead he burst into a huge grin, let out an ear-piercing shriek, and waited to be applauded.

All the adults froze; the only one who smiled was Edward Mackinnon. "Teddy, come on down, I want you to meet some people." The boy descended at his own pace, dawdling as much as he could get away with. Edward Mackinnon said, in a low voice, "We haven't mentioned the gallery," and then led the boy down the last few steps and turned him toward Sharon. "Teddy, this is Sharon Blautner, I knew her when she was as old as you."

The boy stuck out a rigid hand, as he'd been trained to do.

Sharon shook it. "Hello, Ted — great to meet you." He said nothing, wiped his hand off on his pants when she let it go.

"And this is Mr. Karndle — he's an FBI agent. A real one."

"Wow." This was absolutely more interesting than Sharon. He did the same sharp extended hand, but now there was shyness in his eyes. "Do you have a gun?"

"It's packed away," Karndle said.

"Maybe you can show it to me?"

Karndle looked at Mackinnon, who made an expansive gesture. "Maybe later," Karndle said.

"Then we can go shoot Daddy and Mommy, and their brains will all go sploosh, all over the wall!"

Mackinnon took over. "Quick, Teddy, go find Lucretzia. She should be downstairs with your breakfast."

"Okay," said the boy, and continued his stomp, now accompanied by noisy, invisible brain-shooting guns in each hand.

Sharon had never seen a more ill-mannered child in her life.

"This way —" Edward led the adults into a white room with a burning fireplace, deep white couches, mahogany bookshelves, and a desk. Paintings were everywhere: modern canvases Sharon didn't recognize, except for a large Picasso above the fireplace. There were people in the room already; they stood when Sharon entered.

"Now, you already know Special Agent Karndle. May I introduce Gregor Fontin" — Sharon shook hands with a dignified bald man in a fine suit — "his assistant Yves Polap" — Sharon's age, thin, with a ponytail — "and my wife, Melissa — Sharon Blautner." An absolutely stunning ethereal Pre-Raphaelite beauty wafted up from the couch, smiled a sad little smile, and offered a fine-boned, pale hand. She had platinum hair in ringlets down her back, and platinum eyebrows, and great flashing green eyes, and she couldn't have been more than twenty-three. "I've heard so much about you and your family," she said, in almost a whisper. "Coffee?"

"Black, no sugar," Sharon said. "Thank you."

"Sharon, you didn't have to come —"

"Well, if your art was vandalized, I think it might be the person I called you about last night —"

"Last night was an assault on many levels," Edward said, and explained about the sirens.

"Good God! And then your art was attacked —" Sharon said.

"Not just attacked; stolen. Gregor, if you could briefly fill Ms. Blautner in on the details."

The dignified man told the events: the security base had been rendered inoperable; then his gallery had been invaded.

Karndle interrupted: "We're thinking the same perps did both jobs — if they'd had a bigger team, they'd have entered the gallery the minute the computers were out. The gap is travel time." Fontin then explained about the halon tank, the reddish tinge of the chemical that had covered all the paintings. Sharon listened with growing excitement; at last she couldn't stand it any longer.

"Hold it." She stood up. "It's Bill," she said to Karndle. "When he was on the Psych ER, he had this fantasy of paintings changing to blood red if they were viewed by — inappropriate people. He did this."

Melissa Mackinnon looked from Sharon to Fontin. "Was it dye? Or some kind of acid that will actually — change the paintings?"

Fontin looked at the thin man, who spoke up: "It appears to have been a corrosive. There has been damage, but to what extent we can't determine until we get the paintings to a restorer."

"The guy knows chemicals," Karndle said. "Whatever he used, I'm sure it was serious stuff."

Edward Mackinnon considered them all one by one. "He destroys every painting, but takes the van Gogh." He looked at Sharon. "Why?"

"Wiring," Sharon said. "Justice is his electricity, and the van Gogh is part of the circuit."

Kincaide walked into his office balancing a bagel with cream cheese on the lip of his full coffee cup. He set it down on his desk, dried the bottom of his bagel with a napkin, took a bite, and sipped the coffee. The mail was the usual interoffice bullshit, memos about procedure. He tossed them and got to the envelope.

He opened it, and a piece of fabric fell out with the letter, and his heart leapt and started to pound at the first sentence. He went to the door and yelled, "Brannock, get in here!" Then he pulled out his notebook and dialed Edward Mackinnon.

Edward Mackinnon hung up the phone. "He's going to copy it, fax us the copy, and keep the original to dust for prints, do whatever lab work you guys do." He cleared his throat. "Here it is:

> "Mr. Mackinnon:
>
> "We have your van Gogh. One million in cash delivered by you in person gets it back — not bad for a painting worth fifty-three. Pack money loose, in green duffel bag. One communication only @6:00 pm Friday 11/24 tells where to deliver. Edward alone, have money and red BMW ready to go. We have buyer lined up; only offer this one chance to keep Captain Mersault from disappearing from world market. Take it or leave it."

"There's no way, after all this, it's just simple extortion," said Karndle.

Sharon shook her head. "The message at the museum tells us it's something larger."

"How could he sell the painting?" Mackinnon asked, his wife nodding vigorously. "The auction price made every paper —"

Gregor Fontin nodded. "Paintings of this stature disappear fairly frequently. Drug lords in smaller countries tend to be powerful enough, within their sphere, that no one who would see the painting would ever be in a position to question its provenance."

"High-level art's one of the few things valuable enough to trade for mass-quantity drugs," Karndle said.

"In certain countries — Japan and Switzerland are obvious examples, but there are others — title to an object can be declared after mere ownership for three or four years —"

Melissa Mackinnon gestured with her delicate pointed chin. "But once it hits the papers that this particular van Gogh has been stolen — how would anyone buy it?"

"A not entirely implausible story can be concocted," Gregor Fontin went on. "I could see a buyer being told that you only bought the painting to declare it stolen and write off the loss — a complicated maneuver necessitated by business. This would be presented as the inside story, if you will. If the seller took the right tone, a buyer could convince himself it was all true."

Sharon had been listening to all this with rising unease. Finally she blurted out: "As I've mentioned, I was with him on the Psych ER when he saw that piece in the *Times* —" Her heart was beating hard. "I think that's when he decided to do it. He didn't say anything — not directly — but he took an interest."

Mackinnon leaned forward in his chair. "Tell me about that."

For a moment, Sharon thought he sounded like a shrink. "We had a conversation," she said, and then stopped, realizing what she would have to say, realizing the full extent of her culpability, the revelation making the world seem larger and larger, building block after building block sliding into place.

She reached for her coffee, sipped it, wishing she were anywhere but here. "Well, you looked like the perfect family — we talked about that." She glanced at Melissa, looked back at Edward to avoid her patient stare.

Uncle Ed.

"We talked about success in America, how those who achieved it made it look so natural."

They all waited, Melissa, in particular, hanging on every word.

Sharon juggled thoughts madly, and finally settled on: "Well, you know, I lost a son." Immediately, it felt wrong. It was wrong; but it was out there, and it was too late.

"I didn't know," Edward Mackinnon said.

"Uhm, my husband and my son. It was a car accident. Charley would have been about your son's age. Ted." Or had it been Ed?

Melissa's great green eyes showed sympathy for her, at a remove on the couch. An uncomfortable silence spread like oil around the room. Sharon could let it go, she was about to let it go, and then she decided. No, she couldn't.

Karndle started: "Why don't we —"

"We talked about you." Karndle deferred. Sharon drew a breath, straightened her back, and looked Edward Mackinnon in the eye. "The fact that I knew you."

She felt very good inside, even though she knew she was digging her own grave.

"What did you tell him?" Mackinnon was pleasant, factual, and hard as nails.

"About your role in my family," she said.

She watched him look at the minefield, debate how to cross it, whether to cross it, whether he needed to bother. And then he surprised her: "And you would define that role . . . ?"

She smiled to herself, shook her head, and plunged. "I intimated I felt you were responsible for the death of my father."

Martin's eyes narrowed. Sharon picked up her coffee, took a sip. Melissa looked away, a tremble of disgust passing over her features.

"Sharon — responsible? Allen committed suicide."

"After the lawsuit. After the lawsuit you won, that stripped him of five years of work. But I didn't tell that to Bill Kaiser." She sipped her coffee. "There you were in the paper. I mentioned my father's death, and I mentioned you."

Melissa Mackinnon's eyes flashed green with fury. "And then you let him out so he could get us —"

"No." Sharon put down her coffee cup and turned to Melissa. "I was tricked. He tricked me. He used me to escape — I broke a very small rule, with very big consequences. The FBI has investigated me, the police — they know I didn't do it on purpose. Nobody's telling me to come here and explain it all. I'm doing it because I made a mistake. I had no idea he was going to start hurting everyone who'd ever hurt me."

"I never did anything to you," Mackinnon said.

"That's not, strictly speaking, accurate," Sharon said. "I believe you did. But more importantly, evidently so does he, and whether or not I want him to, he's hurting you as a favor. To me." Sharon let the words sink in around the room. Edward Mackinnon just sat there, limp, a man with all the starch let out. Sharon debated not saying the next words, tried to find a way to stifle them, but finally there was no way to avoid it. "That's why I have to be the one who does the ransom."

Nobody seemed to understand what she'd said for a moment, and then they all did.

"What?!"

"Absolutely not."

Martin just watched her.

Mackinnon shook his head. "Very noble of you, Sharon, but finally unnecessary."

"It's not noble, it's practical. There's a trick involved somewhere in this. We don't know what it is; maybe he's got some twisted piece of poetry he'll use you to express, maybe he'll just try to kill you — but whatever it is, he won't pull it on me."

"It's my painting, it's my responsibility."

"Edward, that's completely wrong. It's not about the painting, it's not about you. This is between me and Bill. Let's keep it that way. Let's bring no other parties into it. Martin — you know it as well as I do — it has to be me. I have to be the one who makes the drop."

It was airless at the end of the west tunnel, and hot, and the lights glared around Bill as he worked. First he drilled hole after hole in the cinderblock wall; then, dripping with sweat, he took up his sledgehammer, began slamming the concrete. When he'd punched out a gap, he stopped, moved the light, and peered in.

It was as he remembered it.

He renewed his attack on the wall in earnest. Ten minutes later the hole was big enough to duck through. The room was very large, and pitch-black. Bill pulled in a caged lamp, the long cord running back all the way to his basement.

He was standing on a dirt bed prepared for train tracks; at chest level was a platform. Bill held the light high, illuminated the far wall. "St. Marks Place." He read it aloud, smiled, and shook his head. Whenever he was here, Bill found himself wondering at the sheer miraculousness of it.

For generations, the East Side of Manhattan had been ill-served by the subway system; while the West Side was graced with several competing and occasionally redundant train lines, the East Side merely had one. In the 1960s, a subway for Second Avenue had been planned. Five stations were built, and about three miles of track laid in Harlem, and then the money ran out, and the completed sections were sealed shut, even down to the ventilation ducts.

Bill clambered onto the platform, shined the light at the vaulted ceilings and tilework. Forty feet above him, at street level, was the intersection of Second Avenue and St. Marks. The platforms were about a block long; the tunnels had been bored out another half-block in either direction, ending abruptly in dirt and rock, the rough schist of Manhattan Island.

Bill stood with a grin, thought of all the carpentry and electrical work he had to do, all the materials he had to get, and then gave up, cupped his hands around his mouth, and yelled, as loud as he could: "HOOOOOOOO-WEEEEEEEE."

The echo bounced quickly back and forth, and then died, and no one in the world could hear it at all, except him.

Edward Mackinnon was silent, glaring at Sharon, when Martin finally got off the phone. "Behavioral needs more time, but they are cautiously optimistic about the idea."

Mackinnon shook his head. "I went through the Marines, I led men in and out of firefights in Vietnam, I can handle this."

"Eddie — nobody says you can't —" That was Melissa.

"He doesn't care about you." Sharon looked at Edward. "It's me he wants."

Martin was right with her. "He misses Sharon. Behavioral is very firm about that. He wants her to see his actions —"

"I'm ready to do it," Sharon said. "This is the answer."

Edward put his hands through his hair. "Look, he embarrassed me in public last night. And then he stole my painting — I want him. And besides" — Melissa looked on, mute — "he requested me. If there's any change from the plan, it will be a betrayal, and he'll destroy the painting."

Silence around the room. Sharon's mind was up against a wall, trying to figure the pathway.

"We could tell him —" Martin mused. "When he calls to arrange the drop —"

Mackinnon snorted. "He's not going to engage in a dialogue here. If I were him, I wouldn't ever have two-way communication."

Sharon turned from the window, looked at them all, realized the answer. "HBN," she said. "We communicate the change through HBN."

The minute she said it, she felt a pang about Erik. Damn, he'd never forgive her for this. And that would be a shame.

They were ripping up Third Avenue, burly men with jackhammers noisily chiseling up the sidewalk, and the streets were full of well-dressed purposeful people, and Sharon envied them so much, shopping, going places, living normal lives.

Perhaps, she found herself thinking, volunteering to do the ransom was just another way of attempting suicide.

She took a deep breath, pushed that thought away, and turned down the street toward home. No reporters anywhere about; one woman in a beat-up Impala, sitting and waiting. Sharon ignored her, went into her building, and took the elevator up to her apartment.

Four messages on her message machine. She played them: Crystal, her mother, two reporters. She dialed Bellevue, watched as clouds scudded quickly above the Empire State Building.

"Psych ER." It was Crystal; she hadn't wanted to get Hermione.

"Hey, it's me." Sharon attempted to sound breezy.

"Where the hella you been? You never answer your machine —"

"I've been busy; there's a lot that's been happening."

Silence on the phone. "Sharon, you got me worried."

Sharon said nothing to that. And then Crystal sighed: "Listen, you asked me to find Bill Slavitch Kaiser's mother, and I think I did, and you ain't been around to hear it."

"Crystal, wow, that's great."

There was a pause while Crystal went through some papers. "You said it would have been ovarian CA, mets, admitted fall of last year —"

"Helen Kaiser," Sharon said.

"Helen Czolgosz" — Crystal tripped over the pronunciation, and spelled it — "admitted October twenty-eighth, died ten days later."

"Metastatic ovarian CA —?"

"Bingo."

"This is good —" Sharon beamed at the world outside her window. "I like this."

"Even got an address."

"Crystal, you are a goddess amongst women. Where is it — is it downtown? East Village?"

"Nope, midtown, Forty-seventh Street. Four eighty-one, that'd be — way West Side."

"Okay, give it to me again." She wrote it. "Thanks, Crystal."

"Come by for dinner? Real low-key."

"I don't know."

"Don't make me get mad."

"All right, you got me. 'Bye." Sharon hung up the phone.

She dialed 411, asked the operator for a Bill Czolgosz, anywhere on the lower East or middle West Side. They had no listing for anything like that. She dialed Martin's office, left a voice mail explaining what she'd learned. Then she dialed WHBN.

"Erik," she said when she got him. "A lot of stuff's going on — can I come pick your brain about a couple of things?"

Cars buzzed high above Bill's head as he parked the car in the shadow of the Brooklyn Bridge, got out, and walked along the east edge of the Smith House projects. On his right, the East River glinted, cold and choppy in the sunlight. Four blocks south of the bridge was the South Street Seaport complex, shops and restaurants and bars and cobblestones and a tall ship, an artificial tourists' simulacrum of what had once been a busy port.

Highways up and down the shoreline crossed and converged at various levels above him, creating a cloverleaf below the bridge. Until the recent budget cuts, there had been a Department of Highways equipment area at the center of the cloverleaf. Now that area was abandoned, and a homeless encampment had taken the space for its own. Bill looked through the chain-link fence at the wood and cardboard squatter shacks, at the collection of sorry-looking garbage-bag tents. Couples sat and argued while others worked on their houses. Radios blared, salsa at one end and dance noise at the other. Children who should have been in school chased each other in circles. Two fires were burning in trash cans in the windbreak of a highway stanchion. The wind off the river was cold here; Bill could feel it through his coat.

He counted heads, counted again. There were about fifty people visible. He tried to count shacks and tents, but gave up; they abutted each other; some places housed whole families.

They had been in Tompkins Square Park, but the police had closed the park and chased them south. Now they were here, crowded between the bridge and the river, perching tenuously on a freezing and useless piece of real estate.

It was amazing what people built, the instincts.

Next Bill tried to see entrances and exits. Huge gaps of the basketball fence had been cut opened and rolled back. He looked around at the highways and, high above, the bridge, thought about trying to sleep under all that, the constant buzzing of tires sixty feet overhead, thought of the pollution, carbon monoxide and cancer raining down on these people day after day, night after night.

He walked back up the street. The Smith Houses, twenty-story low-income housing projects, would give him the perfect view of the bridge approach. Getting inside would be a piece of cake.

He looked again at the ragged fence surrounding the homeless lot, and smiled. There'd be plenty of places for them to scurry, he could see, when the world exploded around them.

"Kuhzolgosh?" Erik tried. "Cholgoj? That'd be it if it was Polish, I think."

"I have no idea how you'd pronounce that," Sharon said, and immediately hated how unworldly it made her sound in front of this man. They were sitting in his office at the radio station, Cajun fiddle on the speakers hanging from the ceiling. His desk was only slightly cleaner than she remembered it.

"It's funny, it actually looks familiar," Erik went on. "Like I read it somewhere?" He looked at her. "Did the guy ever, like, put out a CD, or play in a local band or anything?"

"That'd be great, if we could find it."

Erik pushed up his tortoiseshell glasses. "Okay, let's look." He turned to the computer, typed "Czolgosz," pressed enter.

Five minutes later, they gave up. "Nope — I'm not getting anybody with that name at all as a contributor to this station."

Sharon sat back in her chair. "It was just an idea."

"I was thinking —" He swallowed. "For years I've been dealing with loonies who overidentify with this station, and you know what? You're absolutely right. What happens when they decide you're not living up to their vision of what you should be? When do you become one of the things they hate?"

Sharon was serious. "I've worked with mentally ill populations for years. Whenever they incorporate you in their delusions, ninety-nine point nine percent of cases, it's a problem."

"Right. Well, so anyway, I have to show the letters with the swizzle sticks to the FBI."

"Wow, Erik. Thank you." She found herself blushing, and turned away, embarrassed. "I'm really glad you agree," she said, struggling to regain her equilibrium. "Unfortunately there's a whole other thing that's come up, and I hate it, but I'm going to need your help."

In the cab downtown, Erik listened to Sharon with growing discontent. Finally he interrupted her. "So essentially, this guy Bill is threatening the man you've wanted dead since you were nine, and you're going to risk your own life to stop him."

"I know, you think I'm nuts —"

"No, I don't think that at all." He looked at her, something quiet in his eyes.

She looked at her knees. "I was kind of concerned about drawing you into this — all your anarcho-punk disc jockeys aren't going to be interested in helping the FBI."

He shrugged. "They'll hate it, but I can force it. Besides, it's not about helping the FBI. It's about keeping you alive."

Erik and his file full of swizzle sticks were being pored over in another office while Sharon read the paper with her feet on the edge of Martin's desk. Finally he came in, shut the door behind him. "Well, I'll say it: Sharon, between Erik Moore and Czolgosz" — he pronounced it "Cholgosh" — "you've removed any doubts I might have had about which side you're committed to in this situation."

Sharon kept her back straight. "Thank you, Martin, I appreciate that."

"How are you handling it all?"

She considered. "I've been better."

"Well, it's been party time over here, ever since we started plugging Czolgosz into the computers. The first database we tried was the NCIC — National Criminal Information Center — which links arrest records from all fifty states. Nothing, which didn't come as a surprise because we'd already run his prints and we didn't get a match, but sometimes you get lucky. Then we started in on the other databases — ATF, zip. Never registered a gun, never had one stolen. DMV, he owned a car in New York City twelve years ago, sold it eight, and the description on the license fits our Mr. Bill. He's thirty-five, six-one, brown hair, brown eyes, he never got a ticket for speeding and he paid his parking tickets on time. If he's got cars under aka's — other names — we'd only find it if we knew the name. The day has not yet come when you get fingerprinted to get a license — though if it ever gets privatized, watch out. Then we turned to the credit history databases, and things got interesting." Martin wheeled over to the far corner of the desk, plucked some papers from a pile. "William Czolgosz: no credit cards, no mortgages, but his name came up in connection with two companies: Linnet Communications and Unicorn Holding. So we took 'em to good old Dun and Bradstreet, and guess what turned up? Unicorn Holding is a company that controls the rights to three patents, all awarded nice and proper by the United States government to William Czolgosz."

Patents. Sharon smiled. "Computer electronics, right?"

"Bingo. At the age of twenty, he patented a" — he read off the paper — "semiconductor-integrated, high-speed, low-power pipe-lined digital transmission circuit —"

"All three of them are circuits, right?"

He looked. "Yes indeed. We have someone who knows this stuff checking if there's any way of making weapons from his ideas."

"He wouldn't do anything that obvious — he takes elaborate steps to hide his violence. I'm sure whatever these are, they're all about promoting communication. What was the other company?"

"Linnet Communications. Founded eleven years ago, broken up and sold in three chunks for a total of two and a quarter million dollars seven years later. William Czolgosz, founder and CEO. No other names listed. Basically, they installed and maintained office computer, telephone, and security systems. Now, we also ran a couple of searches on Helen Kaiser/Czolgosz, and the story seems to be pretty much as you got it. The building on Forty-seventh is now a parking lot —"

"Did you find Bill's stepfather?"

Martin searched through more paper. "Nathaniel Liebling. Sutton Place — I'd say he's wealthy."

"I'd like to talk to him."

"He's on the list. There are a few people we want to contact — the buyers of his companies, for one. We want to see who his confederates were. And we found out another interesting thing about his name —" He grinned.

"Don't keep me in suspense."

"Ever heard of Leon Czolgosz?"

"Doesn't ring a bell."

"The man who shot President William McKinley at the Pan-American Exposition in Buffalo, New York, in September 1901."

Sharon's mouth opened, and then she laughed out loud. "Well, that fits."

"If he's related. It could be another pseudonym."

Sharon shook her head. "No. That's Bill. That's our man."

Edward Mackinnon stood with the headphones on and waited as they set up the target. Around him were burly men with mustaches, and a couple of women. Usually he liked to see what the other people were doing, but he didn't have the patience for it today.

He thought Sharon's offer was brave and foolhardy; even if Behavioral Science decided it would be the safest way to go, he hated it, and he had no intention of letting it happen.

The green light went on, which meant it was safe for Mackinnon to shoot. He lowered his eye protector, picked the Colt .45 off the Astroturfed tray on the wall, popped in a clip, ratcheted one into the chamber, clicked off the safety, and squeezed off one shot.

Wide and low. That's what he usually did when he wasn't paying attention — same with golf, come to think of it, though he enjoyed shooting more. He steadied himself, relaxed his back — that was a problem sometimes; his back would tense up and it would pull his hands — and fired again.

This one charted in the oblong circle of the man, a gutshot. He fired another, clipped the outline. The old gun was beginning to feel comfortable again.

It wasn't his old Marine Corps .45 — it was the top-of-the-line civilian model he'd bought for himself upon his discharge, after his second tour in Vietnam. Now that the military had long since supplanted the Colt with the Baretta M9, he actually felt affection for the old gun, whereas before he had merely considered it a tool he knew inside and out, and thus not worth replacing. He put the gun down, took off his tie, and draped it over the coat hook. He undid the top button of his peach Brooks Brothers shirt. He undulated his shoulder blades, stretched his neck. Then he took up the gun and aimed at the target, seventy-five feet away.

Paintings. A roomful of paintings sprayed with corrosive acid, permanently destroyed. He fired. The acid shooting out, altering everything it touched. He fired. The paintings trashed, gone, might as well just toss them. He fired and fired and fired.

Head shots, chest shots, not a bad grouping. He dropped the clip out of the gun, slapped in another, took up the position, and thought of those blank-faced police photographs of the son of a bitch who stole his van Gogh.

XIX

Sharon got home, took off her coat, and took out the sheaf of photocopies Martin had given her. She arranged them on her little desk and then sat down and went through them all, making notes. Finally she picked up the sheets on Helen Czolgosz and opened the phone book.

There was only one Liebling on Sutton Place. She dialed the number; it rang four times and a woman answered.

"Hello, my name is Sharon Blautner, and I'm looking for Nathaniel Liebling."

Long pause on the line. "What is this in reference to?"

"I'm trying to track down some information about a former wife of his, and her child —"

Another cool pause. "I'm sorry, Mr. Liebling is extremely ill."

"Well, is he there? I just have a couple of questions —"

"First off, no he's not. Second of all, Mr. Liebling is in no condition —"

"May I ask who this is?"

A complete change of tone. "You call me? And ask me who I am?" A throaty chuckle. "I don't think so."

"I'm sorry — please —" The line clicked, and Sharon was talking into a dead phone.

Damn. She hung up, stood, and paced around the apartment, feeling like a complete idiot. And then, abruptly, she knew what to do.

Sharon sat down at her desk, opened the Yellow Pages to "Hospitals," and started in.

Each one had voice mail, which was frustrating, but eventually on each one she got to patient information. On the fifth, she hit pay dirt.

She stripped off her jeans and opened her closet. She only really owned one true nurse's outfit. She threw on white panty hose, the conservative white dress, a white sweater and ugly white shoes, and headed uptown.

Sharon walked into the cancer ward in her whites, stepped gently down the hall. Wheelchairs and IV poles and wheeled scales lined the hallway. She avoided the nurse's station, then checked the names on door after door.

Liebling, Nathaniel was in 2606, a private room with a view. Next to his name were stickers: a green warning, a radioactivity sticker, and a red sticker admonishing anyone entering to take universal precautions. Below that was a cart with masks, gloves, and a red medical waste garbage bag in a covered pail.

Sharon put on gloves and a mask and pushed into the room.

Mr. Liebling looked to weigh about eighty pounds; obviously he had once weighed more. He was hooked up to an Imed computerized IV infusion pump, a cardiac hemodynamic monitoring catheter, a Foley catheter, and was receiving oxygen through a face mask. Sharon approached the bed.

"Mr. Liebling? Mr. Liebling?" He did not react in any way. "Mr. Liebling? I'm here to ask you about Helen Czolgosz."

At that, his head twitched.

"Or Helen Kaiser — her stage name —"

There was something mute and panicked in his eyes.

"And her son, Bill. Do you remember her son, Bill?"

He stared at her, and then, with great effort, his head tipped slightly and returned.

Unmistakably, a yes.

"Can you tell me anything about Bill?"

Sharon leaned over. Once again, nothing, and then deep in the man's throat, she heard slight gurgling sounds.

"He was in school, right? Can you tell me what school?"

Nathaniel Liebling lifted his hand to the vicinity of his oxygen mask, made a weak gesture to push it off.

"Do you want to talk?" Sharon slipped the mask up to his forehead. The man's lips were cracked and dry; she could see his mouth ravaged by sores.

"Water," he said in a weak and fragmented voice.

Sharon poured him some from the Styrofoam bucket, put the straw in his mouth. Slowly the water rose up — a sip, no more.

"They were poor." The words were soft; Sharon strained to hear. "I married Helen, we sent him to Dalton." He began to gasp for air. Sharon replaced the oxygen mask, waited. At last he gestured again, and she slipped it back up.

"Smart kid — loner. Went on to Columbia. And then Helen — Helen —" He began a coughing fit so racking Sharon was afraid he'd die right there. She put the oxygen mask back on, held his hand, waited for it to subside. Again he gestured to take off the mask. "That woman drove me crazy," he said finally.

"Did Bill have any girlfriends — any friends from then that you remember?"

Long pause, during which Sharon debated other questions. But finally he came back with: "Kat."

"Cat? He had a cat?"

"Kat — von — something." He swallowed. "I forget. Prussian."

Sharon could barely hear him. "Russian?"

"*Prussian.*" And then the door opened, and a blond woman in a sable fur coat swept in, carrying two sleek black shopping bags. "Honey, see, I made it." She made kissing gestures with her overlipsticked mouth, dropped the sable haphazardly on a chair. Sharon decided she was the woman who'd been so helpful on the phone. Once she'd obviously been attractive; now she was too old and too large for the short skirt and boots she was wearing. She stood over his bed. "How are we today?"

"Doing very well," Sharon said brightly.

"I didn't ask *you*." She stared down at Liebling. Sharon noticed the large diamond on her finger, the jewelry on her wrists and neck. "Everybody at the office says not to worry, they're doing fine without you. Oh — and" — she dipped back into one of her bags, came up with a small bouquet of flowers — "Marshall's secretary — the ugly one, I can't remember her name — sent you these. God —" She looked at them. "Money she makes, you would think she'd send something decent. Nurse, could you get a vase?"

Sharon smiled. "Sure thing," she said, and took the flowers from the woman's suede-clad hand.

"And Dr. Tokaido — could you have him paged? Honestly, all these Chinese doctors — the way this place is run —"

Sharon, smiling, backed out the door with the bouquet, set it on the table with the gloves and masks, and got out of there as quickly and quietly as she could.

In the lobby, she found a pay phone and called Martin. "I found Liebling," she said, and gave him the particulars. "Bill went to Dalton and Columbia University. Is there any way you can get yearbooks?"

A pause, and then: "It's not unheard of. May I ask why?"

"If I'm going to go up against him, I have to know if I'm right about the man I think he is."

"And his high-school yearbooks will help?"

Sharon smiled. "Like a Rorschach he can't fake."

Melissa had just negotiated the doorknob with a glass of wine in her hand when Teddy shot past her, tearing in circles around his father in the white room, shooting noisy guns with both hands.

"Ted — I told you not to run in here."

"Powpowpowpowpowpowpowpowpowpow —"

"Ted! Don't shoot your father!"

The gun in his hand became a machine gun. "Pookapooka-pooka — pookapookapookapooka —"

"Stop this right now."

Glee on his face. "POOKH POOKH POOKH POOKH POOKH —"

"Ted!" Ed yelled, and the boy froze, and it took about four seconds as his face slowly morphed into a tragic mask, and the piercing wail started, and got louder, and louder, and louder again.

Melissa grabbed him and rushed him out of the room. "LU-

CRETZIA!" The door slammed behind them, and Edward Mackinnon slumped in a chair and felt trapped in his own life. He wanted to escape, but everywhere he could think of going, the van Gogh would still be missing and his kid would still be a pain in the ass.

Melissa came back in, shaking her head. "He'll calm down," she said, trying to assure them both that this was true. She sat on the couch. "Ed, I don't want to take him to the beach house."

"Damn Thanksgiving pageant has to be tomorrow evening —"

"He has lines to say, Ed. All his friends are in it. I even helped Lucretzia make his Pilgrim costume." Melissa sat on the edge of the desk. Her legs dangled, not touching the floor. "Whether it's you or Sharon, doing the ransom — I'll cover Ted. That way I won't just be sitting here. I'll do the pageant, and by the time we get home you'll all be back with the painting."

She took another sip, and he took her hand, and they stayed like that, each of them silently thinking: if everything goes well.

The apartment smelled a little like a pet store, and it was convivially messy. The dining room was filled with a crowded jumble of bright primary-colored plastic toys, a long fish tank filled with gerbils, and another with fish darting back and forth above the table. The room was bright, with books on the walls and an old fat cat asleep on the couch and a big slobbery mastiff curled up in the corner, watching Sharon and Crystal and Larry and the kids finish their dinners. Sharon had made them all laugh out loud with her adventures of the day.

"So, have you spoken with Dr. Garber? Or Dr. DeLeo?" Larry, Crystal's husband, was a barrel-chested Latino with a short black beard.

Sharon swallowed. "I sent a note to Garber's wife. I don't know what to do about Frank — I mean, I'm sure he doesn't want to see me or hear from me or anything."

Crystal leaned back. "I heard he was going to some Park Avenue plastic surgeon —"

"I don't even want to know." Sharon grimaced. "I didn't ask for this. That's why I've got to track down Bill."

"See," Larry said, "I think that's good." But Crystal was shaking her head.

"I'd let it go, hon. You're telling those stories, I kept thinking, 'Just let the FBI do everything.'" Crystal leaned back. "Guy makes bombs, he's a major-league sociopath —"

"Crystal, he's managed to work his way into my family business, and I don't want him there. I mean, my family's complicated enough without Bill Kaiser using it as justification for his insanity."

"You get in his way, he'll hurt you, I promise it." Crystal eyed her. "I just don't want you to become what they call collateral damage," she said, and finished her wine. "Now, you 'bout ready for dessert?"

Sharon was humming quietly when she got off the elevator and walked down the hall to her apartment. Some dance tune from a few years back, silly stuff. It had been playing in the taxi on the way back downtown. She let herself into the apartment, hung her coat in the closet, thinking of Crystal and Larry and their kids and all those animals. A menagerie. She liked that.

She studied Charley's drawing on the refrigerator. She and Rick hadn't really considered animals. If she ever got another chance, that'd be a nice way to do it — cats and dogs and fish, a house brimming over with life.

If she ever got another chance.

She checked the machine, listened to Martin tell her he'd made an appointment for her at Dalton at ten-thirty tomorrow morning. An agent would meet her there.

All at once, she was anxious. She walked over to the radio and punched it on. A show tune she didn't recognize, emotive, with a full orchestra over big singing. She turned up the volume, opened the top button of her pants — she felt stuffed, after that meal — debated having a drink, and decided she probably shouldn't.

The music ended, and Erik's soothing voice crept out over the airwaves: "WHBN 98.6, from the pulsating primeval heart of the Lower East Side, Erik Moore filling in for Harrison until three A.M., and the word of the evening is this: substitute in the lineup, Sharon will be batting for Ed tomorrow night." Fear suddenly impaled Sharon's heart. It was out there; the world was forever changed. "That's the message, I've been saying it all night, so learn it — know it — use it. In that set we heard Reichart Wagner, the overture to *Tannhäuser,* and then — let's see — John Adams, from *Nixon in China,* Nixon's aria, 'News Has a Kind of Mystery.' Then, 'Being Alive' from Stephen Sondheim's *Company,* which is where we find ourselves this very absolute moment. Here's Fats Waller."

A scratchy old recording of "Ain't Misbehavin'" started to tinkle out the speakers. Sharon dialed the station.

"HBN."

"Erik — Hi. Do you feel like a jerk?"

A pause. "I've felt like less of a jerk at other times in my life. I realized I was the only one who could say it and program music for it, so I've been on air since five this afternoon."

"You poor thing!"

"Yeah, tonight and tomorrow night, just me, the microphone, and the FBI tracing every call that comes in."

"You think he's listening?"

"If he is, he hasn't called. But — remember I had a mental association with Czolgosz?"

"You'd seen it on a record —?"

"Stephen Sondheim's musical *Assassins,* all about presidents and the people who shoot them. One of the songs is 'Ballad of Czolgosz,' a pleasant little ditty about Leon Czolgosz —"

"The man who shot President William McKinley. The FBI's already figured out that connection."

"Yeah, they're debating whether or not to let me play it. But if Bill's related, maybe Great-Uncle Leon was his hero, growing up —"

"Yes." Sharon had thought the same thing. "Brilliant, twisted-up little kid, with that in his mythology —" Then something crumpled inside. "Now I've gotten you involved, and this whole situation is spiraling out of control —"

"You're actually going to face him. I'm amazed you're not scared."

"I'm scared, Erik." She held the phone. "I just spent an entire dinner party talking about how sure I am about everything, and the truth is, I'm scared as hell."

The next morning Sharon sat in the Dalton School headmaster's office with Special Agent Travis Springer, who was affable but clearly had important things he'd rather be doing. The headmaster's assistant was being very helpful, bringing them both coffee, getting them the relevant yearbooks and documents. "We have records of Bill Kaiser coming to Dalton his junior and senior year. He excelled at math and chemistry." Sharon accepted the yearbook, searched the picture, found Bill, third year of high school, lanky and diffident, a half-smile, at the back of the group. She looked at his face — so young, so oddly innocent — and part of her wanted to have known him, wanted to have gone to that school, been his friend.

She looked at the boy he'd been, remembered herself in high school, and knew: no, she would have wanted more.

She read the names under the picture, and when she saw it, her heart gently skipped a beat. *Ekaterina von Arlesburg.* Sharon tried to keep her reaction studious, even as she searched the page to see which, in the crowd, she was.

The blond. Leather jacket. The tallest, most beautiful girl in the class. Nowhere near Bill in the picture, but just as tall, and looking slightly at him, as he looked out at the world.

She handed the book to Travis, didn't say a word. "And here's his senior book —" The assistant headmaster held out the book. "Given what you say, the picture is actually very interesting —" Travis was occupied with the junior book; Sharon flipped through the seniors. The school was small enough so that everyone had a full page. She found Ekaterina's picture first: the blond was hard to miss. She'd chosen to portray herself dramatically lit, in a skintight leather dress, lying on a grand velvet couch, smoking a cigar. Oddly enough, the girl had the presence to pull it off. Sharon kept flipping through.

Bill's was a picture he'd obviously taken by pointing the camera at himself, at the top of a rope hanging from the ceiling of a large gym, students in gym clothes forty feet below. "That's the school gym," the assistant headmaster said.

"So let's see," Sharon said, trying to work it out. "He climbed the rope with the camera, held on with one hand while he took the picture —"

The man checked his papers. "It seems he was quite an athlete, though we don't find any team activities. But track, swimming, the rock-climbing wall — and of course, he went on to Columbia."

"Where it turns out he didn't graduate," Sharon said, and remembered: rah rah rah, the old blue and white. Columbia's colors. "I spoke with the dean there this morning." She turned her attention to his senior quote. There were two:

> *"If you want an omelette you must not be afraid of breaking eggs." — Count D'Artois*
> *"So many eggs broken and so few omelettes." — A. M. Schlesinger Jr.*

"Evidently," said Sharon, "he hasn't changed."

Sharon walked out of the school with Travis. "May I offer you a ride anywhere? I have a bureau car —"

"That's okay," Sharon said. "I'll just head home, relax a bit before tonight."

"Special Agent Karndle is expecting you at three-thirty —"

"At Edward's. Yes, I know. Thanks for all your trouble —"

The man got into the car and pulled into traffic. Sharon waited until he turned the corner, then went to the nearest pay phone and dialed information.

"Ekaterina von Arlesburg, everything you've got. Business and residence."

Sharon stood on a beautiful tree-lined street in the West Village, looking at a converted carriage house's large and ornate bay window. The home residence had been unlisted; the business was here: Ekaterina von Arlesburg Antiques.

She had no idea what she was stepping into, but she knew she had no choice. With any luck, she'd see what she needed to see.

Sharon pushed through the door into an elegant shop, swaths of dark red theater curtain covering the walls, and high-tech lights illuminating expensive-looking tables, chairs, and vases. Everything around her was exceptional, grouped into decorated little arrangements. She saw a bed she immediately wanted, and remarkable lamps, and seductive art nouveau sculptures.

No one seemed to be around. Sharon reached the back of the shop, pushed through a heavy velvet curtain, and saw stairs leading down. She took them, searching for an office. She walked down a hall lined with antique canes and umbrellas, through another heavy curtain. The room that opened before her was moodily lit, and it took a moment for Sharon's eyes to adjust, and for her to take stock of what was around her. At first it looked merely like a collection of antique equestrian equipment until Sharon saw the cage: waist-high, wrought iron, desiccated, ancient.

"It was a ship's brig." The voice so surprised Sharon that she actually jolted. A tall blond woman came out of the shadows. "Seventeenth-century Spanish. This was actually salvaged out of the Mediterranean." She was wearing black leather pants, impeccably tailored, and a long black leather jacket. "There is some modern restoration —" She pointed one long red fingernail. "Here — and here. When the divers found it, it contained the skeletons of three men. Nobody bothered to save them when the ship sank."

"How much?" Sharon had to ask.

"One hundred and seventy thousand dollars." Ekaterina von Arlesburg adjusted her perfect blond hair about her shoulders.

"I'm not in the market for a cage."

The woman smiled a disarming smile. "You'd be surprised at the people I get who are." And she laughed, and suddenly Sharon liked her. Ekaterina gestured, and led her back upstairs into the light. "Are you looking for anything in particular?"

She'd kept her looks, Ms. von Arlesburg. Sharon drew in

breath, and plunged. "I'm here because I'm trying to track down information about Bill Kaiser."

That stopped her, but only for a moment. "Ah, yes. Bill made the papers. I saw that."

"I'm Sharon Blautner."

"Ekaterina von Arlesburg." Sharon shook her hand. Her grip was firm; her skin was the softest Sharon had ever encountered in an adult.

"I spoke yesterday with Nathan Liebling — Bill's stepfather. He said you and Bill had been very close friends. Very close," she repeated.

"Bill and I tried being close." The blond woman picked her words carefully. "We made better friends than anything else."

"But did he ever have a real relationship? Is he capable of it? Or does the political always transcend the personal?"

"May I ask — are you a reporter?"

"No."

"With the police in some fashion?"

"I'm the nurse that managed to help him escape —"

"Ah." Something in Ekaterina relaxed, and she leaned back against a marble pillar. "Then you and I have both tried to help Bill, and both suffered the consequences."

"What was it for you?"

"I assume you're working with law enforcement —"

"As a matter of fact yes, the FBI. But I'm here on my own." And suddenly, saying it, for the first time she felt vulnerable. "I'm trying to get a grasp of his psychological state," she said quickly. "I mean he has patents, he's obviously brilliant —"

"Bill's an exceptionally bright man. Unfortunately, really, he went quite off the deep end."

"When was the first time?"

"Well, when he dropped out of Columbia. He was living in some windowless basement, reading the ancient Greeks and talking about rebuilding civilization. Actually, I think he wanted to rebuild himself — and he worked himself out of it. Or at least I thought he had. It changed him. But even after that, at one point he was institutionalized for a few months."

"Where?"

"Oh, God, some awful place. The worst. In one of the boroughs."

"Do you know where he is now?"

"Really, no."

"When was the last time you saw him?"

She considered the question. "Years. He decided I was terribly bourgeois, with the antique business. He thought I was just cozying up to the enemy."

"But who is the enemy? Who does he want to hurt — I mean, he's got this amazing mind, this amazing ability, but I don't understand what he wants to accomplish —"

"I think," Ekaterina said, "that was always a problem. I couldn't keep it straight. Now, unfortunately, I have to close up the shop —"

"Were you aware of his business?"

She stopped and smiled. "I was part of it. As long as I could stand it."

"Evidently it was quite successful."

"Well, as you mentioned, the patents. But he couldn't handle the mundane realities — I mean, can you see him in business? The day-to-day grind?" She laughed.

"I can see him giving anonymous donations to tutoring programs. I can see him blowing up senators —"

"You don't think he actually did that, do you?"

"I can see him being very disciplined, very clear on what he wants —"

Ekaterina said nothing, and suddenly Sharon felt like she had the upper hand. "Could we sit somewhere, and have a cup of coffee? Or a drink? I just want to pick your brain —"

"I'm afraid today that's just impossible. I have a buying trip coming up, and I've a million phone calls to make. But certainly, when I get back —"

"That would be great."

"Here's my card —" She extracted one from a black leather case in her purse. "And my private line —" She scribbled a phone number.

"Great — thank you."

She ushered Sharon out, set about locking the front door. "Now, I'm really afraid I have to run — Call me!"

Across the street, waiting for her, was a black Rolls-Royce, one of the old-fashioned, heavy Silver Shadows. Ekaterina got in, and then Sharon couldn't see her behind the black windows. Then she noted with some astonishment that the chauffeur was a woman, and an exceptionally attractive one, at that.

As she watched the car roll heavily down the street, she had the sinking feeling that she had lost a lot more than she'd gained.

Ekaterina tapped her cellular phone against her chin, eyed the streets as they drove. Finally she saw a place. "Casa Pescadoro," she said. "The red awning."

The car double-parked; Ekaterina ran across the sidewalk into the restaurant. "Millicent —" She air-kissed the hostess. "I know I haven't been here for months, but may I use your telephone? I'm afraid it's an emergency —"

"Of course, dear — by the restrooms."

"Thank you so much." Kat fished out change, pumped it in the phone, and then realized she didn't remember the number. She found her computerized address book, entered the secure section, and found Lobo's info. She dialed, a machine answered, and she spoke quickly into it.

"Listen, guys, it's me. I just had a strange little visit from our late friend's nurse, if you've been following the papers, and I'm leaving town — and I strongly urge you to do the same. Like, right now. He's boiled over, guys — he's doing it. He's become everything we've ever feared."

XX

"There are several tools and techniques we'll be using in this situation —" Karndle looked from Edward to Sharon. Sharon stared him straight in the eye; she had yet to tell him about her visit with

Ekaterina. After this was all over, she would. "We've already got the money stamped with anthracene-II ink, it only shows under high-intensity UV light. The note asked for the bills loose in a duffel bag; that's done. Now, there is the matter of a dye bomb — size of a cigarette pack, stick it in with the cash, it blows one minute after the handoff, covers everything in ten feet with green dye —"

"I have no problem with that," Edward said.

"Sharon?"

She thought about it. "Will it wash out of my clothes?"

"Ha ha ha. It's not meant to."

"Okay, I'll be advised."

"To arm it, you just click the button. Now, we've got agents monitoring your lines, for when he calls —"

"If he calls." That was Ed.

"Right. Tracing equipment's up and running." He checked his list. "Now, we'll go into this with both of you ready to roll, we'll make a decision on-site whether to use Edward or Sharon —"

Edward crossed his arms. "Sharon, you've never been in combat, you have no idea how things get —"

"Ed, the only way to keep you alive is if I do it."

"You two, stop it right now —" Martin stood. "Look, we want the painting back, we want the deliverer safe, and we want to catch the perp — nothing else matters. Edward, we've worked with all sorts of people in situations like this — if it was you kidnapped, Melissa would probably be making the drop. Now, we're gonna wire you both up with recorders — Sharon is that okay?"

"That's fine."

"Ed?"

He shrugged, glaring.

"Great." He checked it off his list. "Body armor, Sharon, we fitted you up. Ed, you've got your own." He made a note. "Now, when the call comes, they know you've got a red BMW, we'll have it waiting outside. Both of you go in the same car, Sharon in the backseat, under a blanket. We'll be surveilling you — five cars around you at all times, coordinated by helicopter, you'll probably never see the same car in your rearview twice, but we'll be there.

We want to ask you to keep the heat on in the car — uncomfortable, but that way we can pick you up on infrared, from above."

"Thank the Lord it's not mid-August," Sharon said.

"Believe it or not, ransom jobs, that's what we get the biggest complaints about — keeping the heat on in the car. People hate it. Now, Sharon, Ed, whoever ends up doing it, we don't want you going indoors — you go indoors, we lose you. Screw Behavioral; I'd figure if he wants you indoors, he wants to kill you. I'd be prepared to blow the whole deal — just get in the car and get the hell out. Hopefully we'll have enough to grab him right there." Mackinnon looked at Sharon, wondering to himself why she looked so composed. "One more thing — we'll get you rolls of quarters. Sometimes they keep you driving from phone booth to phone booth, so we should have twenty, thirty bucks in change."

Edward Mackinnon stood, reached into his pocket, slapped two plastic-wrapped rolls onto the desk. He fished in another pocket, pulled out two more. "Forty should be enough, right?" he said, and smiled thinly. "I've always believed in being prepared."

The boxes all looked different. Whereas the last little project had involved off-the-shelf technology, these were by and large homemade, cobbled together from a variety of parts and sources. Some were fancier than others; all had to be handled equally carefully. They were all rather delicate.

The first building, a twenty-story low-income housing project, had been a piece of cake — go in, get to the roof, place the box, tape the wires down so that they dangled over the sides, get out. The second, an office tower on the south side of the bridge, had not been much more difficult. The third had been the black-and-white phone company tower on Pearl Street; that had involved a change of uniform and some fancy talking, but now his box was planted on the roof, exactly the way he'd wanted it to be.

The fourth had been on the roof of Pace University; he'd interrupted a pair of students about to light a joint. Bill explained he was from Con Ed, had some testing equipment to set up, and nothing would happen if the young people left the area immediately. The young people complied.

The fifth was on another office building, forty-eight stories on the south end of the target area. The locks to the roof had been resilient, but Bill had gotten through.

The last box placed, Bill stood high over lower Manhattan, wind rippling his clothes like flags. He looked east, at the steel cable bridge glinting in the afternoon sunlight over the river. He took out the reconditioned Walkman for one final test and hoped once again that, when the time came, it would be Edward up there instead of Sharon. That would — no way around it — be a shame.

"Promise me you'll be careful," Melissa said.

"I will."

"Promise you'll do everything the FBI asks."

"I will."

"I'm going to be so nervous."

Edward held her. "Try to enjoy the pageant."

"I just wish you could be there."

"Next time."

She said nothing to that, held him, her cheek up against his barrel chest. She didn't want to let him go.

Gently he disentangled her hands. "Hon —"

"I know, I know. Good little trouper." She looked at him. "If anything happens to you —"

"It won't." He picked up her mink from where it had been draped over a chair, and held it up for her.

She slipped into it, pulled her hair out from under, and tossed it behind. He took her hand and walked her downstairs, into the yellow room. At a nod of his head, the FBI agents dropped what they were doing and scurried down the hall. She looked at their refuse: half-cleaned guns, walkie-talkies, and black baseball caps and flak jackets. She sighed and looked back at him. "I love you," she said.

"I love you too." He held her close. "Go to Ted's play."

She left. He watched her walk out of sight, and shut the door.

"Gentlemen — Sharon —" he called out, "we have work to do. Let's put it in gear here."

Bill was late getting to the corner, but he had the Bendel's bag and the man was still there — homeless, shaking a Greek diner coffee cup for change. His eyes were monstrous, sightless and decayed. Bill kept his steps steady as he approached, pitched his voice low: "Go beg uptown, where people have money," he said, and walked by him.

The man didn't follow the voice; he just kept jingling his change. Ten feet farther along was a metal trash can chained to an apartment building railing; Bill stepped to it, noisily opened the metal lid, dropped the Bendel's shopping bag into the empty space, slammed the lid down, and kept walking west.

The man with the nasty corneal infection waited just a few moments before stepping over to the trash can. He opened it, rooted around a bit before pulling out the Bendel's bag, crammed it under his coat. He walked back to the corner, shaking his cup, and stayed for another ten minutes before starting his walk south.

Bill took the stairs two at a time to the roof, shouldered through the heavy door, and looked at the lights of the city below. It was cold up here; nobody had messed with the locked box he'd left. He took out six wooden doorstops, hammered them into the gaps between the door and the frame.

Down below him, the traffic was fast; taxis weaved in and out, heading downtown.

He unlocked the box. The device itself was a homemade, bedraggled thing: a gutted wooden radio receiver with a badly cut cardboard top, powered by two heavy twelve-volt car batteries. Bill pressed the button to start it; the dial glowed green. Something in him immediately felt calm.

Bill unwrapped the headset from its paper towels, put it on; it only covered one ear. He adjusted the stick microphone to be close to his mouth, plugged the headset in. He heard nothing.

Sitting on top of the radio was an electronics store five-way knob, wired through a hole in the cardboard to the hardware inside. Bill flipped the knob to the first stop, watched the tuning meter on the old radio dial jump to attention. That meant Box Two, on top of the southeasternmost tower of the Smith House project, was receiving him. He flipped the knob again. The needle dipped and shot back up, slightly higher. Box Three, on the phone company building, was getting his signal.

Bill checked Box Four — weaker than the rest, it had always been the problem child — and Box Five, strong signal, ready to go.

Box One, Bill's console, was sending out the absolute bare minimum of power. All the other boxes contained specially rigged receivers, amplifiers of various wattages to boost that power, and crude homemade repeaters to blast it back out.

Bill spent a long moment focusing his binocs on the wooden walkway of the bridge, far below. When he could read the graffiti clearly, he took up the black blanket. This Bill had made years before: a heavy black bedspread with weights hemmed into the edges. He spread it out over his equipment, climbed under with the binoculars. Then he pulled the MAC-10 onto his lap, locked in a clip, clicked off the safety, and sighted it down at the bridge.

He checked his watch, and settled in to wait for the red car.

The woman in the wheelchair was wearing three coats, and missing a leg. She smelled bad, wore sunglasses, and had rolled up to Edward Mackinnon's townhouse with a much disheveled Bendel's bag on her lap. "Look," she was saying, "I was in the shelter, guy walks up to me, say I deliver the package, I get twenny bucks. I say, you deliver the package, you so concerned. He say he cain't, do I want twenny bucks or not. I say is it drugs? 'Cause I don't do no drugs. He say you feel it, it's a Sunny Walkman, ain't no drugs. I say yes, I come up here, now you given me all this shit."

The woman sat surrounded by a circle of hulking healthy white male FBI agents, all with guns in their hands. If she'd been able to see, she would have been scared, but she couldn't, so all she was was irritated.

"Can you give a description of whoever gave you the package?"

The woman turned toward the voice. "Now how am I supposed to do that?"

"His voice," said Martin Karndle. "Was he white or black?"

"Black."

"Was it someone you knew?"

"No."

"Someone from the shelters?"

"I'd never heard him before."

"Did he say a name?"

"Galby, Gabby, some shit like that. Southern black, you could hear it in his voice."

Two men emerged at the end of the hallway, and signaled to Martin Karndle. He held his hand up: Wait. "You have the money he gave you? The twenty bucks?" he asked.

This made her nervous. "Uh-huh —"

"Could you give it to us? We'd like to check it for prints —"

She said nothing for a long moment, and then she exploded: "You doin' all this shit to make an old lady give up her twenny bucks, man, this some kinda piece a shit, I don't know nothin' about you guys, I don't know one damn thing but you want my money!"

Martin Karndle stood up. "Gentlemen, could one of you explain it to the lady?" He turned his back on the mess, walked down to the cluster of agents in the formal dining room. "What you got?" he asked.

"A small piece of the picture frame from the van Gogh, and a Sony Walkman, modified inside. The dogs didn't smell explosives, nothing turned up on X ray. Moving parts all seem to work. There's a tape; it seems normal as well. We haven't played it."

"Not gonna blow up?"

"Nope."

"Not gonna spew acids?"

"Nope."

Martin Karndle moved his hands through his hair, readjusted his haircut. "Tim? Tell me about modifications?"

Tim Sannstromm was a wiry older agent with a hearing aid behind one ear. "Can I open it?"

"Go ahead, as long as it works when you're done." Tim set to with the Phillips head.

Karndle put on a glove, picked up the tape. "Meantime, I'll take this to Mr. Mackinnon."

Sharon and Edward were upstairs, both in dark clothing. Sharon looked blank; Mackinnon looked pained. By each of them were unfinished bowls of pasta with Bolognese sauce. The volume of the TV news was too loud for conversation; Edward pressed it down at Martin's arrival. "We checked it," Karndle said. "It's harmless."

Sharon stood to look. "Any handwriting?" There was none.

"All right, let's play it," Mackinnon said, and punched on the bookshelf stereo, pressed the button for the tape machine. He reached for the tape; Karndle stopped him.

"Gloves." The FBI man held up his gloved hand. "I'll put it in." He slipped the cassette into the machine, and then was confused how to start it. Edward pressed the play button, and the three of them waited. There was the hiss of the leader, then quiet, and the voice started.

"No, the machine is not going to blow up."

The voice was male, hollow, metallic, monotonous.

"Nothing bad is going to happen, unless you don't follow the instructions on this tape very precisely, word for word."

"It's not Bill," Sharon said.

"It's a computer," Martin Karndle said. "They have programs — you type something, choose a voice, and voilà."

"Jesus," said Edward.

The oddly hearty male voice went on:

"As you can see from the piece of frame included, we are the group that currently possesses the van Gogh portrait of the Captain. We are offering this one chance to get the

painting back. If communication fails us at any time this evening, the portrait will be out of the country within thirty-six hours — no second chances. We offer it to you for less money than we have been offered elsewhere. Once again: make no mistake, we have a buyer in a foreign country already lined up. If you want the van Gogh back, you will do exactly as this tape tells you to do. You have the money we have asked for, one million dollars, packed in a green duffel bag. You will get into your red BMW, license plate DPR 169, alone. You will put on the headphones connected to the Walkman we gave you. Do not use another Walkman; this one has been converted to receive transmissions others will not get; these transmissions will guide you. At the end of this message, switch the Walkman to 'Radio' — there is a line of red paint at the spot, on the side. Leave it in this setting, with the headphones on your head, as you drive south, down Second Avenue. You may use your own headphones, if you would be more comfortable with them, though the ones provided are completely safe and unaltered in any way. At some point, a voice will come over the air — only accessible by this Walkman — and guide you precisely where to go. The entire ransom should take about an hour; if everything goes well, you will be back home safe and sound only a short while later. Once again, we mean you no harm; this is merely a business matter. We'll be seeing you within the hour, or we will not see you at all, and you will not see the van Gogh again. This is the end of the recorded section of this tape; the rest of this tape is silent."

The words stopped; the tape kept turning, hissing out over the speakers. Edward Mackinnon stopped the machine.

"He's not acting like he heard the HBN message," Sharon said.

Edward shook his head. "That only clinches the argument that I should do the payoff."

"We make that decision on-site," Martin growled.

Edward looked away from Sharon. "You sure that Walkman thing is safe?"

"We looked it over thoroughly; we didn't find anything wrong."

He checked his watch, and stood. "Melissa's got a Walkman with detachable mini-speakers, that way we'll all be able to hear. Let me get them." He stepped out of the room.

Martin smiled at Sharon. "Tracking a radio signal — piece of cake," he said, and picked up his walkie-talkie. "Get the team ready to roll. Over," he said, as Tim Sannstromm appeared at the door. "Tim! You got a radio frequency we can trace?"

"Well — no, uh — what he's done is quite interesting. It's a receiver, tied to a frequency hopper. It's got a mate, somewhere out there. Like a radio station and a radio receiver that both make pre-programmed jumps all over the dial. Every tenth of a second, or something, this thing's gonna change broadcast frequencies on us."

"Can we trace it?"

"That's the point — you can't jam it, it's hard as hell to trace."

Martin said nothing for a long moment, and then he groaned. "Why does everything always have to be so goddamn difficult?"

The agents and cops formed a cordon between the door and the car, and Sharon was brought through under a blanket and settled into the backseat. Then Edward Mackinnon walked through, heaved the green bag into the passenger seat of the BMW, went back around, and got behind the wheel. There was a helicopter somewhere up above, but living in New York he heard so many every day that it was only with a start he remembered: this one was there for him alone. He had his Colt in his right coat pocket, and extra clips in his left. He had qualified on the FBI range for the privilege.

He slammed the car door. "You okay back there, Sharon?"

She poked an eye out from under the blanket. "I've been more comfortable," she said, "but I'm fine."

"All right." He set the little speakers up on the dashboard, turned the Walkman on.

Silence.

"Let's go." Mackinnon turned on his ignition. Cars roared to life all around him: one moved out, and then another, and then him. In his rearview, he could see he was being followed.

Two blocks south of his house, he drove by a Cineplex Odeon Sixplex — "God," he said to Sharon, "I haven't seen a movie in so long." When this was over, maybe he and Melissa and Ted could go out, see movies, really be a family for a few weeks. Do normal shit. "Funny thing is," he ventured, "Melissa is always saying I get into this mode, I become a business automaton, some kind of deal-making machine — the fact that this all seems as reasonable as any other business deal makes me think maybe she's right."

Sharon shivered slightly at the thought of Edward Mackinnon pretending polite surprise at how ruthless he could be. "Did you tear down the Hammerstein Theater?"

"Yes indeed, to build the Century Tower. Why do you ask?"

"No reason. Are you sure that radio's on?"

Bill checked his watch, sat up on his knees, hit the test button, and whistled into the microphone on his headset.

The sound he heard through the headphone had been electronically downshifted four octaves, making his light whistle bellow like a tugboat foghorn. He had also put some sound gates and filters in, rock-and-roll guitar waveform envelope changers and such, to make his voice even more difficult to identify.

Now was the time. He pressed the appropriate buttons on the radio player, took a breath, calmly said, "Second to Houston, one block west on Houston to Bowery, then south on Bowery" into the microphone, and then set the echo unit to repeat it over and over. Then he listened over the headphone as his voice, lowered so that he sounded like a truck driver, went out over the air.

It was going to happen. The thought made Bill want to blast the bridge across the way with the MAC-10. He kept cool, took up the binoculars, continued his vigil, waiting for the red car.

*   *   *

At first Edward Mackinnon couldn't understand it — second down, block who? — but it repeated and repeated, and Sharon figured it out.

"He's sending us into Chinatown —" she offered.

"Right, right." Mackinnon grabbed the police radio. "We're supposed to go south on Bowery —" Mackinnon yelled into the box.

"Don't shout," Karndle shouted, from several cars away. "We're right with you, over." Karndle clicked off.

"Bill's voice?" Edward asked.

Sharon listened hard. "Maybe. I can't really tell."

Around them kids in leather jackets littered the sidewalks of the Lower East Side. Edward Mackinnon reflected that he never came down here — there wasn't even a theater he'd heard of, or a decent restaurant, just junkies and kids with weird haircuts pushing amplifiers up and down the streets. But he didn't say anything to Sharon — as he remembered it, she lived downtown. Maybe all these choices made more sense to her than they did to him.

They turned on Houston en masse — anyone looking would have thought they were a particularly rude foreign dignitary, late for a curtain or an airport — and then south on Bowery, past block after block of restaurant supply stores. At that moment, the message changed — "Bowery south, past Canal, down St. James" — and Mackinnon thought he heard some quality of breath that made it sound live, but only the first time. He grabbed the radio. "Bowery to Canal, and then south!" he yelled, and then slammed on the brake — he'd almost run a red light. He peered up at the street sign, tried to figure out where they were.

He was looking east at a vast tangle of streets; Edward Mackinnon had no recollection of ever having been exactly here before in his life. He was reminded of getting lost once, in Venice; he meandered away from the San Marco vicinity and ended up on some long street he never found again, Venetians bustling about doing their shopping. To his left, a bridge rose up in the distance; Mackinnon spent a moment juggling bridges. "What's that, the Manhattan Bridge?" he asked.

Sharon lifted her head. "Nope, Williamsburg."

Edward watched as a homeless man with his leg in a cast picked through a garbage can not four feet from the nose of the BMW. The light turned; Mackinnon drove straight. Ahead of them, unattractive low-income housing projects rose into the sky.

High above, in the FBI helicopter, Tim Sannstromm was trying not to let the frustration get to him. He was in a ridiculously tight space behind the pilot and the surveillance coordinator, knees cramped against his equipment, headphones over his ears. He was working his way through a full spectrum scan, carrier and subcarrier frequencies from 20 kHz up through the radio, and microwaves to 6 GHz, knowing full well that the chances of actually tracking Bill's radio signal were somewhere between slim and none.

Still, he'd tracked more impossible radio sources, from bugs in government buildings to the South American numbers stations broadcasting on shortwave to AM and FM pirate stations wherever they sprang up. Sometimes all you needed to beat a truckload of equipment was a clear head; if he was at the right place at the right time, he'd see what he needed to see.

When Bill saw the red BMW turn onto Saint James, he'd smiled. He'd known it would travel surrounded by plainclothes. There were helicopters in the sky; they were noisy as he pressed the button. He cupped his hands over the microphone. "Take a right on Avenue of the Finest to the bridge arch. Stop. Edward Mackinnon, take the money, go into the arch, climb the stairs up to the Brooklyn Bridge alone."

"That's it — he asked for me."
   "Edward, I have to do it precisely because he asked for you."
   "Sharon —"
   "Just drive, all right?" Actually, at that moment, Sharon would have dearly loved Edward Mackinnon to do the damn ransom. But in her heart, she knew: there's a trick to this, Bill's a poet, and I'm the person he wants to see.

Edward Mackinnon rolled to a stop and looked up at the steel-caged maintenance stairs leading up to the bridge roadway, four stories above the city. He picked up the police radio. "I'm doing it," he barked at Karndle.

"Negative, Ed. We're going with Sharon."

"You can't do this, Martin —"

"Ed, all situations have an ideal negotiator, and she's it."

Sharon took a deep breath, threw off the blanket, and sat up. The first thing she grabbed was the Walkman, ripped out the speaker plugs, grabbed the headphones off the dashboard.

"Sharon —"

She shoved the Walkman deep into her bulletproof vest. "Give me the walkie-talkie, Edward."

He gripped it tighter. "Martin, she's taken the Walkman."

Sharon turned the box toward her mouth. "Martin, I'm going." She reached over, opened the passenger door, shoved the duffel on its side so the door stayed open. Then she came out the back door, hands on the bag so if he drove away, she'd have it.

She stood tugging at the bag, and the fucker was heavy, but she got it out. Helicopters thundered overhead. She planted the strap over her arm, and found she could walk it well enough.

Fifteen feet across the cracked sidewalk to the archway. Once inside, she could see two flights of stairs up to the bridge walkway.

She heard salsa music wafting from somewhere east.

She set one foot on the steps, plugged the headphones into the Walkman, and then Edward Mackinnon was there, Uncle Ed. He had come from the car.

"I said I'm doing it, and I am."

"Edward, I'm here — it's all worked out —"

"My money, my painting. Give me the bag."

"Absolutely not. This situation is my fault, and I'm dealing with it." She hoisted the bag, started to climb.

Edward Mackinnon made a smooth move, and there was a gun in his hand, a large automatic, and Sharon looked from it to him, shocked, and then angry.

"How dare you point a gun at me."

"Give me my money, Sharon."

"Go ahead — shoot. I'm bulletproof. Except you'll have to shoot me in the head — or would that remind you of my father —"

"I didn't kill Allen."

"No, you just stole five years of his life, left him with nothing —"

"This is not the time." He shoved her, grabbed the shoulder strap, pulled it from her.

"You prick."

"And the Walkman."

"Last time I try to save your fucking life."

"The Walkman, Sharon."

She stared at him, she stared at the gun. "All right, you do it." She slapped the Walkman into his palm, the headphones dangling down. "Just don't ask me to care." She turned and walked back to the car.

Mackinnon stood for a moment, putting on the headphones, one ear off, one on. He put his left arm through the strap, lifted the bag onto his back. He shifted the .45 to his right hand, clicked off the safety.

A helicopter was hovering, noisy, somewhere above him.

He climbed out into the night.

"Walk towards Brooklyn," the voice in the headphones commanded.

Now that Tim Sannstromm understood where everything was happening, he could begin to try to understand how. Even with all the gear in the helicopter, he had not been able to hear a peep of the communications between the ransomers and Edward Mackinnon, which was pretty much as he expected. He had marked a map of Manhattan with the spot that radio communications were first picked up by Mackinnon. Now he could see that everything revolved around the Brooklyn Bridge; the radio sender had to be within visual contact of the bridge in order to guide Mackinnon. Sannstromm centered a compass on the intersection of St. James and the bridge on his map, opened it to the edge of the radio communication area, drew a circle that included a large swath of lower Manhattan and clipped the edge of Brooklyn.

Well, it was obvious the radio equipment they were using was vastly more powerful than it needed to be. Sannstromm considered the buildings as they appeared before him: low-income projects and office towers, all tall enough to provide visual contact with the bridge entrance. He pressed the button on his headset. "I want a sweep of every building" — he pointed — "in a circle around this bridge."

The pilot touched his mike. "Recon? Or do you want 'em to know we're coming?"

Sannstromm considered. If it was up to him, they'd pull out all the bells and whistles. But this operation was pure FBI. "Keep it quiet," he said, "and put on the infrared. Let's check for heat."

At first, Bill had seen Sharon dragging the bag from the car; he'd yelled "NO CHANGE!" into his microphone, but she hadn't had the damn earphones on. Then Mackinnon had gone under the arch, Bill unable to see them, but finally Sharon had walked back — pissed as hell; he could see that through the binoculars — and now Edward was on the wooden bridge walkway, and everything was back on track. Traffic on the bridge had stopped, a huge blaring traffic jam, and the swooping helicopters were even noisier, cutting about in circles in the sky.

Bill pressed the button. "Faster, Edward Mackinnon," he said. "Faster!" He let it repeat three times, got off the air, watched through his binocs as the man with the sack began to move more quickly. Bill smiled, felt like a long-range puppeteer, pulling the strings from his position high in the sky.

Sitting under his blanket, headphones on and binoculars at his eyes, Bill didn't notice the way the unmarked helicopter hovered for a long moment above his building while the pilot and the passenger conferred. Though not readily apparent to the unaided eye, there was a person-shaped heat source hiding under a cover of some kind down there; the trajectory was good in terms of both radio and visual contact. Sannstromm radioed it in to Karndle, and pressed on to the next building, on the off chance they were wrong.

Policemen on motorcycles had roared across the walkway, clearing the bridge of pedestrians and bicyclists. Edward Mackinnon stopped for a moment, was readjusting the duffel bag full of money when the low voice started again: "Keep walking until you get to a star painted on the bridge. About a hundred more feet."

Mackinnon walked quickly east, lost count of how many steps he'd taken. Then, suddenly, there was the star.

White spray paint. On the ground, north side of the walkway. Graffiti.

"Directly before you is a catwalk over the westbound traffic, to the north edge of the bridge. It's got handrails. Climb on it, and walk to the edge of the bridge."

"Jesus Christ," Mackinnon said out loud. The railing was flesh colored, navel high. He looked around, climbed up, pulled the heavy bag up after him. Twenty-five feet below, three lanes of traffic stood frozen, honking and angry. The catwalk was a girder over the highway, nothing more, with handrails.

The radio voice clicked on. "Be careful of the electrical wires towards the end there."

Mackinnon stepped over them, looked up, trying to figure out where the man had to be to see him that closely.

He was now at the edge of the Brooklyn Bridge, holding on to the cables. But he was not over water; there was some kind of activity below.

"Now," the voice said, "do what we say and you will not be a target, nobody will hurt you. Open the duffel bag."

Mackinnon unclipped the drawstring, pulled it open.

"Any dye bombs they gave you, take them out, drop them on the roadway."

Mackinnon fished them out, did as he was told.

"Now. Hold the duffel bag over the edge of the bridge —"

Mackinnon's arms were trembling as he held the bag in the wind. There were lights below him, fires. Salsa music.

"Now shake the bag out until it's empty."

Mackinnon just stood there, feeling like an idiot.

"Empty the bag, Edward!" the voice commanded.

"What good will that do?!" Mackinnon yelled at the sky, at the wind, at the city around him.

"EMPTY THE BAG, SHAKE IT OUT AND DROP IT OR WE'LL KILL YOU, EDWARD! YOU WANT TO SEE THE VAN GOGH AGAIN? EMPTY THE FUCKING BAG!"

Edward upended the bag and shook it. Instantly the air was littered with a blizzard of bills — some blowing back over the bridge, the lion's share falling in a cometlike clump down into the heart of the homeless encampment below.

There were bills everywhere, and something about it, something about the release of it, the absurdity, made Edward Mackinnon laugh, tossing away all that money.

"THE BAG TOO, EDWARD!"

What the hell, Edward thought, and tossed the bag into the air. Down below, he could hear the sounds of a crowd beginning to yell as they realized what had befallen them: cries of "*Dinero!*" "Money!" "Gimme that!" Edward Mackinnon looked out over the edge of the bridge and marveled at the crowd of people surging and lunging for the money.

"Taped to the underside of the girder on which you are standing is an envelope," the low voice on the headphones said. "There's a note inside. It'll tell you where to go for the picture. This is Radio Free New York, signing off the air."

Edward Mackinnon knelt carefully, felt around, touched the envelope. He figured he'd wait for the police to come and take it off. When they caught up with him, he was just leaning over the side of the bridge, watching the homeless lot empty as the police sirens wailed through the neighborhood, swooping down.

Sharon was sitting in the backseat of Karndle's car when the money dropped, and at first she didn't understand it, and then she did and she began to laugh out loud. She grabbed binoculars and watched as he threw the empty bag out into the night.

"Better him than me," she said to Karndle. "If I'd blown all that money, I'd have never heard the end of it."

Within a minute, there were hundreds of people rushing by the cars, their shirts stuffed with hundred-dollar bills. "Shouldn't you go stop them?" Sharon asked.

"What, the three of us? Like they'll come to a halt if we get out of this car and pull badges? All they know is some rich guy dumped money on them, and it's theirs." He shook his head. "Bill Kaiser one, Edward Mackinnon zero."

Bill yanked the radio pieces apart, stashed them in his backpack, looked out over the bridge again — even from here, it was obvious something was up; the thing was awash in sirens and flashing colored lights. He went to knock out the doorstops when he saw two plainclothes cars rushing up the street toward his building, twenty stories below.

One after the other. And then a third, racing down the block straight toward him.

He looked west; his stretch was where he'd parked it. He pulled out the rope, found a pipe jutting up from the roof. He slipped it over, dropped the two ends down the outside of the building. Then he got himself into position, took up the rope with both hands, and let himself over the edge.

Sharon stood in the back of the FBI van, ripping off the black flak jacket, and then the Velcroed body armor underneath. She spent a moment peeling the duct-taped transmitter from the small of her back, and it hurt like hell, but finally she was free of it. Tucking her shirt back in, she still felt like a soldier, though she was no longer dressed like one.

She presented the small pile of equipment to the agent in charge, who gave her a receipt. Then she stepped down into the darkness, and there, waiting for her, was Edward Mackinnon.

He was in her way, so she stopped. "I'm sorry about that moment before —" he said.

"No sorrier than I."

He had nothing to say to that, but he tried anyway. "Sharon —"

"Look, Edward, I was trying to save your ass, you pulled a gun on me. I don't care if you live or die, okay? You victimize me, that makes you no better than Bill."

"Sharon —"

"Get out of my face, get out of my family, get out of my world." She walked past him, on down the street.

"Sharon —"

She kept walking.

"I loved your father like a brother, Sharon —"

That made her turn around. "This isn't about you and my father, Ed. I didn't ask Bill Kaiser to do long-distance family therapy on us, okay? I am so sick of appeasing terrorists —" She shook her head. "Go get your painting, Ed." And she turned back and kept on walking north.

Bill Kaiser slipped into the Steiner Building wearing a plain dark suit with a white shirt and tie. He used the black leather briefcase in his hand to cut his way through the successful men and their attractive wives all around him, trotted one flight up the marble stairs, and went through the nearly empty auditorium. He climbed the steps onto the stage, crossed past the trees painted on canvas and the piano and trotted down into the prep room.

This was a madhouse — half-costumed kids running everywhere, prepubescent energy bursting now that the show was over, teachers trying to keep everybody from wreaking havoc, get them back into their clothes. A young man with a name tag on his jacket approached him. "Excuse me — parents are to wait downstairs for the children."

Bill smiled broadly, took a leather billfold from his pocket and flipped it. "FBI" he said, and let Mr. Potter look at the ID as long as he wanted. "I'm here to collect Ted Mackinnon."

"Ted?" Potter strode toward a group of young boys, which parted to display Ted Mackinnon, sitting on another boy's chest, hands in fists, the other boy's face etched in a wail. "Ted!" Mr. Potter grabbed the boy up by the arm. "Ted, get changed right now. This man is here to take you home."

Ted looked over at the tall fellow with blond hair. Bill pulled him aside, squatted down so they were eye to eye.

"You're not my usual driver," said the boy.

"No, I'm not," said Bill. He opened the billfold, showed it to the boy. "I'm with the FBI — don't bother to change, just get your stuff and put it in this —" He opened the briefcase. Inside was a walkie-talkie and some kind of fancy pistol. The boy's eyes lit up, and he got the contents of his locker out and jammed them into the briefcase. "They sent us to bring you to your father —" Bill said. The boy put his winter coat on, and thrust the front out at Bill, waiting to be zipped.

Bill didn't get it at first, and then did. He zipped up the coat, stood up, and took the boy by the hand. "Come with me," he said. "We're taking the back way out — there's a car waiting."

XXI

Sharon had walked.

She hadn't wanted to do anything else. There was a simple pleasure in putting one foot in front of the other, moving forward, watching all the people on the streets. She worked her way through Soho, and then east, and she felt fierce and free and liberated and disgusted with the authority figures in her life.

She knew whom she wanted to see, and finally she stopped at a pay phone and dialed the station. Erik answered on the fifth ring.

"I'm glad you're safe," he said. "I'm here until ten, unless the FBI tells me otherwise. Come."

Mackinnon sat in the surveillance van outside the burned-out Harlem tenement, happy to be the central player no longer. Just a cog in the machine, that was fine with him. He wanted life to return to normal: he wanted the van Gogh back, safe and unharmed; he wanted Sharon to be a vague memory and not a stinging indictment of every decision he'd ever made; he wanted to wander around in socks with his wife and kid. He watched the TV monitor as three flak-jacketed FBI agents led dogs around the tenement basement. One was filming the entire invasion; everything they saw was from his perspective. The envelope at the bridge had sent them to a rooftop in midtown; an envelope there had directed them to a second building, where a third envelope had sent them here. At last each man gave the all clear, and the camera focused on the door in the basement's cement block back wall.

There was a lock securing a deadbolt on the front of the door. From the shank of the lock dangled a two-foot blue ribbon. This ribbon matched the one tied to the key in the envelope that had been found by the FBI in the third envelope.

Now, on the screen, Edward could see the agents in their flak coats and helmets letting the dogs smell the lock, one by one.

"Dogs give it a negative, over."

The agent with the camera came close, focused on the lock and deadbolt. A voice said: "Visual inspection, no outstanding wires in evidence." And then a portable fluoroscope was brought in and turned on, the picture patched back into the van.

"Door appears normal," one of the voices said.

"Clear to this point."

"Clear to this point."

Martin Karndle checked his watch, scribbled down notes on a clipboard, and then gave the order: "Okay, B Team, enter at will."

The dogs were brought out and given to a handler. Mackinnon watched as the flak-jacketed agents in the basement flattened themselves against the walls while one helmeted man inserted the key into the lock, blue ribbons fluttering on the monitor. He unlocked it, set it down into a plastic evidence bag. Then he tied string onto the knob of the deadbolt, got as far away as he could — about twelve feet — yelled "Opening!," and yanked the rope taut.

The deadbolt slid open.

In the van, Karndle turned to Edward. "One of the most common booby traps we've seen is deadbolts wired up to be explosive switches." On the screen, agents slammed the door open, and the dogs were brought back down and sent into the small room.

The room was empty except for several suitcases piled to make a sort of stage, upon which was a chair. On the chair was what looked like a burlap bag of potatoes.

"If that's the painting, it's been rolled up," Mackinnon said.

Pinned to the burlap was a cassette tape in a clear plastic bag. And then one of the dogs started barking, lunging up on his hind legs at the burlap bag, and all three agents cleared out of the room. Karndle touched the button on his headset: "What the hell kind of bomb dog reaction is that —?"

And then, over the radio came a voice from inside: "Something in that bag moved; it spooked the dog —"

"Retire that dog!" Karndle yelled.

"Going back in" one staticky voice announced. The camera reentered the room, an agent came in with the fluoroscope equipment, and the weird blue image came up again on the screen.

Skeletons. Perfectly articulated living skeletons moving and struggling and shoving each other in and out of focus. It was Martin who said it first:

"If the van Gogh is in there, it's fucked, because that bag is filled with live rats."

It took a while to properly install the sleeping child in the room Bill had thrown together at the end of the subway tunnel. Bill tucked Theodore Mackinnon into the sleeping bag, arranged the pillows under his head. Then he booted up the computer on the table, set the screen so the boy could choose a game to play once the drugs wore off. He dumped a bag of candy bars onto a tray, put them close by, then just watched the sleeping child, television images of playful babies and happy children jammed in his head. And then, looking down at the boy, the thought bubbled up: *I wonder how you'd cook one of these.*

Not much meat on the arms; you could stuff the chest; corn bread and cranberries. Legs you could probably get steaks. The thought was funny; it made sense at the same time it didn't.

After all, he had the painting and the kid; he could slip through this little crack in time, confound everybody. The more he looked at the sleeping child, the more he knew: I could do anything, right now.

Anything at all.

All right then, he thought. What do I want to do?

The little room was crammed with technology — two turntables and two CD players and two tape machines and a big black microphone suspended from a metal fixture, pushed away from Erik's chair. There were records on both turntables, one spinning and one cued, Ella Fitzgerald singing 'Soon' out over the airwaves.

"I was so angry —" Sharon caught her pale reflection in the studio glass, tried to not think how terrible her hair looked. "And then, all that money dropping on these homeless people —"

"I wish I'd seen it," Erik said.

"It's like a party out there tonight," Sharon said. They smiled, their kneecaps just barely touching, and he looked at her a moment too long, turned to the console, and busied himself with the segue into the next song.

"Any ideas? More jazz? Or something else?"

"More of the same," she said. "I like this."

He flipped through records, pulled one out, slapped it on the turntable and noisily cued up a track, swinging the record backwards with his hand until the needle hit the dead space between songs. She stood, watching over his shoulder. When he turned back to her, his chair bumped her thigh.

"Sorry!" He was nervous.

"I've never seen anybody actually do that — all my years of radio listening —" She stepped back.

"Romance of radio. It seems trivial compared to what you do."

"What I used to do."

"What you did today —" They were staring at each other, he sitting, she standing up, saxophone curling into smoky trails around them. Finally he stood, and said, "I'm not very good at this," took her in his arms, kissed her lips, and Sharon's long fingers pulled him closer; he tasted good, and his lips were really sensual, her tongue dancing into his. She felt him breathing in her arms, his muscular back under the white cotton shirt. Sharon's heart was soaring; this all felt obviously wonderful, they didn't want to stop, and then he did. He pulled back, but not away.

"I've been wanting to do that since the first time you walked in here —"

"I would say that was fairly mutual," Sharon said.

"I — I sort of keep thinking about you — I mean, all today, all yesterday —"

The smile spread on Sharon's face. She tried for words, didn't have them. "I can't even say," she finally said.

"I have a girlfriend," Erik said, and Sharon froze. "She lives with me." Her arms were suddenly so tense they hurt. "She's having an affair with another woman."

They stood for a moment, inches away and not touching, Sharon measuring the swirl of her feelings. "Well," she finally said, and she knew it was a commitment, "now so are you."

"He's gone, Edward. They took him." Melissa Mackinnon's hands were useless to her, laying on her thighs like broken sticks. "I was waiting in the building, they took him, and now he's gone." Her voice was a shattered thing, patches torn from the high end. She closed her eyes, and they seemed sunken in their sockets, as if in an hour she'd aged forty years. And then one wrist began hitting the other, the bones bashing each other hard.

Edward Mackinnon held them to make her stop. "We're going to get him back." It was a hard thing to say; it sounded stupid after the wild-goose chase that hadn't led them to the van Gogh. "I swear to you, this will end. Ted'll be safe, we'll be happy. Melissa — I promise."

And then he held her, and something inside her cracked, and she began to cry for real, a keening wail, instantly familiar, though neither had ever heard it from her mouth before: bereavement and hopelessness exploding out of her, rising higher and higher with such longing that even the FBI men upstairs stopped what they were doing and just stood, listening.

Brassy, raucous horns cascaded out of the speakers in the small studio. Erik sat back in his chair, the headphones in his lap. "I mean, I don't just do late-night fill-ins when the FBI thinks I can help catch desperadoes. I'm here once or twice a week this late. I'm the station manager, I've got a sub-list three pages long — I don't have to be here, spinning records at one in the morning."

"But —?" Sharon asked.

"Well —?" Erik shrugged. "Go home and wait until she gets in: how'd it go? What's the story? Is it a lie or not — or, come in at two-thirty, have her be in bed, asleep, no questions. Or else a note — 'Market week — cranking until late — don't wait up —'"

"Sounds pretty awful," Sharon said.

"It wasn't, for a long time — the first year was great. And it's not like she wasn't totally open about — you know, that women were as important to her as men. That was okay from the start."

"You put up with it — it didn't threaten you —"

He considered. "I was in love with her," he said, simply.

"Are you now?"

He thought about it, and then he smiled. "No. Now, I'm accepting late-night fill-ins so I don't have to go home and face how bad everything's gotten."

"You could end it —"

"I've sort of been working my way towards that — I've been thinking a lot about it in the last month or so. I've even been thinking of seeing someone —"

Sharon didn't like the way that sounded. "Like, another woman, or —"

"Like a therapist," he leveled. "I mean I did that when I was younger — I kind of didn't want to get involved with it again."

"I know what you mean," she said. "Sometimes it's wonderful, sometimes less so. But when your relationship isn't working, it can be hard to extricate yourself —"

"Not so hard," he looked right at her. They weren't touching, not even their knees, their chairs cramped together in the tiny studio.

"Did you think you'd marry her?"

He measured his words. "I thought we'd get there. I thought —" The song was ending. He turned to the equipment, flawlessly segued from the record to one of the CD players. Meditative oud music strummed gently, topped by a wandering oboe. "You know, it's not going to happen with her," he said then. "I've never allowed myself to see it. I mean, she's not going to commit, and at this point I don't want her to commit —"

Coltrane's sax cut in, dreamy and wonderful. Sharon forced herself to stand. "Erik, I have to go," she said, and the music suddenly seemed tinny. She hated herself as he hid his first reaction, which was hurt. "I've been so keyed up all day, I think part of me is starting to crash —"

"May I see you?" He was wiry and resolute behind his glasses.

"I'd like that."

He stood. "I'd like it too," he said, and then there they were kissing again, hope and promise everywhere between them. Slowly, they separated. "I have some stuff to do," he said.

She smiled, glad he'd said it. He walked her to the door, sax and oboe darting in the air about them, and she said "Goodbye" and he said "I'll call you," and they just stood there like idiots for a long moment, not going anywhere. Then she said "Well," and he opened the door and she went up the stairs past the guard and out into the night, the saxophone still playing somewhere in the back of her mind.

The cassette affixed to the burlap was a ninety-minute bottom-of-the-line TDK, just as the first had been. Edward, Melissa, Karndle, and five other FBI agents sat in the Mackinnon's white room. One was at a laptop, typing every word as the hearty male mechanical computer voice droned on and on from the speakers:

> **"As a developer, Mr. Mackinnon has littered the skyline**
> **with tall, architecturally unpleasant towers catering to peo-**

ple of wealth, without attempting any amelioration of the lives of working-class families whose homes he has displaced, whose neighborhoods he has upscaled, whose jobs and businesses no longer fit into Mr. Mackinnon's bourgeois vision of Manhattan.

"These people, however, are still in New York; they have moved to less expensive areas, and have thus created a demand for basic services in neighborhoods already strained beyond endurance.

"In these neighborhoods one often finds beautiful large buildings that once stood proud, whether they were factories, schools, or housing. Now they are empty, often dilapidated, awaiting either destruction or gentrification.

"One such building is the Lower East Side's Carnegie-Hayden Library-Lyceum Science Center."

"Goddamn that building," said Edward, shaking his head.

"Built as a library, gymnasium, and educational center, it has served, in its one-hundred-and-ten-year history, as a school, a military storage facility, a nightclub, and an arts commune. One section, the Annex, is still in use as a day-care center.

"This is the building that Mr. Mackinnon and his recently purchased company, Straythmore Security, Inc., want to tear down to build a prison. In fact, Mr. Mackinnon's plan for the Carnegie-Hayden represents a bold new step in urbanization of Straythmore's ultimate philosophy and goals. It is his marketing game plan for the company to find buildings like the Carnegie-Hayden in other neighborhoods and cities throughout America, large "white elephant" sites in inexpensive communities, to show their privatization scheme's break with the past and ability to forge a new future. But the people who live in these areas can only regard such actions as an insult — a racist corporate occupying force which feels their neighborhood isn't good enough to get landmark status for an old building, much less turn it into a desperately needed school, hospital, or commerce center. Adaptive reuse comes easily to lesser buildings in wealthier neighborhoods. And the callous disregard of the history of the Carnegie-Hayden that this plan represents flies in the face of the peculiar character of this part of the city, its traditions and its future.

"Many plans have been put forward over the years to return the Carnegie-Hayden to its original function as a health and education center, but these efforts have been stymied by developers who used it as a hedge against taxes and allowed it to crumble. The best plan, by general agreement, is the so-called Father Digby Plan, promulgated by an ad hoc committee operating under city council charter in 1969.

"Universally acknowledged at the time as a bold answer to a troubled community, the Father Digby Plan languished for lack of funding, and eventually faded into unjust obscurity.

"Until now.

"This party is now in possession of (1) Mr. Mackinnon's van Gogh painting, *Portrait of Captain Merseult*; and (2) The quite living personage of Mr. Mackinnon's five-year-old son, Theodore.

"This party demands the following actions be taken to secure the freedom and safety of these two particulars.

"1. The painting shall be released into the custody of Sharon Blautner, RN, of 327 East Twenty-fifth Street, Manhattan. Ms. Blautner is in no way an aider or abettor of this party, and is merely being used in this transaction as a personage of honesty and truthfulness known to both Edward Mackinnon and this party.

"2. Ms. Blautner will then supervise the selling of said painting on the open market, at auction, in the upcoming Major Impressionist sale at Christie's auction house, to the highest bidder. The painting will be given freely for sale by

Mr. Mackinnon and his heirs and assigns, and signed papers furnished offering proof of that free act in perpetuity throughout the universe. The painting will be offered with a buying-in figure of fifty million dollars; if that is not attained, the painting will revert to the possession of Sharon Blautner and another attempt will be made to sell it, at an auction house and in a country of her choosing, until the fifty-million-dollar minimum is attained.

"3. All funds raised at auction will be held in trust by Sharon Blautner, in whatever manner she chooses. The sole purpose of the monies raised will be the implementation of the Father Digby Plan.

"4. A fair market price shall be negotiated by Mr. Mackinnon and the city of New York, the current owner, for the purchase of the Carnegie-Hayden. Before the city took it over for back taxes, it was appraised by Derrick Giannelli Associates for $725,500.00. Ms. Blautner will make one million dollars of the painting's proceeds available for this purchase. Any difference between the purchase price and one million dollars will revert to the trust held by Ms. Blautner. The building must be purchased within one week of the auction, or Theodore Mackinnon will be harmed.

"5. The remainder of the money will be spent on the conversion of the Carnegie-Hayden into the medical and emotional crisis center specified in the Father Digby Plan, version 8, dated 4/4/71. This document includes architectural renderings for the conversion; these will, with modernizations, be utilized.

"6. The day that the third phase of construction is begun, as specified in the Father Digby Plan, with no hidden legal impediments, will mark the day Theodore Mackinnon is released in good health. This can take as little as two months. Any attempt to block, thwart, or disrupt any aspect of this plan, either before or after release, will result in the death of Theodore Mackinnon.

"Once again, this party absolves Sharon Blautner of responsibility for any events at Bellevue, the theft of the
painting, the destruction of other property, or the kidnapping of Theodore Mackinnon. These actions are the sole
responsibility of this party.

"This is the end of the recorded section of this tape; the
rest of this tape is silent."

Edward and Melissa sat on the couch saying nothing, dazed into
silence. Finally Edward looked at Martin.

"He's insane," he said simply.

Martin Karndle cleared his throat. "I know what you two must
be feeling now —"

Melissa Mackinnon leveled her green eyes at him. "You have
absolutely no idea."

"Melissa —" Ed said. "It's very important we work together as a
team."

She took a long deep sigh. "Right," she said. "Of course. It
doesn't help." But there were tears in her eyes.

"Martin —" Edward turned to Karndle. "What do you say we
do?"

"Well, it's rough — because what we've already learned about
Bill is, he doesn't allow two-way communication."

"And he has our son —" Melissa paled.

Edward Mackinnon took his seat behind the antique desk.
"Melissa, call Gregor Fontin, tell him we need to get to the head of
Christie's — I've met the man, Cedric something —" Melissa rose
from the couch, pulled a portable phone off the coffee table, held
it in her hands without dialing. "Martin." Mackinnon looked at
Karndle. "There's a phone in the study, I'm sure you want to get
your men under way —" Martin nodded, left with his men.

"Eddie — what are we going to do?" She held the phone as if
she had never seen one before, had no idea what it did or how it
worked.

"We're going to do everything this guy wants. We're going to
get the van Gogh, we're going to sell it, we're going to start to

build the fucking hospital, and when Theodore is released, we're going to turn around and crush this asshole so hard, no one will ever touch our boy again. Melissa — trust me. I've got a plan."

Sharon took a cab back to her neighborhood, paid the driver and got out, and then abruptly two men stepped out of a car.

FBI agents. Christ, what now? "Hi, guys," she said, trying to keep it breezy. "Catch Bill?"

"'Fraid not, Sharon."

"Edward get the painting back?"

The blond one shook his head.

Oh, God. "What happened?"

"May we ask you to come uptown with us? There've been some complications in the case —"

"Guys, I'm totally exhausted. Can't it wait —"

"I'm afraid not, Ms. Blautner. Special Agent Karndle requested to see you immediately."

"Something bad happened."

The agent said nothing, virtually an acknowledgment. He stepped to the car and opened the door.

Sharon stood for a second, debated going upstairs and calling Martin. And then she made the connection. "Uptown."

"That's right."

"Edward Mackinnon?"

The two agents looked at each other. Before they answered she started walking to the car. "All right all right all right," she said. "If he were dead we'd be going downtown, right?"

She got in the car.

Sharon put down the transcript of the tape and looked over the coffee table at Edward.

"Edward — Melissa — I'm so sorry."

"When you were so helpful to him at Bellevue, did you talk about this with him, too?" Melissa's voice was ragged.

Sharon felt the anger and irritation start, but she checked it, just the way she would on the Psych ER with a particularly needy patient. She took a deep breath and straightened her back.

"The first seizure my son Charley had after the car accident was at his father's funeral. For four months, until he died, I took him from specialist to specialist, totally out of control, totally powerless, unable to protect my child. I swear to you, Melissa, I would never ever subject anyone to that nightmare."

Melissa's face reddened slightly, but she was listening. "Melissa, Bill chose me as the go-between because he knew I wouldn't do anything to muck it up." Not just why. She sat back, pressed the ramifications out of her mind. "You'll get Ted back, we'll stop him, everything will be fine."

Melissa Mackinnon had begun to cry. "I'm sorry, Sharon —" Her eyes were brimming with tears. "I'm not being really effective here. I'm sorry." She stood, left the scotch someone had poured her on the table. "I think I need to be alone for a bit." She walked out. Edward rose heavily and followed her, shutting the door behind them.

Sharon looked at Martin. "So the whole thing at the bridge today was just smoke —?"

"Bill Kaiser's special brand."

"Hoo boy," she said with a sigh, and shifted forward. "Okay, just you and me — how are we going to handle this? There's no room to negotiate, if the cops find him, you endanger Ted —"

Sharon stopped midbreath as the door opened, and Edward came back in, dropped down on the couch. "Sharon —" he said. "I know I speak for both of us when I say we appreciate everything you've done, today, all week — you've been amazing. I know we had that fight earlier —"

"Not a problem," Sharon said.

"What are your thoughts on all this? You know him better than anyone —"

"Honestly?" Sharon picked up the transcript of the tape. They weren't going to want to hear this. "Often, when a child is kidnapped like this, people wind up paying the ransom, yes?"

Martin fielded it. "More than we like to admit. But yes. Usually we can make the arrest based on the ransom payment — that's where the perps have to deal with the world outside their little scheme, and that's where we get our best results."

"Well, Edward, he's not asking for money, he's asking for action. So, if we follow that model, you've got no choice but to complete the circuit, dance the dance he's taking you on. Today he showed you can't communicate with him, and you can't buy him out. So Edward — how do you feel about turning your prison into a hospital?"

XXII

An hour later, driving Sharon back through the night to her apartment, Martin Karndle was explaining how it was going to be. "Your life is going to totally change. You're going to have twenty-four-hour coverage — that means an agent living with you at all times, going everywhere you go. And we'll see if we can't rent or sublet an apartment in the building, make a base of operations right there."

"Well, you've been keeping tabs on me —"

"That was not as high-priority. This is a totally different thing. This is an agent-in-place at all times. You go to the bathroom, she'll be with you. She'll watch you sleep."

Sharon looked at him. He looked so obviously drained, she felt like asking if he wanted her to drive.

Instead, she took a deep breath. "Martin, I've got to tell you something that you're not going to like." And she explained about Ekaterina.

His scowl grew deeper and deeper, and finally he interrupted her. "You should have come to us."

She debated various responses; they all seemed paltry. "I thought I could handle it," she finally said.

"Sharon" — at first she thought his tone seemed kind — "if you ever pull a stunt like this again, I will fry you in ways you did not know you could be fried. Do you understand?"

*   *   *

After Karndle's reaming, Sharon had expected the agent spending the night in her apartment to distrust her. But the minute she met Special Agent Fiona Conlin, she instantly felt comfortable: the girl wore glasses and looked like she belonged in a library, handling rare manuscripts. They'd talked late into the night about the case, and then about men and relationships and — Fiona brought it up — falling in love on the job. But even so, when the agent pulled a chair around the corner to read and Sharon finally went to bed, she lay awake staring at the ceiling for a long time, trying to figure out how in hell they were going to save that child.

The damn box was huge, it was taking up most of the coat-check room, and it had been pissing Marcia off all morning. It should have been simple, being a coat-check girl at the Russian Tea Room. Just look good, and match coats with their numbers. And she'd seen all sorts of celebrities and flirted with lots of attractive power-lunching executives. Not a bad job for an unemployed actress: she worked lunches, and somebody else covered dinners. So somebody must have left this box here last night. But who?

Three foot by four foot by eight inches, large and flat, planks and plywood. Finally she couldn't stand it any longer; she looked out over at Lawrence, prepping the bar. "Lawrence, I have a question about this box —"

"Right there," the older man said, and stepped across the luxuriantly carpeted aisle. "What's the problem, hon?"

"I came in this morning, this — thing was here, I don't know what it is, who left it, but I need space for the lunch crowd."

Lawrence opened the half door, came in. He took out his reading glasses, perched them on his nose. "Well," he said, "all I'm seeing is a phone number, stenciled on the side here, we might as well dial it."

In the van downtown, Sharon was regretting that she hadn't even had the chance to shower. But she was grateful something — anything — had happened. And then, once again, the audacity of it made her smile: how the hell did he get the van Gogh into the coat-check room of the Russian Tea Room?

Fifty-seventh off Seventh was filled with plainclothes cars and vans when they got there. Sharon hoisted herself into Martin's van, watched as the X-ray equipment revealed the box's contents, the ghostly countenance of the steamboat captain appearing on the blue screen for a fleeting moment, like a face materializing under-water, before the screen went blank.

From the radio: "No obvious wires, clear to this point, over."

Martin looked at Sharon. "This is where we deviate from the directive. Bill said to take it to Christie's. And we will — after we take it down to the lab, look for prints, hair and fiber, a sweat drop, anything we can find."

"Well, those weren't his instructions —"

"You have nothing to say to this, okay?"

Sharon stopped, surprised at his vehemence. And then she col-lected herself. "Martin, I'm sorry, but my directive is to stay with the painting until it gets to Christie's."

"Sharon, that's not necessary."

"Martin, that's my job. I'm not going to let anybody say I fucked this up. That's the deal: I stay with it until the end."

Man, Bill was thinking, this was going to take forever. Theodore Mackinnon had been screaming at the top of his lungs for four hours; finally he had yelled himself out, and his voice was hoarse.

"Ted, do you have any pills or shots that you get regularly?"

No response.

"If you help me here, I'll get you some ice cream."

No response.

"Come on, Ted — any pills or shots?"

Finally the boy gave in. "Lucretzia gives me vitamins."

"Lucretzia does just about everything, huh?" No response. "Okay, vitamins. Do they come in glass bottles, from the store?" Bill held up a vitamin C jar. "Or little plastic ones like this?" He shook a prescription drug vial with a childproof cap.

The boy stuck out a straight arm at the glass jar.

"How about these?" Bill rummaged in his bag, came up with a brown glass prescription cough syrup bottle and a plastic syringe. "Do you ever get any of these?"

The boy looked at the syringe. "At the doctor's," he said.

"But never at home?"

"Nope. Is my mommy coming here?"

"Any special foods they give you? Or anything that makes you feel bad when you eat it?"

Theodore Mackinnon sized up the man before him. "They give me chocolate and peanut butter."

"That's all you eat?"

"And swordfish and bacon and caviar sauce."

"Over and over? Every day?" The boy nodded. Bill smiled pleasantly. "I don't believe you for a second," he said.

The boy's face turned slowly into a mask of tragedy, and a noise emitted from his mouth that got louder and louder, and then even louder than that.

Bill waved his hands. "All right, all *right!*" The volume crescendoed in the small space. Bill covered his ears. "SHUT UP!" he yelled so fiercely, the child was instantly quiet. An echo of the noise reverberated in the room.

"You'll get bacon, you'll get chocolate, you'll get all the peanut butter you can eat. You work with me, I'll even do swordfish. You figure out the computer yet?"

"I want Dynographix."

"Dinosaur game? If you're good, maybe." He brought out the box he'd been saving for last. "But I have a present for you."

The box was old, the cellophane ripped and crumbling, but Bill had spent twenty minutes with the multimeter, making sure all the parts still worked. Ted didn't say a word. "This was my favorite toy when I was your age." The kid turned his head slightly to watch him. "It's one of the only things I have from my childhood."

"It's all old." Bill knew this was meant to be a put-down, but he didn't mind.

"It is old," Bill said. "And valuable." He opened the box, took out the black steam locomotive. He'd always admired the detail on the thing, the delicate metal rods that turned the wheels; the boy expressed not very much interest. Bill began hooking the pieces of track together. He had forgotten what a pain it was to align the segments so the electrical contacts all touched, but finally he'd made a respectable figure eight about six feet in length. He put the locomotive on the track, plugged in the transformer, turned on the control box.

The black locomotive pushed forward a few inches and stopped.

Bill picked it up, realigned it, tried again, and was rewarded by the sight of the little engine chuffing surely around the track. Ted, lying on his stomach on the bed, watched it go, his thumb in his mouth. Finally, the boy sat up, watched attentively.

"Not bad, huh?" said Bill, and turned to the box to investigate the condition of the other cars.

Ted stood up, took three steps, and kicked the locomotive high against the rock wall. It cracked and shattered and fell on its side. Bill looked up, startled; the boy leaned forward, hands balled into fists, waiting for something to happen.

Bill rose heavily to his feet, crossed the room, and picked up the broken engine. He held it, investigating the damage. A long crack across the engine, and the cowcatcher had shattered, and the wheels were busted. Bill looked at Ted, who was waiting, tense with expectation.

He was a kid. That's all he was. He was a kid in a difficult situation, and Bill found it amazing he'd had the guts to act out at all.

Bill set the locomotive down, leaned back against the mini-fridge. "Ted, it's just you and me here, so get this straight." He kept his voice low, stared directly into his eyes. "Treat me with dignity, I'll treat you with dignity. You know what 'dignity' means?"

The boy sat down on the bed, gulped, nodded up and down.

"We have to work this out," Bill said. "This can all actually be fun. But only if we respect each other, okay?"

Ted sat, watching. Bill shoved the track haphazardly back into the box, sighed heavily as he stood with it under his arm, stepped out and locked the door. As he walked toward the tunnel exit, behind him he heard the boy start crying for real.

*   *   *

When they got to the FBI building, Martin tapped Sharon on the shoulder. "My office. Now," he said.

She followed him down the hall. He held his office door open for her, and then slammed it. "I just want you to know that Ekaterina von Arlesburg flew to Switzerland last night. Interpol is trying to track her movements, but they may have already lost her." He shook his head. "You watch this shit, or I'll nail you for aiding and abetting a fugitive. Got that?" He opened the door before she could say anything, walked out ahead of her. "Don't think I won't prosecute, either, because I will," he said then, in front of the other agents in the office. "You want to be with the painting, get your stuff and go to the lab."

The FBI's rubber gloves were different from the rubber gloves Sharon had used at Bellevue: thicker, greenish, less prone to ripping, more expensive. She sat in the corner of the lab, in the chair they'd specified for her, in gloves and a surgical mask and a white clean-room suit, under the fluorescent lights.

First they X-rayed the wooden box. Then they photographed it. Then they checked the box for fingerprints by skimming laser light across it. They lifted several, with brush, powder, and tape. None matched the prints Bill had given at Bellevue. Sharon had expected them to open the box now, but they didn't. Two agents in hair nets and masks took an excruciating time poring over it with lenses and tweezers, looking for tiny filaments of fiber. Of the several they collected, a few would be found to be appropriate to rubberized cotton work gloves.

Sharon's stenciled phone number had been painted with silver radiator paint. The hair and fiber guys paid special attention to the area around the number; tape used to hold the stencil during painting might have left a slight layer of adhesive, just enough to trap microfibers. But evidently no such tape had been used.

They looked at the nail heads. They cast impressions of the round marks the hammer had made in the soft wood. Then they had long conversations about how the box had been put together; finally they agreed the box's maker had been right-handed, that he had used at least two kinds of nails, and that the stenciled panel they'd decided was the front piece had been the last section put into place. Then they took the front panel off, nail by nail, in as close an approximation as possible of the reverse order of construction.

Sharon stood to watch as they lifted the lid, as the light hit the van Gogh. There, looking mournfully up at the ceiling from the floor of the lab, was the wise, honest face of Captain Merseult. Sharon was not expecting to be emotionally rocked by the painting, by the greens turning to yellows on the bridge of the man's nose, by the swirling haze of purples behind him. But the minute she saw it something welled up in her throat, and she was caught on the edge of how beautiful it was, how tormented and tragic. Vincent van Gogh, the hard, sad-eyed steamboat captain, and somewhere out there, Theodore Mackinnon, a five-year-old boy, alone and no doubt terrified. Even the agents in their gloves and hair nets spent the moment gazing at the painting.

One of the agents opened a shiny metal suitcase, took up a scanner hardwired to a small computer screen. He straddled the painting and moved the scanner slowly over it. There was a beep, and everyone crowded around the monitor. "It's the real thing," one agent said. "Right where it should be."

"Microchip embedded in the painting," an agent explained. "Latest thing with art objects. That way we know it's not a fake."

Sharon stood for a moment thinking of Bill Kaiser's preoccupation with microchips. At this point, she wouldn't have been surprised if he'd embedded his own.

Bill sat back with his feet on his desk and watched the closed circuit feed from Ted's cell. Currently the boy was firing at video aliens, explaining the game as he played to an invisible presence to make himself less lonely.

God, Bill had done that. Endlessly, in his own childhood. The perpetual eye-in-the-sky camera that he had constantly imagined dogging his every footstep, recording his every thought and muscle movement for — for what? For posterity? For retribution?

And now, here he was, creating for this profoundly irritating boy the precise internal imaginings of his own childhood: constant, purposeless monitoring, trapped in a reality he did not make.

Bill peered at the black-and-white image on the monitor and considered the notion that he was watching the tapes he had assumed back then they were making of his own childhood: a little kid alone in a room, playing with electronics, humming to keep the silence from teeming up around him. And then he gulped and squirmed slightly at the surreal corollary: that the boy he was watching was, in fact, himself.

He'd always wondered what his own limits were. This little experiment, he could plainly see, was beginning to test their ends.

XXIII

They arrived at the auction house at ten that night; the huge door glided open, the two vans rolled to a stop at a loading dock, and then everyone waited for the door to shut before making a move to get out. On the dock were three men and two women, all in power suits, and a couple of workmen for the heavy lifting. Sharon was so preoccupied with getting the now rewrapped and recrated van Gogh out of the van that she didn't even notice Edward Mackinnon until he was almost on top of her.

He looked terrible, gray and almost shrunken in his suit. "Sharon —" He shook her hand with both of his.

"How's Melissa holding up?"

His smile was pale. "Sometimes I'm strong, sometimes she is. We trade off."

That stopped Sharon. She hadn't expected him to be so nice.

They lifted the crate onto a dolly, and the whole crowd of FBI agents and Christie's employees marched in a parade behind it. Edward gestured for Sharon to go first, and they followed the group into a huge double-height elevator large enough to be a studio apartment. They descended, the door opened, and everyone filed out through a keypad-locked steel security door into a workroom. Sharon watched, fascinated, as the new wooden crate was deftly opened by two workmen in a matter of moments and the van Gogh was taken out.

Edward Mackinnon stepped up, looked hard at several areas on the canvas, and then sighed and turned away. A scanner confirmed that this was indeed the real painting, with the microchip hidden in the correct location. Then the vault door was opened and the painting ceremoniously taken inside for storage.

Sharon found herself standing next to Edward. "I feel like I should follow it," she said. "Stay with it all the way."

"Not necessary," said a tall, bald man next to Edward. "Couldn't be safer, now."

Mackinnon looked up. "I'm sorry — Cedric Buford, president of Christie's — Sharon Blautner." Sharon shook hands with the dapper man. "His assistant," Edward went on, "Lamont Freyer." This was a thin-lipped man her own age in an elegant suit.

"Tell me" — she rubbed the scar under her chin — "How are you going to publicize this? The auction's in five days —"

"There are only a very small handful of people in the world who can afford a painting of this caliber," the thin-lipped man said. "We've already notified a number of interested clients that the van Gogh will be up again."

"Unfortunately," the bald man sighed, "the press is rather going to have a joke, I fear, at Mr. Mackinnon's expense."

"Not the first time," said Edward with a shrug. "Besides, they don't know the real deal."

Sharon shook her head. "They're going to speculate like mad. You made the papers when you bought it, you're going to make the papers even more when you sell it — right?"

Edward Mackinnon looked up at the ceiling, scratched his neck. It was a gesture that suddenly seemed intimately familiar to Sharon, something he'd probably been doing all his life. "We managed to keep the gallery incident away from the press. The event yesterday at the bridge — the FBI got the three major papers to keep it small, say we were filming a TV commercial."

"I caught that."

"Major media usually plays along in ongoing kidnappings. But we have every reason to believe the stock'll take a hit tomorrow —

people are going to think I'm selling it to get out of a shortfall, re-capitalize the companies."

"My God," Sharon said. A whole other aspect of what Bill set in motion that she hadn't even considered.

"Yeah, we've got a huge shareholders meeting coming up next month." Mackinnon shook his head. "First things first. We'll attend to all that when we get Ted back. Right now — my kid —" His voice floundered, suddenly untrustworthy, and he turned away.

Sharon watched him, this grim, exhausted man, frighteningly close to tears. She wanted to reach out and touch his arm.

But she held back, because she knew this wasn't just anyone.

This was Edward Mackinnon.

And, once upon a time, he had not reached out to her.

From Sharon's vantage point, in a booth on the second floor, the crowd was packed and restive. The auction had started late; because Bill Kaiser enjoyed ruining artworks, the entire building had been scoured carefully by the bomb-search team. Nothing had been found. The audience had been metal-detected, the machine's sensitivities torqued up high enough to be triggered by pens and belt buckles, and the resulting lines had turned well-dressed New York socialites into fulminating smudge-pots of invective. Several licensed handguns had turned up, and one sword cane, antique but quite lethal.

Lamont Freyer stood at the podium, organizing the stately matching of paintings and money. Flanking him on either side were six well-groomed young men and women at telephones, covering bidders unable to attend the proceedings. The FBI had been worried that Bill, or a confederate, would attempt to bid up the picture; Christie's had been more than helpful in letting them install tap and trace equipment on all incoming lines. In addition, there were FBI agents spread throughout the room, watching everything that moved.

Edward Mackinnon and Martin Karndle were in the booth with Sharon when the auction started. Melissa joined them halfway through. She kissed Sharon on the cheek, was bright and friendly, and even though Sharon liked Melissa, her professional training made her suspect strong antidepressants.

A large Cézanne that Sharon had fallen in love with during the preview was hammered down for seven million — "A bargain," Edward Mackinnon said rather sadly. A Braque that Sharon had thought boring went for eighteen, which mystified her. Various little paintings were ushered gently by the auctioneer to expensive new homes. And then, waiting for the final lot to be called, Edward had looked at Sharon with infinitely sad eyes. "If someone had just approached me reasonably —"

Sharon looked at him awkwardly. "I can see why Bill Kaiser might think it's an obscene amount to pay for a painting —"

And then the van Gogh was brought up by two workmen and set on the stand. Captain Merseult looked woefully out at his audience as the crowd hushed and the video lights went on and turned the room to a startling white.

Lamont Freyer gave the press a moment to do their work, then took the podium. "Lot 206, 'Portrait of Captain Merseult' by Vincent van Gogh —" he pronounced the "gh" hard and guttural, "Dutch Postimpressionist, painted in Arles in March 1889. Merseult was a ferryman at Arles; studies for this painting can be found in the Louvre. Merseult was painted by Gauguin, who suggested the subject to van Gogh, leading to the present instance."

"They're really showboating," Edward said. "The Sotheby's sale a month ago was much more discreet."

"Provenance — the painting was given by van Gogh to a nurse who tended him at the asylum at Saint-Rémy —"

"Really?" said Sharon, amazed.

"— stayed in her family until the 1950s, when it was sold to the American industrialist Henry Cabott Suckley. Sold by his estate in 1966 to Israeli cabinet minister Chaim Godwitz. Purchased from his estate last month by Edward Mackinnon, who offers it freely for sale today." Sharon glanced at Martin, who was looking straight ahead. "The painting is in very good to excellent condition. Ladies and gentlemen, I open the bidding at fifteen million dollars. Do I hear fifteen million dollars?"

Sharon's heart was in her mouth. Nothing happened at all that she could see. "Thank you," Freyer said. "Do I hear sixteen? Sixteen million dollars. Thank you. Seventeen. Eighteen? Eighteen. Nineteen million — twenty million dollars."

The tension in Sharon was such that she could barely breathe. She had her hands folded in an uncomfortable way, and her knuckles were bloodless and white, and all she could feel was her heart hammering like a racehorse.

"Thirty-eight five, thirty-nine. Thirty-nine five, thirty-nine five — forty million dollars. Do I hear forty million five hundred thousand —? Forty-one million. Forty-one five —"

It was like brain surgery, it was like a car crash in slow motion, it was like sex. It was unbearable, and it was fascinating.

"Forty-eight million, forty-eight five — forty-nine. I have forty-nine million — forty-nine five? I have forty-nine million five hundred thousand dollars —"

Edward Mackinnon leaned toward the glass.

"Do I hear fifty? Fifty?"

The crowd was hushed. "Fifty million dollars!" Over the speaker, they could hear a smattering of applause. "Bingo," Sharon said, "we made it." She watched two of the young women at the table behind Freyer hang up their phones.

She had been expecting a sigh of relief around her, an easing of tension, and was gently surprised that there had been none.

Edward Mackinnon leaned back in his chair and closed his eyes. He stayed in precisely that position until the final hammer came down, six minutes later, at sixty-seven million five hundred thousand dollars. Then he stood and walked stiffly out of the booth like a man who had just lost his last chip at a roulette table, his wife scampering after to keep up.

At that moment Cedric Buford stuck his bald head into the booth. "Mr. Karndle. Ms. Blautner?"

"Mr. Buford —?" Sharon asked.

"The men from the Justice Department are in my office. They're going to need you to sign some documents about giving them control of the money —"

"I'll do whatever's required," Sharon said, and got up without looking at Karndle.

Once Bill had heard what he wanted, he flipped the radio back from the all-news station to WHBN, listened for a long moment to the African tribal drumming. Then he took up the shopping bag and walked down the pitch-black hall into the subway tunnel.

"Ted, I'm coming in." Bill stepped into the cell.

The child began to bawl, his hands curled into tight Diane Arbus fists.

"Ted —"

The screaming became louder.

"Ted, I'd like you to look at me."

The child turned away, still screaming.

Bill reached into his pocket. "Want a piece of candy?"

The child shook his head no. Bill opened the Clark bar he'd brought, held it out before him.

The child slammed it across the room with one swipe of his arm. The violence of it took Bill aback; the screaming continued.

"Ted, I brought you Disney videos to watch."

The child fell down on the bed on his stomach, covered his head with his arms, and kept screaming.

"And a tape recorder to play with — would you like to play with the tape recorder?"

Ted kept screaming.

Bill had always thought he'd make a good father, but if this was how kids were, the survival of the human race was a complete mystery to him. He dug into his shopping bag, held up three tapes. "Any of these make you quake?"

The child screamed into his bed.

Goddamnit, Bill wasn't leaving. They had to figure out how to do this, and that was that. He considered the tapes, finally put one into the machine, hit play.

Ten minutes later, the boy quieted down. Five minutes after that, he shifted on the bed, so he could see the screen.

Ninety minutes later, Bill asked, "Which one would you like to see now?" and the boy said, "That one" and pointed at another. Bill popped it in.

Halfway through the second movie, Bill took out the tape recorder, started to play with it. When the movie ended, he let Ted play with the thing, make noises and play them back.

Then Bill pulled out that day's *New York Times*, put on his gloves, and opened a fresh cassette and said "Ted, how'd you like to help me make a tape?"

Martin leaned back in his chair. "What we're going to do," he was telling Sharon, "is this: as soon as Mackinnon closes on the Carnegie-Hayden, we'll get some bulldozers and cranes, whatever the bureau can get its hands on, and we'll send some agents down to make a great show of building a hospital. We've got two agents in hard hats down there right now, one guy with the little thing on the tripod, the other fifty yards away with the stick, leaving spray-paint surveyor's marks all over the street —"

"You're not going to be able to fake him out," said Sharon.

"We'll keep it up as long as necessary —"

"Three weeks? Two months?"

"Coupled with an interview in the *Times*, Edward Mackinnon saying he sold the painting to build this thing —"

"Martin — it's exactly what he thinks we'd do. I'd like to see an ad in the *Times* from the architects who did the original Digby studies, thanking Mackinnon for the chance to make their plans a reality."

Karndle smiled. "Good, good — I like it. If the architects agree to it — or if not, we could do our own fake office, set up a number in the ad so Bill can double-check it —"

"Or we could go down there, write a check as a retainer, and get them cracking on the job of updating and redesigning the plan. That's what he's waiting for — that's the circuit you have to complete. He's waiting to see how the updates are going to work."

Martin looked at her as if she were patently insane. "That won't be recoverable money, Sharon. You'll have to take that up with the Justice Department."

"I don't like this, Martin. It's my job to make sure that little kid stays alive, and I do not want to fuck it up."

"Sharon —"

"We'll try it your way for a week. When Edward Mackinnon starts breathing down your neck, trying to figure out why his kid isn't free yet, then we'll do it my way."

The envelope arrived at Sharon's the next afternoon; they didn't open it until they got it to the FBI. Inside was a tape. The lab boys took the original to analyze for physical and audio clues, forwarded a copy to Behavioral to infer Bill's state of mind, and brought another copy to Martin. By that time Edward and Melissa had arrived. She was prim, buttoned-up, holding it together.

The leader hummed, and then: "Congrats on the thirteen million dollars profit," the voice began. "The Carnegie-Hayden sure can use it."

"That's Bill," Sharon said. "That's him." Just hearing his voice galvanized something inside her; suddenly she had a complete picture of him in her mind.

"Consider this a reward," Bill said on the tape, and then there was a click, and the sound changed, and they were in a room.

"That intro was recorded over this," Martin said, and Melissa said: "Shhhh!"

"— ya doing, Ted?" Bill's voice said.

"Fine." The voice was high, a child's.

"Oh my God," said Melissa. Edward took her hand.

"What'd you eat for breakfast?" That was Bill. It sounded as if he was holding the microphone.

"Frosted Flakes." His "r"s sounded a little like "w"s. "You like the Cheerios, but that's not what we eat at our house."

"So I got you what you like to eat, right?"

"Uh-hunh."

"And what did we do today? Did we watch Captain Jack?"

"Captain Jack and the pirates —"

"Is that your favorite video?" No answer from the boy. "Okay, the front page of the *Times* today — what is this a picture of? Teddy? Teddy? Who is that?"

"The President."

"Shaking hands with someone — who's he shaking hands with?"

Martin pushed a copy of the previous day's *Times* across the table, for Edward and Melissa to see.

"Ummm — a woman," Teddy said, proud that he had the right answer to the question.

"A woman in a wheelchair — see, it's an article about disabled people. And then, underneath, it says, 'President meets protesters.' Anyway, that's enough tape-recorder fun for now." There was a flurry of noise, Bill fumbling with the microphone.

Teddy said, "What is the —" and then the sound cut, and was followed by the hiss of blank tape.

"Well, he sounds healthy," Edward Mackinnon said cautiously.

"He didn't know he was talking to us," Melissa said, her eyes swimming in tears. "Play it again," she said. "Please."

Martin hit the rewind, and Sharon began to feel that she was in some terrible group-therapy session that was never going to end, discussing questions that had no resolution, with people who felt they had all the time in the world.

Bill and Theodore had spent an hour making origami birds and animals, and now they were having a war, Bill lying on his stomach letting Theodore make up the rules: cranes could squash hippos because Theodore hadn't made a hippo, while Bill's tiger could eat cranes, but only if Theodore wasn't down to his last one. Theodore had just captured Bill's kangaroo with two tigers, when he said, "My daddy would never have let me come here."

Bill looked at the boy. "Is that bad or good?"

Ted was toying with his origami tiger. "Sometimes he, he doesn't let me do stuff."

"That's not so bad," Bill said. The boy just looked at him. "Sometimes he's probably right; sometimes he's probably wrong —"

The boy pounced his tiger onto Bill's hippo. "Rrrrrr," he roared. "Mine!" He took the hippo into his pile.

Bill smiled. Damnit, the kid had snuck up on him.

He had a way of doing that. Bill had had moments of picturing the child not wanting to leave when the time came. Sometimes he'd find himself thinking that this was his kid, his and Sharon's; he could just see the three of them walking with the boy along some sunset-lit beach in South America.

Raising the boy right.

To get there from here — that was a complicated issue. But not impossible. Because in fact, Bill knew: nothing was impossible, unless you made it so.

Bill considered his next move, looked at his animals, thought about how the Stockholm syndrome had never been applied backwards. Someone should do a study, he decided, of the effects of hostages on their captors.

XXIV

It had been a hard session of therapy, and when she left Dr. Solomon's office, her car was not where she had left it. She looked up and down the street, and finally recognized it double-parked by a mailbox. She walked the forty feet, and got in.

When the door closed, it made an odd noise, as if it had locked. "Hideo — back to the house, please," she said.

Bill looked at her in the rearview mirror. "I'm afraid that won't be possible for another hour or two, ma'am."

Melissa sat bolt upright, and immediately tried the door. Locked. She started banging on the dark-tinted window as Bill pulled into traffic.

"Ma'am, there's no reason to be difficult about this. Ted's fine, you'll be fine. I just want to talk."

"About what?"

"Well, first — hand up your purse. Any beepers, cell-phones, any wireless communication devices." She dropped her purse in the front seat; he dumped it out, found a cell-phone and pulled off the battery. "As you've seen, I've eliminated the door locks. And unless you have a bazooka on your person, the glass is shatterproof. You know, this car's famous — I've read about it in several articles, over the years."

"You're kidnapping me?"

"No, I'm borrowing you for a couple of hours to show you something. After that, you'll be free to go."

"Something's wrong with Ted. And you're taking me to him."

"No, and no. He's fine. I know you're concerned. I just want to show you what's at stake —"

"Besides my child's life."

"Right."

"What about Hideo — my driver? What have you done with him?

"He's downtown. He'll wake up in several hours."

"Bill — you know, we could end this right now. I'll make you a promise that the building won't be a prison, and you release Teddy —"

"I'm afraid that would be a very one-sided bargain."

"I know Edward. You're doing this the wrong way — it's no good getting him angry. It just stiffens his position."

Bill kept silent.

"We're heading downtown."

Bill didn't say a word.

"Please God, Ted's okay, isn't he? Tell me he's okay —"

"From the bottom of my heart, I'm not lying to you. He's fine."

"Because you could give up Ted, and take —"

Bill knew what was coming, and pushed the button to raise the soundproof glass between the driver and the passenger. Then, alone with his thoughts, he headed downtown.

"All right — so I see it." Melissa turned back around, unimpressed. "Behind us — the Carnegie-Hayden center. This is what you wanted to show me —?"

"You know, everyone says this building's completely abandoned. But it's not. Did you know that?"

"Well, yes, but I didn't really think —"

"There's a day-care center right across from us, it's actually part of the building — what was originally called the Annex. That's the entrance — the brown door. Been there for years."

"Really?" She was trying to play along with him, and acting badly.

"Indeed," Bill said, and then he saw what he'd been waiting to see. A plump dark-haired woman walked quickly in the cold evening, hurrying down the sidewalk toward the Carnegie-Hayden. Bill checked his watch; same time as the night before, and the night before that. "You see that woman?" Bill asked.

"Lucretzia!" Melissa banged the dark glass window with her hand, trying to attract attention, but the woman kept walking.

"Notice where she's going," Bill said. They watched as she climbed up the steps and pushed open the brown door. For a moment they saw lights inside, kids running around. Bill put the car in gear, glided up the street and turned uptown. "Where do you think Lucretzia puts her kid when she takes care of Teddy? Did you ever wonder that?" Bill asked, and for once the woman was silent.

Bill drove uptown, let her think. Finally he pulled over to the middle of a residential side street, no pay phones in evidence. He kept the battery to her cell-phone, crammed the rest into her purse, and handed it to her. "You can do day care when they're young, or you can put them in prison when they're older. Tell Edward that's the choice, all across the country. Now, you're five blocks from your house. Get out and spread the word."

The next morning, Sharon sat on the stoop in her coat and gloves, drinking coffee from a Greek diner cup through a triangular hole she'd ripped in the lid. Next to her was Fiona, in jeans and a windbreaker. Across the street was the Carnegie-Hayden. Wooden construction walls had been put up around it, topped with barbed wire. Square holes had been cut into each panel, so that sidewalk supervisors (and Bill Kaiser, should he come along) could see the work going on inside. A cement truck rolled its belly by the entrance next to a small trailer plastered with permits. Lights shone out the windows like on a movie set; guys with hard hats carried bricks up and down the main stairs.

"They're not dirty enough," Sharon said. "Usually construction guys wear clothes caked with plaster and concrete."

Fiona studied the men across the street. "Good point," she said, and scribbled a note. "Do you think they look busy enough?"

"I've never seen a New York construction site where they did," said Sharon.

"Damn straight. Now — you said you wanted to go inside?"

They stopped in at the trailer, were issued hard hats by the agent in charge. Then they climbed the steps into the Carnegie-Hayden. The ceilings were high, and the stairs were marble, with carved wooden balustrades. Yes, Sharon could see, with a great deal of money, the place would make a wonderful community health center.

"There's a swimming pool downstairs," Fiona was saying. "Total wreck, it's all filled with garbage. Imagine — a hospital with a swimming pool —"

"Lenox Hill has one," Sharon said. "You could do physiotherapy in it." Fiona looked at Sharon, didn't say a word. "Where's the grand auditorium that used to be that nightclub?"

"Upstairs." They took the marble stairs up to the second floor, crossed a long atrium, and opened a door. Caged bulbs on extensions had been hung in the French windows, to make the place look like work was being done. Sharon stopped, looked around, and after a moment realized her jaw had actually dropped in wonder.

The room was vast, wood- and marble-paneled, with a shallow proscenium stage in the back wall. "You could do a lot with this," Sharon said, finally. "Put in movable office three-quarter walls, leave a little space in front of the stage for presentations and staff meetings. It would be a nice place to work." Fiona just watched her. "I mean, if we ever got that far —"

"Big if." Fiona went to the door. "Come on; this is only about a third of the second floor. There's a gymnasium, and what looks like a bunch of classrooms — and then the day-care center, and the basketball court on the roof." Sharon turned to follow, but then her eye was caught by three columns of benefactors' names chiseled into each of the six large marble panels at either side of the entranceway. Each group of names was partitioned off by the Roman numeral for the year they had contributed. Astors and Morgans had all given money at one time or another. Sharon stood, thinking about a different, more civilized time, when a large public ballroom might be regarded as something in a community's interest. And then she saw the name, chiseled toward the bottom of the second panel, and suddenly she was dizzy; she ran her fingers along the letters cut deep into the marble.

"What?" Fiona said.

"Look." Under her fingers was the name: WLADISLAS CZOLGOSZ.

Fiona knelt, figured out the year — 1905. And then they found another Czolgosz, and another.

There'd been a Czolgosz on the board, evidently, from the very beginning.

"No wonder he doesn't want this building ripped down," Sharon said finally. "He's part of it, and it's part of him."

Bill sat at his desk, surrounded by three days of newspaper, a bologna, bacon, and cheese sandwich ready for Ted at his elbow. He was waiting for his tea to finish steeping, when he remembered he hadn't read the *Village Voice*'s gossip column. He flipped through, found it; halfway through, his heart started to pound.

> *. . . Tout le monde is speculating about Edward Mackinnon's whirlwind of activity. First came that bizarre broadcast at the recent Museum of Natural History benefit, against him building that prison he's so fired up about. Then the even more bizarre bridge incident, reported here last week, which Mackinnon's office claimed was a film shoot for an upcoming TV commercial. Now comes word from a very high source that Eddie and Melissa didn't see a dime off last week's record-setting van Gogh sale. The Justice Department went to the auction house and whisked it all away — though what they have against poor Edward, no one's telling. . . .*

Adrenaline burst in his chest, soured everything it touched.

He'd been betrayed.

His instructions had been explicit. He had intended Sharon to get the money.

They were fucking with him.

No more. He took a frozen container from the fridge, chose a knife. He grabbed a sealed cassette off the shelf.

They challenged him, he'd challenge them right back.

Out the door, down the pitch-black hallway, through the wall to the door of Ted's cell. He slammed the door open, ripped the plastic off the tape, slapped it in the recorder, and pressed it on. Then he grabbed Ted, held his head down tight — the boy was screaming — and ripped the knife through the back of his frilly costume shirt.

Ten-forty in the morning, and Melissa Mackinnon was at her desk, flipping through the Gucci catalog, avoiding the phone when it rang. She was sick of people; they kept asking, How are you? How are you? As if how she was made any difference.

As if it mattered one bit.

Dr. Solomon was concerned. He tried not to show it — he tried to act like having a child kidnapped in exchange for a hospital was the most common problem a girl could have. All he really ever fretted about was her intake of antidepressants — making sure she was always fully saturated. Well, she hated the things. Being depressed would be better than this stupid false elation, this eminent agreeability with the world. Her despair was real; there was no sense in hiding it.

She'd been impressed by Bill. But in her heart she knew that whatever his charm, they were in a war, and no subterfuge was out of bounds when her child's life was at stake. The thing of it was, Bill seemed somehow such a reasonable man. He wasn't, of course — but he had almost made sense, in a frightening kind of way. At her behest, both she and Edward had read the Digby Plan. In truth, it was a logical and sincere proposal. In another universe, perhaps, at another time, it might have gotten done.

Absorbed in her thoughts, she didn't see Edward until he entered her peripheral vision, and then she looked up, startled. He stood, uncomfortable, an ashen look on his face.

"A package arrived in the mail," he started. "From Bill. Addressed to you. The agents X-rayed it, and then — called me."

"And —"

"Melissa, I'm sorry."

"What is it?" Fear in her eyes.

"It's a tape. And — Ted's costume for the pageant, the shirt he was wearing, it's cut open and soaked with blood." And he crumpled to the bed, weeping.

Sharon got out of the cab and ran to Edward's front door; it opened as she reached for the bell. Martin was there. "Pig's blood. Not human," he said.

"What?"

"On Ted's shirt. Pig's blood. Frozen and defrosted, according to the lab."

Something in Sharon relaxed so suddenly, she thought she would cry. "So we have no reason to think —"

"So far as we know, Ted is okay. You'd never know it from the tape, though. He must have scared that kid something awful."

Not as bad as what he did to the parents, Sharon thought. She followed Martin up the stairs. Edward and Melissa were in the white room. They appeared utterly exhausted.

"I'm so glad to hear —" Sharon said, and Melissa just nodded.

"What's on the tape?" Sharon asked. "Can I listen to it?"

"I can't hear that scream again," Melissa said.

"He's such a bastard to toy with us —" Edward was angry.

Melissa stood abruptly. "I'm going to — make some calls." She walked out.

"What intrigues me," Edward said then, "is that he couldn't do it. In some measure, he didn't have the guts."

"He's killed before," Martin said. "Assassination. This was a warning. Sharon, you wanted to hear the tape —" Martin went to the machine. "This is a copy; lab's already faxed us a draft report on the original. The first tape was entirely computer generated. The second opened with Bill doing a prologue, and then revealed Ted. This one" — he swallowed — "begins midscene, shall we say. I warn you — it sounds bad. Ready?"

She nodded. He tapped the play button, stood uncomfortably with his arms folded.

The hiss of leader, and then a jumble of tape-recorder noise and an awkward sound of struggling, Bill saying, "No, hold it —" Ted howling with tears, and then, the boy's voice: "What, what — NOOOOOOOO!" A full-throttle scream, open and piercing.

Sharon grimaced, teeth clenched, as if she'd taken a punch. Martin stopped the tape. "You okay?" Martin asked.

"I know — it's there to shock. But it gets you."

"The next part was recorded over, without Ted in the room." He hit the button.

Another moment of Ted screaming, and then an abrupt cut. A quiet place, Bill close to the microphone. "The money was supposed to go to Sharon. You might think it's a small point; I'm sending you a small shirt. I'd say we're even. Since you've proven yourselves untrustworthy — new demand: I want a completion bond. Publish it as a supplement to the Sunday *Times*. I want specs, cost breakdowns, architectural plans, accounting sheets, everything. And I want a business plan that will apply Digby to all the other buildings Straythmore is considering. One week. Next time what you'll get in the mail will make the jump from porcine to prehensile." A click, and silence.

"Amazing how he keeps his discipline," Sharon said.

Martin hit the off button on the machine. "Engineering lab's having quite a time with it." He opened his notebook. "Recorded with a cheap mike, diminished frequency response, probably a few years old."

"Very helpful," Edward said, cold. "Forgive me, Martin, I've heard all this. I'm going to check on Melissa." He walked out.

Martin and Sharon exchanged a glance. "Go on," she said.

"Just like last time, the tape was recorded, and then a section was recorded over. On this as well as the last one, we actually have been able to rebuild the stuff underneath, looking for car noise, firetrucks, insects, anything."

"And —?"

"Nothing that easy," Martin said. "But the absence of any urban noise is actually rather interesting."

"Out of New York —?" Sharon asked. "In the country?" She shook her head. "He'd never leave Manhattan."

"Behavioral thinks that too. Okay, check this out — during the scream —" He gestured at the cassette machine. "You can barely hear it, but when they enhanced the original tape, equalized it through filters — there's bounceback."

"Like an echo —?"

"It's quite subtle, and he makes so much noise that it's hard to get, but it's measurable."

"Play it." He rewound the tape, hit play. The hiss of leader, and then Ted started screaming. Martin held his hand up, pointed at the ceiling when it came. Sharon nodded.

"It's tiny," she said.

Martin stopped the tape. "It's not a huge room, but obviously reflective —" he flipped a page in the report. "Probably rock or concrete walls, possibly tile."

"And a high ceiling." She closed her eyes, tried to picture. "Like the Oyster Bar," she said. "At Grand Central."

Martin frumped his lips. "That's noisier. This has a much faster decay. There's something — not cloth, more like wood — absorbing the sound."

"And no traffic noise," Sharon said, and looked up. "I'll bet you he's underground."

The book was a history of New York nightlife, and it was dauntingly thick. Sharon took a seat under the huge paintings in the main room of the Public Library, while Fiona worked the card room, searching the computerized index for other sources. Sharon opened the thick book randomly, read a little about the five versions of Delmonico's, then flipped to the index. She found Kaiser, and her heart sank: a substantial German population had settled in Yorkville on the East Side of Manhattan; at one time it must have been very popular to name your bar after the Kaiser.

Before tackling that, she flipped back a few pages and looked under "C," knowing full well that this would be a waste of time, that the whole attempt reeked of grasping at straws.

There, in the index, was "Czolgosz, Charley, 448." For a long moment, Sharon forgot to breathe. And then the excitement took over, and she flipped quickly back through the thick book, to 448, scanned the page quickly, looking for "Cz."

There it was.

> *One of the largest speaks on the lower east side, Cholly's, was owned by the colorful Polish gangster Charley Czolgosz, a man whose sartorial tastes ran to checkered suits. Cholly's, two stories beneath 236 E. 7th, was noted for its tunneled raid exits as well as its drink; its large room was said to hold fifty comfortably and five hundred less so. Charley liked to regale the crowd with stories about his cousin, Leon Czolgosz, the man who killed William McKinley; unlike many saloon legends, the connection may have been true.*

Sharon looked up from the book, and the lights around her seemed to shake with intensity; the room seemed different, clearer, as if the clouds had parted, as if someone had ripped off the top of her head and allowed the sun to pour in. She stood, took up the heavy book and her bag, and walked across the long room.

She could get Ted. Right now. Without the FBI. No helicopters, no body armor, no law enforcement to pressure Bill into shedding real blood. Just her and him.

The way it should be.

If only Charley had been this simple.

She turned into the card catalog room, and there was Fiona at a computer terminal completing her search, her back to Sharon, and for one moment she wanted to tell her, blurt out the truth. But she knew: if she went alone, she could solve this thing.

The circuit would be complete.

She ducked back into the big room, picked a random shelf just above the floor, and hid the thick book inside. Then, holding her bag, she walked confidently up to Fiona.

The shame of it was, she actually liked the girl. "Fiona, hi. Listen, I just have to hit the restroom a moment —" Sharon pointed out the door.

"I'll go with you."

"That's okay —"

"No — I'll join you." Fiona finished writing her last reference, and she and Sharon walked out, past the marble stairwells to the restrooms.

Walking, Sharon was on the verge of telling it all, letting it spill, but then Fiona said, "How was that book you found? Anything in it?"

"I'm not sure yet," Sharon said, and realized she was committed. They entered the bathroom.

"Because I found a couple of things that might help us —" Sharon stepped to a stall, watched as Fiona did the same. The agent actually had to pee.

"Great." Sharon, in the next stall, waited until Fiona took her pants down. She hated herself for doing it, but she knew: it had to be just Bill and her.

Finally the moment was right. Sharon stepped quietly but briskly out of the bathroom, and then ran for the stairs. She headed down, expecting any moment to hear her name echoing through the marble halls. The main floor, the security guard — damn. She took a left, went around the side to Forty-second Street, ran down the stairs and found an exit, showed her purse to the security guard, and she was out.

Eddies of wind wisped around her. She ran across the slate sidewalk, stuck out her hand. If Fiona caught her, she'd have a lot of explaining to do, and then the FBI would mount a full-scale military assault operation on Bill Kaiser.

She could avoid that. She knew she could, knew it in her bones.

A cab cut across three lanes, came to a halt, and she got in.

XXV

Now that she knew what she was looking for, Sharon was surprised nobody had ever questioned the dilapidated building bristling with cameras on East Seventh Street. But there it was — a five-story tenement, old people periodically shuffling about behind the upper windows. A camera on the roof, a camera overlooking the entrance, a camera, she could see, above the elevator at the end of the well-kept front hall.

It was as if Charley were in there, alive, unharmed, and all she had to do was go in and get him.

The building's inner door opened, and an old man in a debonair hat stepped through, leaning on his cane as he walked. Sharon hustled across, looked down the list of occupants by the buzzer.

A neat roll of press-taped names, most Russian-sounding, none she recognized. And then the man came through the outer door.

"Excuse me, sir, I'm looking for Bill Kaiser."

The man, in his eighties, wore a three-piece suit and well-shined shoes. He shook his head. "The name," he said, in accented English, "is not familiar."

"Bill Czolgosz?"

A long, slow pause. "Our superintendent is Mr. Czolgosz."

Sharon bit her lip. "Is he — good?" That came out weirdly.

The man made an expansive gesture. "He is superb. The building is immaculate." Sharon smiled. Of course, it would be. "Often he can be found in the basement."

Underground. Sharon thanked the man, accepted the open door, and walked the length of the hall, under the camera. The elevator opened when she pressed.

Inside it was beautiful, well-kept old wood and gleaming polished brass, with another small closed-circuit camera in the corner. She pushed B, nerves gnawing in her stomach as she descended.

The door opened onto a tidy little foyer, red paint shoulder-high and green paint above. "Bill?" she asked. If a tenant with a backed-up sink could get him, she could get him.

No answer; no sound from anywhere. She stepped into the laundry room. Above the washers was yet another closed-circuit camera swiveling gently back and forth. The red light was on; a wire went into the wall. She stood before it, staring up, not having a clue what to do next. And then she noticed that this camera had a microphone built into its body.

There it was.

"Bill?" She sounded timid and stupid and awful. She cleared her throat.

"Bill," she said, more emboldened. "I'm here to pick up Theodore." Like this was an afternoon play group. "Release him, Bill. The cops have no idea I'm here. You know as well as I do they'd've never let me come alone. And I am alone, Bill — check your other cameras. Please believe me."

Damnit, there was no way to know if he was watching. "They're going to come here, Bill. They'll have guns, and firepower, equipment beyond your dreams. They'll rip this place apart."

The unblinking red light of the video camera stayed on.

"I know you haven't hurt Ted, Bill. The pig's blood tells me that. You know there's no need to hurt the boy." Every instinct inside told her not to display any anger whatsoever. "What'll it take to free him? Do you want me? Because I'll exchange myself for Theodore. Look — I'm not wearing any weapons, Bill — just me, no guns, no wire recorders —" The camera stared down.

"Damnit, I'll show you." She pulled one arm off her jean jacket, and then the other, and she remembered Charley, the way she would have done anything.

Now she didn't push it out of her mind. She allowed herself to ride the calm certainty of her panic as she unbuttoned her black shirt, slowly, from the neck, slipped it off, and laid it on the cement floor before her. She shook her hair out, made no move to undo her bra. "Please, Bill, let me see you. Stopping Edward Mackinnon is a noble goal. With the Digby Plan, we can make the Carnegie-Hayden a model for any city, anywhere. We can do it together. Take me, Bill. Take me and give them Theodore."

She'd had him when she walked in. He'd been tempted just to turn on the intercom to the laundry room and answer her. Just her being there, something in him had melted — the earnest pleading of it, it had made him want to cry.

When she took off the jacket, laid it like an offering, the perfection of her every movement had almost seemed holy.

When she started to unbutton her shirt, Bill looked around his basement, his computers and clutter and work desk and the paintings on the walls and the unmade bed in the next room, and the sadness was thick inside him, arcing and twisting in his chest. He'd had this, he'd been happy here, and of course he'd spoiled it, played too high and mighty, and soon he'd lose it. She knew where he was.

It would become some kind of goddamn tourist site, a holocaust memorial, people filing through and pointing.

He remembered his old pubescent fantasies of satellites, of microchips in his testicles and constant computer tracking. It would have felt like this, he realized. It would have felt exactly the way he felt right now.

Sharon opening her shirt on the monitor. Why he needed to make his life like his worst nightmares, he didn't know, but — he could see it plainly — evidently he did.

That's when he'd left to get the canisters, two large, cool ten-gallon cans of gasoline next to a twenty-pound sledgehammer. He took the cans out, opened the first, walked through the basement, glugging clear distillate over everything, the smell roiling up, making him think of gas stations and sticky summer asphalt. Then he got the hammer, hoisted it up, and calmly and methodically began to smash his main computer to bits.

Sharon had begun to wonder what to do next. She'd needed to make a statement, force a level of intimacy as quickly as possible. Now, though, a sharp-edged debate was rearing up in her mind about whether or not she was actually engaged in any sort of communication with anyone at all, praying with all her might to a red light on the wall.

It wasn't enough. She felt too vulnerable and crazy without her shirt; she slipped it back on, left it unbuttoned, desperately looked around for some other way to reach him, some way that involved meeting him as an equal.

It was a nicer laundry room than the one in her building. Washers and double-stack dryers and chairs and a table with some old magazines, a large clean ashtray and a bowl of matchbooks. Somebody in the building smoked when they did their laundry, and that somebody had been planned for by the super. In the corner was a plant, one of those big green bushes that doesn't need much light. She reached out and touched a leaf. It was real, not plastic.

She looked at the camera, looked at the dryers, and then she had it.

Eight dryers in four units, each taller than her head. She looked between the units and the wall: each had two plastic accordion-pleat hot air exhaust pipes out, and two valved bendoflex natural gas lines into the machines. She pushed her shoulder against the first dryer, worried it was anchored to the cement floor, shoved it hard and it rocked back.

Perfect. She got behind the first machine, spent a moment unscrewing its two bendoflex pipes from the two valved metal gas pipes that came out of the wall. She ignored the accordion-pleat exhaust, got behind the dryer and started to push.

It weighed hundreds of pounds. She put her back to the wall, jammed her hands high against the machine, pressed with all her might, and then it slid and rocked and began to tip and she strained every muscle and finally it crashed to the floor with a terrifying slam, dust and dryer lint rising to the light fixtures. Sharon moved to the next, undid the gas pipes, and pushed it over — the noise was monumental; glass broke and steel dented and she didn't care. She crashed the third to the floor — that one nearly caught her on the shin, going down, but she'd jumped — and then the fourth.

The nice, clean laundry room looked like an earthquake had hit it.

Sharon looked up at the camera, and realized it had stopped moving. It was just staring down at her, the red light glaring.

Sharon opened the valves all the way on each of the eight gas pipes. The smell was dizzying, but she stood her ground. She grabbed a magazine, ripped out a page, and ripped fringes in it and held it in front of each gas pipe so he could see streaming movement from the dense, clear gas.

She went back to the bowl, picked up a book of matches, and opened it. She ripped out three, held them next to the striker.

"Show me where you are, Bill," Sharon said to the camera, "or I'll blow this nice building of yours to smithereens."

Bill had taken all his computer disks, upended the microwave, put them in, and set it for an hour. Within moments, microwave had touched metal, and sparks began to turn to fires beneath the glass. Then he had worked his way through the basement, sledge at his shoulder. He'd debated his bookshelves, all his rarities, then slammed them with the sledge and eight years of cross-indexed computer books and magazines came crashing to the floor.

He pulled the Pollock down off the wall, took up a long kitchen knife and cut it off its frame. He rolled it up, set it by the lab door.

He opened the second gas can, started splashing it all over the kitchen, brought it through the basement, over his books, his magazines, his smashed computers. The smell was virtually unbearable; it brought tears to his eyes.

He kicked open the door to the lab room, soaked the table with gas, poured spiraling rings around, out the door into the bedroom.

He set the gasoline down, took up the painting, and ran back into the lab. At the far end was his metal-frame backpack, loaded and heavy. Bill tied the Pollock on the side, hoisted the pack, slipped his arms into the shoulder straps, let the belt dangle.

Forty pounds of dynamite and five pounds of C-4. If he left it here, it would take out most of the block.

His head was swimming from the gas fumes; he felt he was going to drop and vomit. He pushed himself back into the office, and there was transfixed by the monitor. It surprised the hell out of him: Sharon was doing exactly what he was doing — wrecking the place. He pressed the button to stop the back-and-forth movement of the camera, waited to see how far she would take this.

All the way. He watched her with the matches in her hands and couldn't help but admire.

Well, he couldn't have the building upstairs fill with gas; that was too dangerous. He went to the east exit, punched in the code for the trapdoor lock. Somewhere above, the bolts rammed open.

Then he went to the intercom, pressed the button. "Turn off

the gas," he said into the microphone. "There's a hinged metal plate on the floor around the corner. Open it, and come down the ladder. And Sharon? Open a window before you come. You're scaring me."

Sharon turned the valves off, checked the ends of the pipes — no outflow — and then ran to the two high, barred windows and slid them open and breathed. The smell was noxious around her. She sucked in deep lungfuls of air, and then stepped back over the downed dryers, buttoned her shirt, and found the corrugated metal plate. She pulled it up, revealing a square cement-lined hole perhaps thirty feet deep, with a steel ladder bolted to one wall.

She climbed down into the darkness.

Bill opened the north exit, set his backpack against the wall of the pitch-dark hallway, and then heard her, banging the east door.

He walked quietly across the room, pressed his back against the wall next to the door, reached one hand to the keypad, and typed in the door's code. The bolts shot, and there, in the basement, a vision in the shimmering fumes, was Sharon.

He grabbed her, spun her around, pushed her up against the wall, his hand high on her windpipe, under her jaw. "God damn you." He looked her straight in the eye. "You should never have come."

"I had to — see you —" She thought he was going to take her apart with his bare hands.

"*God Damn You,*" he said again. He was furious, shaking his head. And then there was a moment of realization, she saw it in his eyes, and he said, almost amazed: "I'm going to have to kill you."

The quiet in his voice told her he meant it. "Why?"

There was water in his eyes. He reached over to the table, moved some papers, and abruptly there was the long kitchen knife in his hands. All at once Sharon had no saliva in her mouth. "Because this place is going to burn." He gestured around the room. "You destroyed it. And you're going to die with it."

"Where's Theodore?"

"He's safe. I planned for him. You betrayed me."

"I swear to God, I didn't —"

"Shhh — shhh — shhh—" he said, a father to a daughter. "I'm doing this for you, so you're not trapped in a superheated room, trying to crawl out of your own flesh —" And he put the knife hard to her throat, the muscles in his arm tightened, and he began to cut.

She couldn't breathe. She could feel a line of wetness as the knife drew her skin. Sharon could not believe it — not this man. Not the man she knew. Not the man she —

"Since when —" she said, "were you —" she said, "the body and breath of God?"

It stopped him.

"It's me, remember?" And she grabbed his wrist, forced it away from her neck, took the knife from his hand, and tossed it away. "First of all — I didn't betray you. If there were cops involved, they'd've never let me get this close."

"I meant about the money," Bill said quietly.

"That wasn't my choice. I have broken every rule to get here." She wiped the blood off her neck with her thumb, considered it for a moment, and then angrily smudged it on his cheek. "I'm not afraid of you, Bill. You and I, we complete a circuit."

"You don't know shit about any of that."

"Three patents. Unicorn Holding and Linnet. I talked to Liebling — he's dying in New York Hospital, if you care."

"I don't."

"I didn't think so. I even saw your senior picture. And —" The ace in the hole. "I talked to Kat."

He looked at her, and a thin grin spread across his features, and suddenly she was afraid, because everything about his reaction was wrong. "You don't know what she is," Bill said.

She didn't allow herself to be unnerved. "She's a monster. I'm not. *You're not.*" She took a breath. "Give me Ted."

He watched her for a long moment; finally, Sharon saw him make the decision: "He's safe, Sharon. He's fine. He's a hundred yards away."

"Don't burn this place."

"You were about to do the same thing, upstairs."

"I needed to see you. Why'd you stop me, if you were just going to torch it yourself?"

Bill pointed to the ceiling. "Twenty-five-foot firewall above us. Totally isolated from upstairs. No chance of burning the building."

"Just your little piece of it. Look, I'll be totally straight with you, I love the idea of Digby — a family crisis center that makes its money from the bars and music clubs in its building. That's free enterprise. I don't like the shit Straythmore Security has planned for this country. I think the Carnegie-Hayden can be a model for any city anywhere. But Ted's a kid, Bill. He has nothing to do with any of this." She searched his eyes. "Release him, take me." He said nothing, watching her. Sharon considered how far to push the idea of seduction — and then she knew. No. That's how his mother had tried to control him. Seduction wouldn't work.

That was his discipline. He didn't allow himself to be seduced.

"Bill, I don't know how to give you what you want. It's not Theodore, not the Carnegie-Hayden. It's you and me, right? To hell with Kat, from the start it's been you and me —"

He bowed his head.

"Bill, how do I get you to release Ted? If I act seductive, I remind you of your mom, right? How do I get over that?"

He smiled. "It's my job to get over that," he said.

"Right. Mom being seductive — she only did it when she needed something from you, right?"

"She was selfish," Bill said. "Something you aren't."

"You're not either. I know that about you." She took a step toward him, tried to keep her breaths shallow. "Okay, so what do you want out of this situation?"

"Well, the Carnegie-Hayden —"

"No. Right now. This minute."

He looked at her for a long moment. "I've always wanted to fly," he said softly, and shook his head. "I used to think intimacy was such a shuck —"

"A what?"

"A lie. Not possible."

"But now you see things differently."

"Well, I get more about what love is."

"We all want it."

"I used to not."

Sharon took a breath. "Ted deserves it too, Bill. Release him, and you can have me. I don't know how to tell you that without intimidating you or scaring you. And — yeah, I want something from you, so maybe it's not so clean. But it's me here, okay? Release Theodore, and we'll be together, and we'll see what happens."

They were looking at each other, and suddenly Sharon wouldn't have been at all surprised if he'd kissed her, and she found herself wanting to kiss him back. And at that moment, the light of flames began shimmering in the kitchen, the microwave was burning, the rubber sealing gasket emitting choking black smoke, and — *Wump!* — a tongue of fire ignited a splash of gasoline, and the burn was on, a wall of flame racing out in all directions, cutting between them, and Sharon, startled, jumped back.

"GET OUT!" he yelled across the gulf of flames.

"WHAT ABOUT TED —?"

"TRUST ME. *GO!*" He turned and ran out into the hallway, grabbed the backpack, and was gone.

Sharon turned back, ran up the metal ladder, smoke and heat everywhere around her as she crawled out onto the floor of the laundry room. The gas fumes had lessened. She shut the trapdoor, ran upstairs, banged on doors and pushed buzzers, yelling, "FIRE! FIRE!" as she tore up to the next flight above.

Bill hoisted the backpack onto his shoulders, ran down the hall, turned the corner, and scraped through the narrow section and ran until he got to Theodore's door. "Ted!" he yelled.

Ted was wearing a Knicks T-shirt, one of several Bill had bought in his size. His swordfish had gotten cold; he was absorbed in Dynographix.

"Ted, you're going home."

The boy's face opened; it was an amazing thing to see. Then he was tearing around the room, yelling in his excitement.

"Ted!" Bill grabbed him by the shoulders. "We've got a situation, there's a fire, there's smoke, there might be explosions. You've got to keep with me, not get scared, 'cause at the end of it all, I'm going to take you back to your parents. Okay?"

"Okay." Ted was so happy it made Bill sorry, suddenly.

"Okay, climb on." Ted grabbed him around his neck, held on tight as Bill stood, balancing between the child on one side and the heavy backpack on the other. He brought the child through the doors, trotted down the subway channel, holding Theodore close. He ducked through the wall into the thin passageway.

It was pitch-black. He could smell the smoke.

Bill ran as fast as he could. Where it narrowed, he let the boy down, sent him first, squeezed through with the backpack. Theodore waited on the other side, and the two of them ran straight forward, at Theodore's pace.

Not fast enough. "Turn coming up," Bill yelled. And here the smoke was belligerent; it was nasty to breathe. It got thicker, and they could see the red gleam of flames up ahead, right in front of the door to Bill's basement. "What's that?" Theodore asked.

"Just keep running."

"There's fire." Gasoline had drained down the doorsill into the passageway; there was a pool of it, about fifteen feet long, and it was burning.

"How do we cross it?"

"Climb on me." Bill knelt.

"No, Bill!" the boy cried.

"Climb on me! Now, Theodore! There's no other way!" The smoke and heat were intense: Bill was shouting, the boy was bawling. Bill took one of his little hands, put it around his own neck, took the other, picked the boy up, and stood and hugged him close.

The heat was ravaging and fierce, and Bill took a breath of useless smoky air, held it, hugging the boy, prayed that the gasoline wouldn't splash, that the backpack wouldn't catch, that the dynamite wouldn't blow, that they would survive the next ten seconds. And then Bill ran splashing through the flames, past the door and past the heat emanating visibly from what had been his basement, and his shoes were on fire, and the cuffs of his pants, and Theodore was screaming and screaming, and Bill kept running, running not from the heat but from the dynamite strapped to his back.

Twenty yards later Bill stopped and set Theodore down and stamped the fire off his feet, slapped it out of his cuffs. He knelt. "Get back on," he said, and Theodore hugged Bill's neck, and Bill lifted him and continued down the passageway through the smoke, one block and then another.

By the time they came up from the basement of the building on Avenue D, it was dark. They walked across the street to the garage, a man and a little boy, bone tired and sooty and ragged looking as they went in to get the stretch.

Bill hadn't been to Serendipity III in twenty years. He'd had a terrible thought that perhaps it no longer existed, this oddball psychedelic-Victorian ice-cream parlor he'd been to with his mom, but when he saw it he slammed on the limo's brakes. "Here."

In a squalid bathroom at the garage, he had put on wrinkled clothes from the bottom part of the backpack, cleaned Ted's face and his own as well as he could with toilet paper and hand soap, and combed the boy's hair. Now he put on the blinkers, opened the back door of the limo, walked Ted into the restaurant.

Toys and gewgaws in the front; tables in the back, under art nouveau woodwork and giant clocks. "Table for two anywhere," Bill said, and the rather sniffy greeter tossed her pretty hair at them, man and child who looked like they'd just hiked in from Appalachia. She took them to a table hidden in a corner on the second floor.

Bill ordered Ted a cheeseburger and a chocolate malted and the largest banana split they had. Then he gave Ted a fifty from the bottom pocket of the backpack and told him to wait there, his parents would come to pick him up.

Bill walked out of the restaurant, got back in the limo, and drove uptown. When he saw a pay phone, he pulled over.

*   *   *

The first call Sharon made from outside the building was to Martin, telling him where to come. When she realized he was just going to get angrier and angrier, she hung up on him. Then she checked her machine.

She could barely hear it as the fire trucks rolled up, sirens wailing. A message from Crystal, a string of messages from Fiona, and then Karndle. And then, the last one: Bill Kaiser.

"Ted's safe, Sharon. I dropped him off at Serendipity III, a restaurant on the East Side. Tell the Mackinnons, would you? And let them know, you know, nothing sexual happened." Suddenly, there on the tape, he sounded awkward. "Just so it's not a mystery. That's not who I am. Anyway, it was great to see you again —" Like standing in a burning room with him had been the equivalent of a high-school reunion. "And, you know, maybe they'll implement Digby in the Carnegie-Hayden, take it from there to every city that needs it. That'd be nice, right? I mean, I'd still like to see that. See you 'round," and he hung up.

She called Edward, and then she called Karndle back. "He dropped Theodore at a restaurant." She gave the name. "I'm going there now."

"Stay right where you are, Sharon —"

"No. I want to make sure Ted's okay, so that's where I'll be."

Bill headed west through the park, and then back downtown. He left the car in a garage, walked through the West Village. The night was clear, the wind cold off the Hudson. The apartment building was old; a ten-story elevator prewar with nice detailing on the front and thick walls inside.

Bill got his keys out the side pocket of the backpack, opened the etched-glass front door, rang for the elevator. Eventually it came; a young woman got out. Bill avoided her glance, got in, and pressed PH — the highest floor. Then he stepped back out before the door closed, unlocked the basement stairwell, went downstairs to the elevator's operational room. On each side were huge steel cable drums and well-greased motors spinning cable up into the shaft.

Bill opened the half-door to the shaft, looked up to make sure the elevator was high above, and then quickly pushed his backpack in and shut the door behind.

Far above, the elevator he had sent up to twelve was coming slowly back down.

Across the shaft was another half-door. It took three keys to open it; no one else in the world had all three.

The door opened out, revealing a wooden panel. Bill gave it four solid, well-placed kicks before it fell. Two steps down, and he was in a clammy, damp little room with no light. He pulled the explosive-laden backpack in after him. There were matches in a jar in the corner, where he had left them. He lit one, peered around.

A mattress, a bucket and a sleeping bag, some cans of beans and some books, all in a room twice the size of the elevator next door. The place smelled musty and dead. Bill had forgotten how noisy the elevator machinery was, through the wall. It had been a while since he'd stayed here for any length of time.

Cholly Czolgosz had kept whiskey here, during Prohibition. Bill doubted anybody in the building knew about it. Bill doubted anybody in the world knew about it, except him.

He shook out the match before it burned his fingers, stashed the backpack in the corner. Last time he'd been here he'd brought a battery-operated reading light; he groped around until he found it, switched it on. The batteries were dead.

Okay then, candles. He struck another match, found a candle stub, lit it. Then he kicked the wooden panel into place behind the door.

He took off his shoes, lay on the mattress. Just before he fell asleep, he forced himself to put out the candle.

"Are you a friend of my dad's?" the boy said when Sharon found him, eating the banana split.

"We met at your house," Sharon said. "Remember?"

He stared hard at her, and said, "Maybe." And at that moment Theodore Mackinnon's eyes widened like saucers, and he yelled "DADDY!" at the top of his lungs and Sharon turned and there was Edward Mackinnon at the top of the stairs, and Sharon watched what happened when he saw his son, watched the way his face changed and he ran between tables, husky and clumsy like a bear, and the boy stood up, practically scrambled over her, and then the father swept the son into his arms, held him and rocked him back and forth, and the restaurant was silent, everybody was watching, everybody knew who this was, and Sharon suddenly realized she had never seen Edward Mackinnon cry.

He was now, tears leaking down his cheeks. "Theodore Theodore Theodore —" he said, over and over.

The boy didn't want to let him go.

Edward Mackinnon looked over at Sharon, and she suddenly had the giddy, slightly terrifying sensation that all this was familiar, that she'd lived through it before: the Tiffany lamps and the white-painted wood and the faces of the people, forks frozen in midair. She looked at the father and child, not her father, not her child, and it was as if the entire moment had tumbled out of a dream.

PART

THREE

XXVI

"We have hostage negotiators, we have teams that are experts at this — WHY DID YOU DO IT?"

Sharon held the phone away from her ear. She had never heard Martin so furious.

"We could have HAD HIM, Sharon."

"Look, Ted's safe —" she tried.

"YOU'RE NOT! We could have FINISHED HIM OFF!" He was so filled with rage he actually sputtered. "What were you THINKING?"

Sharon arrived late the next morning, stepped quietly into the crowded room just as the Mackinnons' PR guy was winding up his remarks at the podium. She took the seat Erik had saved for her.

"I'm surprised they didn't want you up there," he said.

Sharon waved it away. "I'm not really up for any awards in law enforcement, currently." She stopped, suddenly aware that two reporters in front of them had cut their conversation in midsentence and tuned in to theirs. And then Edward stepped onstage in a somber suit and tie and strode over to the podium. "Ladies and gentlemen of the press," he said into the forest of microphones, "do I have a story for you."

Erik adjusted the level on his handheld tape recorder. "He thinks he's such a showman," he said to Sharon.

". . . As you know," Mackinnon was saying, "ever since I announced that the Mackinnon Group was going into the hospital business, the net worth of our stocks on the New York Stock Exchange has gone down thirty-eight points. Well, I am here to tell you all, we are not building any hospital in the Lower East Side, we are not building any hospitals in New York City, we are not building any hospitals at all.

"The reason we said we were is that my son, Theodore, was kidnapped by a madman, a new kind of terrorist —"

It was the story, but it was the story bleached white and spin-dried, and after a while she tuned out. It was just so many words. She was tired; she was thinking about her mother; she was thinking about the future.

"— Next week, when we have our shareholders meeting," Mackinnon kept on, "we will be presenting a plan for a maximum-security prison on the site of the Carnegie-Hayden that will do more to clean up that neighborhood than any mental or medical hospital ever would."

Sharon looked at the man behind the podium, shook her head. "Erik," she whispered, "I think I have to leave."

"Right now?"

"Right now."

Erik turned off the tape recorder. "Wherever you're going, I'm coming with you."

"At last," Erik said, "I actually get to see your apartment."

"It's tiny," said Sharon. "It's even tinier when you have to share it with shifts of FBI agents twenty-four hours a day. Can I get you something?" Sharon slipped by Erik into the kitchen, opened the refrigerator. It was embarrassingly empty. "There's — umm, a wrapped sandwich, cottage cheese and pineapple —"

"What happened with you and Bill in that room? I mean, if you don't mind me asking —"

Sharon touched the thin inch-long line of dried blood on the left side of her neck, thought how best to explain. "We both played roles," she said finally. "They were based on the people we are, but not fully," she said. "Not realistically."

"Because I find myself worrying — I mean, forgive this, it sounds awful, but here I am trying to work my way out of an impossible relationship, and you seem to be working your way into one —"

"Erik, I had a job to do. I was willing to do anything, say anything —"

"I just don't want him in your head."

She smiled. "He won't be — when this is all over. I promise."

And then Erik looked away. "Well, who am I to bug you about this — I mean, you saved that boy's life, and meanwhile Janine's been in Hong Kong. It's impossible to have a serious conversation, between the time change and our schedules —"

Sharon leaned back. "Well, of course, it's complicated."

"I don't want to do it over the phone, Sharon. We've talked all around it. She knows, she has to know." Sharon said nothing. "Look, she was supposed to be back yesterday. She called at three-thirty in the morning to tell me they'd extended it." And then he heard himself, hated how he sounded, and his shoulders slumped. "Oh hell," he said finally. "How tiresome." He took up his coat. "I've got to get back to the station."

"It's not the worst thing, wanting to face her in person," she said. "Playing out the roles."

"Right." He looked at her, held out a hand, and she took it, and suddenly they were in an embrace, pressing against each other, wanting to be together. Then he turned, and walked out, and she sat in her chair and looked out at the Empire State Building.

Something had happened with Bill. Something that was not over. Sharon touched the short, thin scab, and worried that somewhere inside, something never would be.

* * *

Bill was awake when the alarm went off, at six the next morning; he grabbed the travel clock, felt for the button that stopped the noise, set the clock down, and sat up.

The room was so dark he could not see his hand before his eyes. He scratched his fingers through his hair, trying to untangle it. Then he pulled the panel away from the door.

It had been thirty-six hours since he'd set foot outside; he had a feeling he was scary to behold. The elevator was somewhere high above him; he crossed the shaft, listened for any human presence. Nothing. He opened the half-door, walked through the elevator control room, washed his face in the laundry sink. He hit the elevator button, got in when it arrived, and went to the tenth floor.

Nobody there took delivery of the *Times*. He walked down to nine, and found one, waiting in front of an apartment door. He took it, walked down a couple more floors and found a *Daily News*.

Those would do. He went back down to the basement, sealed himself back in his cubbyhole, lit a candle and read all about Edward Mackinnon's press conference.

One foot in front of the other, higher and higher, step after step after step. There was a camera in the elevator, and Bill hadn't liked that much, though rationally he knew it didn't matter. Besides, he'd been cramped so long in his cell downtown, just walking up these stairs was a pleasure.

It was a glorious clear day in New York City, not too cold, and it made Bill melancholy that he couldn't just stroll through it, walk about the island and see the faces around him. But he'd done that for years, drifted about the population. Now his life felt as focused as the stairwell he was climbing.

Step after step after step. And Sharon, out there, waiting.

On the thirty-first floor, cartons of empty Moet bottles testified to a party; Bill continued up. Finally, on the forty-fifth floor the stairwell ended; down a short hall was a door. Bill unbolted it, stepped out onto a pebbly surface, and a blast of wind hit him.

He was on the roof. Around him were the skyscrapers of midtown, steel and brick towers looming above him, even at this great height. There was a calmness here, the sounds of the city almost distant. A battlefield a long way off.

Across from him stood the monolithic Citicorp Building, a square stick shoved high into the sky, horizontal stripes of aluminum and glass in orderly precision. He could see women in skirts and men in ties walking on carpets and sitting at desks behind the glass. Above them all was the wedge.

The Citicorp Building was famous for the wedge. It was probably the most easily assimilated change of the New York skyline in the last generation; it had started a fad in architecture for silly roofs on towers, and had outlived its imitators. The roof rose high on one side, then plummeted down ten stories, steep as a ski slope. It had originally been sold to the public as a solar panel for the building; of course, Bill thought ruefully, that idea had long since been abandoned as uneconomical.

On the upper floors of the Citicorp Building was a spacious business conference center. Next week, Edward Mackinnon would welcome his shareholders there.

The building was so massive, Bill's stash of explosives would pop like a firecracker, in comparison. But if he used it right, he knew he could make it pop with a particularly loud bang.

The stretch looked incongruous in front of the rubble-strewn lot, but it was late enough that it didn't matter. Bill had cruised the neighborhood for half an hour before seeing Paulie, walking quickly down Avenue C. He'd pulled around the corner, found a spot, followed the dealer on foot.

"Yo —" Bill looked him in the eye. "What you got tonight?"

"Hey, bud —" Paulie shook Bill's hand. "Got nickels of Nightzone, cleanest smack around —"

"Can you get me quantity? I'm leaving town, going down south, I do not want to fuck with scoring heroin in Lafayette, Louisiana."

The pale man smiled broadly. "I hear that," he said. "What ya need, an eightball?"

"'Bout right. And maybe some downs, some Percodans."

"Not Percs. Butes." Butisol. "I got ten on me right now. Or, if you wait, I can get you Percs."

"No, no, fine, Butes'd be great. Listen, I got a big ol' stretch parked down the street. Full liquor cabinet, the works. Come have a drink, we'll hang, do it in the car."

Bill walked him up the street, opened the car door like a chauffeur, and the blond man got in. Bill climbed in after, shut the door, opened the ice bucket, took up the cloth soaked in ether, and clamped it over Paulie's face. He struggled and kicked in the tight space, and for a moment they were equally matched. Bill was aware his opposite number could have overpowered him, but then the ether took effect, his eyes rolled back, and he went limp.

Bill cuffed his hands and roped his feet together, spread the cloth over the unconscious man's nose and mouth, then locked him in and opened the driver's door, keyed on the ignition, and glided gracefully west.

Radu had called in sick, and Erik had been going down the sub-list, trying to track down somebody to take the ten-to-two shift. For some reason very few of his disc jockeys were home, and those that were had other plans for the evening. He was in the act of leaving yet another message on yet another answering machine when the key went in his lock, and Janine stuck her head in and said, "Erik, hi, could you help me with my suitcases?"

Erik hung up, stood and approached her, and their two heads bubbled around each other like repelled magnets, and finally he leaned in and kissed her cheek, part of her lip.

Uncomfortable. She half smiled, and they hustled in her suitcase, her sample cases, her shopping bags, the trunk on wheels.

"I'm sorry," he said, "I would have met you; I didn't know when you were coming back."

"I should have called, but we barely made the plane."

Planes always have phones now. But he didn't say it because he didn't want to sound niggling. "You look great," he said.

"I haven't really slept in days."

She looked it. She shut the door and stood in the middle of the room. Artemis wandered in, circled around her, diffidently sniffing the luggage. "I think a glass of wine," she said, and turned into the kitchen.

He followed her. "Listen, lots of things have been going on here — but you had me concerned because all your messages kept talking about some emergency." She had her head in the fridge, pulled out an opened bottle of white, glugged wine into a glass. She drank a gulp off the top, leaned against the wall, and looked him in the eye.

"Erik, Gillian's asked me to move in" — she tilted her head, rubbed her thigh with the heel of her hand — "and I've said yes."

Erik considered that, thought about it within the context of his own life. Then he stood up, and without a word walked out of the kitchen, through the living room, and into the bedroom. He opened the closet door — all of Janine's things, all her beautiful clothes, all smelling like she smelled. He dug his arms deep into the closet, hugged as many as he could get, and lifted them off the bar. He walked with them back into the living room. Janine stood there, dumbfounded, as he dropped the clothes into a pile on the floor.

"I keep the cat," Erik said.

"Well, that's another thing I wanted to talk to you about — Gillian's allergic to cat hair —"

"Good." Erik took up his leather jacket. "Get your stuff out tonight. I'm going out. When I come back, you'll be gone."

Sharon was typing up her seventeenth résumé cover letter on her old Smith Corona when a blast of noise came over the radio. She had been listening to HBN enough in the past month to know Nietzsche Prosthesis when she heard them; at first she'd hated them, but now, she had to admit, they had a certain rough charm. The song ended with a long feedback squeal, and Erik's voice came over the airwaves into her room: "Radu's not here; I am. I'm Erik, and I ain't gonna play Hank Williams because I ain't sad. Here's Brian Eno's immortal 'Burning Airlines Give You So Much More.'"

Sharon reached for the phone as the song started, found HBN's number and dialed it. "Erik — it's Sharon. You okay?"

"She came back. Tonight. It's over, Sharon, the whole damn thing is over."

She couldn't help it: something she'd been keeping tamped down broke; some part of her heart immediately filled with warmth. "You sound awful," she said.

"I'm not, really. I mean I'm weird. I'm giddy and I'm sad and — I don't know. Weird."

"Want company, over there?"

"Well maybe — I mean, would you like —?"

She thought it, and then she thought, Just say it. "I don't think I can take sitting in this room and listening to you on the radio and not being with you."

"Then come," Erik said. "Come right down."

When Sharon got to the station, Erik buzzed her in and then met her at the door and she sunk into his arms, and he didn't let her go, and they felt a perfect fit, their heights and their bodies instantly comfortable with each other. They didn't even kiss; they just held each other and felt each other's strengths. Then Erik found her mouth with his own, Sharon delighting in the way his lips felt, delighting in the hard and soft of teeth and tongue, relative strangers utterly surprised to find they spoke the same language. Finally Erik pushed her away with a loopy grin on his face, adjusted his glasses, and said, "Let me go cue up some records."

She followed him into the studio, sat in the tight room as he slapped records onto turntables, faded down the CD player, and pressed the button to start the first record playing out over the airwaves. "Where were we?" he said, and Sharon asked, "Are we alone?" and when Erik said yes, she straddled his chair, sat on his thighs and held his chin in her hand and began gently kissing him, then biting him, in control by silent mutual assent.

She stood, gestured for him to stand, knelt in the limited space below the console and opened his thick brown belt, unbuttoned his jeans and pulled down his fly. White underwear. She coaxed out his penis, which was gasping and raising and searching. She slipped his pants to his knees, reached down the front of her dress into her bra, took out the condom she'd placed there, tore open the foil, and slipped the rubber between her teeth. Then she took his penis into her mouth, rolled the condom down the shaft with her tongue.

She kicked the rolling chair away, pulled down on his hands until he sat on the floor, stripped her panties from under her dress, straddled him, and kissed him as she guided his penis inside.

She pushed him back onto the carpeted floor of the studio, and smiled down. He was really such a beautiful man, she thought, so intelligent and sweet and sexy, and he began to pump, his hands reaching for her, and she gave in to him, and there the two of them were, rocking and sweating and moaning. She wanted his shirt open, she wanted to see his chest, but there wasn't time for that; he was thick inside her, filling and expanding and she closed her eyes, she could no longer really think, there was so much going on, so many sensations coming to her at once, now, faster and faster. And then there was something complicated, his rhythm changed, the song was ending, and she opened her eyes to see his arm stretched high, his fingers groping along the console edge for the button, and he got it, and the sound from the turntable died just as the song ended. She watched him reach one over, press another button, and the other turntable started up. "Press —" he said, "the slider —" he said, "to eight," and she arched forward without leaving him, poked the plastic lever where he'd asked.

Intelligent guitar chords in counterpoint provided a new rhythm. God, his taste in music was impeccable — and they began again, the new beat breathing around them. It took a moment for them to find it, but then they did, and she wanted to melt all over him, she wanted him to melt into her. And then she couldn't control herself; sounds began in her throat, a high atonal song louder and louder with each breath and somewhere below her she heard him say "Sharon, I'm coming," and that sent her over the top, the song turned to a cry in her throat, her neck arched, her dark hair behind her, and the orgasm grew in waves until it was over.

She felt his hand grasp the condom, pull himself out of her. And then she lay with him on the floor, his arm around her back, feeling his breathing and hers slowly come down to normal.

"I can't tell you," he said, "how nice it is" — he breathed — "to be with you."

"I was about," she said, "to say exactly that" — she breathed — "to you."

Bill was finding it hard to read.

Candlelight was complicated enough. Even in this airless room, the flickering interrupted his concentration, made him think of the centuries humankind had lived by candlelight, the way the flicker made the words shadow and bounce on the page.

And then, of course, there were the intermittent moans and shrieks from Paulie, when the heroin and the Butisol wore off and he came out of sleep and struggled against his bonds.

Bill had mummy-wrapped him in blankets, and then wound the blankets with cord. The gag was one of Paulie's own socks tied into a knot around a stretch of rope; he couldn't speak, but when he was awake he had a full range of expressive grunts and cries.

Really, it was most annoying. The Butisols weren't as strong as Bill had hoped; Paulie had had a fair supply of heroin, and had been carrying works, so Bill had to keep him narcotized, always careful not to give too much. Dead, the man was useless.

But truthfully, hour after hour, the constant whimpered pleading and sobbing was just too irritating. Finally, Bill opened the toolbox, looking for something long and sharp.

A screwdriver. A delicate, slender one, thin as an icepick, with a flat edge. Yup, this would work.

Bill took up his candle, went over to the moaning lump. He sat on the man's chest, pulled the blanket away from his head.

Paulie had nearly bitten through the rope. Clearly, this had to stop — the man was just too much trouble.

Bill held up the candle, looked at the fear in the man's eyes, the way they dilated and followed the flame. His lips were cracked;

dried spittle and tears had turned to salt on his cheeks. From his throat came elephantine pleading noises.

Bill didn't care. He set the candle on the ground, clamped his left hand on the man's forehead, pulled his eyelid up with his thumb. When Paulie saw the screwdriver enter his field of vision, he tried to shout, and squirm. Bill shifted, fixed the drug dealer's head between his knees.

He touched the steel tip of the screwdriver to the fleshy red meat on the underside of the eyelid. He was not touching the man's eye; one slip and he'd put the eye out. He pushed the screwdriver up; obviously more force was required. He gathered his strength, gave it a good strong jolt, and the screwdriver slid and then caught and there was a delicate crunch of bone, and Bill was in. He shoved the screwdriver deep into the man's brain, tried to get a sideways motion going. The resistance was like pudding, with occasional clouds of membrane and gristle.

It was easier to pivot than swish.

It was interesting to see the changes going on in Paulie's face, all sorts of twitches and expressions. But it was obvious: he was immediately calmer.

Bill worked the screwdriver in gradually larger circles, and then brought it out, slimed with blood and gray matter. Paulie was trying to speak, but it was arduous. Bill pulled up the left eyelid, positioned the screwdriver, and jabbed straight up.

This time it went in easily.

When Bill was finished, Paulie seemed awake, blinking, the blood trickling into his eyes. But he was quieter. Much quieter.

That, really, was all Bill had wanted. Bill watched him for a while, and then grew bored and took the candle back to his mattress, opened his book to his place, and continued his reading.

When Sharon opened her eyes the next morning, the first thing she saw was gray daylight around the edges of her upturned Venetian blinds. And then she saw Erik, his head propped on his hand, his elbow on the pillow. "Hi," Erik said.

"Hey," she said, smiling. He leaned over and kissed her.

Funny how she didn't feel anxious. She kissed him back; the kiss grew and lingered, all her attention focused on the softness of his wonderful lips. Then she broke away, a stretch working through her body ending in a wide yawn, her arms arcing in the air.

She wasn't wondering how to get him to leave.

"So you've been watching me sleep?" she asked.

"Just a few minutes," he lied. "You have a wonderful nose."

She reached out, touched his. "So do you."

"How do you feel? About everything —?"

About being with him. She considered it. "Calm," she said.

"Calm is nice." It wasn't shallow. He meant it.

"Calm," Sharon said, "is ardently to be desired." And then she drew him to her, and he shifted to gather her in his arms, and they began, again, to make love.

Damnit, Bill missed his basement. His computers, his books, all his equipment —without it he felt like a blind man traversing the edge of a razor. Gone, all gone.

His first stop, at nine that morning, had been the hospital auxiliary thrift stores on the East Side; he had purchased a blanket and an oversized fat man's suit at the first, but he'd had to look through two more before finding the other things he needed. Then he'd gone back to the second and purchased a sewing kit. That gave him a uniform: enough identity for now.

He took the subway up to the 125th Street office of the phone company, got copies of the Yellow and White Pages phone books.

He found himself hungry, noted a clock in a store window, and for a melancholy moment thought of Lobo, probably digging into beans and rice right now at La Lengua Larga. But that was gone as well; instead he stopped into a supermarket, purchased tuna fish and no-salt sourdough pretzels and bottled water, sponges and paper towels and garbage bags and some malt balls for his houseguest.

If he hadn't liked malt balls before, Bill reasoned, he probably would like them now. And then Bill laughed: who'd really had the frontal lobotomy? Who's past had been completely erased?

Bundled with a scarf over his face, he went back to the building. There were maids in the laundry room when he got there; he had to wait a perplexing few minutes until he had privacy enough to get back into his cell.

His houseguest was beginning to smell.

Bill undid the ropes and cleaned the man's behind and wrapped him in the new blanket. Throughout it all, the man did very little complaining; he hadn't really said much at all since Bill had scrambled his frontal lobes.

Then he lay back on his mattress and began flipping through the Yellow Pages. He would need a box, of course, but as the first advertisements he checked proved, that could wait until evening.

"Martin? It's Sharon —"

"Sharon, yes. What's up?"

"Listen, I know all the arguments against it, but I think it might be an intelligent idea for me to go to Edward's shareholders meeting —" Silence on the phone. Sharon rushed to fill it. "It's the perfect forum for Bill to try something —"

"Sharon, absolutely not. In terms of security I've got a logistical nightmare on my hands, three thousand VIPs in midtown Manhattan, every paper in America is onto this story, there'll be press coming in from all over — I don't want you anywhere near the Citicorp Building."

"Martin —"

"Sharon, I cannot risk you doing your loose cannon bit again, all right? I'm not asking you, I'm telling you — stay home, or I'll have you arrested."

Bill's first stop was a tiny little Spanish hardware store, where he purchased a hammer, nails, gloves, and a saw. Then he raced over to the lumberyard five minutes before it closed, bought the two-by-fours and dowels and rectangles of plywood he'd need. He took a cab back to the Lower West Side, got out, and walked several blocks with his purchases. A yuppie couple had been happy to hold the door as he struggled his lumber into the building.

He brought everything down to the basement, stashed the wood behind the row of dryers, went back into his cell. His house-guest had peed on himself again, but Bill didn't really mind; in fact he'd gotten rather used to it.

He had a lot of work to do before morning.

Dinner had been wonderful, the two of them at a corner table of Erik's favorite sushi place, drinking hot sake against the cold night. Afterward Erik had said, "I live four blocks over — if you'd like to come up —?"

"Will Janine be there?"

"Nope. It's my damn apartment. I had it for seven years before she ever happened." In fact, Janine had done a singularly incomplete job of getting her stuff out. That afternoon the place had been littered with her detritus; Erik had tidied everything up before meeting Sharon for dinner. "Come," he said, and led the way toward his building.

Erik opened the apartment door with great exuberance, but even then, they walked through the place with trepidation, as if they had sneaked into someplace they didn't belong. Artemis spent a long time smelling Sharon's ankles — "Artemis likes everybody," Erik said, while waiting to see if it was true — and then the little cat rubbed Sharon's stockinged shin with the side of her head.

They were alone. Erik put on water, set out glasses with tea bags in them, and then joined Sharon on the couch. By the time the water boiled, they were too enmeshed in each other to care about tea. Erik bolted up to turn off the whistle, and then led Sharon by the hand into the bedroom. An hour and a half later he put on his glasses, went back into the kitchen, got some ice water in an oversized glass for them both to share.

When he returned, she was sitting with her knees up, not really looking at anything, lost in thought. "Talk to me," he said, sipped on the water, and handed her the glass.

"Oh, it's Bill Kaiser, this whole situation."

"The shareholders conference."

Sharon looked at him, this gentle, bare-chested man in bed beside her. "He's going to do something, I know it. He has to complete the circuit." Erik took her hand. "In this whole situation," she went on, "I'm the one he's talked to; I'm his connection to the world. I'm it." She looked at him in the half-light. "I have to get in there, Erik. If I'm not, and something happens —"

"So go."

"Well, when the FBI says no, it gets complex."

"I could go as press —" Erik said. "Maybe you could too —"

"Too tight — that's how they expect him to get in."

Erik let her hand go, and a benevolent grin spread wide across his features, a grin of delight tinged with something darker, and in a flash he was up. He opened Janine's dresser, pawed through her trinkets, opened the drawer below it. Finally he emerged, victorious. He strode back to the bed, naked, holding an envelope high above his head. "Voilà — your invitation, madam."

She accepted the envelope, a thick wad computer-addressed to Janine Lowell at Erik's apartment.

"Open it."

"Really?"

"Open it."

She stuck her finger in the flap, ripped it apart. Inside was a letter, and a program, and cards and envelopes, Mackinnon Group logos on everything. Suddenly Sharon understood, and her heart beat hard. "She's a shareholder."

"Twenty thousand shares, left to her by her aunt. Call them tomorrow, tell them you're Janine, you're in town, you want to go. With that many shares I'm sure they'll find a way to squeeze you in."

XXVII

The main desk of the Citicorp Building was staffed by three white men, all with weight-room builds. They had a wall of closed-circuit monitors and fire alarm equipment and phones, one of which was ringing now. Mark, the security guard closest, picked it up.

"Jason?" Male voice at the other end.

"No, Mark. You want Jason?"

"Mark, fine, listen, this is Marvin Sorenson at Sorenson Cox. There's a technician coming with some equipment for us, from DCI. Don't make him go through the mail room — send him right up."

"Send him right up."

"Thanks, that'd be great."

"Thank *you*, Mr. Sorenson."

God, Bill thought, hanging up, they really did the Thankful Lackey bit to the hilt.

Twenty minutes later, he pushed a hand truck bearing the crate into the Citicorp Building, aimed straight for the front desk. "Sorenson Cox?" he asked, loudly.

"You from DCI?"

"That's me."

"Freight elevator to forty-six, they're expecting you." The man scribbled the time and destination on a visitor's sticker, gave it to Bill, who slapped it on his chest, right under the DCI patch. Bill jerked the hand truck into motion, pushed the bulky box toward the far elevator bank, hit the button, and waited.

Paulie hadn't made a noise. But then, he hadn't really been feeling much like himself, lately.

The door opened; Bill got on, pushed eighteen. A legal office had recently vacated: management had office space ads in the papers. With luck and a little creativity, he'd be able to stash the box somewhere high up in the building, then stay in the empty offices for a day or two, until he'd really gotten to know the lay of the land.

There were trucks bearing satellite dishes and vans with microwave television transmitters all around as Erik and Sharon got off the subway and came up to street level, the monumental bulk of the Citicorp Building above them. Sharon was looking rather like a fifties Hollywood starlet — large round impenetrable sunglasses, and a Hermes scarf over her head with red bangs peeking out from under.

Sharon and Erik had spent a lovely afternoon the previous Saturday at the wig counter of the House of Field, one of the more outrageous downtown boutiques, laughing at the dubious complexities of Erik trying to figure out how to make his new girlfriend look like his old. They had purchased the wig, and a sweater. Sharon had noticed Erik eyeing a complicated bit of rubber lingerie; the next day she came alone, bought it, and wore it home.

Now, blue police-line barricades were everywhere, along with motorcycle cops and cops on horseback. They were herding everybody who had business in the building onto one endless and seemingly immobile line. "This is such a mess," Sharon said, holding her wig down against the wind.

"It's like trying to get into the Garden to see some obnoxious teenage rock act," Erik said, exasperated.

They had decided to dress her as rich-looking as possible, and the most Chanel-like thing Sharon had was a black summerweight suit. After forty minutes, they had moved sixty feet to the front door, and Sharon was shivering in Erik's embrace. Inside, they could see cops passing all carry-ins through an X-ray machine, and making people walk through metal detectors torqued so high one man had been asked to remove his belt and shoes.

Through the glass Sharon saw one of the FBI agents she had met in the last month. "See him?" Sharon pointed.

"He was at the radio station a couple of times. I should probably get to the press entrance before he sees us together —"

"I hate to make you wait on line again —"

Erik smiled. "Yeah, well, that's life."

Sharon looked at him with something approaching awe. "You are really a nice man," she said, and then it was her turn. She kissed his cheek, adjusted her glasses, and marched through the door.

Erik stood by the glass as Sharon dumped her pocketbook onto the belt, and stepped through the metal detector. They had planned for her to wear as little metal as possible. She picked up her purse at the other end, and walked right past the FBI agent to the next security checkpoint.

Erik left, walked around the building, and found the press entrance, where he was greeted by another long line.

*   *   *

Bill kept low amid the pipes, shimmying up the slope on his stomach. Above him the wind howled loud; patches of sky could be glimpsed through the interstices between the panels of glass. Here it was shaded, an oddly calm little universe few had ever seen.

For days, cops had been everywhere, in suits and out; it had been like playing chess solo against a team. But now, he saw, his little contraption on the east edge of the building was as he had left it.

It was risky to be out here, but he'd had to be sure.

In the lobby, Sharon found two lines — one for the building's workers who had to be in their offices on Saturday, and one for the Mackinnon Group shareholders meeting. Sharon got onto the second, terrified of seeing Martin or Fiona at the desk. They weren't there, but one of Karndle's agents was, Jimmy, along with an older agent she didn't think she'd seen before. Both men were matching invitations and IDs with names on lists, and then Jimmy let the man in front of her go in, and there she was, about to get stared at by this man who'd seen her countless times, days on end.

Sharon took a step, unzipped her purse and opened it wide and fumbled. Lipsticks and compacts skittered across the floor. She dropped to her knees, began scrabbling to pick them up, and the man behind her stepped around with his invitation and driver's license out for Jimmy. Sharon stood just as the other man became free, stepped up, handed over her invitation and ID.

"I'm sorry the license is expired," Sharon said. "I haven't gotten around to getting a new one."

The man in the jacket peered at the picture on the card, looked up at Sharon. "Take off your glasses, please."

Sharon glanced over at Jimmy, who seemed busy. She took off the glasses, smiled at the man.

"Do you have anything more current?"

"Of course." Her hands were shaking as she dug back into the wallet. A health club membership, Janine's library card, a ragged social security card with no signature, and an old ID from Janine's last job. Not exactly authoritative. Sharon picked that, handed it over. The picture looked nothing like Sharon — narrower eyes, a longer face. Then Sharon handed over the health club card. That picture, as far as Sharon was concerned, resembled her even less.

The man peered at the pictures, peered into Sharon's eyes, looked at the driver's license. Janine's eyes were light brown. Sharon's were hazel, browner in some lights. She hoped this was one of them.

He looked at her, he looked at the picture, then back at her. "Social security number?"

"707-38-4889," Sharon said, effortlessly.

"All right, Ms. Lowell," the man finally said. "Go on in."

The elevator was packed with men in suits, wealthy testosterone muffled by clashing colognes, and Sharon had never felt more like a spy in her life. The buttons were controlled by a woman who Sharon was sure was FBI. When they arrived at the fifty-seventh floor of the Citicorp Building, the first level of Citicorp's famous slanted roof, the doors opened onto a different world.

Edward Mackinnon knew that because of his recent troubles this convention had to be a media event, and a media event it was. The elevator hallway had astounding views of the city below. Sharon walked on into a reception area, which had been turned into a photo exhibit of the Mackinnon Group's holdings, with charts showing how profits on each had climbed. All the charts pointed up toward the ceiling. Coffee bars in each corner dispensed cappuccinos, espressos, and mimosas, along with various fruits, cheeses, and pastries. Sharon took a cappuccino and a piece of melon wrapped in prosciutto, and walked up a grand flight of stairs into the auditorium.

This was a vast, modern assembly hall, all blond woods and steel and row after row of comfortable chairs. With a start Sharon realized that the hall's ceiling was the same angle as the Citicorp tower's roofline: they were that high up, actually in the wedge.

Above the stage was a large Diamondvision screen, upon which a documentary about the Mackinnon Group was being ignored by people sipping coffee, talking in sporadic clumps in the aisles. At the back of the room was a press area, with television cameras aimed at the dais, reams of mixers and light boards and Nikons on tripods. Sharon walked the length of it, back and forth, looking for Erik and not finding him. Then she took up a position next to the entranceway, to the side of a television crew. She sipped her coffee and watched idly as the crew's small black-and-white monitor showed Edward and Melissa Mackinnon standing in what looked like a hallway, waiting, bored, as cameras were set up and meters flicked in front of faces and lights adjusted. This scene, she realized, was happening live, somewhere else in the building.

And then Erik walked up to her and said "Hi" and kissed her cheek, and she held him for a moment. "Martin was covering the press entrance. They actually opened my tape recorder, to make sure it wasn't a bomb —"

Sharon pointed. "Look —" On the little monitor, Edward was pulling Theodore onto his lap, they were joined by Melissa, in a Valentino suit and pearls.

"She looks like skin and bones," Sharon said.

"Ah." Erik looked at the screen. "The nuclear family, reunited and shedding quarks."

"Teddy," Edward was saying, "are you doing okay? Do you want anything?"

"No, thank you." Theodore looked out the window, enjoying the vast view. Edward looked at Melissa, holding her child's hand, not paying any attention to anyone but him.

The funny thing was, Theodore had been so damn well behaved ever since he'd come back from being kidnapped. He shook hands, he listened more, he didn't shriek in public. Edward watched the change with near wonderment — suddenly the rules were important.

He checked his watch. They were in a small reception area above the main auditorium. Edward had an office on the other side of the floor, but the camera crew following him around today had vetoed it, and so here they were in this open room, pretending to be comfortable. Edward had hired them to do an in-house corporate film about the personal crisis and the stock slippage; the current corporate video style looked like music television had five years before: all jump cuts and grainy cinema verité black and white and endless "casual" shots "backstage," and the cameramen were having a field day shooting each other shooting Edward, Ted, and Melissa idly staring out the grand windows and periodically making distracted comments. These would be the only views of Ted in the film, though Edward was considering including some pre-kidnapping home videos as well. In three minutes, Melissa would take the boy, and the interview would begin in earnest, Ed alone acting nervous before the Big Event. In fifteen minutes the speakers downstairs would begin, preparatory to his entrance in an hour.

Out the window, Edward could see all New York. He felt calm, his family around him, his company about to fight back. Mackinnon stock had risen since the press conference, but not enough; by the end of the shareholders meeting he would use this personal debacle to push it higher than it had ever been.

He checked his watch, excused himself to Melissa, shouldered past the camera crew, and walked down the hall to the bathroom. He was standing at the urinal, peeing, when there was a commotion above him, like an animal scuffling about, and a marble panel slid open, and one leg, and then another, poked down from the ceiling, and then a man dropped noisily into the room between Edward and the door. A blond man, burly, in a suit. Edward zipped his pants, had his .45 out before he even knew it was Bill Kaiser.

"You son of a bitch, you took my kid —" Edward clicked off the safety.

"Oooh, bad idea, Ed —" Bill opened his jacket, exposing the parallel red sticks of dynamite bound with thick black tape that ran all the way around his chest and back. "The dynamite," said Bill, "is really a rather noisy trigger for the real explosive, the C-4 underneath." He tapped his heart, then held up his hands to show the open copper wires that fanned out across his palms, twisted at the back of his fingers like rings. "If I clap my hands" — he gestured, stopping his hands an inch away from each other — "we lose the top half of the Citicorp Building. If I touch my neck" — he pointed at the wires running up from under his shirt and around his ears, "ka-blooey. If I touch my ankle, cross my legs" — he gestured at the wires running out the cuffs of his pants and into his shoes — "same thing. Now, give me the gun." Bill held one hand at his neck, as if scratching behind his ear, and extended the other to Edward.

Edward did nothing.

Bill took a step forward. "The gun, Edward."

Edward's lips were moving; the rest of his body was still.

"Shoot me and you and all your major shareholders die. Not to mention your wife and child, and who knows however many more innocent people. Don't shoot me, and you know what? We'll go upstairs, have a little talk, we'll come to a moral and philosophical agreement, and then you'll go back down and announce that you're going to be the hero that the city needs — you're going to build a city on a hill, and at the top of that hill will be a shining castle, a beacon of hope for all, called the Carnegie-Hayden."

"How do I know that's real dynamite?"

Bill considered this, and then reached in his pocket and took out a lighter. He pulled the electrical blasting cap off one of the sticks on his chest, jammed in an eight-inch length of fuse, and lit it. "Wanna find out?" Bill asked, as the sparking fuse got shorter. "I've never lied to you, Edward."

"Okay, okay —" Edward was looking a trifle green. "You are completely psychotic," he said.

Bill snorted out laughter. "If I was psychotic, it would have been Ted's blood on that shirt, not pig's blood. Okay?" He took the fuse out, dropped it on the ground, and in the same motion plucked the gun out of Edward's hand. He dropped the cartridge out into the palm of his hand, put it down his pants, and tucked the gun into the dynamite under his arm. Then he clapped Edward on the shoulder, took a pair of handcuffs from his inside jacket pocket. "Turn around."

Edward didn't move.

"Don't give me shit about this, Edward. Listen, what I want, you have to be alive for, so don't worry."

Edward turned warily, extended his hands behind. Bill snapped the metal cuff on one, and then the other, careful never to hold the cuffs at any time with both hands. Then he moved in close to Edward's ear. "You were a Marine, right? Like Sharon's dad." Bill shoved the stick of dynamite under his nose. "Smell this?"

"Yes," Edward croaked out.

"Real, right?"

"Yes."

Bill stepped back, replaced it in his arsenal, reconfigured the blasting cap. "Let us go then, you and I, when the evening is spread out against the sky like a patient etherised upon a table." Bill smiled. "We walk out this door, take a left, toward Melissa and all them at the end of the hallway. You say a word, try to signal —" Bill mimed clapping his hands. "Boom. There's a door to your left, about seven feet down. Go through it; I'll be holding on to the handcuffs behind you. Head upstairs. Anything I don't like — Boom. I promise you, I don't want anybody to die — not me, not you, not Teddy or Melissa. Smile, Edward. Are you smiling?" Bill turned him toward the mirror to check, jabbed his lips up with his finger. "Good boy. Open the door and walk."

Bill grabbed the chain between the cuffs, followed Edward through the door. At the end of the hall was the arched doorway and the couch and the camera crew and the window. Teddy had his back to them, his hands cupped to the window, looking out. Melissa saw Edward and waved. "Ed — they're ready —"

The documentary camera swung around just in time to see Ed turn and go through a door with a burly man who looked like a plainclothes cop.

Sharon was draining the last dregs from her plastic coffeecup when Edward Mackinnon appeared on the monitor and went in the door. And then her throat locked, and she gagged. "Erik —" she said.

"What?" He was looking around the room; he hadn't seen.

"Bill Kaiser — there — damn, they're swinging back."

"Sharon —" He didn't believe her.

"Edward Mackinnon just walked down that hall — there." She pointed at the edge of the screen. "Through a door, Bill Kaiser behind him." She turned to the attractive man behind the video board, waved her hand. He cocked one ear off his headphones.

"Can you rewind that?"

The man shook his head. "We're supposed to begin the interview upstairs in one minute."

"Is Edward Mackinnon there?" Sharon was hitting one fist with the other. "I mean, he should be there — did he just disappear? Or do they know where he is?" The man said nothing. "Look, it's urgent — just tell me. Is he in the room? Or do they not know —"

He listened to his headphones. "They're looking for him now," he said, at length.

"He went into that door with that other man, and he's just gone, right?" But the man was no longer listening to them.

Sharon looked around, chose an exit sign by the stage, started to run to it, Erik loping along behind her. She slammed through a metal double door into a brick hallway; twenty feet down was a security man sitting on a stool with a Rottweiler at his feet. Sharon wheeled back, looked around the huge room, hiked up her skirt, and climbed onto the stage.

Erik followed Sharon as she barreled past curtains to another steel door. "Same hallway," Sharon said, and at that moment a plainclothes agent, probably FBI, began running down the middle aisle toward the stage, and Sharon looked at him, and said, more to herself than to Erik, "I do not have the time." There was a door in front of her, and she ran through it into a carpeted lounge. Through that was a hallway, executive types milling about. To her right was a stairwell. She went in as casually as possible, took it up, two steps at a time, followed closely by Erik.

"How do we know he went up?" Erik said, climbing behind her. The question stopped Sharon for a moment, made her grab the railing. "Because Bill Kaiser always goes up," she said, and began climbing again. "He did it" — she breathed — "at Bellevue, he did it" — she breathed — "at that senator's —" And then the stairwell ended at a door. Sharon opened it, looked, shut it again. "Fuck," she said; she leaned back against the wall to catch her breath.

"What?"

"Another rent-a-cop."

Erik looked at her. "They're on our side, right?"

"Oh, right, you try to explain that." Her eyes flared. "This guy radios for his superior, that guy'll radio for *his* superior —"

"Okay, okay —"

"You run toward him, I'll run away from him."

"What?"

"As a sacrifice. If we get cornered." And then, because of the way his eyebrows arched in the air: "I'm the only one who can talk to Bill Kaiser, all right?"

"Well, he did like my radio show —"

Sharon smiled, looked at him cockeyed, kissed his cheek. "True. Let's go." And she strode out the door and away from the cop in gray. "Hey, you two," he said, and then Sharon jabbed Erik in the side and walked more briskly. "Stop right there," the man said, and then they heard the clink of a chain and the man said "Get 'em," and Erik looked behind and a large black Rottweiler was bounding at them down the cinder-block hallway.

Erik ran and Sharon ran and there was a door up ahead. Sharon grabbed the knob and pushed with her shoulder and nothing happened. "Locked," Sharon said, and up ahead was a corner. The cop running up yelled "FREEZE" and Erik froze and the dog skittered on the linoleum, did an about face and sat.

Erik said to the man, "You've got to help us!" and Sharon ducked around the corner and there at the end was another rent-a-cop with another Rottweiler, running toward them, but to her left was a doorway, and Sharon took it. A red exit sign beaconed over a door at the end of a carpeted hallway; next to it was a fire extinguisher in a glassed-in niche. She got it out just as the door behind her opened. A dog bounded toward her down the carpet; Sharon hurled herself through the exit, found herself in another stairwell. She set the extinguisher down, turned it so the short rubber hose sat between the door and doorframe, slammed the door with all her might, pushed until the door and frame were flush, pulled the ring, and jammed the lever down against the wall.

That would hold them for a minute.

She ran up the steps three at a time, pulling herself up by the railing as the guards banged on the door beneath her. Up four more flights, each one with a doorway back into the building. Sharon kept on, was finally stopped by an access-blocking locked steel cage door set over the stairs; a couple of flights above was obviously the roof, but this was as far as she could go.

Below she could hear the door slam open, dogs barking and men shouting. They were coming up. She ran down a flight, opened the door, and found herself in a well-carpeted wood and steel hallway.

Nothing to her right but a dead end. She ran left, around a corner, and there were four men running toward her with guns out, and two more came from a room on the side, and she stopped and put her hands up, and Martin stepped out of the room behind the other agents and said, "Sharon, there's no time — take off your wig; we're going up to the roof."

XXVIII

"American business," Bill spoke loudly, "is addicted to short-term thinking. All those assholes in suits down there" — he waved his arm over the city before them, beyond the sloping roof — "are totally convinced that the social contract is in the toilet. Now, either they don't think it's their problem, or they blame the poor people and start building prisons for them, without realizing the rich people are just as responsible for the death of the social contract as the poor."

Edward Mackinnon just stared over the city.

"Prisons don't make it better, Edward. Living, growing, thriving communities make it better."

When they'd first come out, the wind had hit them full force. They were at the high end of the wedge, higher than any building around them. Bill and Edward were seated at the middle of a walkway on the north side of the roof, next to a massive ventilation unit, their backs to the north wall, in a pocket of relative quiet. Here they could converse; four feet above them the wind howled and raged. "Democrat, Republican, doesn't matter," Bill continued. "Everybody thinks short-term, because they can't afford the luxury of long-term thinking.

"You can, Edward," Bill went on. "You're the permanent government. You have that luxury."

"You kidnap my son, God knows how he'll be traumatized for the rest of his life, and you lecture me about short-term thinking —"

Bill shrugged. "He'll be fine. He's a pretty good kid, actually. And besides, it got us here, didn't it?"

"You son of a bitch —" Edward said, arms jerking, hands cuffed behind his back.

"Oooh, machismo, very helpful." Bill shook his head. "We're talking about a place that can support itself without any state funding while it brings families together, Edward. We're talking about a place that can educate, offer people jobs — do whatever's required without costing the taxpayers a dime. Read Digby. It's not just a mental health facility or a hospital — it's a self-perpetuating therapeutic machine to fix broken families — and it can be set up over a summer, all for the price of one van Gogh."

"What you're talking —" Edward had to clear his throat. "What you're talking about is much more expensive than that."

"Yeah, well, sell another painting."

"You destroyed them all, remember?"

Bill shrugged. "Use the insurance. Edward, you're worth six hundred mil. You could put Digby facilities in neighborhoods in New York, Chicago, Los Angeles — all you have to do is commit." Edward knit his brows. "Look —" Bill continued, "the social contract isn't going away. You are part of this time, you are part of this city, whether you like it or not. And you're the only person I know in a position to actually do something." Bill sighed. "Ever read Jung?" he asked. "On individuation?"

"Jung — God, years ago —" Edward said, and at that moment, fifty yards away, the door under the airplane beacon at the end of the roof slammed open.

Edward half expected Bill to twist him around, use him as a shield, but instead they watched and waited. After a long moment, a hand put a bullhorn on the ground in front of the doorway. A curled wire stretched taut into the building. "Bill," the voice came from the bullhorn. "It's Sharon."

A big grin worked itself all across Bill's face. "Wonderful! It's Sharon. Isn't Sharon great? You really shouldn't have driven her father to suicide —"

"Bullshit," Edward Mackinnon said, but there was something behind his eyes.

The bullhorn scratched back to life. "I'm coming out there," she went on. "Is that okay?"

"She's always so polite," Bill said.

"I'll be alone. And I'll shut the door after me —"

Bill, behind Edward, made a come-on-over gesture. Nothing happened for a long moment, and then she appeared in the doorway, looked down the fifty yards at the two figures huddled together in a lump. She started toward them gingerly, almost as though she were setting foot after foot on a tightrope; she stepped over the bullhorn, keeping her eyes on Bill. Then, one foot in front of the other, she walked down the long alley, the wind fierce and blowing.

All New York spread south, before her: beyond the endless sheet of solar panels, she could see the curve of the horizon and the ocean. She cursed her stupid light clothing, trembled in the cold. She was trying to group her thoughts, figure out what on earth she could possibly say that would somehow save the situation.

Whatever the situation was.

Finally when she was twenty feet away, the cold got to her, and she ducked her head and ran.

"Bill Czolgosz," she said, when she'd gotten near. "You okay, Ed?"

"Fine," he said, but he had a look in his eyes she had never seen before, a look of bewildered defeat.

"So —" She took a step closer. "You guys just shooting the shit up here? Or what?"

Neither said anything for a long moment. And then Bill opened his jacket. At first Sharon didn't completely understand what she was seeing, and then, suddenly, she did. "Oh, God —" she said.

It was like he'd shown her his incurable disease.

And then Bill smiled at her, and she had an odd sense of what he must have looked like as a boy, wide-eyed and open and smart as hell. "There is time," he said, "to prepare a face to meet the faces that you meet."

"There will be time," she corrected.

"Well, one hopes," Bill said.

Edward looked from one to the other, desperation in his eyes. "Please — what the hell are you two talking about?"

"'Prufrock,'" said Sharon.

"T. S. Eliot," said Bill.

Sharon touched Edward's shoulder and sat down next to Bill. "It doesn't look to me like you're going to survive this," she told him.

"You said that last time."

"This time is different," Sharon said. "You can't get people to do stuff this way, Bill —"

Edward looked up. "It's terrorism," he said.

"Terrorism is when you make decisions for other people without their consent," Bill said. "Which, Edward, you do all the time."

"I've never done it by violence."

"You've ripped up neighborhoods, wiped out the ethnic small businesses, all to fill the city with people who can afford luxury housing. And now, you're planning to get money from the state to lock up all the people whom your customers are afraid of. You're single-handedly widening the gulf between rich and poor in the richest city on earth."

"I've never damaged anyone."

"Some of us might beg to differ," Bill said softly.

Edward Mackinnon shook his head, sat up, backbone stiffer. "I don't negotiate with terrorists."

"Oh, come on —" Bill smiled. "From the day we are born to the day we die, we spend every waking moment negotiating with terrorists. The basic condition of childhood is constant negotiation with terrorists. The basic condition of adulthood —" He shook his head. "Sharon, this man terrorized your childhood, did he not?"

"That's not why we're here."

"Sharon —" he made a clapping gesture, hands a foot apart. "That's the whole point. Did he or didn't he?" Sharon said nothing. "Sharon, in your childhood, who was this man?"

She debated how to answer that, what to tell and where to take it. "He was my uncle Ed," Sharon said. "He was my father's best friend —" And then something surprised her, the tiniest essence of a smell unlocked deep from her memory, Sunday dinner and spaghetti and sauce, the four of them. Except it wasn't Sunday, it had been every day, suddenly she knew that now. Every day and — she looked at Mackinnon. Here he was. "Hey, Ed, you remember spaghetti? The four of us around the table wolfing it down after you and Dad spent the day with the computer in the basement — you remember that?" Edward said nothing. "Why do I only ever remember spaghetti?"

"It was fifteen cents a box."

"We were that broke."

"We were all that broke."

"So —" Bill leaned back. "There was a lawsuit? Some kind of court deal?"

Sharon looked from Bill to Ed and back, and suddenly she saw it, a way of uniting the personal and the political, a way out. "Edward and my father met in the army," she started, "saw how screwed up things were, got out and worked together for two years on this computer program. You could keep track of benefits for massive numbers of individuals, with all different variables and pay scales, and it would even mail out checks. This was, what, twenty-four years ago. Right?" She looked at Ed, who didn't answer. "Anyway, they get it done, they have a disagreement. Edward tries to buy my father out — there's some piece of paper they signed early on. Edward sues him, my father countersues, they end up in court. Edward wins because of this fucking piece of paper. He starts a company called Mackinnon Systems, markets the program to the government — it's perfect for the welfare system. Then he starts buying real estate, putting up buildings, he goes public and becomes the Mackinnon Group, and that's where we find him today."

"And your father?" Bill asked.

Sharon sighed. "Three days after the court decision against him,

Dad blew his brains out. I found the body." It was amazing how she felt saying it in front of Edward. Like suddenly she could breathe with every part of her lungs, with absolutely no parts blocked off.

"I was always sorry for that," Edward said, looking down.

The swing set. Leaving the swing set. Fuck, now it all made sense. She tried not to say it, but it just came out: "You left us with nothing — we couldn't even keep the house."

That's what Sharon remembered. They'd had to leave. Her father pouring cement in the postholes to fix it in place.

He'd built it for her. It had stayed; she and mom had left.

Sharon lowered her head, rubbed her eyes with the palm of her hand.

"Edward?" Bill said. "That kind of the way it went?"

Edward Mackinnon just sat, slumped over, hands behind his back and his chest on his knees, staring out at the horizon.

"Yeah," he said at last. "Pretty much."

"Really?" Bill sat up. "You're not just saying that because I'm strapped with dynamite and your hands are cuffed?"

Edward turned his head to the two of them. "No," he said with a long sigh. "That's about how it went."

"So," Bill went on. "I'd say you owe Sharon something, wouldn't you?"

Edward Mackinnon said nothing, staring right at him, his mouth slightly open.

"I said —" said Bill, "Edward, it would seem you owe Sharon something."

Very slowly, in tiny increments, Edward Mackinnon's head moved up and down. "Yeah," he said finally.

"Sharon," Bill smiled. "What would you like Edward Mackinnon to do?"

Sharon took a deep breath, shook her head sadly. "Bill, Bill, Bill. It's such a good setup — you want me to ask him to drop Straythmore, take up Digby with the same fervor, fund the Carnegie-Hayden as the pilot project and I'll be a nurse there and everything'll be great. But it doesn't work that way."

Bill just stared, something wounded in his face.

"I never asked you to do any of this for me — I mean, Digby's a great idea, the Carnegie-Hayden's a perfect building, but still, I can't do it." Bill just watched her. "Bill, I lost my father, I lost my husband, I lost my son. The one thing I've been able to figure out is that there's a difference between justice and vengeance. If you force people to do things for a good cause, it's not a good cause anymore. The ends don't justify the means."

"Actually —" Edward Mackinnon cleared his throat. "Actually, I've always rather felt they did."

They both looked at him as if he'd appeared out of nowhere.

"Life is war. The Marines, Vietnam, and then the business world — that's what I know. And your father — I've never forgotten him, you know. The man was brilliant, he was unstable, but he had principles, Sharon. And I — I didn't. I didn't think it would ever matter. And here we are, all these years later." He shook his head. "I made a mistake back then — I went for the short-term, same thing I did with Straythmore." He looked at Bill. "I never liked their long-term goals. Short-term, I thought we could do some business. But that's the way I've trained myself to think: to hell with the long-term consequences, we'll pay that price when we get to it. Well" — he turned to Sharon — "you've been paying that price your entire life. And that's unacceptable. I lie awake at night because of you, because at the time, *I knew what I was doing.* Just like I did with Straythmore. And that's why" — he cleared his throat again — "that's why I'm going to fund the Carnegie-Hayden."

"Edward, absolutely not —" Sharon was furious.

"Wait a minute —" Bill shushed her.

"You win, Bill. It's war, and you've made a perfect checkmate. Sharon can fight it — but I can't." He looked at Sharon. "I screwed your father, I screwed your family — that was war, too. I thought it was over, but it's not. I'll dump Straythmore and build this damn thing. That's not vengeance, that's justice."

The three of them sat for a long moment, listening to the wind. Then Edward went on: "You know the weird thing, Bill? You think you and Sharon are somehow spiritually identical. But you're not." He looked straight at him. "You and I — we think alike."

Bill stared at Ed for a long moment, and then, with an odd half-smile, looked at Sharon. "And you never liked him —"

Sharon considered Uncle Ed. "Nope."

"And you don't like —"

"I did." And there they were across a void, ineffable sadness between them, three inches away from each other, not touching, not able to touch. She closed her eyes slowly, and when she opened them, she was staring right into his. "I could have. But then you — started to remind me of him." Her eyes glanced to Ed and back.

Bill considered that for a moment, then sighed. "I know," he said at last, with a strange, galvanized acceptance. And then he rose to stand.

"Bill, they've got sharpshooters —" She pointed. "There — and there." She pointed at the low corners of the wedge. "Take off the dynamite. You've gotten what you wanted, let's go. You know how fucked up the courts are, you've got a fighting chance —"

He was shaking his head no. "Tell them I'm a bomb."

"Bill, sit down, we'll take the shit off you —"

"Thirty pounds of dynamite over four pounds of C-4!"

"Bill, don't do this —"

"I'm a Bomb!" He was clambering up the wall, up to the railing. "I'M A BOMB!" he yelled.

"BILL!" She stood, grabbed his calf. "No. NO!"

"I'M A BOMB!" He kicked her hand away, climbed up higher, out of her reach, and the shots sounded distant, far away, and he seemed to jump, or the wind seemed to kick him — he was up in the wind now, and then he was tumbling. Sharon pulled herself up and Bill was falling down the glass slope of the Citicorp Building, it took forever, a dead weight rolling over and over, arms and legs akimbo, the glass cracking under him as he fell, and the wind and the gravity seemed to be dragging him to one side, to the edge of the sloping field of glass. "For God's sake, Sharon, get down!" Mackinnon yelled. "They'll shoot you!" But Sharon ignored him and climbed higher to watch as Bill fell off the glass, into the maintenance alleyway between the glass and the east edge of the building. She ran to that side to see him, but there was a forest of pipes and ducts in her way. She sprinted back, and when she finally saw him her heart stopped — he was clambering back onto the glass, walking unsteadily, looking up at her, at the sky above, and then he

slipped, the wind blasted him, and the riflemen were standing —
he rose, shaking his head, got to his feet, hands out, looking at the
perfect blue sky —

"NO!" Sharon screamed, and suddenly there was fire emanating from his chest, and he had no balance, but he was running, or
trying to run, and then the first explosion blew and the wind actually picked him up and slammed him into the air, sent him up and
twirling, and the explosions kept coming, the building shuddered
like an earthquake, loud booms rocking the roof; he was in the air
and he was reaching for something, and then his entire body
seemed to detonate, the fireball was tremendous — Sharon actually felt the jarring change of force on her face — and everywhere
glass was cracking, and he just came apart and the wind blasted
whatever there was of him over the side.

And then the last explosion came; a monumental blast like a
warhead exploding that drove glass shards into the air and made
the building actually rock. Sharon dove to the ground, covered
Mackinnon, her ears immediately reacting with a soft, high tinni-
tus. She lay there, and hoped to God the building wasn't going to
crumble and fall beneath them.

Thirty seconds passed, forty-five, and they were still alive.
Sharon opened her eyes, found herself stomach down over Edward
Mackinnon, protecting his head. They lay there for a moment,
breathing, and then Sharon rolled off Edward. "Are you okay?"

"You saved my life," Edward said.

Sharon said nothing.

"This whole thing, you saved my life, you saved Ted's life."

Sharon said nothing, catching her breath.

"Whatever you want to do," Edward Mackinnon said, "that's
what we'll do."

XXIX

"So he was talking normally —?" Martin asked, over the phone.

Sharon, sitting in her apartment, sipped her coffee. "You heard
him on the wire, didn't you?"

"Because we've been studying the footage, and it's as if there were an explosive charge in his head —"

"Well, he had those wires going up his neck — maybe behind his ears —"

"We also think he had a stick of dynamite up his rectum — possibly more than one."

Up his rectum? That didn't sound very much like Bill. "Quite possibly," Sharon said, dully.

"When you were with him, was he sitting normally? Did he seem comfortable, or —"

Suddenly the questions tallied up in Sharon's mind. "Are you worried it wasn't Bill?" She tried to keep her voice as normal as possible.

Silence. Then: "We're just kicking around some ideas, here, you know, tidying up the loose ends —"

"Because now that you mention it, he did seem uncomfortable. He was totally straight-backed — he didn't slump at all."

"Really?" Sharon heard Martin scribbling on a pad. "Reason I ask, the lab at Quantico has been beta-testing a new computer program, it works out height, weight, and other identifiable characteristics of anybody in a picture or videotape. All the lab guys keep saying it's full of bugs, but anyway. They fed it the FBI footage from the low end of the roof, basically Bill from behind, and they came up with a slight statistical variation in one factor — Bill's weight — before and after he dropped into that maintenance gully, just before the explosions started." Sharon couldn't help it; her heart began to beat a little harder, and suddenly she was on her feet, pacing back and forth across her apartment. "It's within the program's margin of error, so nobody's really excited about it, but I don't like it."

Sharon stood for a moment, trying to sort through her emotions. "Martin, we all saw him die. How many witnesses?"

"Twenty. Officially, the case is closed. And to do another full battery of tests — DNA and the others — that's another huge expense, on an incredibly expensive case, when twenty agents saw the guy blow apart — I mean, everybody in the office is happy —"

"Except you."

"Right."

Sharon stood with the phone to her ear, and looked out the window at the Empire State Building. The sky was a glorious blue, tousled with occasional swift clouds. "You have slides made up of your samples from the roof — "

"Of course."

"Well, then, if something comes up in the future, you'll know. But I promise you — that was Bill Kaiser. He's dead. I believe it was him."

"Great. That's just what I wanted to hear. Listen, I told you about my Christmas party next week —"

"Thanks, Martin — I appreciate the invite."

"You're welcome — see you then."

Sharon hung up the phone, stood and stared at the Empire State Building a moment longer.

The guy hadn't moved like Bill.

Bill's movements had always been quick, sharp and focused. But after he reappeared on the roof, his gait had been more like an overmedicated schizophrenic on a ward, kind of shambling, on the edge of losing balance.

Organic neurological disorder, 293.10 or so on the DSM-IV classification, which Bill, whatever his problems, had not had.

She sat back at her desk, the Smith Corona humming under the lamp, took another sip of her coffee, and got back to her place in the Father Digby Plan. She was reducing it to a list of priorities and requirements, so that when she met with Edward Mackinnon's architects two days from now she'd know what she regarded as important to fight for, and what she didn't consider worth sustained argument.

The Nietzsche Prosthesis show started at ten, Erik was picking her up at seven-thirty, and she wanted to get as much work done as possible before she had to start getting showered and changed.

The sky was gray and full of rain and the ground was flat as a table and Bill wanted nothing more than to pull over and go to sleep.

He'd been driving all night, with the intention of getting out of Texas by daybreak, but Texas just seemed to go on forever; no motels or border markers yet, and the sun was just a glare in the rearview of the used Chevette he'd purchased in Pennsylvania two days before. He'd alternated all night between classic rock, country-and-western, and all-news, and none of them had been particularly satisfying. Finally he crossed the border into New Mexico, drove a little ways into the state and up a dusty county road before pulling in to the Nara Visa Motel and Restaurant. The old man behind the counter seemed singularly unsurprised to see him. Bill presented his driver's license — Jon Booth; he'd still been on his presidential kick when he'd established that identity — paid thirty-five dollars up front for a day, and was given a key. He bought all the newspapers available in the lobby vending machines, drove around to his room, went inside, and considered the musty smell and the green bedspread and "Western" lamp shades and the cable television. He pulled the curtains, opened the window. The air did not appreciably change. He took off his shoes, lay on the bed, and read, for the first time, that the FBI was officially declaring the case closed.

There, across the road, was a package store with a pay phone out front, next to a small grocery. Bill slipped back into his sneakers, stepped out, and walked to it. No need to look back and forth; no traffic in sight. In the grocery store, he bought some magazines and bottled iced tea and two prewrapped sub sandwiches. He paid with a twenty, asked for five dollars in quarters.

He stepped back outside, set his purchases on a bench, picked up the pay phone receiver, dialed the number. When the recording came on telling him how much to put in, he spun quarter after quarter into the slot, until finally the voice shut up and the ringing began.

It took a while for anyone to answer, but finally a woman did. "WHBN," she said.

"Could you put me on hold?" Bill asked. "I'm trying to tune my radio."

"Sure thing," the woman said, there was a click, and then intelligent, abstract jazz came over the line.

Bill listened for a long moment before finally hanging up the receiver. Never again, he thought.

It wasn't New York he missed, he realized as he walked back across the street.

It was Sharon.